MASTER PLAN

ANDY DANE NYE

ARTAVIA
PUBLISHING

First published in 2021 by Artavia Publishing

1 3 5 7 9 10 8 6 4 2

A CIP catalogue record for this book is available from the British Library.

ISBN 978 1 913351 03 8

Typeset in Crimson Text by Google Fonts

Printed and bound in Great Britain by Clays Ltd, Elcograf S.p.A.

No animals were harmed in the writing of this book.

Dedicated to each and every one of you who enjoyed *Master Piece* enough to come back for more.

Things are never what they seem...

for what they seem is prejudiced by perspective.

Only with omnipresence could you hope to understand it all.

Donald Tucker-Jenkins studied himself in the mirror and agreed with his reflection that, for the most part, they both looked extremely dapper. There was just something not quite right... and, for the life of him, he couldn't put his finger on it.

He examined himself again, hoping that, by methodical and forensic scrutiny, the cause of his unease might be ascertained.

Bow tie evenly spaced and perfectly level with the floor.

Check.

Dress shirt immaculately pressed and as white as the day he'd removed its pins.

Check.

Dinner suit crisp and clean, fitting as snugly as his bespoke tailor had intended.

Check.

Patent leather shoes polished to the point of reflecting the hem of his Savile Row trousers.

Check.

2.7 metres of tin foil wrapped around his head.

Mmmm.

He gave the matter some thought.

Perhaps it was the socks?

Having given the matter even more thought, he shook his head... which was a bad idea.

Okay... It was the foil, he deduced, hastily preventing his makeshift turban from unravelling. But he could hardly forego *that.*

It had been a while, but uninvited voices were once again using the inside of his cranium as a sounding board, and he desperately needed something to keep them out. He'd considered using lead flashing from the roof, but he'd been unable to locate a long enough ladder.

Not that those voices had ever *completely* deserted him. He often found himself having to put up with the odd intrusive conversation... usually from disgruntled, disembodied souls griping about a lack of material comforts in the spirit world. However, recently, things had gotten out of hand.

'ALRIGHT... I'LL GIVE YOU IT LOOKS BLOODY RIDICULOUS... BUT IT'S STAYING WHERE IT IS!' he shouted at a more familiar and begrudgingly tolerated visitor to his head. *So now that intrusion included fashion critique?* Donald tutted loudly. His spirit guide, Whitebait, could hardly talk.

He meant that in a facetious and non-literal way, of course... given the incorporeal one was required to use Donald as a conduit in order to get his thoughts across. He was referring to the fact that the expired, nineteenth-century trawlerman from Grimsby did so whilst still attired in an oilskin jacket, sou'wester, and bottle-green Wellington boots. If *anyone* was going to criticise Donald's appearance, it certainly wasn't going to be *him*.

The headgear was staying. He couldn't risk those *other* voices ruining his big night.

A sharp tug added weight to his trousers.

'Get down, Mendelssohn!' He chastised one of a number of cats that had been desperately craving his attention for the past half hour. 'Goodness knows why daddy's so popular all of a sudden. But... be that as it may... he's got more important matters to attend to! You'll have to make do with each other's company while he's gone!'

Nodding extremely carefully at his reflection, he received confirmation back that it was, indeed, time to leave. If comments were passed that evening pertaining to his appearance, he'd respectfully point out that at least it was a far cry from how it *used* to be before his "accident". For one, his trousers weren't stained with urine... and for that, whoever it may concern – and the rest of the theatre – should be extremely grateful.

'YES... I'M WELL AWARE YOU ARE TOO!' he acknowledged loudly, his eyes rising to somewhere in the vicinity of his turban.

Hygienic trousers were just one part of a tidal wave of change that had swept tsunami-like through Donald's life in recent years. Accordingly, he'd made a great effort over the last five of them to attend the premieres of his stage plays looking every bit the literary genius he was internationally hailed as being. "The new Shakespeare", the critics had pronounced, "leading the vanguard of a worldwide renaissance in art".

And the world had certainly needed it. Pursuit of more cerebral pleasures had helped lift the mood of a shattered global society as it struggled to rebuild its devastated economies and re-evaluate the purpose of it all.

Ironically, Donald had been at the vanguard of that devastation too.

It had all started innocuously enough with a spate of art exhibitions that sprang up around the world, despite his prophetic warnings that things weren't as they seemed. His well-intentioned actions indirectly contributed to some of the world's wealthiest investors questioning the value... and wisdom... of their art portfolios. Were pictures of past-their-prime sunflowers – wilting in vases that wouldn't impress at a car boot sale – *really* worth the eye-watering multiplier of value of the paint, canvas, man-hours and ears it took to produce them? Come to think of it... it wasn't as if there was anything interesting to look at in the background when it came to *those* particular ones. At least the Mona Lisa had winding paths and a curious little bridge to hold your attention. Vincent – on the other hand – hadn't even bothered with wallpaper.

A seed of doubt having been planted, a handful of concerned industrialists decided it prudent to offload their own portfolios, precipitating a sudden glut in the market. With supply vastly outstripping demand – and panic, as to why this might be occurring, gripping fellow investors – the negative ripples quickly spread, sending the market into a catastrophic freefall. As bullish optimism became replaced by a sense they'd just caught a glimpse of the emperor's private parts, investors around the world began questioning the true value of their *other* portfolios. In a time of crisis, would cocoa beans, pound for pound, *really* be worth more than a staple such as wheat? Even if a few of them *had* passed through the anus of a civet, would that *still* justify the answer being *yes?*

As questions arose, prices fell. Pessimism became contagious. No sooner had the market sneezed, than the collapse became viral and the patient close to death.

Floundering in the aftermath, the world found itself without a *raison d'être*. The pursuit of wealth had proven to be unreliable... an ephemeral goal that had literally lost its value. What was the point of it all? In fact... what was the point of *anything?*

Desperately needing answers as to why one should bother reaching for one's slippers in the morning, people began exploring their spiritual side. Not only did it provide comfort... it didn't cost a penny.

It also came with another benefit. Life seemed easier! Suddenly the Joneses weren't of interest. Greed hadn't just been bad... it had been extremely hard work.

Established religions wore a smug, *we-told-you-so* look as they delivered their pious sermons to ever-swelling congregations. Faith offered the disenchanted a broom for a clean start that conveniently doubled as a crutch.

But old habits die hard.

As collection plates became the new growth market, a plethora of enterprising souls set themselves up as self-appointed messiahs... reasoning that if God had been against fleecing the lazy and gullible, he wouldn't have allowed them to procreate in the first place. Televised, well-coiffured smiles in suits claimed religion had just gotten easier. Now you didn't even have to pick up the broom. You could sit at home in your favourite armchair whilst they did the sweeping for you... provided you had a credit card, of course. Salvation was just a pin number away. And if God was against *that*, he wouldn't have allowed the invention of plastic either.

But not everyone handed their spiritual well-being over to others. Seeking reasons of their own for their three score years and ten, many unexpectedly discovered answers in the work of the artists of this new age... those who had taken advantage of a sudden upsurge in inspiration from the heavens... or wherever they'd been looking for the meaning of it all.

Enter Donald...

...exiting.

The cats tumbled down the stairs behind him like a furry waterfall, threatening to trip him all the way to the front door, their consternation at his leaving curiously out of proportion to all previous occasions.

'Daddy won't be long,' he assured them, trusting in at least a rudimentary grasp of English on their part. 'There's something very important he has to do.'

There certainly was. He still found his phenomenal success hard to believe. I mean... one minute he was climbing on the roof of a lorry in an attempt to save a young man from being burnt to death in his own bedsit... The next... he'd been struck by a strange-looking fireball and instantly and inexplicably able to write the most sublime poetry and plays.

Tonight would be the opening of his twenty-third – *Wonders Will Never Crease* – the story of an ironing board salesman who gets mistaken for a bored iron salesman, and finds love in the guise of someone he thought was his long-lost twin sister... but turns out – after an admittedly implausible but fortuitously comical twist – to be an unrelated nymphomaniac. But it was the deeper meaning in the play that would leave his audience spellbound... his words awakening in them something reassuringly familiar yet paradoxically intangible.

The mystifying thing was... it wasn't as if he even had to try. The words came spinning out of the ether and into his mind faster than his writing hand could sometimes cope with.

Coincidentally, he'd acquired this new gift at precisely the same time the more insistent voices in his head had ceased their chatter. Not because they were unable to compete for his attention anymore, but because the danger they'd been warning him about seemed to have passed.

The trouble was – as his wearing of the tin foil testified – they were now back...

...and with a vengeance.

*   *   *

Worker One rammed his wooden pole into the wet grass of the hillside and strained to use it as a lever, trying to prevent the huge slab of stone sliding off the logs that were inching it towards the river below.

Worker Two – whose job it was to take the logs already rolled over from the back and transport them to the front – grunted his concern for his fingers. He only had seven left, and if it was alright with Worker One, he'd quite like to keep those.

Worker One managed a scowl through a strained grimace, leaving Worker Two in no doubt that he deemed his grunt petty and inappropriate, given the weight of rock he was battling to control. Maybe one day, Worker One reasoned, someone might take the time to sit under a tree somewhere and work out just why it was that a magic force insisted on constantly sliding the slab of stone towards Worker Two's fingers further down the hill... but until that time...

Worker Three – pulling on a rope from the other side – gazed up at the sun. He'd been told not to do this on countless occasions... but usually by men who were blind, so he was hardly going to take *their* advice. To his horror, the sun god seemed to be slowly removing his presence from the sky. The birds were startled too, having stopped their singing in bewilderment at the onslaught of bedtime halfway through the afternoon.

Worker One gave Worker Two a look that suggested it was all his fault. The sun god was clearly showing his displeasure with Worker Two's attitude towards their task.

Worker Two, incensed by Worker One's accusatory stare, instinctively gave him the finger.

Worker One, seeing Worker Two raise his fist in the air,

assumed he was being challenged to a fight and immediately withdrew his pole from the ground in order to defend himself.

Worker Two, having forgotten that his middle finger wasn't one of the seven he had left, suddenly realised the futility of his gesture and the fact the block of stone was now heading towards his remaining digits.

Worker Three, feeling his rope snap, yelled out a warning in a language that has since disappeared.

Worker Two let out a yelp in a universal language that hasn't... as something pink and covered in blood plopped onto the ground.

* * *

Norman Penkridge peered over the top of his book and at the gardener tending the plants in front of him. The old man seemed at ease with himself and the flora he was busying himself with, having clearly done so for much of his working life. Norman had only just been thinking that the garden had been looking a little untidy recently and was in need of some loving care.

The gardener noticed him staring. 'Fatsia Japonica,' he said softly. 'It's perfect for this kind of climate, being equally at home in both full sun and shade.'

Norman nodded his understanding and pretended to go back to his book. He'd not seen that particular member of staff before... but that was nothing new. Xanthia was always hiring and firing them, never content with their attitude. She was convinced they were looking down their noses at her, despite Norman's repeated assurances that denim hot pants and dangerously low necklines were the prerogative of the lady of the house.

Bored, he chanced another surreptitious glance at the old man and felt sorry for him. Though he clearly enjoyed his work from the attention he was giving it, a lifetime's exertion in the Mediterranean sun had clearly taken its toll on his aging body. He could see from the slight hump bulging beneath the man's worn, linen work shirt that his spine had taken the brunt of too many years hunched over his floral charges. He wondered if he was in pain.

As if by way of an answer, the gardener straightened himself up with surprising ease and moved on to the next plant.

It had large, deeply lobed leaves and a tall flower spike covered in small, white flowers, each with a purple bract. Norman had never taken the time to appreciate its construction before, let alone acknowledge its presence in his garden. *Perhaps it was similar to discovering the beauty of art... and more time should be taken to value plants and marvel at their existence.* He wondered what *this* one's name might be.

'Acanthus Mollis,' announced the gardener, with uncanny timing. 'Whilst it's happy in full sun, its leaves are much glossier if you allow it a little shade.'

Norman's eyes darted back to his book... but it had lost his interest. A handful of cicadas – impatient for the dark – were doing their best to entertain him. But the immaculately blue sky and accompanying heat had sapped his powers of concentration.

His eyes strayed to the old man's deformity.

Was it his imagination... or did that hump now look more pronounced?

The old man continued with his work.

It must be the angle at which he's bending, surmised Norman, applying the logical thought process at which he excelled. It was a skill that had once had him called upon to save the Universe. Whilst he hadn't been *entirely* successful... the fact he and it were still there clearly counted for something.

He sighed heavily as those memories skirted his consciousness. It all seemed so distant, now... like an obscure dream. If it wasn't for the acres of French coastal hillside and the large, white house occupying the centre of them, he'd have thought he'd made the whole thing up. But his substantial abode and accompanying boat bobbing gently on the water below were tangible proof he hadn't.

Not that he'd been out on it recently. Once you'd seen one

set of coastal hills, you'd seen them all. Even the pretty, small, stone harbours into which he occasionally ventured had acquired a predictability that numbed his initial excitement.

The same, however, couldn't be said of the vast collection of paintings that wallpapered his numerous rooms... paid for courtesy of the thinning chequebook securely locked away in a safe behind a particularly valuable Matisse. Not that price was an issue.

The chequebook was proof positive of the strange circumstances in which it had been acquired... coming with no strings attached or limit to the amount that could be withdrawn with each individual page.

He'd certainly made good use of it up to that point.

Whether the Archangel who'd given it to him would agree was a matter for conjecture. For, whilst indulging in a limited number of philanthropic ventures, the majority of its use had been for purely selfish purposes.

Original works of art by some of the greatest masters in history had featured foremost... and at knock-down prices, given recent market conditions. Xanthia's own tastes were a little more prosaic... even though they were usually of a pink or sparkly nature.

And *there* was the biggest change in his life... the one he found hardest to believe. Having fantasised over the glamour-model-cum-pointless-celebrity for most of his extended adolescence, he'd wasted no time in exploiting his unexpected acquaintance with the girl of his wet dreams... actually managing to convince her that even *his* personality could sparkle if you viewed it through the bottom of enough champagne and cocktail glasses... all provided courtesy of the chequebook, of course.

He was well aware of what had done the trick... but the result was all that mattered. Children were an occasional thought on the horizon. But he was more than happy if they took their time getting there. It was the practice that counted... and he certainly needed it.

Wondering if she was back from having her nails done, he

let out another extended sigh, envying her a reason to leave the house. His skin was beginning to burn under the late afternoon sun, but the lethargy it induced prevented him from doing anything about it.

How did the gardener cope?

He watched as the old man went about his business without so much as a single drop of sweat on his weather-beaten brow.

Norman thought it strange.

But stranger still... the old man had spoken to him in perfect English... and

... hadn't that hump just got even bigger?

He dropped his book and stared at the strange protuberance stretching the old man's shirt. Just as he was beginning to think it possessed a life of its own and was struggling to escape its confines, a small rip appeared in the material restraining it.

Norman's blood froze as the rip became a larger tear and exposed what appeared to be...

... feathers? It's not possible!

'All things are possible,' said the gardener, looking round at him. 'It's just a case of you thinking them so.'

'That's precisely what I *was* doing,' said Norman aloud. '*Thinking!*'

'As I've told you before... it's all the same thing where I come from.'

Norman's eyes widened. 'Gabriel?'

'If you want me to be.' The old man stood fully upright, causing a magnificent set of wings to burst forth from beneath his shirt. 'Which clearly you do.' He flexed them so as to admire Norman's handiwork.

'But I *didn't* want anything!' blurted Norman excitedly. 'I mean... I wasn't thinking of you!'

'Everybody wants *something*,' said Gabriel. 'And you're obviously not thinking of the answer if you ask the question.'

'I don't believe it!' A broad grin lighting up his face, Norman scrambled to his feet.

Gabriel raised a hand. 'Just like the old days. But it's not going to work.'

'*What's* not?'

'The embrace you're about to give me… Remember?'

'Oh… right…' Norman stopped himself before his arms scythed through the air. 'Of course! I forgot!'

'I fear you've forgotten far more than that,' said Gabriel, blunting any further enthusiasm.

Norman's earlier thoughts waved at him uncomfortably. 'Is it about the money? Only…'

Gabriel sighed with a weight Norman felt. 'Was it all for nothing?'

Norman wasn't quite sure what he meant. 'The world's a *slightly* better place,' he offered optimistically. 'You were right about everyone reappraising their priorities, the last time we met. The world's been through quite an upheaval since then. Though much of it's returned to normal, our actions at least caused people to look at themselves and question what life was about for a while.'

'And what conclusion did *you* come to?'

Norman felt another reproving wave engulf him. He gestured at his opulent surroundings. 'You're angry about all this, aren't you?'

'I understand the plants,' conceded Gabriel.

'I knew it was about the money,' Norman grimaced.

'You really *have* forgotten what I taught you, haven't you. Material things are nothing more than a temporary illusion. They're an irrelevance. It's what you choose to do with them that marks their *real* value.' Gabriel stretched out his arms. 'So… does all this make you a wealthy man, Norman?'

'I take it you mean in *spiritual* terms?'

'There's no point in any other.'

'I'm *happy*,' Norman winced, as if starting a list of positives he'd struggle to extend much further.

'Does it stretch to content?'

Norman felt a chill permeate his being. He realised his visitor already knew the answer.

'I've missed you,' he side-stepped smartly. 'Without you here to keep me on my toes, it's all been so…'

'Pointless?'

The word struck Norman with the clarity of a bell. He had to admit that it was *precisely* the one he would've used, had he managed to get as far as choosing one that honestly encapsulated everything about his life. True... he'd managed to indulge his newly found passion for art to a degree he'd once have thought impossible and become the custodian of some very important works of art. As well as that responsibility, he now also had another which entailed considering someone else's demand for a share of the duvet. But beyond that... 'You *see... that's* why I feel so comfortable around you,' he nodded sanguinely. 'You have all the answers.'

'You're supposed to be working those out for yourself,' returned Gabriel. 'Otherwise your time on this plane is a complete waste of it.'

'You once told me time doesn't exist!' Norman challenged him with a twinkle in his eye, recalling with fondness their verbal sparring.

'I see you still haven't lost any of that obstinacy,' sighed Gabriel, showing less enthusiasm for it. 'Time *doesn't* exist in the spiritual realm... that's true. There's only *being*. I was using terms it would be easier for you to understand.'

'I'm happy to try harder ones!' parried Norman.

'I meant easier as in "kinder to you",' said Gabriel dryly. 'But if you want me to put it in a more succinct way... You're completely wasting your *being*.'

As Norman contemplated how appalling that sounded, a cry from the direction of the house broke his thoughts.

'I don't believe it!' yelled a high-pitched voice. 'What on earth are *you* doing here?'

Norman turned and was taken aback to see Xanthia running as fast as her lack of a sports bra allowed, her face beaming as she hurried to embrace Gabriel like a long-lost lover.

Gabriel seemed surprised too.

'I was just thinking about you the other...' She came to a sudden halt, her faced twisted by confusion.

'Xan?'

'Sorry, Normy. I thought it was... someone else,' she said awkwardly, staring at Gabriel as if struggling to access a memory.

'Are you alright, darling?'

She didn't answer... her rotating jaw slowing, as the gum she was chewing became more and more an irrelevance.

'Don't worry,' said Gabriel. 'It's not always easy for material entities to place me. It depends on their beliefs. So if they've never *had* any...'

'It's Gabriel,' Norman prompted gently. 'He's come back to see us.'

'Does he want his money back?' she chewed, still in a daze.

'I don't know. But I assume he wants *something*.'

'Ah... there it is,' Gabriel smiled. 'That sublime logic of yours. I'm glad to see your appreciation of the more colourful things in life hasn't dulled its black and white application.'

'I'm right, though... aren't I?'

Gabriel ruffled his wings. 'Shall I give it the whole "clouds parting, cherubs circling" routine... or do we know each other well enough to understand that what I'm about to say is of immense importance?'

Norman considered the options. 'Oh... go on,' he smiled. 'It's been a while!'

Gabriel shrugged.

The sky above them began filling with clouds blown through a hole in its centre. As that hole widened to accommodate evermore cumulonimbus, the sound of a heavenly choir set the mood for what was about to follow. Winged horses pulling golden chariots charged out at breakneck speed and scattered to the four corners of the unfolding tapestry. The chariots' occupants – abandoning their transportation – proceeded to float randomly about Norman's head, blowing long, thin horns at him or strumming golden lyres in time to the celestial crescendo.

'Norman Penkridge,' boomed Gabriel grandly above it, now looking nothing like a gardener. 'You have been chosen, once again, from all of humanity to save the Universe from complete and utter annihilation. But this time... it's even *more* serious.'

Norman wondered how on earth such a thing could be possible. It had seemed pretty serious the *last* time.

'Unlike last time,' Gabriel read him, 'we cannot fail.'

Norman raised his hand.

'Yes?' said Gabriel testily.

'I assume you don't mean "cannot" as in "we're destined to succeed"?'

Gabriel had to think about that one.

'I mean "cannot" as in... we no longer have the luxury of time. If we *do* fail, the destruction of the Universe will begin immediately, and everything that has ever been, is or ever will be... will not be.'

'You mean...?'

Gabriel nodded solemnly.

'How *much* time?'

'Twenty-three days,' answered Gabriel phlegmatically.

Norman expelled an appreciative whistle. 'That *is* serious.'

'I haven't finished yet.' Gabriel allowed himself a slight pause so as to regain his authority. 'The forces arraigned against you will number a thousand fold and more, and present a far greater danger than before... being not of this realm. For the time foretold as Armageddon has finally come upon us, heralding the ultimate battle between good and evil... the continuation of existence itself... or a cold, lifeless void for eternity.'

Even the cherubs looked anxious.

The choir gave forth one more soul-swelling burst, before fading with the scene they had been accompanying... presumably to ponder on whether they might have just given their last performance.

Norman waited for the final horse's tail to disappear before daring to speak. 'Perhaps I should've gone for the informal version,' he croaked. 'I think it might've seemed less apocalyptic!'

'It is what it is,' said Gabriel grimly. 'There will be no second chances this time. It is all or nothing... To be or not to be... Do *or d_'*

'Ssssh!' hushed Norman, putting a finger to his lips and nodding nervously towards Xanthia. 'I'm not sure how she'll cope with such dark dilemmas. She even struggles with *Trick or Treat* every year!'

Xanthia, for her part, had stopped her chewing... along with every other faculty she'd ever possessed.

'I understand,' whispered Gabriel. 'Perhaps it's best if I leave you two alone for a while, to digest what has just been said, and come back later.'

Before Norman could offer an opinion, the Archangel began to fade.

'Do I have to digitise artworks again?' shouted Norman desperately after him.

Even the cicadas seemed to be awaiting the answer.

'Oh, no,' came Gabriel's faint voice from the ether. 'You'll find it's going to be *much* harder than that!'

As Norman found himself alone with the stupefied love of his life, he glanced at the flowerbed Gabriel had been attending.

There wasn't one.

*   *   *

It wasn't quite the performance the theatre audience had been expecting... nor the actors, come to that. Whilst the obligatory announcement had been made regarding everyone switching off their mobile phones so as not to ruin the play, it hadn't included the request that they also refrain from shouting at the top of their voices as it was being performed. To complicate matters... the person doing the shouting seemed to be the playwright himself... an embarrassing and difficult situation for those currently having to suffer it.

'I KNOW THY WORKS, AND THY LABOUR, AND THY PATIENCE, AND HOW THOU CANST NOT BEAR THEM WHICH ARE EVIL!' bellowed Donald, much to his *own* embarrassment.

There was a loud "Shhhhhh"... which only confounded the

audience more, given it had come from Donald himself.

It had always been obvious to the great and the good – assembled to witness yet another of the gifted man's works – that the gifted one himself was a little... how could it be put...?

...*different.*

But that was the convenient thing about being in the presence of a genius. If they turned up to the premiere of their play sporting an aluminium turban, one politely enquired as to the name of their milliner. Take the genius out of the equation and one politely phoned the police. But Donald had always managed to contain his eccentricity just enough to make himself look on the riskier side of interesting. Not that he was seen that much in public. Such sightings were rare... and interviews non-existent. He was too busy writing plays to be talking about them, his prudent publishers would say. It was a situation that suited him perfectly.

Unfortunately, one had to show one's face at some point.

'REMEMBER THEREFORE FROM WHENCE THOU ART FALLEN!'

'I do beg your pardon,' whispered Donald, addressing those around him.

'NO... THAT *DOESN'T* INCLUDE YOU!' he bellowed. 'YOU SHOULD BE STOPPING THEM... NOT ENCOURAGING THEM!'

'Would you like a glass of water?' enquired one of the dignitaries who thought he'd been clever in engineering pride of place next to the renowned playwright, but was now beginning to regret it.

'Well... I *could* try pouring it on my head,' said Donald. 'But I'm hardly likely to be able to drown them... am I?'

The dignitary smiled inanely, struggling to interpret the great man's deeper meaning.

'YOU'RE RIGHT... IT *MIGHT* NOT BE WORKING EFFICIENTLY... BUT I'M NOT BLOODY WELL TAKING IT OFF!'

And so the evening continued... Donald mortified, the audience mystified and the struggling actors onstage petrified.

But his words had won through... albeit not the ones that had reluctantly spewed out of his mouth that evening. He would be lauded in the morning... the critics gushing with ever-spiralling superlatives, as they outbid each other to demonstrate that they were clever enough to understand his deepest insights. "He could do no wrong," they gushed.

Unfortunately for Donald... the next twenty-three days would prove that wasn't strictly true.

*　　*　　*

It must be assumed that camels possess a morbid fear of straw. It's understandable. Their trepidation on being loaded with the stuff must be immense... not least if the person doing the loading rubs their chin and contemplates whether to put the last bit on.

But camels would do well to note that whilst proverbs and maxims allow communication of thoughts in the laziest possible way – substituting somebody else's imagination in place of one's own – they are not always worthy of closer scrutiny.

Take *"you can't have your cake and eat it"*.

Which puritanical pessimist came up with *that* counter-intuitive piece of masochism? Surely the whole point of having a cake is that you're *supposed* to eat it. In fact... it would be exceedingly strange to have a cake and *not* eat it. It would – in the minds of the unimaginative – be as pointless as *"having a dog and barking yourself"*.

"A bird in the hand is worth two in the bush" is a further example of such lackadaisical thinking. Try imparting *that* nugget of wisdom to a screaming ornithophobic, finding themselves clutching a handful of flapping feathers, eight sharp claws and a disgruntled beak.

As for *"better the devil you know than the devil you don't"*... is it *seriously* being suggested that prior acquaintance with the Prince of Darkness will ultimately be any more beneficial to your soul than having to deal with him in an unfamiliar manifestation?

The flaws are there for all to see. For crumpled camels... whilst it could've been the final straw that did the damage, it might just as easily have been the last grain of rice, drop of myrrh, or bite of whatever took its owner's fancy prior to mounting. Paradoxically... this last, calorie-based scenario has given rise to a popular adage amongst long-suffering camels for hire in holiday locations that holds... *"Overweight tourists shouldn't have their cake and eat it."*

In truth... it would be more accurate to say it was the final *sub-atomic particle* that made the difference... taking the saying to a *far* more interesting level.

There has to be a point – no matter how infinitesimally small in scale – when such a minute piece of matter really does... matter. Somewhere, the line has to be drawn and the most seemingly insignificant speck of stuff finds itself with unimaginable power and responsibility in relation to its size.

Take the microscopically precise zenith of a failing rocket or the exact moment an entire mountainside of snow decides to become an avalanche. Having reached a tipping point, *something* has to give and decide it's had enough. And as no two events can happen at *precisely* the same time... if the timeline is dissected minutely enough, you will eventually discover the single particle that made the difference.

In the case of the errant rocket, this will be the particle that finally succumbs to the laws of gravity and says to its neighbours... 'Do you know what, boys...? I think I'm going back!' Having looked forward with excitement to their interplanetary jaunt, his colleagues might unimaginatively advise the contrary rascal that *"birds of a feather flock together"* and *"there is strength in numbers"*. But having reminded them that *"pride comes before a fall"* and doffed its cap to Sir Isaac Newton, it will fulfil its destiny and tip the balance... prompting a few sympathetic shouts of *"all for one and one for all"*... followed by the inevitable clamour of *"if you can't beat 'em, join 'em!"*.

One final point to ponder... If the Universe is not to end in a cosmological big freeze, but by some cosmological catastrophe instead, there exists right now a single particle somewhere in its unimaginable vastness that holds the tipping point for its demise... assuming, of course, it isn't ended by the failure of a mortal named Norman Penkridge... an act of God... or the devil you *didn't* know.

As particles are indestructible and live many lives, in its present incarnation, that particle may not be so far away... part of a teacup in someone's cupboard, the breath propelling an expletive or within your very own body. It may even – if an intelligent designer possessed a sense of humour – be part of a piece of straw.

But tipping points aren't exclusive to matter, of course. They are also found in thoughts... and just as potentially catastrophic.

*   *   *

There once was a time Chad Cheadle would have been appalled at the mountain of junk in front of which he was slouched... had he gotten over the shock of being slouched in the first place. All things paper – spent drinking cups included – competed with some-things-not-paper to claim its summit... its only positive feature being it signalled the whereabouts of a perfectly good desk beneath.

Battling the clutter was a computer screen displaying a game of solitaire, whose prospects of a happy ending appeared as bleak as the person playing it.

The only activity in the room belonged to the second hand of a wristwatch. And though logic would once have suggested to its owner that the minute and hour hands must also be up to something... it no longer seemed that way.

To kill a few of those seconds, Chad stroked the stubble threatening to become a beard and gazed aimlessly out of the window; his apathy momentarily put on hold by action taking place behind others across the street. There was also once a time he would have envied the people engaged in it their sense of purpose.

Not anymore.

What was the point?

You spent years developing a highly disciplined sense of logic to establish yourself as the best in your field... in control and working diligently to maintain order for the rest of the world... only for fate to intervene and pull the rug from beneath you, bringing everything you ever believed in crashing down around your neatly pigeonholed theories on life, the Universe and your part in it.

He sighed... to pass a few more seconds.

At least he could take comfort from the fact his own part didn't matter anymore.

Switching his attention to a map of the world that was unsuccessfully trying to make a peeling, vanilla wall appear interesting, he found himself drawn to an arrogantly shaped island a little north-west of centre. Fate had deemed *his* rug be pulled by a wayward eccentric who hailed from its shores.

The memory tugged like an old scar.

Leaning back, he placed his trust in two legs of a chair whose condition suggested he shouldn't and cupped his hands on top of his head.

Fate!

The mere fact he now acknowledged the concept was testament to the extent of his decline. That *other* time would have had him arguing furiously against such an abstraction... confidently stating that if it couldn't be quantified, it didn't exist.

But that was then and now was reality. Things had changed.

The sign on his door read *Private Investigator*... though given the only thing he'd investigated in the past week was how to avoid being evicted for failing to pay the rent, that claim was starting to look a little spurious.

Prior to that, his skills had been under-utilised recording the activities of a pair of surgically enhanced breasts as they flirted their way through endless days of tuition from athletic males hired to coach their pucker-lipped owner in the skills of tennis, golf, yoga... or anything else that involved suspiciously close body contact. Her husband had broken down in tears when handed the final report... and yet more when handed the final bill. But with the remuneration for his efforts having gone on servicing debts, Chad figured he'd reached a professional and personal nadir.

The little island on the map seemed to smirk in agreement. Sitting defiantly alone on its fat, Anglo-Saxon haunches, it wore a grin stretching from North Berwick to Falkirk. And why not? History had proved it could punch well above its weight.

It had certainly got the better of *him.*

He'd left its shores a broken man... the blame for failing to help prevent the collapse of the international art market and resulting global chaos forever engraved on his CV. From golden boy to whipping boy in the space of an Atlantic crossing... his fate had been well and truly sealed.

See... there it was again... that friggin' F word!

He winced at its continued intrusion into his thoughts and reflected on the possibility that if he allowed his mental standards to sink any lower, he might... a non-existent God forbid... find himself resorting to prayer.

Mind you... if it meant getting that previous life back...

'So this is where you've been hiding that ego-inflated carcass of yours all this time!' boomed a voice.

Absorbed in his melancholia, he hadn't heard the door with the spurious claim on it open.

'Jeez, Cheadle... you look friggin' awful!'

The shock of company jarred him from his torpor. The shock of who it was dropped his jaw to the ground and his feet from the desk. 'Bob?' he gawped.

'Good to see you still haven't lost those outstanding powers of observation!' his visitor beamed.

'Forget observation. I'd recognise that body odour anywhere... even after all *these* years! But what in hell's name causes it to waft *this* way?'

Bob drank in his insalubrious surroundings and flinched.

'The need to rescue you, from the look of things!'

Embarrassed, Chad opened his mouth to object. But his visitor disarmed him with the cheekiest of grins... flinging open his arms and giving a nod of encouragement.

Accepting the invitation, Chad scrambled from his chair and embraced his old partner with a warmth that would've surprised them both had it happened when they'd worked together. 'God, Bob,' he laughed, cupping his friend's sweat-drenched face affectionately in his hands. 'It might've been a while, but you're *really* not smelling any sweeter!'

'Not my fault you can't afford an office with an elevator. And *you* can talk!' Bob ran his own across Chad's ungroomed stubble.

Chad shrugged awkwardly. 'Well... you know... I wasn't expecting callers today.'

'Business *that* good, eh?'

'I'm doin' okay,' said Chad... though even to him, the words sounded unconvincing.

'Not from where I'm standing! What the hell's happened to that clean-cut, golden boy I once knew?'

Bob's bluntness caught Chad off guard. 'He became tarnished,' he blurted, downgrading his enthusiasm somewhat. 'Anyway... you should *know* what happened. You were with me... remember?'

Bob pulled back to allow his old friend his moment of martyrdom. 'And I'm with you now,' he smiled sympathetically.

Chad didn't reply.

Bob telegraphed his surprise. '*Really...?* Still hurtin' after all *these* years? Is *that* what all this is about?' He nodded at the pile of apathy obliterating the desk.

'So... I'm not yet able to stretch to an office cleaner. Big deal!'

'I meant the reason you've been hiding yourself in these godforsaken backwaters for so long. What's it been... a little under five years... a little over four?'

The question provoked another silence.

'Okay, then... let me do the reasoning.' Bob stepped back to

445

assess the situation. 'Could it be the only way you thought to cope with the stigma of failure was to remove yourself from those who knew you bore it? Is *that* why you've not been back to visit the old team?'

Chad was becoming increasingly irked by the conversation's negative direction. Having not spoken for a number of years, he at least thought they could have started with pleasantries about the weather. 'I seem to remember being given the impression the department no longer considered us part of the team,' he answered coldly, his initial excitement having all but evaporated.

Bob's brow creased. 'How could *that* be? You and I were the *A team*... remember?' He flung out his arms again.

Chad ignored this second invitation. 'Given the successes we regularly delivered, I'm hardly likely to forget. But we were only given that epithet when things were going well. As soon as the situation turned, our triumphs were spectacularly overlooked, and you and I were hung out to dry.'

Bob lowered his arms, realising the car wreck he'd walked in on was more serious than first assumed. 'Wow! I really thought you'd be over all that by now! You've just gotta face facts, Chad. We might not have been to blame for the outcome of our last mission and everything that followed, but the truth is... organisations like ours aren't funded to fail. *Someone* had to take the wrap for what happened.' He shrugged philosophically. 'You know how these things work. There's no way it was ever gonna be anyone above *our* pay grade.'

Chad stared back unconvinced. 'Anyway... it's all in the past now. I don't have to worry about such things anymore. That's *your* world, seeing you were fool enough to stick with it. *Mine's* one of self-determination.'

'And total friggin' mess,' snorted Bob, with his trademark indelicacy. 'I mean... look at this place! You used to beat up on me if I so much as dropped a candy wrapper in your virtuous presence!'

Chad now rued his initial welcome. 'I take it you haven't come all this way just to gloat?' he scowled.

Bob fixed him firmly in the eye. 'Now... how on *earth* could I be doing that, if everything here's so hunky-dory?'

'I'm doing okay,' Chad mumbled, looking away.

Bob puffed out his cheeks. 'If you say so.'

'I ain't hiding. I just needed a change of scenery and time to sort my head out. What happened back then was a shock to everything I ever believed in. And I'm not talking about a lack of support from those who put me in that position in the first place. I'm talking about a set of firm, logical, commonsense beliefs that got stood on their head by a raving lunatic who communicated with the dead!'

'Tucker-Jenkins?' squinted Bob. He raised a finger. 'Interesting. I notice you didn't say... *claimed to.*'

'Precisely. So you'll excuse me if I also happen to have changed my attitude towards workplace litter and a few minor areas of personal hygiene.'

Bob lifted his hands. 'Hey... you'll hear no complaints from me! Makes me feel right at home. What I'm *really* curious about is how the mighty Chad Cheadle – one-time supreme champion of logic – hasn't managed to convince himself, after all these years, that a *raving lunatic who communicated with the dead* simply got lucky with his predictions or was in on the scam from the start. That *old* Chad Cheadle would've had no problem listing every possible alternative... and in strict order of probability. How the tables have turned! I remember *me* struggling to convince *you* that Donald might be onto something back then... and *you* who suggested he was deliberately leaking information to act as a decoy. Well... I've since come to the conclusion you were right. The question is... what happened to *your* beliefs?'

'Things have changed,' Chad muttered.

'They sure have! But how come? Tucker-Jenkins was a stooge. Pure and simple. He said as much as he was carted away on that stretcher... *a herring still resembles a herring, even when it's red...* remember?'

Chad flinched at the reminder. 'D'ya wanna know how many times I've run those words through my head these past years? It was a warning against relying on logic. And he was right. It failed me!'

Bob looked at his friend, stunned. 'And you've given up on everything simply because of one man's parting taunt?' He gestured towards the sign on the door. 'If that includes your legendary approach to problem solving, might I suggest you're now in the wrong game?'

'It's all I know to do,' Chad shrugged. 'Besides... Tucker-Jenkins' comment was merely the catalyst. I lost my belief in quantifiable certainties because of all the other inexplicable crap surrounding it.'

'Like what?'

Chad's head jerked. 'Are you serious? Take that old fool's sudden, meteoric rise to fame. I mean... how on earth do you explain *that*? Have you *seen* his plays?'

Bob winced. 'I'm waiting for the film versions. I hear they don't do popcorn in theatres.'

'They're *genius*, Bob. That one-time fruitcake... previously incapable of making sense about *anything*... suddenly and miraculously acquired the ability to communicate from his soul directly to the deepest part of yours.' He looked beyond his former partner's vacuous expression. 'Well... most people's, anyway.'

'He's an eccentric,' shrugged Bob. 'Maybe he always had it in him but never bothered. He simply saw an increased enthusiasm for the arts as a bandwagon to be jumped on.'

Chad looked him square in the eyes. 'Do you know the discipline it takes to write, Bob? Let alone write at the rate *he's* been doing since that *red herring* incident. He's churned out twenty-two plays in the last five years!'

'Twenty-three, actually. I heard them lauding his latest one on TV last night.'

'There you go... I rest my case! Most people would settle for *one* of his in any given lifetime. It's unheard of... and all after he got struck by that weird ball of...' Chad stopped himself and quickly dropped his eyes to the floor. 'Forget it,' he frowned. 'Let's talk about the weather.'

Bob's open mouth suggested that wasn't going to be an option. His default *laissez-faire* expression had morphed into one of nervous expectation. 'Go on,' he prodded. 'What were you gonna say?'

Chad raised his eyes and stared at his former partner imploringly.

'Chad? Weird ball of... *what?*'

Chad shook his head, wrestling with a memory that was preventing him from answering.

'You were gonna say *light*... weren't you? Only it kinda *wasn't*... if you get my drift.'

Chad scrunched his eyes shut, as if willing the image in his head to go away.

'Well, I'll be damned! You saw it too!'

Chad capitulated with a nod.

'SHIT!' Bob walked himself around in a tight circle to expel his adrenalin. 'After all these friggin' years!' He looked up at the ceiling and drew a deep breath. 'Man! You never said! I thought it was just *me*! I thought I'd gone mad!' He let out a loud, cathartic whistle and ruffled his hair with his hands, as if to reassemble his thoughts. 'It was just a fleeting glimpse, so I told myself I'd imagined it... the result of too much stress and adrenalin that day. There was no point mentioning it in the heat of battle... and as *you* never said anything...'

Chad acknowledged the absurdity of the situation. 'Probably for the exact same reasons as you. We were drowning in enough shit at the time. Things were fucked up as they were. I sure as hell wasn't gonna bring it up in any debriefing... official or otherwise. The last thing I wanted was my sanity questioned! They were already out to crucify us. I definitely wasn't gonna hand those arseholes the hammer with which to strike home the nails!'

'What about *my* sanity? I saw it too!'

'I was never sure. Everything happened so fast. My attention was glued on whatever it was emanating from that window... not on whether you were experiencing it with me. Given your *own* silence, I pretended it hadn't happened. I guess that's what you do when your sense of logic gets severely challenged. But the experience became harder to bury as time passed. The more it dominated my thoughts, the more I believed what I saw. Not that your confirmation makes it any easier. Now it's *definitely* real. We can't *both* have been hallucinating!'

Bob wiped the shock from his face with an unsteady hand. 'So... given we can consider ourselves sane, rational human beings once again... what the *fuck* d'ya reckon it was? I mean... it had pulsating veins and shit.' His eyes widened. 'I've never seen anything like it. It was like... real... but... *not* real... if you know what I mean.'

Chad knew *exactly* what he meant. An expression of wonderment transformed his face. 'I just remember thinking it was the most beautiful thing I'd ever seen.' His eyes glistened. 'It made me feel for a brief second that...' He paused... struggling to express precisely what that experience had been. 'I know this sounds weird and hippy... but that I *understood* what everything was all about!' He stopped, as a less welcome image took hold. 'And then... after that explosion... nothing... a void... just a frustrating feeling like I *used* to know. Like when a name sits on the tip of your tongue and refuses to take that final step to put you out of your misery.' The light disappeared from his eyes. 'The thought of it's haunted me ever since.'

'Same for me!' exclaimed Bob. 'I can't tell you the number of times I've questioned what I witnessed! At least now I know I wasn't seeing things!'

'Well... we're both agreed on that,' Chad nodded. 'And therein lies my problem... No matter how many angles I approach it from, I simply can't explain it. The systematic application of logic, in which I once put all my faith, has finally let me down. That's why I can't trust it anymore.'

Bob took a moment to appreciate the enormity of his friend's admission. For anyone else, such a realisation would've been a shock. For the man in front of him, it had been a total disaster. 'So... *that's* what's reduced you to all this,' he empathised.

'Not on its own,' Chad grimaced. 'But when you're forced to

accept the existence of something you would've once regarded as impossible, it lessens the implausibility of everything else you never believed in... like communicating with the dead. And then you find yourself floating in a world of all possibilities, without solid ground on which to anchor your beliefs. That's a difficult place for someone like me to inhabit.'

Bob gave a sympathetic look. 'I guess I owe you an apology... bursting in on your life like this. You know me... I never did do sensitivity or tact. I'd no idea things had gotten so bad. Maybe I should've come sooner.'

'It wouldn't have made any difference if you had. There's nothing you could've said or done that would've helped. Real or imagined... that ball of light isn't the *only* mystery that's been eating away at me all these years. There's another, far more fundamental one.' Chad looked his former partner squarely in the eyes. 'What exactly *was* going on in that room, Bob? What the hell was it all about? I mean... one minute we're put into the field to investigate a mysterious conspiracy involving every religious institution on this planet... the next... we've traced its source to a single room – no bigger than this one – where a nobody kid is handling some of the most valuable artworks ever created. Then... just as we're about to discover the answer, something otherworldly takes the place apart and sends any evidence we might've collected up in smoke. The only thing that survived was that nobody kid!'

'Penkridge.'

The name stung. 'And not such a nobody anymore.'

'Now... there's a curiosity!'

'You're not wrong! Up until that point, a penniless nonentity... completely off everyone's radar. But following that explosion, someone who starts spending money like it's rained down on him from heaven! So... given the one fact we *do* know is that they weren't actually *stealing* the paintings... where did his sudden wealth come from?'

'You know my theory on that. It's never changed. It was all a scam to play the markets. You start with a fickle one... then destabilise it further by sowing seeds of panic. Maybe we were unwitting pawns... promulgating the idea that a large proportion of valuable paintings were being replaced by fakes. Having invested in commodities that would increase in an economic crash – gold... precious stones... that kinda thing – he and his cohorts simply sat back and watched as market forces got to work and sent the value of their investments through the roof!'

'Your argument perfectly illustrates my predicament. In a previous life, I would've applauded the logic behind it and wholeheartedly agreed. But the logic *doesn't* work. The facts say that never happened. Despite meticulously studying the data of every exchange in the world, no abnormal trading patterns were ever discovered.'

'Maybe they invested over a longer period of time to cover their tracks. Don't forget... he also benefited from massive, knock-down prices when he started accumulating his own art portfolio.'

'The value of which has risen little in the intervening years,' pointed out Chad. 'From what I've seen... none of it makes sense. *None* of it! And that's what consumes me... day in, day out. I can't let go of the fact there's stuff out there I ain't ever gonna be able to explain, no matter how hard I try.' He looked at Bob, the weight of the thought sitting heavy on him. 'So maybe *now* you understand why I don't give a damn about anything else.'

Bob winked. 'So perhaps it's time you asked me why I'm here.'

'It's not because you've missed me?' tried Chad, a thin smile creasing his lips.

'What do *you* reckon?'

'I reckon not. If you *had*, it wouldn't have taken you this long to track me down.'

'Interesting to see you trusting logic, there.'

Chad frowned as a thought struck him. 'You've not been sent to persuade me back, have you?'

'To the Agency? You gotta be kiddin'!' Bob snorted. 'We couldn't handle you moping around the office all day!'

'In which case... you've not quit your own position and are here looking for a job.'

'There it is again... that logic you claim to have lost faith in. You're damn right I'm not. But you're getting warm.'

'I'm getting pissed off... is what I'm getting!' Chad pointed to his stubble. 'You'd better cut to the chase before this becomes a beard!'

'What if there was a third scenario?'

Chad's eyes narrowed. 'You haven't come to *kill* me, have you?'

'You *have* lost it. I'm not wearing gloves. My prints would be all over the place.'

'I may need to put on a pair myself if you don't get to the point!'

Heeding the threat, Bob utilised the only corner of the desk capable of accommodating a buttock and beckoned for Chad to sit. 'Okay... here it is. It seems there's someone *else* out there keen to find the answers to all those questions that have been torturing you.'

'Regarding the conspiracy?'

'Not in general.'

'Then, *what* in particular?'

'Penkridge. I think they're looking to punish him.'

'Sounds like another disgruntled bankrupt. I guess they'll just have to join the queue.' Chad's countenance suddenly changed. 'Hang on, though... Penkridge's involvement was only ever known to the intelligence community.'

'Precisely... and this guy certainly ain't bankrupt!'

Chad lent forward. 'Go on.'

'I believe he could be our ticket to finally solving this puzzle.'

'*Our?*'

'Yeah... as in the *A-team*... back together again... you and me... the old partnership.'

'You're thinking of freelancing?'

'Let's just say... I'm due some leave... and if we get it right this time, I won't be going back. I've been promised we'll never need to work again!'

Chad cast a glance at the game of solitaire on his computer screen. 'Sounds interesting.'

'*Very!*'

'Okay... Tell me more.'

'Like I say... there's someone out there with money who wants the same answers we do.'

'And who exactly *is* this mystery benefactor?'

'Dunno,' shrugged Bob, unconcerned by the vagueness of his answer. 'But he tells me I don't need to.'

Chad considered the situation. 'Fair enough. I can live with that. But is he part of an organisation?'

'I told you... I dunno. And I reckon that's how he wants it to stay.'

'He contacted you without leaving a footprint?'

'Absolutely. I was sitting on a bench minding my own business...'

'You mean being a pervert.'

'That *is* my business. So... this guy sits down beside me. At first I reckon he's a wino or some kinda weirdo. He smells funny and his clothes are a little unconventional. But he knows who I am. He comes straight out with it ... telling me he wants Penkridge brought to his knees and that he's prepared to pay whatever it takes to achieve it.'

'Just like that?'

'*Exactly* like that.'

'He definitely referred to Penkridge by name?'

'Directly.'

Chad skewed his jaw. 'Then he clearly has access to classified information... especially if he knows of your involvement in the case.'

'And yours.'

Chad looked at him cagily.

'Well... you didn't reckon I was here outta pure altruism, did ya? Cut you in on a lucrative deal and halve my earnings... just to rescue a troubled ex-colleague from having to locate old ladies' missing Chihuahuas? My fondness for you don't stretch *that* far! It was my *client* who insisted I use you. Seems his access to classified information extends to him also knowing about *your* involvement in the case. He was very specific about his wishes. He instructed me to arrange a meeting between the three of us... refusing to divulge anything further until then. Hence the reason I tracked you down and braved these provincial backwaters. But this is the best bit... He made it clear money is no object. We can name our price! Chad... this could be that retirement in the sun we always fantasised about on those long surveillance ops! It seems like all our prayers might've been answered in one!'

'You know I don't believe in such things.'

'Then maybe it's time you started. *Someone* up there clearly likes you!' Bob looked at his old partner eagerly. 'So... what d'ya say? You and me... our mystery benefactor... and one more shot at finding the answers to all those lay-awake questions that have been tormenting you these past years?'

Chad narrowed his eyes and scoured Bob's expression for the hint of a telltale smile. 'This better not be one of your famous wind-ups,' he warned. 'Otherwise I really *will* be putting gloves on.'

'This one's straight from the hip,' said Bob earnestly. 'Even *I* wouldn't joke about a subject as serious as this.'

Chad considered the proposition in front of him... then looked at the years of accumulated neglect swamping his desk. 'Okay,' he said heavily, with a breath that drew in ghosts from the past. He glanced across at the map on the wall and the odd-shaped island that had been taunting him for so long. 'Maybe I'll live to regret this... but at least I won't die regretting having never tried!'

Bob stood and removed the corner of the desk from his backside. 'So... does that mean you're in?'

Chad nodded his reply... knowing he was about to prove the other two hands of his wristwatch did move after all.

*　　*　　*

After much patient coaxing and gentle brow stroking, Norman

had finally managed to get Xanthia to relax her bulging eyes just enough for them to close and allow some sleep. It had also taken repeated assurances that apocalyptic revelations were renowned for being open to interpretation... not to mention a handful of the strongest sleeping tablets available without prescription.

It had pained him to see her childlike mind struggling to come to terms with what she'd witnessed in the garden. Perversely, that was one of her qualities he most adored... the way her mind appeared so delicate and fragile when threatened by anything... *well... complicated.* She was his wounded fawn, and he the caring woodsman whose duty it was to nurture and protect. Not that he'd ever owned an axe.

He embraced the vision of her struggling, in need of his help. *That cute, little pout she gave when things got difficult. Her doe-eyed stare gently and alluringly refreshed by the innocence of those long, Bambi-like lashes.* His heartbeat quickened. *Her trembling and vulnerable body, quivering like that of a young, distressed creature cowering in the forest, unsure as to the intent of her would-be benefactor's large chopper...*

He shook himself from the analogy.

Suffice to say... he would safeguard her from the evils of the real world – and the *apparently-real-but-you-wouldn't-necessarily-admit-at-a-dinner-party-to-having-personally-conversed-with-entities-from-it* world – as much as he could.

It wasn't going to be easy. She always struggled with visualising anything further than one day in the future... let alone having to visualise the notion there might not be one at all. So trying to explain why he'd be less attentive to her needs during the coming weeks would demand an awful lot of tact and patience on his part.

Not that he knew what his task would entail... which is why he was sitting downstairs in the living room, apprehensively waiting for its ceiling lights to dim and for Gabriel to make an appearance... just like the old days.

Up until that afternoon, it had been his favourite spot in the house... a place where he would sit for hour upon hour, surrounded by his most treasured artworks, wallowing in the mind-boggling fact that canvasses once sat upon the easels of great masters such as Holbein, Renoir and Vermeer – and on which they had imbedded their souls in paint – now hung on *his* walls... effectively meaning that they had ultimately done so for *him*.

The view away from the paintings wasn't bad either. Staring out through the imposing patio windows, he drank in the breathtaking, night-time panorama beyond. Whilst the twinkling lights of boats and waterfront properties that delineated the coastline were still as impressive as the day the estate agent had smugly introduced him to it, he couldn't seem to shake the feeling that the contents of the room had somehow lost their lustre... the paintings hanging with a new and uncomfortable sense of ostentation.

As he was contemplating this fact, a bronze table lamp away to his left flickered momentarily... then blew its bulb.

'Gabriel? Is that you?'

A familiar ball of orange light appeared above a rug that had once nonchalantly grazed upon the Serengeti... a little *too* nonchalantly, as it transpired.

The ceiling lights Norman had expected to dim obliged... with various other electrical items joining in the commotion for good measure. The ball of orange light pulsated rapidly before finally exploding in a bright flash, releasing a brief wave of what felt like euphoria and the splendidly robed figure of the Archangel Norman had been expecting.

'You really don't have to go to all this trouble,' said Gabriel, carefully steering his unfolding wings away from a number of endangered artworks. 'I've told you before... this is all in your mind.'

'I can't help it,' Norman shrugged. 'It's how I've been conditioned.'

'Those Renaissance painters have a lot to answer for,' tutted Gabriel. 'You know... I wish... just once... *someone* would have the vision to see past the hype and put me in a leather jacket!'

'Wouldn't that be blasphemous?'

'Depends which biking fraternity you belong to, I suppose.' said Gabriel, retracting his wings. 'It certainly wouldn't make one jot of difference to what it is I have to say.'

'I'll see if I can be a bit more creative next time,' Norman promised.

Gabriel flinched. 'I can't say that makes me feel any easier. Creativity has never been your strong point.'

'I think you'll find things have changed.' Norman pointed proudly at the works of art surrounding him, deciding it was time he stood up for himself and blew his own trumpet. 'I've come a long way since we first met. As you can see, I've used your gift of the chequebook to better myself. Owning some of the greatest artworks ever produced has enabled me to study them in the minutest detail and fully appreciate their construction. The last five years have been *far* from wasted. They've allowed me to understand how such exquisite beauty is created. In fact... I'd go as far as to say I now consider myself a bit of an *expert* when it comes to creativity!'

'Understanding how beauty is created is not the same as knowing how to create it,' replied Gabriel phlegmatically, his words scything through Norman's defence.

Having blown it, Norman's trumpet sounded like a bugle signalling retreat. Once more, the clarity of the Archangel's words made ownership of the room and its contents sit heavily on his sagging shoulders. He sensibly changed the subject. 'Talking of understanding... I'm sorry about Xanthia's lack of it earlier. She has trouble grasping things sometimes. I think it was all a bit too much for her.'

'On the contrary,' said Gabriel. 'I would say she grasped the severity of the situation perfectly. Her reaction was in direct proportion to the message... unlike yours.'

Norman bowed his head and sighed.

'Your frustration is due to the fact I have confirmed that the truth of what you have achieved here is not as you would wish it to be,' counselled Gabriel. 'I'm sure it comes as no surprise to learn I've always found your lack of deference and detachment frustrating. I've never encountered anyone who treats what I have to say with such casualness.'

'You wanted me to put you in a leather jacket a couple of minutes ago!' objected Norman, his eyes widening.

'See what I mean?'

Norman realised further protestations were futile. They would only strengthen Gabriel's case. He held his tongue, knowing full well the Archangel could read his thoughts anyway.

'Correct on all three assumptions,' confirmed Gabriel. 'The message I bring is far more consequential than the defence of your ego. Whatever nightmares Xanthia is currently experiencing are as nothing to what will follow should you fail the mission we need you to undertake. Your previous efforts merely bought us a little time.'

'Well... at least I did *something* positive, then!' offered Norman sardonically.

'Not when you consider it's just run out,' said Gabriel.

Norman felt the weight of the Archangel's words squash any last resistance.

'Good,' said Gabriel, feeling it too. 'Now we can get down to business.'

'You mentioned *Armageddon* in the garden,' ventured Norman.

Gabriel didn't answer.

'*That* bad, eh...?'

A further silence suggested it was.

'So... what is it you want *me* to do?'

'Trust me,' said Gabriel.

Norman looked at him blankly.

'That bit's very important. The danger I'm about to put you in is beyond anything you've encountered before... paradoxically because we are trying to keep you safe for as long as possible. You will need to succeed in your task alone this time. There will be no outside support to assist you, as it is imperative we keep targets to a minimum.'

'*Targets?*' Norman gulped.

'It is a fundamental law of spirit that like attracts like. Whilst

431

love draws love, and positivity is strengthened in similar fashion... the same is also true of negativity and evil. Dark forces will be drawn to each other and increase their threat as the threat against *them* increases. In limiting the scope of their retribution, the paradox is that it will all be focused on the one area. *You.*'

'I understand,' croaked Norman.

'As in... you now *know* it. That alone has started the clock ticking. But the least you do know, the better... for the very reason I have given. That is why I say you must trust me.'

'I guess we shouldn't waste time, then,' said Norman stoically. 'Shall we get started?'

Gabriel embraced the positive ripple. 'Very well. We need you to generate a vibrational confluence that effectuates a molecular dissonance.'

Norman twitched.

'I suggest you get a pen,' Gabriel advised.

'I'll grab a dictionary whilst I'm at it.'

Gabriel waited until Norman was ready. 'It is vital you do *exactly* as requested, without deviation. You must work out a way to generate a continuous pattern of two individual frequencies, being those of 587.33 and 554.365 cycles per second... each frequency being separated by an interval of 1,481,481,481 nanoseconds and delivered at a level of 145 decibels.'

Norman hastily scribbled the specifications on a notepad and awaited further instructions.

'There aren't any... for now,' said Gabriel.

Norman read back what he'd just written. As the precision of the numbers left nothing to chance, he intuitively felt it would be easy.

'You're wrong,' said Gabriel. 'It will be anything *but.*'

'Am I allowed to ask *one* question?' The thought of all those dark forces gathering hadn't *quite* blunted Norman's inquisitiveness.

'It is safe to ask the one you are currently thinking of,' Gabriel replied.

'Okay... Why have you chosen *me* again?'

The Archangel looked at him fondly. 'Because you need it to be so.' He ruffled his wings. 'Now... you must start immediately. We have great faith in you. For all your faults... giving up isn't one of them. Once you have found a way to accomplish what is required, I will return with further instructions.'

'I'll try and forgo the wings, when you do,' Norman quipped, trying not to think about the danger further instructions might attract.

Gabriel looked around uneasily. 'You must be careful. As stated... we have set the clock ticking in this room. Now the start of our plans has been made manifest, malevolent entities will already be drawing towards them.'

'Does that mean I'm going to meet Satan again?' groaned Norman.

'He will keep his intentions as guarded as ours. But let's just say... I wouldn't bet against it.'

Norman suddenly felt vulnerable.

'No! Be strong!' Gabriel encouraged him. 'You have the whole of the Universe within you. It is important you remember that! You are never alone... even when you think you are.' As if to disprove that very point, he started to fade.

Norman felt the urge to call out and stop him, but couldn't think of anything to say.

As the image of the Archangel became a surreal memory, Norman experienced a massive sense of unease. The atmosphere in the room held a different stillness to that which he'd experienced on previous partings. The space Gabriel had inhabited still seemed charged with energy. But it now felt nothing like the warm, friendly glow that had just vacated it. It was negative... dark and brooding... like a menacing void.

The clock on the mantelpiece moved its hands and chimed the arrival of midnight... the once pretty bells tolling like a death knell as they intruded on the silence.

Norman could swear the room smelt... *damp?*

He felt a cold shiver enter his body, as he turned for comfort

429

to what lay beyond the window and saw that the twinkling lights had ceased to be.

*　　　*　　　*

'BEHOLD, HE COMETH WITH CLOUDS... AND EVERY EYE SHALL SEE HIM, AND THEY ALSO WHICH PIERCED HIM... AND ALL KINDREDS OF THE EARTH SHALL WAIL BECAUSE OF HIM!' Donald clamped his hand over his mouth and appealed with suffering eyes for the scattering cats to forgive their daddy's unwarranted outburst.

The taxi driver bringing him home had looked similarly alarmed... though *his* options of escape had been rather more limited. The poor man had politely – if nervously – pretended to ignore the incessant ranting, only chancing the occasional troubled glance at Donald via the rear view mirror when things seemed like they might be getting out of hand. The look of relief on his face as he'd pocketed his tip and hastily put his cab into gear said it all.

But Donald hadn't said enough... not as far as those planting the words in his head were concerned.

'FOR THE GREAT DAY OF HIS WRATH IS COME... AND WHO SHALL BE ABLE TO STAND?'

'Please make them stop!' he implored higher vibrations he hoped might be listening in... if just for their amusement.

But to no avail.

'YOU'RE A FAT HELP!' he chastised Whitebait. 'CAN'T YOU HAVE A WORD WITH THEM? AFTER ALL... THEY'RE *YOUR* NEIGHBOURS!'

It appeared the expired seafarer couldn't.

Donald felt he had no other choice. Grabbing a shamefully grubby tea towel from the kitchen drainer, he stuffed it into his mouth.

'Mmmm Mmm Mm Mmmm Mmmmm Mmm Mm Mmmmmmm!'

Not only was it not working, it wasn't helping. The bacteria were making him gag.

428

He pulled it out and gave the matter some thought. It was obvious the words were being delivered as a warning, much like they had been a few years earlier. Only *then*, the vague cautions were about paintings and acts of deception, with the odd bit of Shakespeare thrown in for good measure. But now it was phrases of a far darker nature, along with what appeared to be hints at a large-scale desecration... though of what, he had no idea.

'IF THEY INSIST ON BEING SO PERSISTENT, ASK THEM TO BE MORE BLOODY *SPECIFIC* WHILST THEY'RE AT IT!' he implored his spirit guide.

He waited for Whitebait to relay the message.

'WHAT DO YOU MEAN... *THEY DON'T KNOW EITHER?*'

The explanation received was that the spirit world was awash with vibrations from increased activity at a higher level. Stuff was leaking through, which those who hadn't quite made the top grade assumed should be passed on to those even further down the vibrational ladder. Having a foot on the first rung, that meant Donald.

A thought struck him.

Much to his relief, it was one of his own.

Perhaps if he in turn passed on this information to others, those supplying him with it might stop, having considered their work done.

It was certainly worth a try.

When he'd previously warned the world about an artwork conspiracy, its response had been lukewarm... any reaction usually manifested via a fist. But that was back in the days when the state of his trousers *alone* would scare people away.

Now he was *someone*. He had a voice... a *global* voice. He was listened to. His plays had elevated him to a position where millions of people around the world analysed and interpreted every word in them. So... what if he made his next opus include the warnings he was being presented with? That way, they would reach a global audience.

The thought seemed a brilliant one... and the more he considered it, the better it got. He would write his twenty-fourth play to encompass what he was being told. He would trust in his muse to dictate the flow of words and put a stop to whatever mischief was being planned. He would start right away and leave nothing to chance. Not only would he write the play... he would produce and direct it himself. Taking total control, he wouldn't stop until his work was done. Even baths would have to wait.

'YES... JUST LIKE THE OLD DAYS!'

Invigorated, he strode purposefully out of the kitchen and into his study. 'Out of my way, Mahler,' he instructed an inquisitive cat who'd chanced a return to his feet. 'Daddy's got extremely important work to do!'

The cat knew better than to argue and sprang sideways to a safer distance, though still doggedly in attendance alongside its peers.

'Daddy seems popular today,' he addressed them brightly. 'I really can't think why!'

They purred their acknowledgement.

Settling himself at his desk and picking up his favourite pen, he ceremoniously unwound the tin foil from his head. The voices could flood in as loud as they liked now.

As a piece of chicken fat plopped onto the blank sheet of paper in front of him, one of those flooding voices suggested it might have been wiser to have used a fresh bit of foil... rather than recycle some from the kitchen bin.

The cats pounced on the discarded wrapping.

Donald shrugged and composed himself.

It was extremely important he attain the correct state of mind. Inspiration lurked on the periphery of thought. The trick was to stare inwardly at nowhere-in-particular for as long as it took for that first flash to announce itself and ignite a flow of consciousness that would surprise even him.

He didn't have long to wait.

Almost causing him to topple backwards in his chair, it struck with unprecedented force.

'YES! YES!' he shouted excitedly, as a torrent of words spewed into his head. 'THAT'S IT! I SEE IT! I SEE IT!'

He brushed the chicken fat from the paper.

'SCENE ONE,' he hastily scribbled. 'THREE MEN ARE MOVING A LARGE BLOCK OF STONE.'

*　　*　　*

'What time is it, Normy?' Xanthia slouched in the doorway, her tousled hair curtaining her bleary eyes, a pink baby-doll nightie struggling to protect her modesty.

'Eleven o'clock,' he replied, grateful for an excuse to break from the computer screen in front of him.

'At night?'

'In the morning,' he smiled.

'But it's dark... sort of... and cold.'

'It's the sea mist.' He looked towards the window and the blanket of grey beyond. 'It's the worst I've ever seen. It's refusing to burn off. It rolled in late last night.'

'I don't remember,' she mumbled, rubbing her eyes with the sides of her fists.

'Of course not,' he soothed. 'How did you sleep?'

'Like this.' She clasped her hands beside her face.

He tried again. 'I meant... did you sleep well?'

'No... I had the worst dreams *ever*,' she pouted. 'There were all these nasty creatures watching me. Only... it was as if they were real! They didn't do anyfink... just watched me.'

'Any*thing*,' he corrected her. She'd been having elocution lessons, but the results could be sporadic.

'*Anything*,' she mouthed silently.

Norman dreaded it when she recounted her nightmares. She would reel them off as if they'd actually happened... then blame him for not having assisted her in them. The repercussions could last for the best part of the day, if he'd been particularly unhelpful.

'You were really horrible,' she sulked. 'You didn't do any... *thing* to help.'

'I'm sorry... I was busy elsewhere,' he quipped.

'Doing what?'

425

Norman happily changed the conversation. 'I'll show you. Listen!' He inputted a command on his keyboard, causing two computer-generated tones to seesaw back and forth in a regular rhythm.

'That's nice,' she yawned.

He knew she was being polite. What he didn't know was how much he should tell her. He'd never forgive himself if he gave her knowledge that would make her a target of anything more unpleasant than the creatures in her dream.

The alternating notes were the frequencies Gabriel had given him the night before, their performance in strict accordance with his instructions. Except for the volume, that was. For when he'd come to *that* bit of the equation, the enormity of his task had hit home. He now knew why Gabriel had said it wasn't going to be easy.

That had been an understatement.

145 decibels was *unfeasibly* loud. To appreciate just *how* loud, one needed to take into consideration that the threshold of pain lies between 120 and 130 decibels... and that a jet engine one hundred feet away would send the meter needle rocketing to 140.

But that wasn't the worst bit.

As he discovered from his research, the decibel scale was exponential... meaning that 5 decibels more than having a shotgun discharged next to your ear meant hearing that same sound half as loud again... not to mention a bit of a headache in the morning if the sound being generated had to be continuous... which, according to Gabriel, it did.

'Aren't you gonna ask me what it's for?' he asked.

'Is it a burglar alarm?'

'No... Gabriel asked me to do this... last night, after you'd gone to sleep.'

'He came back, then?'

'Yes... but...' Norman stopped the notes and sighed despondently.

'Somefink wrong?'

He raised an eyebrow.

424

'Some*thing*,' she corrected herself.

'You could say that.'

Her forehead creased. 'I thought I just did.'

Norman decided there'd be no harm confiding in her. As she wouldn't understand the problem anyway, he figured her thoughts couldn't possibly attract anything untoward.

'Those notes I've just played you... Gabriel says I have to be able to generate them at a level of 145 decibels.'

Xanthia gave a long, descending whistle. 'That's *very* loud,' she said at the end of it. 'I fink you might have more than a little difficulty achieving that!'

Norman's head jerked.

'The loudest music ever played was 140 decibels,' she confounded him. 'And that took an *awful* lot of equipment!'

He stared at her, speechless.

'Are you sure you heard the number right?' she asked.

Norman tipped his head slowly.

She puffed out her cheeks in sympathy. 'I see your problem. That's gonna take some solving.'

'I know...! But how come *you* do?' he stuttered.

'*Duh!*' she mocked him. 'I lived with the lead singer of *Trouzerbulge*... remember? They hold the world record for the loudest rock band *ever!*'

'140 decibels?'

'Exactly. They were *that* good!' She smiled, as a thought stole her attention. 'Stump was so proud of the fact, he had the number tattooed on his...' she stopped and giggled coyly.

'You're kiddin' me,' Norman winced.

'No... wait a minute,' she frowned, concentrating hard. 'Come to fink of it... that was the number 12... followed by two little lines, top right. I fink it must've been somewhere else.' She ruffled her hair. 'You wanna get in touch with Deaf Pete. If anyone can help you, he can.'

'Deaf Pete?'

'Stump's old soundman. He was with the band for years. It was him who helped them achieve their world record. Only... he went by a different name back then.'

'And what was that?'

Xanthia thought long and hard. 'Pete,' she eventually announced.

'You're right,' nodded Norman enthusiastically. 'Perhaps I should give him a call.'

She shook her head. 'There's no point.'

'But you said...'

'He wouldn't hear the phone ring. I suggest you email him instead.'

'Great idea!' Norman scrabbled around for a pen. 'What's his email address?'

The corners of Xanthia's mouth turned down by way of an apology. 'I don't know.'

'You don't?'

'No... but Stump does.'

There was an awkward silence. Xanthia gazed at the floor some way in front of her, prepared to ignore the moment until it passed.

'I hardly think he'll want to hear from *either* of us,' said Norman, tackling it head on. 'I'm sure he's still a little sore about a "loser nerd" like me stealing his girl.'

'Loser *geek*,' she corrected him. 'As well as *"retentive arsehole"* and...'

'Yes, yes,' he interrupted uncomfortably. 'It's not a meeting I'm likely to forget!'

In truth, Norman thought Stump had behaved as reasonably as could be expected when the former had appeared at Soddem Hall to pick up Xanthia and all her worldly possessions. Stump had only *threatened* to "*ram his head up his arse until it popped out of his neck again,*" not actually going through with the action... and the black eye had healed remarkably quickly, given the venom with which it had been delivered.

'Wait a minute!' she said excitedly, bouncing on her toes. 'There's someone else who'll have Deaf Pete's email address.'

He smiled at her affectionately. 'Oh... how I love you! Who's that?'

'Stump's roadie, Sharky.'

'And how do I contact him?'

'Stump will know,' she said brightly.

Norman sighed. 'Looks like I'll have to do a little digging of my own.'

Xanthia offered her usual look of confusion. '*Gardening?* How come you suddenly know how to use a spade?'

'Don't you worry your pretty little head about it,' he cooed. 'You've been a great help... you *really* have.'

'Good,' she said proudly, turning to leave. 'In that case... I'm going to go and feed the dog.'

'That might be difficult,' he advised.

'Why?'

'We don't have one.'

'We did last night,' she insisted.

'That was a dream,' he said gently.

Xanthia let out a huff. 'Well... it's just as well.' She gave another of her pouts. '*He* didn't help me in it, either!'

Norman extrapolated from her unforgiving tone the level of difficulty he expected to endure for the rest of the day. He quickly calculated moderate to moderately heavy.

He wasn't even close.

*　　*　　*

The high-pitched squawking of macaques jarred painfully against the guttural whoops of howler monkeys; the frenzied chaos slicing the languorous air and adding to Chad's irritability. The sun was at its zenith, and he was suffering its effect.

'Whose crazy idea was this?' he moaned, tugging at his collar and stopping to survey his surroundings.

'Our mystery benefactor's,' said Bob, glad of the respite and using it to drain the remains of the bottle of water he'd been clutching. 'I told you he was weird.'

Chad's neck craned forward, as he tried to identify an animal a short distance ahead of them. 'What the hell's that?'

'A leopard,' said Bob, wiping his mouth indelicately with the back of his hand.

Chad considered their options. 'Okay. I need to think about this.'

Bob waited patiently.

'And that over there... the one looking at us like we're breakfast?'

'*Panthera onca*,' announced Bob, through a squint.

'In English, smart arse?'

Bob mopped the sweat from his brow with an already-sodden sleeve. 'I think it says *Jaguar*.'

'Then we must be close.' Chad folded up the small guide he'd been studying and moved briskly on, pushing through a swarm of schoolchildren brandishing clipboards and multi-coloured backpacks.

'He said he wanted to meet somewhere public again,' explained Bob, scurrying closely behind. 'Out in the open. My guess is he's watching us to make sure we've come alone.'

'It's his call. But you can tell him I'll be sticking the entrance fee on my expenses when we're done.'

'I don't reckon that'll be a problem,' ventured Bob, chancing a glance at his wristwatch.

'How are we doin'?'

'Spot on. But just remember what I told you. Don't stare. It's friggin' disconcerting, if you do!'

'I don't give a damn what he looks like!' said Chad. 'It's what he's got to say that interests me.'

'Just thought it best to be warned,' wheezed Bob, struggling to keep pace with his partner's determined stride. Having reached a bench seat in front of the largest of the surrounding enclosures, it relented.

Chad examined the guide again. 'This must be it. So... *now* what do we do?'

'Sit and wait... I suppose.'

Chad nodded and took the weight from his feet, though a cocktail of nerves and excitement prevented him from relaxing. He drummed his fingers impatiently on the bench. 'Is this where you met him last time?'

'No… That happened over by birds of prey.'

'I guess he has a season ticket.'

Something you wouldn't want to come face to face with in a cave let out a powerful roar in the distance.

'Sounds like my stomach feels.' said Bob.

Chad didn't answer. He was watching a magnificently maned lion that had taken a sudden interest in its latest audience. Gracefully rising from its prone position without breaking its stare – and with a menace born of confidence – it sauntered arrogantly towards them. Chad gave as good as he got; raising his head defiantly so as to return the animal's penetrating gaze… determined not to show fear. The wire fence helped.

It was a reaction the lion was used to. He'd encountered many a potential meal who thought they'd demonstrate from the safety of the other side that *they* were king of the jungle. He was just surprised that *this* particular one didn't have the usual female mate next to it to prompt such a false display of bravado. No matter. It never lasted long.

Refusing to back down, Chad found himself compelled to keep the game going. Upping the ante, he gave a sneer of contempt and childishly bared his teeth.

Without warning, the lion sprang forward, using the full force of its muscular hindquarters to crash against the wire.

'Shit!' yelled Bob, scattering from his seat. 'What the fuck was *that* about?'

Chad remained seated, not wishing to allow the animal the satisfaction of knowing how fast his heart was beating beneath his shirt. In an attempt to expunge his adrenalin, he roared as loudly as he could… much to the amusement of some children nearby.

Bob scrambled back onto the bench. 'What the fuck are you doin', you crazy son of a …?'

The lion increased its aggression, pawing at the fencing that stood in the way of his stomach and a choice of meals.

Stuck in an embarrassing impasse, Chad was considering enacting some pawing of his own when the animal suddenly froze. The background chatter of competing primates also eerily ceased. The lion shrank back on its haunches.

'Hardly a fair fight,' said a voice, low in tone and dark in delivery. 'I'd have thought such an unequal challenge wouldn't have interested you, Mister Cheadle.'

Bizarrely and inexplicably, a once familiar smell flashed a childhood memory across Chad's mind. It was of the dark, dank cellar below his parents' house, where unmentionable things lived. On the harrowing occasions he'd been forced to descend its depths – to retrieve something or other for his parents – he knew switching on the light only kept its secret occupants at bay for so long. If he wasn't quick enough, they'd grow accustomed to its glare and eventually make themselves known. He'd always managed to stay ahead of the game; running up the stone steps as fast as his little legs would allow and firmly slamming the door shut as quickly as possible before they'd crawled from their hiding places and given chase.

The smell appeared to emanate from the clothes of the man who'd made the comment. Chad turned to see him bizarrely dressed for a visitor to the zoo at that time of year. Wearing a brown, stained, weather-beaten trench coat and wide-brimmed Stetson that had seen one-too-many seasons, he appeared to be making a deliberate attempt to hide his face by keeping it turned away. From the little Chad *could* see, the man's skin appeared coarse and cracked, as if the result of an unpleasant medical condition.

'I take it you're our prospective client, given you know my name,' Chad offered in reply.

The gentleman merely tipped the brim of his hat in acknowledgement.

'In which case... it's *your* challenge that interests me,' added Chad.

'I never doubted that,' replied the man, still standing and keeping his head turned. 'No one wants to go through life the victim of another. It's only fair they get a chance to restore the balance.'

'I take it you're referring to Penkridge?' Whilst the man seemed keen to promote an air of mystery, Chad simply wanted him to get to the point. 'My former partner here tells me you *too* are interested in seeing the scales of justice balanced as far as that kid is concerned.'

'Justice depends on your viewpoint,' said the man coldly. 'Mine is from an angle it's best you know nothing about.'

The remark and manner in which it was delivered only fuelled Chad's intrigue. He was trying hard to heed Bob's advice not to stare at the individual standing to his side, but was finding it extremely difficult. 'So... what is it you want me to do? I mean... it's not as if this Penkridge kid has broken any laws.'

'He's broken *you*,' said the man, with something approximating a laugh.

Chad sucked in the full force of the remark and was about to come back angrily when he felt Bob's steadying hand on his shoulder.

'Your partner is right. I'm not the enemy,' said the figure calmly, without turning his head. 'I'm here to help you.'

'Help *me*?' retorted Chad, irritated by the man's aloofness.

'To give you a chance to redress the imbalance.'

'And what's in it for you? No one's *that* altruistic!'

'Let's just say... in achieving it, you'll be doing me an enormous favour.'

Chad looked at Bob, who returned a shrug.

'Okay... I understand not wanting to elaborate on your motive or identity. That's *your* affair. But what *exactly* is it you want us to do?' asked Chad. 'We're not in the business of hurting people... let's get that straight from the start. And as far as the authorities are concerned, the kid hasn't committed any crimes. Officially, he's clean and in the clear. If we'd had anything on him, we'd have taken him down years ago.'

'I simply want you to do what you claim to do,' answered the man calmly. '*Investigate*.'

'I'm telling you... it's already been done! The Agency spent months checking his history and looking for anything untoward. But there was nothing! He came up clean.'

'Then why are you here? I trust your partner informed you that that's who I was interested in. If you're now telling me he's an irrelevance and that I'm wasting my time...'

'Wait!' said Chad hastily, as the man motioned to leave. 'I'm here because I *know* there's something to find!'

'Precisely. Even the purest of individuals casts a shadow, Mister Cheadle. You just have to shine a bright enough light on the subject. Penkridge is no exception. I suggest the boy's finances might be a good place to start. It can't have escaped your attention he has a completely unaccounted for source of income. Well... perhaps it's time it *was* accounted for.'

'The authorities in Europe are fully aware of his financial situation,' returned Chad, 'From what I understand, they're not concerned. He's been living in France as a tax exile and filling in his returns like he should, making welcome contributions to their treasury.'

'Then shine a brighter light than they have!' said the man forcefully. 'He may have been clever enough to escape being weighed on their judicial scales... but if you believe there's something he wishes to keep hidden, it shouldn't be too difficult to make things extremely uncomfortable for him.'

'*Uncomfortable?*'

'The more, the better, as far as I'm concerned.'

'That's not exactly *justice*.'

'As I said before... justice depends on your viewpoint. Believe me when I say... from mine... it will have an enormous effect.'

Chad shrugged. 'Fair enough. You're the client. But what I don't understand is... Penkridge has been living his life of luxury for a number of years. So why now?'

The man seemed to be considering how best to formulate his answer. 'I have information that he's about to embark on something big,' he finally said. 'Another *project*. Your job, Mister Cheadle, is to try and put a stop to it.'

'And mine,' pointed out Bob, not wishing to be excluded from the conversation.

416

The man didn't reply.

'A *project?*'

'Its nature is not your concern. I merely want you to make it impossible for him to complete it.'

'And that's it?'

'It'll be more than enough if you succeed. You can leave the rest to me.'

'And the financial side?'

'I take it you mean *your* side?'

'I don't come cheap,' Chad lied.

'I wasn't looking to save money. You'll find a sizeable deposit has already been placed in your bank account. The same applies to your partner. He needn't worry. I'm not interested in hourly rates or invoices. As long as you continue doing the work, payments will be made... and more than you will ever have thought to ask for. I stand by the promise I gave him on our first meeting... Give me the result I desire and you'll never need to work again. You won't have any problems paying your landlord now.'

His last remark startled Chad. 'How did you know about...?'

'I know many things,' the man replied swiftly, reaching up and straightening his hat so as to signal his intention to leave.

The lion – having remained cowed during their conversation – kicked up a large cloud of dust as he awkwardly scampered backwards.

The man's parting shot only added to Chad's curiosity. 'I appreciate you not staring too much, Mister Cheadle. After all... I'm not the one you must investigate.'

Chad felt as if his mind had just been read. He had to confess that at that particular point in time, he was more interested in the strange figure in front of him than the actual target he'd been given. The meeting had been short, if not so sweet... and the strangest client introduction he'd ever undertaken. 'Will we be seeing you again?' he pressed.

The man gave the matter some thought. 'That depends on you,' he answered enigmatically.

'Maybe we could do reptiles next time,' chipped in Bob.

415

'They're my favourite.'

'I understand the connection,' said the man. 'Goodbye to you both.'

With that, he departed.

Chad watched his progress along the path until the sun in his eyes made it impossible.

'I told you!' sung Bob, in response to his friend's expression of bemusement. 'It don't get much weirder than that!'

Chad couldn't disagree.

'But if he does what he says and his money's for real...'

'How come he knew so much about me?' cut in Chad, with less enthusiasm. 'It's as if he's had someone investigating *us!*'

'Well... I reckon we can assume he's definitely not with the Government! And... let's face it... does it matter? You and I get a chance to make Penkridge atone for whatever sins it is he's committed... and when we find out what they are, you'll have the answers you've been searching for all these years.' He put a hand on Chad's shoulder. 'Besides... there's an additional bonus.'

'You're right,' said Chad, shaking off his doubts. 'I won't deny the money will come in useful.'

Bob removed his hand. 'I meant we get to work as a team again,' he said, wounded.

Chad gave an apologetic nod. 'And this time, to the bitter end. Our client may be prepared to settle for Penkridge just being made to feel uncomfortable... but if he's up to something new, we're gonna be the ones who stop him. This is our chance to right a long-standing injustice.'

'I thought you said the kid was officially clean, as far as his past was concerned.' Bob reminded him.

'I was talking about the one done to us,' said Chad determinedly. 'And this time, it's that kid who won't know what hit him!'

*   *   *

Worker One helped push at the river bank with his staff, as the

414

enormous raft on which he and all but one of his fellow workers were standing was cast off and sacrificed to the whim of the current.

That exception – Worker Two – was sitting sullenly at the back, his legs dangling lifelessly in the passing water, a newly acquired pendant hanging around his neck. To Worker One, the pendant looked suspiciously like the missing appendage Worker Two had been lamenting. Worker Three had done his best by wrapping a piece of antelope hide around where it had once been, having first smeared it with badger faeces in accordance with cutting edge shamanism... but it still hurt.

Worker One, determined not to be affected by Worker Two's negative self-obsession, gazed in awe as the bank grew further away, the river's current drawing them towards its fast-flowing centre. It never ceased to amaze him how the great *god of water* made such a heavy block of stone – and all its attendees – float... provided, of course, enough offerings were given and invocations performed beforehand... not to mention ensuring it was placed on a raft whose dimensions were of a magical enough proportion in relation to the weight being carried. But even after all *that*, the ability to float was not to be taken for granted. There had been the requisite incantations to the *god of the woodland* before the timbers from which the raft had been constructed had been felled... along with thanks and apologies to the *god of grass* – whom they'd treated quite shoddily over the past few days – as well as individual "big ups" to the gods of the earth beneath one's feet and the twine that bound the wood together.

It had all taken some time... a fact not helped by Worker Two's brooding intransigence when it came to the final ceremony. For – as he was only too keen to point out – he belonged to a different tribe to Worker One; petulantly refusing to acknowledge the existence of the *god of the riverbank* and failing to contribute to the votives offered. He'd insisted that the riverbank came within the jurisdiction of the *river god* – whom he considered a separate entity from the great *god of water* – and that, as far as *he* was concerned, was schismatically that.

River god?

Worker One – having never entertained the notion of such an autonomous being – found himself faced with a major dilemma. Was Worker Two a delusional zealot... or did he have a valid point... (if not a physical one, given his missing digits)? If there *was* a separate *river god*, Worker One could consider himself to be in very serious trouble, having unwittingly angered the very deity now required to keep him afloat. Worse still... hadn't he just wasted his second-best bracelet burying it in mud in order to compensate for Worker Two's assumed impiety?

Worker Three seemed to think he had... complicating matters further by claiming he'd never heard of the *god of the riverbank* either. As far as *he* was concerned... although that particular territory *technically* fell in the diocese of the *god of the river* – though existentially within the province of the *god of the earth beneath one's feet* – its parochial responsibility lay firmly with the fickle *god of erosion*, and *that's* who they should be trying to appease. Worker One and Worker Two had looked at him aghast... and then in horror at the riverbank on which they were standing, as they realised the foolishness of such an obvious oversight.

It was then that Worker One had hit upon his brilliant idea. An inspirational thought had struck him like a bolt from... well... somewhere up in the sky. He knew it sounded crazy, but it wouldn't half save a lot of time... not to mention bracelets. Wouldn't it be better, he suggested, if instead of all the individual gods, they combined their roles and worshipped just the one?

You could have heard a pin drop.

Worker Two had looked anxiously around, sheltering his remaining fingers beneath his tunic, lest divine retribution rob him of his dwindling ability to pick his nose... whilst Worker Three had stared nervously at the ground below his feet.

Worker One, unperturbed and clearly still alive, had continued promoting his idea. It would solve the problem of inter-denominational boundaries, he'd insisted. There simply wouldn't be any!

Worker Two had loudly ridiculed the idea, hoping his enthusiastic denouncement might appease all those blasphemed. Wouldn't Worker One's single god be kept extremely busy, he conjectured via an exaggerated sneer? Surely that would make his workload impossible?

Worker One was forced to admit he hadn't thought of that.

Worker Three had shaken his head in bewilderment, astounded that Worker One might have assumed that anyone would believe such a thing *remotely* possible.

Having gingerly withdrawn his hand from his tunic, Worker Two had then told Worker One it was sloppy thinking like that that had lost him his finger.

Worker One, angry at Worker Two's turning the subject back from such a laudable notion to his own, petty misfortunes, threatened to put a drowning curse on him... once they'd agreed which deity he should approach to carry it out.

Worker Three had sensibly intervened, pointing out that they'd *all* be cursed if they didn't hurry up and get their important cargo to where it was intended.

*   *   *

'Is that Deaf Pete?' asked Norman, having waited an interminable time for the phone to be answered.

'Pardon?'

'IS THAT DEAF PETE?' yelled Norman into the receiver. He realised the conversation might be difficult. But having finally tracked down the sound engineer's email address and sent him a message, Deaf Pete had written back stating that, due to his severe dyslexia, it would be easier if they were able to "spake on the phine". *Chance would be a fine thing*, thought Norman.

'Hello... This is Deaf Pete,' came a voice from the other end.

'It's Norman,' said Norman.

'Who's that?' asked Deaf Pete.

'NORMAN!'

'Is that you, Norman?'

Norman removed the receiver from his ear and banged it against his head. If it wasn't for the fact he was on a mission to save the Universe again, he would have given up at that point.

'YES!' he screamed as loudly as he could into it.

'I got that,' returned Deaf Pete. 'You sound stressed.'

'I WASN'T WHEN I STARTED!' yelled Norman.

'Keep going at that level,' prompted Deaf Pete. 'That's hitting the spot! Now... tell me what this is all about. I'm all ears.'

'Just a shame they don't bloody work', said Norman at normal volume. 'I NEED YOUR HELP,' he bellowed. 'I NEED TO PLAY SOME MUSIC IN MY HOUSE AT 145 DECIBELS AND XANTHIA SAID YOU WERE THE MAN I SHOULD SPEAK TO.'

'That would be some party if you managed it!' Deaf Pete chuckled. 'I hope you're not planning on putting out your best crockery!'

'I KNOW IT'S LOUD,' shouted Norman.

'No you don't. That volume under a roof would probably ensure you ended up without one. Anyway... How is the old thing?'

'MY ROOF?'

'Xanthia... the dirty slapper.'

'LIVING WITH ME!'

'Oh... I didn't realise. I meant it as a term of endearment, of course,' Deaf Pete furiously back-pedalled. 'But that's even more reason not to have her or anyone else you care for listening to your music, if you intend playing it at *that* volume. It's gonna do some damage!'

'I ASSUMED IT MIGHT. I JUST WANTED TO KNOW IF IT WAS POSSIBLE AND... IF SO... HOW I COULD GO ABOUT IT.'

Deaf Pete appeared to be giving the matter some thought.

It was only when a few minutes of patient waiting failed to secure an answer that Norman realised Deaf Pete probably hadn't heard the question in the first place.

He repeated it, even louder.

'You'd be pushing at the boundaries of what's currently possible,' Deaf Pete advised. 'It's current speaker technology that sets the limit. It's a question of them being able to survive the power that'd have to be fed into them. You put too much in and they'll simply blow. It's the sub-woofers you *really* need to worry about.'

'WHAT ARE THEY?'

'They deal with the bass end. That's the hardest to crank. You're talking serious vibrations.'

'I DON'T THINK THAT'LL BE A PROBLEM.'

'You'd be surprised. Those low frequencies can do a helluva lotta damage.'

'I MEANT... IT WON'T BE A PROBLEM BECAUSE THERE SHOULDN'T BE ANY. I ONLY NEED TO PLAY TWO NOTES... AND THEY'RE BOTH ABOVE MIDDLE C.'

'Jeez!' exclaimed Deaf Pete. 'What are you planning on playing at this party of yours... ultra-minimalist techno?'

'LET'S JUST SAY... IT'S A SCIENTIFIC EXPERIMENT.'

'Oh, I see! Well, that makes more sense. I thought for a minute you were a ravin' fruitcake. Okay. In that case... you wanna look at doing it outside, for a start. Not only will you need to construct one helluva rig... there'll be less chance of incurring structural damage... though no absolute guarantee. I hope you get on well with your neighbours!'

'THAT WON'T BE A PROBLEM EITHER. HOW SOON COULD YOU START?'

'Pardon?'

Norman took a deep breath. His throat was feeling sore. 'I SAID... HOW SOON COULD YOU START?' he yelled as loudly as human biology allowed.

'No need to shout,' said Deaf Pete. 'I heard you the first time. It was just that I didn't know you intended for me to do the work.'

'I DIDN'T,' admitted Norman. 'BUT I'M IN A BIT OF A HURRY. I NEED TO DO THIS EXPERIMENT AS SOON AS

POSSIBLE AND YOU'RE CLEARLY THE MAN TO HELP.'

'The thing is... I'm retired,' said Deaf Pete. 'I don't know if you've heard, but my hearing isn't as good as it used to be.'

'YOU DON'T SAY,' yelled Norman politely.

'Though I must admit... I've missed working with my old crew. They were the best. It would be great to get everybody back together one last time. I've always wondered what it would be like to push beyond 140. Never thought I'd get a chance to do it, though. I always assumed that record-breaking day with *Trouzerbulge* would be the pinnacle of my career. But...' He sounded wistful. 'Just maybe...' There was a brief silence. 'Are you sure it'd only be the two notes?'

'YES. ABSOLUTELY,' promised Norman.

'Shame.'

'IT'D PAY WELL.'

Deaf Pete gave the last comment some consideration. 'It'd have to! You're talking quite a spend,' he warned. 'We'd be looking at putting together the best-spec'd festival rig ever devised... and then some!'

'DON'T WORRY ABOUT THE FINANCIAL SIDE. I'M MORE THAN GOOD FOR IT. XANTHIA WILL VOUCH FOR ME ON THAT.'

'Okay... then say no more!' said Deaf Pete, the excitement rising in his voice. 'Consider me in! I'll make the necessary phone calls!'

That'll be interesting! thought Norman.

*　　*　　*

Worker One gazed pensively at the scenery serenely passing him by. The gods had clearly forgiven his wishing to have them annulled, for they were graciously allowing the raft on which he was perched to be carried along by the river's current, aided only by the occasional prodding of long, wooden poles into the depths below when it looked like they might be changing their minds.

The severe and bleak barren slopes that initially determined the river's passage had gradually morphed into softer, gentler ones; allowing vegetation to find a footing and cloak the landscape in a garment more pleasing to the eye.

The more it changed, the more Worker One realised how big the world really was… further compounding his dilemma. For he still believed his idea of monotheism was an excellent one… if only he could get around the niggling problem of his new god being everywhere in that big world at the same time.

The more of that world that passed, the more he realised how difficult it would be.

Worker Two was continuing his sulk at the back of the raft, ghoulishly caressing the pendant around his neck. Not a single word had passed his lips since they'd set off with their cargo, a fact Worker One would normally have applauded. But the constant stroking of the shrivelled object was beginning to get on his nerves… not least because he knew Worker Two held him responsible for its being around his neck in the first place.

Unable to endure the reminder anymore, Worker One squelched over to where Worker Two was sulking and threatened to drown him personally, with or without the help of any deity.

Worker Two instantly responded by boldly holding up the pendant and claiming such a thing could never happen, as he was now protected by the *god of severed digits*.

Worker One accused him of making that particular deity up.

Incensed at being called a liar, Worker Two scrambled to his feet.

Worker Three quickly intervened by telling them not to be so childish… and for both to sit down before the erratic *god of balance* decided to get involved.

Worker Two suggested that now Worker Three was making things up.

Worker Three rose angrily, causing the raft to tip to one side.

Really?

Worker Two grasped his pendant tightly and quickly sat down.

Worker One – seizing the opportunity to promote his idea again – pointed out that this was just the kind of awkward situation a one god scenario would help eliminate. Life would be so much easier. Everyone would know where they stood. Furthermore, there'd be a Universal benefit to mankind that no one could dispute... As brothers and sisters of the one god, there'd be no need to go to war with neighbouring tribes because your gods had been offended by theirs. The world would unite under the one god and there'd be Universal peace for the first time in its history. The logic was immutable. Only the completely insane would find reasons to think otherwise.

Worker Two – suddenly embarrassed by the crudity of his pendant – found himself drawn to the expression of contentment breaking out on Worker One's face. He'd never seen such a thing before and wanted that contentment too. Perhaps, he admitted as he rose to his feet, Worker One really did have a point. There'd be no need for rivalry, hate or jealousy because you'd all be looking to please the one god.

Worker One agreed and embraced Worker Two warmly, causing the *god of balance* to send a sobering reminder that they hadn't got rid of him just yet. What could *possibly* go wrong?

Worker Two asked what name they should give the one god.

Worker One responded by saying that it wouldn't matter. As long as everyone accepted its authority, its title would be an irrelevance... nothing more than a quirk of your particular tribe. You'd all know who you were talking about because, if there were only one god, he'd have to be the same one. It wouldn't even matter how you individually chose to worship the one god... for that wouldn't matter either... just so long as you did.

Worker Three – starting to show an interest – stopped work on the large phallus he'd been carving. After all, the goddess of fertility would become an irrelevance if Worker One's plan was adopted. But it caused him to raise another important issue.

Would the one god be a *he* or a *she*?

Worker One didn't want to admit that he hadn't thought of that either. He was still wrestling with the sticky issue of omnipresence. Panicking, he reproached Worker Three for even contemplating that such an all-powerful one god wouldn't be male... like them.

Worker Three was horrified. Surely Worker One wasn't suggesting that the one god would also replace the goddess of ladies' problems... *was he?*

Not wishing to lose the momentum his argument was gaining, Worker One suggested that even though *they* knew the one god would be male, the idea might be more palatable to those who didn't if it was not given a man's name but just called... god.

Worker Two thought designating a supreme being such a brief nomenclature was not only disrespectful, but incredibly lazy and unimaginative.

Worker One pointed out to Worker Two that it was grammatically incorrect to have *a* supreme being... it should be *the* supreme being.

Worker Three suggested – if they were arguing points of grammar – his name should at least start with a capital letter.

Or even *His* name, threw in Worker Two sarcastically.

Worker One mulled the name God over in his mind. It certainly felt more respectful and important than just... god.

Worker Two still thought it sounded silly.

It didn't really matter, counselled Worker Three. It was an irrelevance anyway. For, despite the idea being a great one, there was only one problem to the one god scenario as he could see. As wonderful as it sounded... much like Worker One's other heretical idea of using iron instead of bronze to make their tools and weapons stronger... it would never catch on.

*   *   *

After an impressive display of manoeuvring, the huge articulated lorry finally managed to negotiate the narrow, winding drive that was usually only required to cope with a local merchant's battered *Deux Chevaux* or the daily delivery of *La Poste*. It had taken the collective shouts of numerous denim-clad, tattooed individuals to ensure it didn't bring any of the overhanging *platanes* with it. But it was clearly something they were used to, confidently working together in a laid-back manner that suggested they'd seen worse.

That same well-organised team spirit was in evidence as the vehicle's contents were efficiently emptied via a metal ramp that landed a continuous stream of large, wheeled flight-cases onto the temporary wooden surface that had been laid to protect Norman's immaculate lawn.

Working as a well-rehearsed collective, each man busied himself with his own particular tasks, trusting his colleagues to complete theirs in order for the whole to come together. Copious amounts of beer provided an incentive against the climbing sun... along with the barely adequate bikini Xanthia had chosen to almost wear that day.

As the day wore on, Norman witnessed in her a previously unseen persona... coming alive as she enthusiastically followed proceedings, revelling in the attention she was getting and the fact that many of those enjoying the scenery were acquaintances from a time he inwardly knew she missed. It came as no surprise. She never talked about those days or about her life with Stump. But Norman knew that, despite the opulent lifestyle he provided, what he personally had to offer in terms of excitement fell far below what she had been used to in the past. To her credit, she never complained or made him feel uncomfortable about it. Any discomfort was of his own making, stemming from the fact he'd always known he was punching ridiculously above his weight. He'd learnt to live with that feeling... believing himself to be the luckiest man on Earth and that such insecurity was a small price to pay. He didn't doubt that each ogling member of the road crew would clearly have swapped places with him in an instant.

He was also relieved to see Xanthia happy. The last few days had been especially difficult for her. Since being set his mission, an increasing air of melancholy had enveloped the house; even the staff had commented on it. Where once the bright, Mediterranean sun had freely gifted its rejuvenating energy, an inexplicable gloom had appeared to seep in with its heat. He'd refrained from discussing it with her, lest she encountered even more trouble sleeping than was already the case. The distraction of the sound crew and the positive energy they'd brought with them seemed a tonic for them both.

Deaf Pete had taken a relaxed approach to being in charge. He knew his skill would manifest itself later, once the equipment had been assembled and the dark arts of pushing a fader were required. He'd been deep in conversation with Speaker Jim and Mick the Juice, as two giant generators had been wheeled into place and the necessary wiring attached by Cable John and Phil the Socket.

It seemed to Norman everyone on site possessed a sobriquet... some connected with their activity... others reflecting a lack of it. Virgin Merv, for example, gave Norman's former image a run for its money. Whilst comfortably in his mid-thirties, Virgin Merv looked as if he'd not only failed to come into contact with a member of the opposite sex, but had also failed to do the same with soap, deodorant, spot cream, washing powder, a barber, a decent optician, literature other than porn, friends, or the sun. As he was now getting a massive dose of the latter, his pale skin was beginning to warn him of the fact by turning the colour a traffic light goes when it wants you to stop. He was, however, extremely adept at clambering about the rigging being constructed to fly a series of wedge-shaped speakers high in the air... much like an unhygienic monkey. Coming close in the *when-did-I-last-use-my-flannel?* department... Bob the Belly waddled aimlessly about... his only job as far as Norman could ascertain being to ask people – between substantial belches – where the spanner was or if it was them who'd just farted. Still... someone had to do it.

As for Donkey Dave... given he *wasn't* particularly being used to carry things or in possession of an unusual laugh, Norman could only speculate.

Speaker by speaker, two gigantic towers slowly rose into the cloudless sky until – by the time the sun and an exhausted workforce had given their best – Mick the Juice was given the signal to fire up the generators.

Hands were placed on hips as they spluttered into action.

A smell of diesel pervaded the air.

Deaf Pete theatrically cracked his knuckles as Speaker Jim looked on nervously. 'We're about to make history, ladies and gentlemen,' he proudly announced from behind a sound desk that would normally have accommodated a multitude of individual feeds... not the single, rather pathetic-looking stereo input from Norman's laptop. 'This is the first rig of its size ever assembled!'

'Let's hope it works, then!' said Norman, with as much joviality as his nerves allowed.

'Pardon?'

'I SAID, LET'S HOPE IT WORKS!' he yelled.

'I've never yet been unable to get one to do exactly what I tell it to,' Deaf Pete assured him with a wink. 'Don't worry... With only two notes and no serious bass end to contend with, I'll squeeze this baby until she delivers the goods... speaker cones permitting.'

Speaker Jim scratched his nose.

Norman hoped he was right. 'HOW WILL WE KNOW WHEN WE'VE BEEN SUCCESSFUL?' he shouted.

'That's down to Donkey Dave,' replied Deaf Pete. 'I've got him standing at the far end of your grounds with a decibel meter. We don't wanna overcook it... so as soon as we hit 145db he'll give us the nod. Any further and I think you'll have to re-tile every roof within half a mile.' He waggled a finger in his ear... as if that would make the slightest bit of difference. 'Well... are we good to go?' He looked to Norman for confirmation.

It was then that the thought suddenly struck Norman that he had no idea what the Archangel's instructions were meant to achieve. Had he been a little hasty in assuming it was okay to go ahead and actually put Gabriel's instructions into action? *What were they for? Would the notes trigger something that wasn't yet meant to be?* In all the excitement of arranging the necessary equipment to be brought to France and constructed in his garden, he'd overlooked the need to inform Gabriel that his task was close to completion and about to be tested.

He looked around anxiously, hoping to see a new crew member discreetly keeping himself to himself and observing proceedings in the way Gabriel might. But to no avail. Every face expectantly looking at his was now a familiar one.

'Well?' asked Deaf Pete, chomping at the bit.

Norman knew he could hardly change his mind at this late stage.

He took a deep breath. 'Let's do it!' he said nervously.

'This track just runs and runs, does it?' asked Deaf Pete, leaning over and activating the sound file on Norman's laptop.

'It's on a loop,' confirmed Norman. 'It'll keep going until we run out of diesel.'

'Or roof tiles!' chipped in Speaker Jim.

'We'll ramp it up slowly,' Deaf Pete advised, dramatically licking his fingers before putting them to use.

Two large faders were carefully coaxed into action.

At first, the seesawing tones were just annoying. Some of the crew looked at one another and shook their heads. *Theirs not to reason why.* But as Deaf Pete pushed the faders ever higher, the increased volume started to jar painfully. Birds began vacating the trees and anything in the ground burrowed deeper into it.

'Ask him how we're doing,' Deaf Pete instructed Speaker Jim.

Speaker Jim placed a walkie-talkie to the side of his face and relayed the question. 'WE'RE ONLY TOUCHING 133,' he shouted back after a short wait.

'Strewth!' grimaced Deaf Pete. 'You better get the boys to protect their ears. I reckon this is gonna hurt!'

'IT'S THE PURITY OF THE TONES,' shouted Speaker Jim above them. 'IT WOULD BE KINDER IF WE HAD A BETTER SPREAD OF FREQUENCIES!'

'It is what it is,' yelled Deaf Pete. 'So... brace yerselves... I'm taking her higher!'

'GENTLE AS YOU CAN,' advised Speaker Jim. 'IF MY NEW BABIES CAN'T TAKE THE PAIN, I'D RATHER WE STOPPED BEFORE THEY ENDED UP FRIED!'

Deaf Pete nodded in agreement and slowly pushed the master faders higher. Norman had sensibly provided himself and Xanthia with a smart pair of orange ear protectors, much to the amusement of the crew. But as the level increased, even the hardest of them found themselves forced to place their fingers in their ears.

'I THINK WE'RE AT 140!' shouted Speaker Jim, struggling to hear what was being said on the walkie-talkie pressed to his ear.

Deaf Pete signalled to the crew with upright thumbs that they'd equalled their previous world record. They returned a macho cheer – though barely audible – but thought it prudent not to applaud, given their hands were being put to better use.

'Well, folks... we're about to venture into uncharted territory!' beamed Deaf Pete who, unsurprisingly, had forgone any ear protection.

'I THINK WE NEED TO GET IT OVER WITH AS QUICKLY AS POSSIBLE,' yelled Speaker Jim. 'I DON'T KNOW HOW MUCH MORE OF THIS PUNISHMENT MY BABIES CAN TAKE!'

'Okay... Then, let's do it!' hollered Deaf Pete. 'We're going for the big one!' With that he pushed the faders higher still. As they rose, Norman felt the frequencies ripple through his body. Xanthia – who'd been jumping up and down excitedly – suddenly looked like she was going to be sick. The air around them shook.

Bob the Belly thought he'd be clever and use the situation to sneak out a massive fart... though, judging by the screwed-up faces that turned to accuse him, he'd overlooked one vital component.

Deaf Pete blew out his cheeks and made the final increase. A couple of crew members recoiled in agony as the sound waves assaulted them. Speaker Jim peered anxiously at the speaker stacks.

Just as Norman felt he couldn't take the sonic battering any longer and that his chest would implode, the deafening sound of the tones suddenly changed, becoming less pure and causing the vibrations he was experiencing to feel rougher and angrier. For a brief second, he thought his cheeks were about to shatter along with his Adam's apple.

Speaker Jim reacted instantly, waving his arms wildly in order to get Deaf Pete to stop. 'THEY'VE BLOWN!' he mouthed in despair.

Immediately, the sound ceased... though the nausea that had built up in Norman's body still threatened to spill the contents of that morning's breakfast onto the lawn.

'Bugger!' grimaced Deaf Pete. 'I thought we were gonna do it! We must've been within a mouse's fart!'

Speaker Jim ran over to one of the speaker stacks in order to examine his "babies"... then despondently shook his head.

'I'll pay for any damage,' offered Norman contritely.

Deaf Pete gave him a searching look.

'I SAID... I'LL PAY FOR ANY DAMAGE!' Norman yelled.

Deaf Pete continued staring at him blankly.

'Oh dear,' said Norman quietly, as a swaying Xanthia grabbed his arm for support. 'I think Deaf Pete might have to look at changing his name again.'

'To what?' swooned Xanthia, struggling to steady herself.

'*Stone* Deaf Pete.'

'It has a certain ring to it,' she pouted.

'Much like his ears, I should think,' muttered Norman.

The crew were standing around not knowing what to do... sharing in the disappointment.

'That's a first,' said the former Deaf Pete, stretching his jaw and prodding the side of his face. 'I've never failed to get what I want out of a rig. I guess we've pushed the boundaries of technology as far as they're prepared to go.' He bowed his head despondently.

'Looks like what I've been asked to do is physically impossible,' said Norman quietly to Xanthia.

'Does that mean we're all going to die?' she asked, gripping his arm tightly.

'I need to speak to Gabriel,' he answered diplomatically.

She looked behind her. 'Well... on a positive note,' she said brightly, 'at least the house is still standing!'

Norman gave a thin smile. He was about to suggest they leave the guys to dismantle the equipment on their own, when one of the crew came running towards them. His ear protectors slung around his neck, he was clutching a small electronic device. It was Donkey Dave.

'We did it!' he shouted ecstatically. 'One hundred and forty-five! Right on the money!'

A brief moment of stunned silence was followed by an eruption of cheering and impromptu dancing.

'My babies didn't expire in vain!' cried Speaker Jim exuberantly, wiping the hint of a tear from his eye. 'I'd make a few adjustments, if we did it again. But we've shown it can be done! Incredible!'

'Not as incredible as what happened when we reached our target,' commented Donkey Dave.

Norman looked at him expectantly. *Might the purpose of the task now be revealed?*

'Two blokes fell out of a tree next to me... then scampered off clutching their heads!'

Norman had to confess... it wasn't quite the revelation he'd expected.

*   *   *

'It's not just my friggin' ears that are wrecked,' howled Bob, scrambling to drag an unwilling leg into the car. 'I reckon I've busted my goddam knee!'

'It'll heal,' said Chad, unmoved. He hastily threw the car into gear and signalled with a curt nod for Bob to shut the door. Before his partner could oblige, the accelerator felt the full force of his adrenalin... the wheels screaming their objection and drowning out Bob's own.

'I can't stop the friggin' ringing!' Bob exclaimed, hitting the side of his head with the flat of his hand. He forced a wide yawn in a futile attempt to reboot his ears. 'What the hell d'ya think *that* was all about?'

'Dunno,' grimaced Chad, trying much the same technique... his other hand struggling to keep the car on course along the narrow lane. 'All I know is that every time we investigate something that boy's connected to, it gets weirder!' He chanced a glance in his rear view mirror and contented himself with the fact that at least they weren't being followed. 'But what happened back there was *beyond* bizarre!'

'Yeah... we simultaneously fell out of a tree!' attested Bob.

'I meant that whole two-tone, giant car alarm trip. What the hell d'ya reckon they're up to?'

'Maybe they're developing something that can be used as a sonic weapon. Perhaps they're going for extortion this time.'

'Blackmail through *terrorism?*'

'Who knows? Your guess is as good as mine.'

'Whatever it is... our mystery benefactor was spot on the money... That kid's definitely up to *something!*'

Bob turned his attention to his knee. 'It's weird seeing him in the flesh. Hardly comes across as the master criminal type.'

'He's not!' asserted Chad. 'I always figured he's a puppet for a far more powerful master.'

'More monkey than organ grinder, you mean.'

'Yeah... and you know exactly how *that* works!'

Bob ignored the slight. 'It's certainly an advantage getting someone off the radar to do your dirty work for you, I'll give you that.'

'Though our mystery benefactor clearly knows about him,' pointed out Chad. 'Which makes you wonder how.'

'Perhaps those above Penkridge are getting careless. Orders have to be prepared before they're given.'

'Talking of which... any news on abnormal activity from the God squad? Given they figured in the equation last time, there might just be a connection this time around.'

'Negative,' affirmed Bob. 'I've got a few trusted ears back at

Langley listening out on our behalf... but, so far, they're reporting "all quiet on the Charles Heston front".'

Chad looked at him and winced.

'That's quite an efficient team he's assembled back there,' continued Bob. 'They sure knew what they were doing.' He gingerly pulled his trouser leg up, so as to investigate the source of his pain. 'Just a shame *we* didn't!'

'That should come as no surprise... He might be the monkey, but he's a very wealthy one. He can afford the best.'

Bob delicately manipulated his knee. 'Which is why we should've taken our client's advice and started by investigating the roots of his money tree... instead of looking to climb a real one!'

'I told you on the flight over... I needed to smell our quarry first. He's only ever been a frustratingly sparse file to me. I wanted to get as close to him as possible.'

'Trouble is... we may have got a little *too* close. Now he knows someone's watching him.'

'I seem to remember you thinking that was once a useful tactic,' said Chad, momentarily taking his eyes from the road to remind his partner. 'Stirring up a hornet's nest... I believe that's how you referred to it.'

Bob returned a blank stare.

'The Amish...?'

'Oh, yeah,' nodded Bob, the penny dropping.

'Well... not that we have a choice now... but maybe it'll cause them to panic... make a mistake. When people get desperate, they get sloppy.'

'You speaking from experience?'

Bob found his knee cruelly acquainted with the dashboard as Chad applied the brakes on a bend with more enthusiasm than was warranted.

'Perhaps you'd like to do the same with my head,' Bob scowled. 'Help clear the ringing from my ears.'

'That might not be a bad idea. We'll need those working if we're gonna stand any chance of discovering what was going on back there.'

'More surveillance?'

'Yeah... but something less impractical this time. What are your contacts like in this neck of the woods?'

'Are we talking electronics?'

Chad nodded.

'I know a few people who should be able to help us out. It'll cost... but that shouldn't be an issue, given the depth of our benefactor's pockets.'

'In that case, I'll draw up a shopping list.'

'No problem... But isn't there a bigger one you're overlooking?'

'There is?'

'Too friggin' right! You can't seriously be thinking about placing electronic surveillance in or around that property!'

Chad removed his eyes from the road again. 'Why not? It's the only way we'll get a handle on what Penkridge is up to. It's also what we were once best at... remember?'

'Granted... if you mean in relation to climbing trees. But a break-in would be *totally* out of the question! With the value of those paintings he's rumoured to have hanging on his walls, he'll have an alarm system worthy of Fort Knox! There's no *way* we'll be able to sneak in undetected.'

'There's always a way,' countered Chad. 'And maybe the answer is not to sneak.'

'Well... when you finally come up with how we're gonna do it, may I suggest we look at throwing in some high-definition visual alongside the audio,' Bob advised.

'No point,' said Chad firmly. 'It'd only increase the risk of detection... with no obvious upside.'

'Are you kiddin'?' smiled Bob, forgetting about his knee for a moment. 'Did you *see* the framework over which that bikini was stretched, back there?'

'Okay. Be serious. This is gonna be difficult enough. We'll go over what we need and get in touch with your contacts. I take it they operate outside official channels?'

'We can trust 'em, if that's what you mean.'

'We need to,' Chad squinted. 'If the authorities here or back home get wind that someone from the Agency is freelancing on foreign soil with an ex-employee, they'll have us in handcuffs and on a plane before we can offer a Gallic shrug.'

'Leave it to me,' said Bob. 'You just concentrate on how the *hell* you're gonna get us into that house!'

*   *   *

'WHEN YE HEAR THE SOUND OF THE TRUMPET, ALL THE PEOPLE SHALL SHOUT WITH A GREAT SHOUT... AND THE WALL OF THE CITY SHALL FALL DOWN FLAT...' Donald looked pained. 'REALLY?' he asked aloud. 'IS *THAT* WHAT I'M SUPPOSED TO WRITE?'

He was answered by a ghostly howl from the wind seeking refuge from the storm outside, forcing its way through a series of gaps in the window.

Donald waited patiently for a proper reply, tapping his pen irritably on the desk when it failed to materialise. 'ONLY... IT SOUNDS A LITTLE FAMILIAR, IF YOU DON'T MIND ME SAYING SO,' he prompted. 'I WOULDN'T WANT TO BE ACCUSED OF PLAGIARISM!'

Concentrating hard, he tried to ignore the lights in the study that were flickering aggressively in collusion with the storm.

The voices in his head seemed confused over the issue. It was all getting too much for them... if not him. In the past, his writing voice had always overridden that of his spirit guide and any spontaneous outbursts he occasionally found himself forced to utter. The distinction had been clear. But things had now become blurred... muddled... not at all what he was used to.

'PERHAPS I'M THINKING TOO HARD,' he suggested. He tapped his pen harder. 'OR PERHAPS... I'M NOT THINKING ENOUGH.'

It wasn't easy trying to reconcile the random, vague warnings he was being fed with the assuredness of his powerful muse. Attempting to combine the two was like juggling a combination of feathers and cannonballs. Stranger still... he was writing a play without knowing how it would end. At least

394

on previous occasions, he'd been struck by a general idea and then expressed it in a linear fashion, comfortable in the knowledge of where he was headed. *Now* he was writing blind... trying to incorporate warnings, even though those doing the warning were unable to tell him *exactly* what it was he was being warned about!

Be that as it may, he concluded that his struggles were an irrelevance. He *had* to persist... if the lights allowed.

As if on cue, they immediately dimmed, draining his enthusiasm further.

'YES... *PLAGIARISM*,' he confirmed loudly, addressing Whitebait. '*YOU* MIGHT NOT HAVE SPOTTED IT... BUT I THINK OTHERS JUST MIGHT... GIVEN IT COMES FROM THE BIGGEST SELLING BOOK IN HISTORY!' he added, with as much irony as his tired head could muster. He rubbed the bridge of his nose and considered giving up for the day. A creeping wave of melancholia had started to engulf him. 'PERHAPS I COULD PUT IT IN QUOTES?' he suggested wearily. 'AT LEAST THE ORIGINAL WRITER ISN'T AROUND TO SUE ME FOR COPYRIGHT!' He tilted his head back in exasperation. 'ALRIGHT...ALRIGHT... I ACCEPT THAT FROM WHERE *YOU'RE* STANDING... HE IS!'

In response to an almighty crack of thunder – that temporarily separated his skin from his senses – the lights gave up their struggle, plunging the room into total darkness.

That was it. He'd definitely had enough. Perhaps in the morning, on a clear head... and daylight... everything would make sense.

He fumbled around in the drawer of the writing desk for an old torch he kept for such emergencies... but its batteries struggled to remember their purpose. Irritably capping his pen by a waning half-light, he rose swiftly from the desk, determined to get to where his candles were before the torch gave up completely.

As its dwindling beam endeavoured to locate the door, he felt an overwhelming sense of sadness envelop him, placing a further burden on his already tired body.

He empathised with the dying torch.

'What is it, Donald?' he asked himself.

Had writing finally become a chore?

The thought shocked him. Normally, having spent uncounted hours converting inspiration into words, he would feel elated... rejuvenated... worthy... as if having presented a wonderful gift to mankind. Now – despite originally thinking it a good idea – he felt sullied... put upon... some of the more unpleasant voices he'd encountered leaving behind a feeling of unwanted social intrusion... like having to engage with strangers you wish you'd never invited into your house.

As he groped his way towards the door, the all but extinct illumination brushed pitifully across the wall... just strong enough to swipe a shadow over something not quite right.

His blood froze.

Was he seeing things?

His breathing suspended, he gingerly retraced the beam's path.

As the last vestige of light located its target, his feeling of confusion turned into one of paralysis.

The torch wasn't happy either. In an act of cowardice, it vacated the situation altogether, leaving him to deal with what it had highlighted on his own. A picture of him on the wall – looking exceptionally happy and taken at his very first premiere – had been deliberately turned upside down.

A dramatic flash of lightning confirmed the fact before plunging Donald into darkness once again.

Exhaling the shock, he endeavoured to regain control of the situation.

'WAS THAT YOU, LANCELOT?' he enquired, his voice higher than usual.

It seemed the only logical explanation; given the poltergeist was the only other inhabitant of the house. The cats didn't count. Their paws couldn't reach that high.

There was no reply... just the violent rattling of angry glass in an increasingly frightened window.

Donald apprehensively reached out and returned the picture

to what he calculated to be its correct orientation, before rapidly fumbling his way towards the open door.

For he'd noticed something else out of place... something equally baffling.

Normally disturbing him with their passing tails and constant cries for food, the cats were nowhere to be seen. They'd long since vacated the room, not one of them wishing to remain in it. He'd become so engrossed in his work he hadn't noticed.

Moving swiftly into the hall, he slammed the door shut on whatever it was that had been spooking them and tried to steady his breathing. But he couldn't shake the feeling of impending doom now enveloping him.

'DO *YOU* KNOW WHAT THIS IS ALL ABOUT?' he quaked nervously, grateful for the company of his spirit guide.

Whitebait didn't answer. Instead, a strange noise he couldn't place filled the gap.

'IS THAT ME?' he enquired timidly.

There was still no answer.

'I THINK THAT'S ME,' he confirmed to himself, realising the sound was in his head.

He listened harder... then promptly wished he hadn't.

'FLIES?' he gasped, the torch slipping from his hand.

It was as if a host of them were swarming somewhere in the distance... though in the realm of spirit.

'That's not happened before! I didn't think they *had* souls!'

For the first time in his life, he felt intimidated by his isolation in the old house. The noise growing louder, he scurried along its unlit corridor, as frenzied flashes of lightning threw out temporary shadows that threatened to trip him up. Pointlessly swatting the air around his head, he regretted having opened himself up so willingly to any entity that fancied a dalliance with its former realm.

Why flies?

The sound was becoming unbearable. Instinctively, he put his hands to his ears, even though he knew it wouldn't make a difference.

Hang on a second...

He stopped.

...or were they bees?

And then the penny dropped.

'Oh no!' he whimpered, any remaining colour draining from his face.

He wanted to be sick.

Flies and bees he could've coped with.

'IT'S POINTLESS!' he shouted, by way of a bluff to make it stop. 'Handel... Tchaikovsky!' he called out nervously, hoping the appearance of some friendly faces might distract him from his thoughts... even if they did have whiskers attached.

One of those summoned poked his head out from under a chest of drawers in the hallway, his chin low to the ground, his eyes looking up with a cautious uncertainty.

'GO AWAY!' screeched Donald at the top of his voice, sending the confused animal scampering across the floor and disappearing up the stairs. 'No... not you, Tchaikovsky!' he called out despairingly after him.

The sound in his head was now intolerable.

His eyes having become accustomed to the gloom, he groped and staggered his way to the kitchen, then rummaged feverishly about in one of the drawers. Grabbing a roll of tin foil, he hastily tore off a large strip and wrapped it speedily around his head. He was in great pain.

'I CAN'T TAKE MUCH MORE OF THIS!' he warned, his eyes beginning to water. 'I'M ONLY MADE OF FLESH AND BLOOD... EVEN IF *YOU* AREN'T!'

The foil made no difference.

Stumbling to the sink, he pulled a colander from the draining tray and stuck it on his head.

'OH... STILL NOT ENOUGH, EH?' he shouted defiantly, despite his head feeling it was about to split in half. 'ALRIGHT... I FORGOT ABOUT THE PERFORATIONS... BUT LET'S SEE HOW YOU COPE WITH *THIS!*' Desperate to be released from his torment, he staggered towards the oven and swung its battered, enamelled door wide open. Sinking to his knees, he placed his head inside and pulled the door back on himself as tight as he could.

His actions still had no effect.

It was the final straw. He'd had enough. Something inside him snapped.

'I'VE HAD TOO MANY YEARS OF BEING ABUSED! YOU'VE FINALLY GONE TOO FAR! I DON'T WANT TO DO THIS ANYMORE!' he screamed. 'THE VOICES WERE BAD ENOUGH!'

His hand shaking, he reached up blindly and groped around for the oven's controls.

'I WOULD JUST LIKE TO HAVE HAD A LITTLE BIT OF TIME IN MY LIFE WHEN I WAS LEFT ALONE!' he cried. 'JUST ENOUGH TO HAVE BEEN ABLE TO HAVE ENJOYED BEING *ME* FOR A SHORT WHILE!'

His hand located the one he was after.

'WAS IT REALLY TOO MUCH TO ASK?' he sobbed, yanking it sharply to the left.

*   *   *

Norman sat, excitedly awaiting his guests. He was glad of the distraction. An air of melancholy had descended upon the house once again, after Deaf Pete and his men had packed up their equipment and headed back to England.

Xanthia seemed to be feeling it the most. She'd bid them *adieu* with a crestfallen look that suggested they'd also put her newly found sense of fun in the truck and were taking it away with them.

The unseasonably bad weather that followed their departure hadn't helped. His guests would come as a welcome relief.

He'd decided to entertain them in the living room – even though this was ostensibly a business meeting – knowing that they, of all people, would appreciate the collection of artworks he'd managed to assemble on its walls. It was important he impressed them.

A Louis XIV timepiece struck eleven.

Xanthia had taken a trip into town for a hair appointment, it being four days since her last one. Unusually, it had been Norman who'd pointed the fact out, thinking it probably better if she were elsewhere when his callers arrived.

According to the assertive chimes of the doorbell, they had.

Smoothing his hair with his hand, he listened as his housekeeper, Genevieve, ushered his visitors into the hall. He straightened himself up, trying to appear as important and grown-up as he could. Despite what the last few years had accorded him, he still felt a fraud... as if bedsit Norman, the unsuccessful computer geek, could be unmasked by the merest scratching of the surface. It was crucial these particular visitors didn't realise that.

'Monsieur Penkridge will see you now,' came Genevieve's voice from behind the door, in her best English.

The door opened.

'Ah... gentlemen!' said Norman brightly, rising to greet his guests. 'I hope you've had a pleasant journey.'

'Despite the unseasonable weather, I'd say it'd be impossible not to in this beautiful country of yours,' returned one of them with an American drawl, extending his hand.

'Not mine!' Norman reminded him, accepting it.

'No... of course not,' his visitor corrected himself.

'My... what an impressive collection of artworks you have, Mister Penkridge,' sung the other in a squeal of delight. He too was American, but smaller and squatter than his compatriot. 'And such a diverse range! It's a delight to see so much creative genius displayed in just one place,' he cooed. 'Danny... don't you think it just *wonderful* that Mister Penkridge has such discerning taste?'

'Of course, Crispin,' enthused the other. 'Though isn't that why we're here? I doubt there's another art collector in the *world* who'd appreciate what we have to offer more than our exquisitely cultured host.'

Norman tried his best to look unaffected by the flattery, though his quivering mouth gave that lie away.

'Wouldn't the Van Gogh just fit *perfectly* between the Titian and the Hockney?' gasped Crispin, visualising it between his hands.

Norman could barely contain his excitement.

'Vincent would have wanted it that way,' affirmed the other earnestly.

'I can't believe it's on the market!' said Norman ecstatically. 'I never thought I'd have the chance to own one of the most famous painted images in the world!'

'Tsk, tsk, Mister Penkridge,' said Crispin, wagging a finger at him. 'I think we can safely say... *the* most famous painted image in the world. Poor old Mona is so passé these days. They should never have allowed her to be put on biscuit tins.'

Danny nodded wildly in agreement. 'Which is precisely why we have to be extremely careful who ends up purchasing such an iconic work. We can't allow any old Tom, Dick or Harriet to get their grubby little paws on such an important masterpiece. It may never be seen again... consigned to some corporate vault... or, worse still, appreciated purely for its monetary value.'

Crispin closed his eyes in disgust and sucked in his fear of such a vulgar thing happening.

'Talking of which,' said Norman, 'Am I right in understanding that I'll be bidding against other carefully vetted parties.'

'Assuming we've been able to verify your *own* security precautions, of course,' pointed out Danny respectfully. 'It was bad enough Vincent losing his ear. To lose one of his most famous paintings for all time would be unthinkable! We have a duty to mankind to ensure its new home will be a safe one.'

'Indeed we do,' seconded Crispin.

'There's none safer. The security here is the best you'll find in the world,' Norman assured them. 'It has to be. I've spared no expense in installing a state-of-the-art system... with some improvements of my own in the programming department,' he added proudly.

'*Really?*' said Danny, raising an eyebrow.

'Yes... I had pressure sensors buried in the immediate

grounds around the house which feed into the main system. I can control everything... including security shutters that will block every exit. If it's impossible to get in, it's even more so to get out!'

'Is this an early Tiffany?' called out Crispin, having wandered to the other side of the room. He was holding a table lamp and examining it keenly.

'Please... Mister Van der Beer!' said Norman nervously, holding out his hands as if telepathically helping his visitor support the object in question. 'It's one of the first prototypes and *extremely* valuable!'

'I'd expect nothing less, given it belongs to someone so culturally enlightened,' gushed Crispin, fondling the object enthusiastically.

Norman didn't dare breathe. He feared such a distraction might upset his guest's concentration.

'I never realised these were so heavy,' said Crispin, sizing it up in his hands.

'I really must insist...' Norman reigned in his panic as the table lamp was carefully replaced in its original position.

'And what have we here?' sighed Crispin, raising his hands in awe as he studied a painting in front of him.

'It's a Salvador Dali,' replied Norman, flustered by the man's energy. 'One of my favourites... and I consider myself very lucky to have obtained it. It's quite a long story.'

'Oh... do tell,' begged Crispin, clasping his hands together.

Norman did... revelling in having someone finally appreciate – if rather animatedly – every twist and turn of the unfolding tale. It was only as he was concluding it that he realised the two of them were alone. 'Your partner?' he asked, looking around awkwardly.

'Probably didn't want to interrupt,' finished Crispin. 'He has such a weak bladder. I've told him... he really should get it looked at.'

'Perhaps I should see if he's okay,' said Norman, anxiously moving towards the door.

'Danny's never needed help with it in the past,' smiled

Crispin, putting his hand out to stop him. 'I'm sure he'll be okay. He's probably taking the opportunity to give your security a once over whilst he's at it.'

'He'll find nothing wrong there,' insisted Norman, trying to regain control of the situation. He was beginning to feel railroaded.

'As I'm sure we won't with your finances,' ventured Crispin.

'I beg your pardon?'

Crispin feigned a look of discomfort. 'Please don't take this the wrong way, Mister Penkridge... but we need to be able to guarantee that your ability to purchase such a valuable artwork... assuming your bid to be successful, of course... is not in dispute.'

'I don't think you'll find that's a problem,' blustered Norman, wondering how it was he now found himself batting on the back foot.

'I'm sure it isn't,' said Crispin. 'But, as you will be only too aware... you are a bit of a "mystery" as far as the financial and art markets are concerned... and we do need to have complete confidence in the fact that there will be no controversy or problems surrounding the sale of this unique work. Such publicity would be disastrous... not least given the fragility of the recovering market. We would therefore need to validate your financial position.'

'It's never been a problem in the past. Whatever price I bid for the Van Gogh, I have the funds to cover it,' Norman assured him... though he could hardly elaborate and say that was the convenient thing about possessing a chequebook with no earthly limit.

Crispin smiled diplomatically. 'Then I'm sure it won't be a problem us confirming that with your bank. We will, of course, need your permission to contact them and have an audit produced of your finances.'

'An *audit*...? But I've never had to undertake such a thing before!' said Norman, alarmed.

'With respect, Mister Penkridge... You've never purchased such a valuable artwork before!' pointed out his interrogator politely.

Norman's confidence wobbled. Whilst his ability to produce the necessary funds was beyond question, his own bank held but a small amount of what was available to him. He'd been acutely aware from the very first withdrawals using the chequebook that, whilst the amount for which he could write each cheque was unlimited, the cheques themselves were not. His solution had been to use each precious one to top up his own account with amounts that – whilst considerable – wouldn't overly raise suspicion. As the Van Gogh would obviously exceed this self-imposed limit, he'd been considering using the chequebook to pay for its sudden and unexpected appearance in the market outright. The trouble was... it wasn't in his name.

'I intend to use a holding company to make the purchase on my behalf,' he said, forced to think on his feet.

'I see. So you're saying you have an external source of finance available to you?'

'*Kind* of.'

'And the name of that company?'

Norman felt extremely uncomfortable. Had he not been so keen to secure this once-in-a-lifetime opportunity, he would have told the stranger in front of him to "mind his own business". But that response wasn't going to get him what he wanted.

'Templar Resources,' he blurted, a split second before wishing he hadn't.

'Templar?' queried Crispin. 'As in...'

'Knights Templar... I suppose,' answered Norman cagily and feeling very foolish. Something was wrong. He'd never had to prove himself before. This wasn't how it worked.

'Interesting,' said Crispin slowly.

'I know this sounds a little silly at such a late stage,' said Norman, 'but I guess I should validate *your* position. I assume you have some identification with you, Mister Van der Beer?'

His guest looked astonished. 'I am Crispin Van der Beer,' he responded indignantly, pointing at his own face. '...of the

384

famous Van der Beers.'

'It's just that...'

'I think we may have been wrong about you, Mister Penkridge.' Crispin turned his head sharply and strode towards the door in a strop. 'Your clear lack of knowledge is telling. I fear Vincent's flowers might wilt in these conditions. Good day to you!' With that, he made his exit.

Norman hurried after him, panic gripping his confused mind. He wasn't sure whether he'd just lost out on the greatest artwork he would ever possess or was letting a potential conman escape. 'Mister Van der Beer... Crispin!' he called out searchingly, hoping it was the former and that the opportunity could still be rescued. Entering the hall, he saw Danny exiting one of the side rooms.

'Just checking your window locks,' Danny explained hastily. 'First class. I can't see there being any trouble there.'

'I can,' huffed Crispin, now at the front door.

'What's going on?' asked Danny, confused.

'We're leaving,' announced Crispin firmly.

'What?'

'Don't argue, Chad!'

'*Chad?*' queried Norman.

'Yes... Danny Chad,' said Danny Chad smartly.

'I thought you said on the phone your surname was Wentworth?'

'Mister Chad-Wentworth only bothers to hyphenate in front of genuine class!' sneered Crispin, giving his partner a *let's-get-outta-here* stare.

They did... leaving Norman standing at his own front door wondering what on earth had just happened.

* * *

Donald's body lay motionless.

The cats circling around and occasionally jumping onto it were hungry. Their feeding bowls were empty and the mice in the house were sensibly keeping a safe distance.

The storm that had ridden in with the dark had long since blown itself out and it was now early afternoon.

Everything outside the house was as it should be. A rusting wheelbarrow was exactly where it had always been, its deflated front wheel a prisoner of the grass that now ensnared it. A motley collection of bird feeders hung in various states of decay, momentarily teasing new arrivals, until the sparse, mouldy remains that clung to their sides were passed over for a garden whose owners cared. The grounds themselves were overgrown and untidy. A potting shed stood defiantly at the far end of the ghost of a lawn, covered in moss and bindweed, its roof bowed by neglect and the burden of too many English winters.

It hadn't always been that way.

Back in the day – when the mere mention of Bostock Tucker-Jenkins, Donald's father and original owner of the wheelbarrow, would inspire thoughts of the greatest ironing boards mankind had ever produced – the grounds had brought gasps of admiration from those fortunate enough to be invited to the splendid tea parties regularly held on its immaculate lawn. His mother, Dyllis – architect and instigator of all that impressed – had gaily laughed her way through many an idyllic summer's day, with the carefree abandon that had brought her into so many people's hearts... and them to her "little spot of paradise". It was a laugh that was cut cruelly short as the wind blew through her hair, her adoring husband, Bostock, by her side, as their beloved Austin Healey reached a speed it had never attained before. It was just a shame it hadn't been whilst driving *along* Beachy Head as opposed to *over* it.

The croquet hoops never saw action again. In fact, they never saw *anything*... having become as overgrown as Bostock's wheelbarrow, the memory of them fading with those who'd once enjoyed their challenge.

The cats were fading too. It had occurred to one or two of them that, if their master didn't get up soon and rectify the problem, they might have to look at nibbling the flesh that had so far failed to move.

After another half-hour of inactivity, the thought became a plan. A large, grey tabby – having suffered enough – jumped on top of Donald's waistcoat. Cautiously sniffing at the neck sticking out of it, it reached out with its paw and stuck a claw into the wrinkled skin.

'For Heaven's sake, Mussorgsky! Can a man not have some time to himself?' cried Donald angrily, shoving the animal off. 'I'm sick and tired of everyone making demands on me!' He rolled over on the floor... only to be confronted by a sudden increase in activity from the cats who were now expecting to be fed. Their tails were up and Donald figured that maybe... for all their sakes... he should be too.

He'd been lying there for quite some time. He'd had a lot to think about... though nothing made any sense. It wasn't just the events of the previous night that had caused him to remain on his kitchen floor for hours in numb introspection. It was everything about his life.

What had it all been for?

He'd only ever tried to do his best. But, for all the suffering it entailed, his efforts had never been appreciated.

He accepted he was different. He'd been made to feel that way by virtually every person he'd ever come into contact with. Not that it bothered him. As far as he was concerned, it was *them* who had the problems.

Take the way they never said *exactly* what it was they were thinking. A peculiar trait, if someone wished to be thought of as honest. *Surely you said what you thought? Made your feelings crystal clear, without dressing them up to be cloaked versions of what you really meant to say? After all... why would you lie?* But when *he* happened to say what was on his mind, people looked shocked and considered him rude.

What was wrong with the truth?

It never ceased to amaze him – as he observed people going about their daily lives – how they pretended not to have the psychological scars and burdens his psychic ability glaringly illuminated. At times, he could read them like a book. On exceptional days, the high street was *extremely* entertaining.

And people thought *him* odd!

Admittedly, hearing voices in your head wasn't normal. He accepted that. But then again... given they were indisputably there, wasn't it abnormal *not* to hear them?

Either way, they couldn't be ignored. Now... that *would* be rude. So why was it that those shunning his snippets of advice from the other side – when offered with the best of intentions – were the very same people who considered him offensive? He was only trying to help!

He'd never properly understand the world... which is why he'd been fortunate – if you ignored the great personal tragedy that had prefaced it – to be left a substantial inheritance in his early years... enabling him to survive without having to get too closely involved with it.

His solitary lifestyle had never bothered him. With the traffic that crowded *his* head, he was never truly alone.

But last night had been different. That's what had unsettled him and driven him to take such drastic action. Not that he'd known you could no longer kill yourself that way. All he'd done was run up his gas bill and make himself extremely nauseous. He'd just wanted the appalling commotion in his head to stop.

For the first time in his life he *had* felt alone... abandoned... insignificant... immaterial to and at the mercy of something new to his psychic experiences... something vastly dark and overwhelming. He knew the cats had felt it too, so it couldn't be put down to the result of an overactive imagination or the mould on the stale cheese and pickle sandwich he'd eaten that night.

It was *what* was in his head that had gotten to him the most. Not the sound, as first thought, of swarming flies. Whilst flies possessed a life force, they didn't have souls... so he should've known they couldn't pass over into spirit.

It was only as the sound increased that he'd come to realise its true, baleful nature. It was *whispering*... though not of the gentle kind heard in libraries. It was nasty... mean... sinister... threatening... secretive and angry... the kind that would definitely get you thrown out before you'd had the chance to get your book stamped. It was the scale of it that had tipped him over the edge. The vindictive babble – the combination of thousands upon thousands of discontented souls – had increased in volume until it had finally broken him.

But what shocked him the most was that, as soon as he'd attempted to end it, the cacophony of taunting voices had stopped... instantly and without explanation. It was as if, hectoring as they were, they didn't want him to die... as if they were actually *scared* of him doing so.

Why that should be, he didn't know.

No wonder he'd spent so long trying to make sense of the whole situation. His *other* voices had respectfully left him alone during his ruminating... curiously, a courtesy they'd never afforded him before.

But all good things had to end.

'YES,' sighed Donald wearily, as he struggled to his feet. 'I'M LISTENING.'

It was Whitebait... enquiring as to his well-being.

'OH... SO *NOW* YOU CARE! WELL... IT'S A SHAME YOU DIDN'T HAVE THE SAME CONCERN LAST NIGHT. A FAT LOT OF GOOD YOU WERE TO ME THEN!' Donald rebuked him. 'WHAT'S THE POINT OF HAVING AN INTERMEDIARY ON THE OTHER SIDE, IF YOU'RE GOING TO TURN TAIL AND RUN AT THE SLIGHTEST HINT OF TROUBLE. I MEAN... IT'S NOT AS IF YOU'VE GOT ANYTHING TO BE SCARED *OF!* THEY CAN HARDLY *KILL* YOU, CAN THEY?' His joints did their best to complain about their lengthy period of inaction on the cold floor, but deeper thoughts overshadowed them. Turning to examine the oven, the fact he'd tried to kill himself hit home.

He stood for a moment in silent reflection.

It wasn't allowed to last for long.

'YES... I KNOW IT WAS A STUPID IDEA! I'M CLEARLY OUT OF TOUCH! I DIDN'T KNOW YOU COULDN'T KILL YOURSELF WITH NATURAL GAS,' he said. 'MIND YOU,' he added via an ironic half-laugh, 'APPARENTLY, NEITHER DID THOSE DOING THE WHISPERING! I GUESS I'LL

HAVE TO THINK OF SOMETHING ELSE NEXT TIME.'

As the possibility of a "next time" struck him, even the half of that laugh disappeared. He shook himself from the thought.

'Dinner time!' he announced quickly, the cats heeding the cue. 'Then daddy's got to get back to work.'

The prospect didn't exactly inspire him. Having survived one psychic attack, he doubted it'd be long before he found himself subjected to another... and who knew what form *that* would take?

'He doesn't know exactly what it is he's supposed to be saying... but what he's supposed to be saying is clearly important, given the attention he's now receiving. You'll have to forgive him if he neglects you all a little. It's not that he doesn't love you... it's just that he's got an awful feeling his time is finally running out.'

*   *   *

'Just like the old days!' beamed Chad, as he and Bob huddled behind a rack of equipment, acquired courtesy of Bob's French contacts. Concealing a host of short-range receivers, the van in which they were doing the huddling had been discreetly parked on a small trackway dissecting a strip of woodland adjacent to Norman's property. It was close enough for their needs, having just heard Xanthia ask Norman – via a miniature microphone attached to the Tiffany lampshade – if Austria and Australia were next to each other. They'd also heard his reply.

'Only in the dictionary.'

An eavesdropping Australopithecine would probably have raised an objection, had they not had the misfortune of having been extinct for the last two million years.

He'd previously asked her if she'd seen anything suspicious on the way back from her hair appointment... to which she'd replied:

'Yes.'

Having asked her:

'What?'

She'd replied:

'*A cherry gateau with cream all the way around it, in a shop window.*'

Norman having responded:

'*I think you're thinking of "delicious"... not "suspicious".*'

She'd said that she hadn't been thinking of *anything* before Norman had asked his question and chastised him for trying to trick her. She'd then gone on to tell him about an article she'd tried to read in a magazine at the hairdressers about:

'*Some funny jumping animals called kangaroos.*'

'The closer I get to this Penkridge kid, the more I'm convinced we've got the wrong fella,' said Chad, shaking his head. 'I'm struggling to believe this guy has the brains to front some devious master plan. With all that wealth displayed on his walls, is she *really* the best he can do?'

'I'd settle for a few hours with her,' smirked Bob, 'and we wouldn't be discussing geography!'

'Probably just as well,' said Chad dryly.

There then followed a conversation between Norman and Xanthia in which Norman expressed doubts about his two earlier visitors. Though still beating himself up over the thought they might have been genuine, he was beginning to come round to the idea that they were up to no good... and that there could even be a connection with the two men who'd fallen out of the tree.

'Brilliant,' Chad mumbled. 'I rest my case.'

Assuming they might have been '*casing the joint*', he was now keeping every room that wasn't being used alarmed... so Xanthia was to keep him informed of her movements.

Having told him she was thinking of scratching her nose, Norman explained what he meant in a little more detail. He also told her he was angry with himself for divulging the name on the chequebook... and that he had let desperation to own the Van Gogh overrule common sense.

'I'm just greedy,' he berated himself.

'I could get you that gateau I saw in the window,' she offered.

Norman looked at her the way he always did... through rose-tinted contact lenses. 'I love you,' he said.

She smiled.

In a van nearby, two fingers were sarcastically jabbed into a mouth.

'I need to speak to Gabriel,' announced Norman, 'and I think it'd be best if I do it alone.'

The finger jabbing abruptly stopped.

'Wouldn't it be better to do it *with* him?' she asked.

'I mean... without *you* here.'

'I'll leave you to it,' she said, turning to leave.

'Ah, ah!' cautioned Norman, raising a finger. 'Don't you have to tell me something first?'

Xanthia looked at him blankly. 'I love you too?' she tried.

'Where... you're... going,' Norman reminded her affectionately.

'Oh,' said Xanthia, trying hard to get the hang of the game. 'Through... that... door,' she replied with equal measure.

'*Bedroom?*' persevered Norman.

'Normy!' she giggled. 'I'll ruin my hair!'

'I meant... are you going there? The alarm... *remember?*'

'Oh, this is silly!' she said, stamping her foot. 'I don't always know! I just do it!'

'Don't worry,' said Norman, conceding defeat. 'I'll switch it off for now. Gabriel's arrival would probably cause havoc with it anyway.'

'Looks like he's expecting this Gabriel character to visit him soon,' noted Chad, twisting around so as to get a clear view down the trackway to the road from which it ran. 'One of us needs to get to the front of the house and get a visual on this new target.'

'Let's see what the conversation's about first,' advised Bob. 'He could just be the gardener. There's no point in risking compromising our position unnecessarily.'

Chad nodded, acknowledging a point well made.

They waited patiently as doors were opened and closed... and footsteps listened to with upward eyes.

Eventually, Norman broke the boredom. '*Gabriel... are you there?*'

Chad snapped to attention. 'I didn't see a car go by,' he said, having been diligently observing the road. 'Maybe he *is* the gardener.'

A crackle of interference sounded.

Chad and Bob anxiously scanned their equipment.

'*Oops!*' exclaimed Norman. '*Well... at least I tried. I'll see if I can lose the crash helmet next time!*'

The two men looked at each other, perplexed.

'I didn't see a bike either,' Chad frowned.

There was a brief silence, at the end of which Norman said, '*I have to admit, it's not quite you.*'

An even longer silence followed before Norman spoke again. '*I've managed to do exactly what you asked. You were right... it wasn't easy... but it is possible. I guess that means we're ready to move on to the next stage.*'

Chad pushed the headphones tighter to his ears. 'Here we go!'

'Sounds like we've found the organ grinder,' whispered Bob.

Chad put a finger to his lips.

He needn't have bothered. 'What's with the silences?' he asked, having to endure another.

'*What!*' Norman exclaimed. '*You can't be serious! Do you know how difficult that would be?*'

'I don't get it,' said Bob. 'What's going on?'

Chad clicked his fingers. 'He's on the phone!'

'And the crash helmet?'

Chad shrugged.

'*I can't see how it can be done!*' groaned Norman. '*I'd be arrested before I even got started!*'

'Got 'em!' hissed Chad, clenching his fist. 'They're *definitely* up to no good!'

A familiar silence followed.

'*I know how important it is. But that doesn't make it any easier. The authorities would come down on me like a ton of bricks! What you're asking is absolutely impossible!*'

Another silence.

'If that's the case... I might have to enlist the help of friends. It sounds like I'm gonna need all the assistance I can get!'

A shorter silence.

'Yes, I do!' objected Norman indignantly. He paused. 'Alright... I have one... sort of.'

Silence.

'Okay... I'll concede he's more of an acquaintance.'

There was a loud tut.

'Of course I'm not gonna tell him what it's about!'

More silence.

'Well, okay... if you really wanna know... I call him the Provider and he calls me the Master... and don't ask. But I may need help with something, so he could turn out to be useful.'

The next silence carried on for so long, Chad assumed their equipment had malfunctioned. It was only when yet more interference cut through the air, and Norman could be heard quietly moaning to himself, that Chad realised the conversation had been terminated. 'Close... but not close *enough!*' he grimaced. 'If only we'd had a chance to put a tap on that phone! What I'd give to have heard the other end of that conversation!'

'At least we've got a couple of extra names to play with,' said Bob positively. 'Gabriel – who could be our Mister Big, given it looks like he's the one running the show – and this *Provider* guy.'

'The last one sounds like Penkridge's supply man.'

'Of *what*, though?'

Chad shook his head.

'And we've had it from the horse's mouth that the kid's a loner,' said Bob. 'Apart from his love interest, that is.'

'He may look ordinary, but... contrary to his choice of women and my initial assumption... he's smart. No friends equals no chance of betrayal or being put at risk by someone else. It's obviously how he kept himself below the radar for so long.'

'Well... *that's* about to change,' said Bob. 'Sounds like they're planning to take one helluva risk with something!'

Chad's brow furrowed. 'Yeah… and though that could tip the odds in our favour, we're still none the wiser as to what that is.'

'Not yet. But give it time. We're the closest anyone's ever been to nailing this kid… and with a healthy ear to the door. I'd rather be in our shoes than his. All we gotta do is sit tight and wait for him to feed us more information.' Bob rubbed his hands together. 'And on another positive… we'll be spending that time in a country where a girl can blow your mind with just her accent, food's considered an art form, and wine appears to be compulsory!'

'Talking of which…' Chad leant over the front seats and grabbed a bottle they'd purchased earlier. 'Where's that corkscrew of yours?'

'A toast?'

'To the fact we haven't lost our golden touch after all these years!' Chad grinned smugly.

'See… What did I tell ya… You can't keep a good team down!' Bob handed over his pocketknife.

'*Xan!*' broke in Norman's voice. '*Can you come in here for a second, please?*'

'For the first time, we have Penkridge *exactly* where we want him. It's *us* in the driving seat now!'

'*What is it?*' she asked.

Chad removed the cork with a flourish. 'And whilst the weather ain't quite what it's supposed to be for this time of year… at least his good sense in moving out here means we're not having to endure that abysmal climate we'd be forced to suffer back in Britain!'

'*We're leaving this house immediately and returning to England,*' said Norman, '*and I've an awful feeling we won't be back here for quite some time!*'

*   *   *

Worker One watched as the bank grew nearer… a large and noisy crowd tempting the *god of erosion* as they stood excitedly on it, awaiting the arrival of the raft's cargo.

Two columns of huge, wooden poles delineated a wide trackway that ran from the jetty in front of them up a soft slope beyond; its final destination hidden by the brow of a small hill. Multi-coloured sheets of cloth, strung between the poles, fluttered grandly in the wind like giant sails, alerting anyone that came upon them that this was a place of great importance.

Worker Three placed himself at the front of the raft and readied himself for the rope he was expecting to be thrown.

As it flew through the air, he deftly caught it and attached it to their craft, a shout of encouragement going up from the river bank as they were slowly hauled in.

A figure draped in animal fur and boasting an imposing headdress fashioned from deer antlers stood purposely apart from the others, quietly waiting to greet them.

As the raft came to a juddering halt, he stepped forward and spoke.

What he said was much along the lines of what he always said... that he hoped their journey had been as easy as the gods thought fit and that the fact their cargo had reached its destination was proof that those gods were pleased with everyone's work.

With a ready-made audience assembled, Worker One considered that maybe now might be the perfect opportunity to put forward his one-god theory... the figure with the antlers on his head being the very man with whom he should develop his idea. But he thought better of it, as he caught Worker Three fixing him with a warning stare.

Worker Two was quietly thanking the *god of severed digits* for getting him that far without losing another. Although he was aware he'd made that particular deity up... the more he'd asked it for safe passage... and the more that safe passage had been granted... the more real his new deity had seemed. *Perhaps, like Worker One, he was a visionary. Perhaps the god of severed digits existed after all. In which case... where did that put Worker One's one god? And more to the point... where did that put Worker One?*

The fur-clad impersonation of a hat stand raised his hands solemnly. It was at this point that his well-practised speech took an unexpected turn. Instead of requesting that the gods involved look with equal favour on the transportation of future cargos... *blah, blah, blah*... he stated to the assembled throng that their work at that particular site was nearly done. All that remained was to drag the rock to its final destination so that the purpose of their many years of labour could be revealed.

It is a curious fact to note that, many thousands of years later, as experts studying that site struggled to explain exactly why a group of individuals had gone to such extraordinary lengths to build the awe-inspiring structure they had, those doing the building hadn't known the answer either.

*   *   *

The local theatre manager welcomed Donald with the unabashed enthusiasm of someone realising that the person on the other end of their sweating hand could award his venue prestige beyond imagination.

'This is such an honour,' he gushed, trembling slightly as he finally let go of Donald's appendage. 'I am such a great admirer of your work, Mister Tucker-Jenkins... as is the rest of the world... and to think that you might consider bringing the premiere of your next play to this particular theatre is beyond anything I or our trustees could ever have dreamed of.'

'Call me Donald,' said the object of his fawning... causing the theatre manager to let out a strange squeal as he tried to suppress one and failed.

'I don't need to tell you what this would mean... *Donald*,' he obliged self-consciously, 'to a provincial theatre such as ours. The grants we traditionally relied on to keep our cultural programme running dried up like a thespian in need of a prompt when the markets crashed. We've been struggling to keep ourselves afloat ever since. Such international awareness of our venue and the possibilities it would open up for us are incalculable!'

'I'm only too pleased to help a local facility,' replied Donald... knowing full well the reason for his being there – as opposed to a much more prestigious, *non*-provincial, West End theatre – had less to do with altruism and more to do with its potential availability at such short notice. 'The thing is, Mister Knight-Lee...'

'Oh... do please call me Kieran,' the theatre manager interjected obsequiously.

'The thing is, Kieran,' tried Donald again, 'my new play must premiere on a specific date... that is of the utmost importance.'

'I can't see that being a problem. Let's look in the diary,' enthused the theatre manager, grabbing the one from his desk and flamboyantly spinning it and the rest of him to face the great playwright. 'And what date were you thinking of?'

'A fortnight today,' said Donald.

The theatre manager let out a faux laugh and waited for the real answer.

Donald stared back expectantly.

The theatre manager, realising his smile would soon start hurting him, raised his eyebrows so as to conduct Donald's proper reply. When it still didn't come, he blinked encouragingly. 'The date... *Donald?*' he prompted, like a ventriloquist unable to release his overstretched mandible.

'June the twentieth,' replied Donald, trying a different approach.

Relieved to be able to release such a socially embarrassing facial contortion, the theatre manager smartly licked his finger and swished through the pages of the diary.

Seeing how far the finger was travelling, Donald repeated the date a little louder.

'As in next year,' nodded the theatre manager.

'As in... a fortnight today,' Donald corrected him.

The theatre manager's face fell. 'But Mister Tuc... *Donald,*' he stammered, his finger frozen in mid-swish. 'We couldn't possibly fit you in at such short notice! We are fully booked for the next nine months!'

'I was afraid you might be,' said Donald. 'But it was worth a try. I'll just have to enquire somewhere else. Well... thank you for your time. I'm sorry to have wasted it.' He turned to leave.

'Wait!' shrieked the theatre manager in desperation.

'Yes?' enquired Donald hopefully.

The theatre manager grinned at him inanely. 'I don't know,' he admitted, shaking his head. 'It's just that... I can't believe we're losing you. Is there absolutely no flexibility on the date?'

Donald shook *his*.

The theatre manager looked to be in excruciating pain. 'I cannot let this opportunity escape,' he cried, fighting it. 'Please... give me a minute.' He started breathing heavily, hurriedly looking inwardly for a solution to his problem.

Just as Donald thought he wasn't going to find one, his expression suddenly changed... though the quivering edges of his mouth suggested the one he'd just found was going to cause him even more discomfort. 'You *will* premiere your play here in a fortnight,' he announced, with as much defiance as the quake in his voice permitted. 'I just have to make a phone call.' The last line delivered with eyes that appeared to be watching his own execution, he gingerly turned and picked up the phone... then inputted a number from a paper on his desk. 'Hello... is that the production manager for *Taps, Toffs, Top-Hats and Tails?*' he asked delicately. 'Ah, good... Just the man. This is... er... Kieran Knight-Lee from The Tivoli... Yes, yes... that's right... We had you due here in a couple of weeks' time.' He looked at Donald and grimaced. 'No,' he said awkwardly, 'It's not a bad line... I did say *"had"*.'

Donald waited patiently for the next five minutes whilst the theatre manager tortured himself in front of the great man. As the conversation from the other end of the phone became longer and louder, Kieran seemed to be steeling himself with the thought of the eyes of the world being upon his venue a fortnight next Thursday.

As a final, terse exchange of words ended his ordeal, he replaced the phone and smiled weakly. 'All done,' he sung nervously. 'A fortnight today it is.'

'That's wonderful,' beamed Donald. 'All I've got to do now is go home and finish it.'

The theatre manager's eyes watered. 'Finish *what... Donald?*' he asked hesitantly, as if fearing an answer he assumed would surely be impossible.

Donald proved it wasn't. 'The play,' he said matter-of-factly.

What colour was left in the theatre manager's face followed wherever the rest of it had gone.

'You mean... it's not written yet?'

'I wish,' tutted Donald with raised eyes.

'Mister Tucker-Jenkins,' said the theatre manager, trying to control his delivery. 'I've just upset one of our major and most important clients... and been threatened with everything from legal action to having our proscenium arch shoved up a place I'll leave to your imagination. I also have the not-so-small headache of ticket refunds to consider. Whilst I appreciate your phenomenal reputation for writing quickly... and am cognisant of the fact you've only just premiered your last play... I had at least assumed that this latest one was... *in the can*, as they say.'

Donald chewed his lip and shook his head.

'*Nearly* in the can?' the theatre manager pleaded.

Donald widened his eyes as if for understanding.

'I take it we couldn't possibly be talking... only just started?'

Donald nodded.

The theatre manager gripped the edge of his desk. 'But you know the ending,' he risked, grasping at a final straw.

'Chance would be a fine thing,' snorted Donald.

Further complicating a previously examined adage... a straw... that *wasn't* there... finally broke the camel's back. The theatre manager crumpled against the desk and began sinking towards the floor.

'I seem to have this effect on you gentlemen in the art world,' said Donald, watching his victim's downward progress.

The theatre manager never heard this last comment, his mind having gone to a safer, cosier place... one where proscenium arches didn't exist.

*   *   *

368

Peter Snogden-Lambert drew a breath so deep it reached the tip of the shoes he'd obsessively polished the night before. He did so in order to steady nerves that were awakening unwelcome memories from his recent past. The former gallery director was facing the greatest challenge of his life... and given the last few years of it, that was saying something.

His challenge stared at him blankly... non-committal... neither approving nor disapproving... waiting for him to make the first move.

It was now or never. He had to be assertive.

Drawing back his head, Snogden-Lambert gave his challenge the sort of contemptuous sneer often radiated in the direction of Mrs Snogden-Lambert whenever she'd tut loudly and complain about having been dealt a poor hand of scrabble tiles.

His challenge remained unmoved... which was hardly surprising, given it was a door.

Things might have been a little easier, had it not been for the fact this particular one had his name stuck on it.

It might also have been easier had this denoted ownership of said portal. In such an instance, passing through would have been as undemanding as if the offending letters etched into a utilitarian, aluminium plaque attached to it had spelt the words *TOILET* or *MENTAL ASYLUM*... for he'd frequently visited both during the last few years.

But the door belonged to others... the reason for his anxiety. *Others* who'd seen fit to offer investment in a name plaque and position of trust to a man slowly crawling his way back from oblivion via the support of an understanding network of old friends who'd benevolently pulled strings on his behalf.

He couldn't let them down.

No... correction...

He couldn't let *himself* down.

He reminded himself that he was staring out at the door from inside the new Peter Snogden-Lambert... mended and rehabilitated... not at all like the old Peter Snogden-Lambert...

who'd taken a knife to an original work of art by one of the greatest English painters that had ever lived and left it looking like tagliatelle.

Not now, Peter, he counselled himself, as the memory flashed a little too brightly.

That old Peter Snogden-Lambert belonged to a previous life that needed to be forgotten.

He read the name on the plaque again.

His trouble was… it looked exactly the same as it always had. 'Fear is only in your head,' he mumbled to himself. 'Reality is what we allow it to be.' He clung to the mantra delicately fed him during his institutional "breaks" much like one might spoon-feed a bewildered baby.

Gripping the door's handle, he wiped his tongue along a quivering set of dry lips. How he wished it could have been welcomingly opened for him by his personal assistant of so many past years, Joan Fanshawe-Whittingham. The mere thought of her name acted as an anchor for his bobbing thoughts, his mind transported to a happier time when *his* name carried with it an aura of respect in certain circles. Back then, he would often sit behind his luxurious desk and wonder – as she leant over and settled a tray of tea and biscuits on it – what it would be like to be married to her. For instance… would he not have been forced to endure bedroom décor that seemed more suited to a cross between Miss Havisham and a senile, octogenarian Barbie? Joan Fanshawe-Whittingham might have been of similar years to Mrs Snogden-Lambert, but he bet *she* had a duvet. And would such a hypothetical union have meant the end of pointless, crocheted toilet roll covers and the permanent, all-pervading smell of lavender water?

He had never mentally undressed her, mind. Respect for her as a work colleague – and the inconvenience of him being married – prevented such an imposition. That and the fact he could never quite psychologically get past the industrial strength brassiere – warning off would-be perverts – that threatened from beneath her blouse. Theirs would have been a union of minds, had fate decreed it… hers efficient… his in need of hers. The ideal combination in his book.

He certainly needed it now. But an earlier than anticipated retirement – due to her having witnessed him foaming at the mouth and uttering words she wouldn't have encountered in Reader's Digest, whilst being carted away on a paramedic's trolley – had put paid to that possibility.

Ironically, Mrs Snogden-Lambert had also embarked upon a retirement... from *him*. Having a husband who frequently smelt of alcohol and bins didn't go down well with the bridge set.

He was on his own.

Besides... the budget attached to this new "position of trust" didn't go anywhere near stretching to a personal assistant. But that was alright. It prefaced less responsibility.

He applied the full weight of his misgivings to its handle and pushed the door open.

The room that confronted him was friendly enough, possessing a basic chair, desk and solitary filing cabinet that promised an easier path to his own retirement than his previous job.

For that, he was truly thankful.

It wasn't quite the plush surroundings that had earmarked his reign as director of one of the country's most prestigious art galleries. The furniture then boasted history. But at least there were no wooden radiator covers through which he could ram the head of one of the Vatican's most eminent art experts.

For that, future visiting dignitaries should be thankful.

The atmosphere in the room was of new carpet and provincial peace. It also promised a new life... a fresh start.

This was his born-again moment.

His responsibilities were minimal... his job, merely a question of turning up in the morning and overseeing a simple, rural operation.

How difficult could it be?

*　　*　　*

'Normy... be a darlin'! Call down to room service and get them to bring up more fresh flowers, would you?' sung Xanthia from the dressing area that was just one of many excessively luxurious spaces the penthouse suite offered its wealthy guests. 'If we're gonna be here for any length of time, it may as well look and feel like home!'

Norman lifted the receiver by the side of the pointlessly wide bed and did as he was told... even though he couldn't recall their house in France having ever resembled a florist's shop.

He wasn't going to argue. It was good to see Xanthia back to her old self... worrying about her appearance and spending his money.

Just how long that length of time she was referring to would be was anybody's guess. He'd complied with the first part of Gabriel's latest instructions and got himself back to England. But the second part sounded as if it was going to be considerably more difficult. Although he didn't know exactly *where* he was to perform his two-note opus, he'd been informed that it was to be done in a public place... hence the reason for his alarm and protestations. Heaven, he realised, clearly had no concept of health and safety, let alone belligerent councils and their draconian licensing laws.

He was now patiently awaiting the winged-one's ethereal presence, in order to be given the final details.

The hotel employee on the end of the phone was obsequiously accommodating... which was hardly surprising, given how much Norman was paying for the privilege.

'They're asking what kind of flowers,' he shouted back.

'Pretty ones that smell nice,' came the reply, 'and lots of 'em!'

Norman sheepishly conveyed the message, then hung up. 'They'll be here within the hour,' he passed on.

'Good,' said Xanthia, emerging from the dressing area in a cloud of *eau de parfum*. 'But I won't! I'm off to visit an old friend. It's been a while. I'll leave you to have your boys' chat with Gabriel.'

'It's not exactly *that*,' said Norman, noting the lack of skirt length, but knowing an objection was pointless. 'We've never casually chatted about *anything*.'

'Then, perhaps it's time you did!' she suggested, fixing her hair in a mirror for the umpteenth time. 'Perhaps he'd like it if you got to know him a little better. I mean... is there a *Mrs* Gabriel, for instance?'

'I hardly think so!' laughed Norman. 'I wouldn't think that's appropriate in *his* world.'

'What... when you and I die, we won't be together?' she asked.

'That's... erm... different,' he stumbled, defending a position of ignorance. 'I think you should view Gabriel like a man of the cloth... only in spirit form.'

'What... a dead tailor?'

'I mean... like a priest or something.'

'*Vicars* get married,' said Xanthia petulantly.

'Yes... well... I think you'll find he's slightly higher up the ecclesiastical chain than that.'

'I haven't a clue what one of them is,' she pouted. 'But if he's so important, he should be able to bend the rules a little.'

'I guess he's too busy,' said Norman, hoping to seal the conversation.

'You told me he said time didn't exist where he came from,' insisted Xanthia. 'In which case... he can hardly have a lack of it!' With that, she blew him a kiss and tottered out of the door on shoes that made her look like she was walking downhill.

Norman savoured the silence he'd been left in, quietly reflecting on the fact he'd just been comprehensively outsmarted.

The tranquillity was short-lived.

As the sound of the hotel's fire alarm presaged panic and commotion in the corridor outside, he prepared for Gabriel to sort out his vibrations. He wondered whether – if his thoughts now focused on what was considered to be cool in fashion – Gabriel might appear in a form closer to the one he desired. The problem was... dressed in corduroy trousers battling a burgundy and yellow check jumper, Norman had already proved himself incapable of such thinking.

With a throbbing ball of orange light finally producing the awaited vision, the Archangel materialised in a pink and blue Kaftan mercifully covering excessively flared jeans. Norman might just have got away with it, had it not been for the tan-coloured brogues poking out from underneath.

'I think I preferred the wings,' Gabriel sighed, reflecting on Norman's attempts at couture. 'Then again... I guess I should be grateful for not having to look out at you through a visor this time.'

'Maybe it'd be easier if you controlled it yourself,' suggested Norman, hurt... especially given how fabulous he thought the brogues looked.

'I've told you many times, my form is merely a product of your imagination. I simply provide the energy to make it manifest.'

Norman toyed with the idea of asking how Mrs Gabriel envisaged him, thus killing two birds with one stone... but knew the actual words were an irrelevance, as Gabriel shook his head in exasperation.

'I've got my sound crew on standby and ready to go,' Norman announced, attempting to regain some credibility. 'Whilst it's a dead cert we'll all be carted off to the nearest police station before the second piece of scaffolding is in place, I assume you're now able to tell me *where* that arrest will be taking place?'

'I can give the location you require for your task,' said Gabriel, ignoring the sarcasm.

'With the volume involved, we're obviously talking an open air one,' prompted Norman.

'It'll definitely be that,' conceded the Archangel.

'With reasonable access for a large truck?'

'You won't have a problem there.'

'Good.'

They stared at each other.

'Then, what are we waiting for?'

'The summer solstice,' replied Gabriel matter-of-factly. 'Which will be occurring in precisely...'

'Wait...' Norman staved off the answer with his hand and subtracted the number of days since he'd been given the figure of twenty-three. 'Fourteen days?'

'Correct.'

'Well, at least *that* part now makes sense.' The rest clearly didn't. 'So... what is it you want me to do in the meantime?'

'Prepare for your performance,' answered Gabriel.

Norman awaited further instructions.

Gabriel looked at him.

'That's it?' Norman exclaimed. 'No other special tasks between now and then?'

'I think you'll find that'll keep you busy enough,' Gabriel replied. 'I shouldn't think it'll be easy obtaining the permissions you'll need to execute your mission successfully.'

'I told *you* that!' declared Norman, with widening eyes. 'No one's gonna allow me to set up a sound system in this country to blast out two continuous notes that can shatter masonry, let alone eardrums!'

'We have no choice,' said Gabriel. 'And remember... you must achieve it without breaking any laws.'

'God forbid!' exclaimed Norman petulantly.

Gabriel raised an eyebrow.

'*Well...*' sung Norman in his own defence. 'I'm sure those dark forces you say are amassing against me will be doing just *that*. It hardly seems a fair fight!'

'That's what makes them dark,' said Gabriel soberly. 'Ours is a force of goodness and righteousness. Its supreme power lies in those very principles. We cannot risk weakening it by having it tainted with anything that represents its opposite. It will only work for us if applied in its purest form.'

'Surely there are ways around such things, though? I overrode the Devil last time on the point of copyright,' Norman reminded him.

'You did,' acknowledged Gabriel. 'And look what happened!'

Norman appreciated he'd just been outsmarted for the second time in less than five minutes.

'The path is simple,' Gabriel expanded. 'The power of God is not subjective... even if attempts to apply it on your earth plane usually seem to be.'

'I know, I know,' sighed Norman, resigning himself to the inevitable. He raised his hand in oath. 'I promise to play by all the rules.'

'Then we must begin in earnest.' Gabriel drew himself up, exposing the tassels on his brogues.

Norman tried not to be distracted by them, sensing the Archangel was about to make an announcement more important than their allure.

'Everything will change from this moment,' Gabriel warned. 'Those opposing us will be considerably stronger with the knowledge I'm about to impart.'

'Finally... the location!' exclaimed Norman impatiently.

'It is at a point that is a vital confluence of spiritual energy within the material plane,' Gabriel announced grandly.

Norman squinted. 'Something I can find on a map would be better.'

'Of course. Do you want a fanfare?'

Norman shook his head wearily. 'Just the name.'

'As you wish.'

Norman swore he heard the hint of a muffled trumpet... but let it go.

'You have given it the name... *Stonehenge*,' said Gabriel, without further theatricality. 'I trust you are familiar with it?'

Norman's eyes bulged. 'What... *the* Stonehenge?' The revelation nearly caused him to choke.

'The very one you're currently thinking of,' Gabriel confirmed.

'But that's impossible!'

'The site... or the fact you've managed to think of the correct one?'

'The fact it's our most revered ancient monument... and you want me to set up the most powerful and destructive PA system ever assembled... at precisely the one time of year when it's surrounded by its heaviest security! Are you completely *mad?*'

'As madness is a product of insanity... which your world defines as a state of mind preventing normal perception, behaviour or social interaction... I'd rather not answer that question.'

'But they'll never allow it! It's *absolutely* impossible! We'll just have to do it somewhere else.'

'We can't.' said Gabriel bluntly. 'I've already explained... it's an extremely significant site. It's been waiting for this moment for thousands of years. Why do you think the ancients went to so much trouble to build it in the first place?'

'I don't know!' exclaimed Norman, throwing up his hands. 'I doubt you're going to want to tell me *that* bit!'

'Correct,' said Gabriel. 'All in good time.'

'We all thought it was some sort of calendar!'

'I'd have thought there are far easier ways to mark the passing of time,' remarked Gabriel. 'Those stones were dragged there at huge sacrifice for a much greater purpose. It is your job to ensure that effort was not in vain.'

'I don't believe this!' said Norman, burying his head in his hands.

'Don't encourage the forces of negativity,' Gabriel admonished him. 'Remember what I told you... like attracts like. You must believe in yourself and draw the positive forces towards you. There are enough dark ones heading your way as it is.'

'I know! I believe I've already encountered some of them! Apart from a disturbing air of menace that's been shadowing me these last nine days, I've had strange visitors acting suspiciously and people falling out of my trees!'

'That'll be the start of it,' nodded Gabriel. 'But no matter how strong those forces become, they can never be more powerful than that of love. It is very important you remember that.'

'Is love also more powerful than Wiltshire County Council and English Heritage?' enquired Norman facetiously. 'Because that's who I'm gonna need to overpower if I'm to achieve what you want!'

'You *have* to achieve it,' insisted Gabriel. 'You *must* find a way. As the sun rises on the twenty-first of June, the frequencies I gave you *must* be generated in strict accordance with my original instructions at the place described. Nothing less will do!'

Norman couldn't see how it would be remotely possible... but knew further objections were pointless. 'If I'm to do so without breaking any laws, I'm going to have to be *extremely* creative!'

Gabriel's presence flickered slightly. 'Not your strongest point, if I recall,' he said, braving a glance at his footwear. 'Let's hope those paintings on your wall really *have* done you some good!'

Norman hoped so too. On the positive side... at least he'd be able to justify their costly acquisition.

'That's better,' said Gabriel. 'At least your thoughts are now going in the right direction!' With further conversation unnecessary, he prepared to depart. 'I'll leave you to it,' he said, adjusting the sleeves of his kaftan.

'Wait!'

Gabriel paused what he was doing.

Norman fidgeted awkwardly. 'Erm... You don't possibly fancy a little... er... *chat* before you go... do you?'

'I beg your pardon?'

'A chat,' repeated Norman, not sure how to rephrase it.

'I thought we'd just had one,' said Gabriel perplexed.

'We could have... another,' ventured Norman.

'About what?'

'Other... *things*,' suggested Norman timidly.

'Is there something bothering you?' asked Gabriel, forgetting about his sleeves.

'What... beyond having a deadline in which to do the impossible in order to save the Universe? No... I just thought it would be nice if we talked about something *else* for a change.'

Gabriel considered the idea... though more from a point of politeness. 'Alright... what would you like to talk about?'

Norman wished Xanthia was there. *She'd* know what to ask.

It had been her idea, anyway. 'What's Heaven like?' he blurted out, in the absence of anything else springing to mind. After all... he could hardly ask an Archangel what car he drove.

'Pure love,' answered Gabriel.

Norman looked uncomfortable.

'Anything else?' asked Gabriel.

'Er... what does it *look* like?'

'It doesn't.'

'Right.'

Gabriel waited expectantly.

'I take it... there aren't any roads, then,' said Norman quietly. Even *he* appreciated the foolishness of the question the minute it stumbled from his mouth.

Gabriel smiled. 'Look, Norman... if you want to know more about me... I'm everything in your heart that's good. If you look at yourself and understand what that is, you'll understand me. As for Heaven... that's what makes it possible.'

Norman felt the words touch him like the memory of a favourite embrace. The experience was something new... yet reassuringly familiar. He couldn't explain it.

'That feeling you just had,' said Gabriel. 'That's you connecting with your inner spirit. You should do it more often.'

'I think I'd like that,' said Norman, drinking in its warmth.

'Good,' said Gabriel. 'It means you're *definitely* going in the right direction! As for me... I have a car to wash.'

Norman stared in disbelief.

'It was a joke,' said Gabriel. 'I leave that job to the wife.'

With that, he started to fade.

Norman was just dwelling on how well the conversation *hadn't* gone when Gabriel unexpectedly came back into focus.

'By the way... Just a thought... Don't you think it would be wise to join the others?'

'Others?' queried Norman.

'Yes... those assembling outside this hotel's main entrance.'

Norman was suddenly aware of the fire alarm still ringing in the background.

'Oh... I get it!' he laughed. 'Very funny!' He liked this new Gabriel. He'd always wondered why an Archangel couldn't possess a sense of humour. 'I wonder how long they'll be standing there until it's discovered to be a false alarm!' he sniggered.

'False alarm?' Gabriel looked concerned. 'I hope you don't think *I* had anything to do with that?'

'You didn't?' asked Norman awkwardly.

Gabriel shook his head. 'Not guilty,' he grimaced.

Norman tentatively sniffed the air.

'Shit!' he exclaimed loudly, as his nose returned the smell of burning carpet.

*   *   *

The short taxi ride from the airport to one of the numerous, formula hotels that lined its perimeter did nothing to lift Chad's foreboding at being forced to return to his least favourite place on Earth. The weather didn't help... having swapped the warm, clear blue skies of Southern France – that had miraculously reappeared just prior to their departure – for the dismal, grey ones currently shrouding the West of London. Even the endless parade of traffic lights had been against them... the drab, urban landscape a mocking disappointment after the promising medieval patchwork of abundantly green fields that had welcomed them from the air... on the rare occasion a break in the clouds had allowed. But he knew they had no other choice. France had proved a cruel waste of time, only providing further questions that needed yet more answers.

What to do next was the one currently being debated over a meal as bland as the hotel in which it had been microwaved.

Both men agreed that the contrast between the last forty-eight hours could not have been more depressing. They'd gone from the hubris of believing themselves to be in the driving seat... to the stark realisation that – whilst having the steering wheel firmly in their hands – all four wheels had fallen off.

Their problems had been further compounded when

discovering the last-minute flight they'd overheard Norman telling Xanthia he'd booked was full. With their surveillance effectively ended at the departure gate, they'd been forced to follow on a later flight... leaving them clueless as to their quarry's whereabouts.

Even an investigation of the livery of the truck that had transported the sound equipment to Norman's property in France had proved fruitless... turning out to belong to a large, UK-wide haulage contractor with depots the length and breadth of the country.

With little alternative, they'd chosen to assume that Norman had headed into the city on his arrival and booked into one of its many plusher hotels. Their only hope of discovering exactly which one lay in the audaciousness of a few individuals Bob referred to as his *inner circle*... trusted colleagues from within the agency, who'd agreed to see if they could garner information regarding the location of Norman's cellphone or the use of his credit cards. Whilst they'd already been keeping an eye out for unusual activity regarding religious orders meeting in secret again, their latest assistance came with a health warning. Worthy of a major felony charge if exposed, these additional favours had to be undertaken in an extremely cautious manner. It was taking time the two men feared they didn't have.

The sound of panpipes murdering classic love ballads providing the perfect accompaniment to their misery, Bob threw a name into the conversation.

'Donald Tucker-Jenkins,' he mumbled, through a mouthful of *crème brûlée*.

'What about him?' asked Chad. 'You're not thinking of killing time by taking in one of his plays, are you? I'd have thought there was more chance of getting you in a *bath* than a theatre.'

'Perhaps we should pay him a visit,' said Bob, piling in yet more dessert before the previous mouthful sensibly allowed.

'What... so that we can have cryptic insults about red herrings thrown at us again?'

'You may scoff,' Bob spat. 'But think about it. That particular gem was lobbed from right outside Penkridge's apartment! Now... we can believe one of two things about that old wacko. The first is that he was employed as a decoy, but got so wrapped up in his part that he ended up giving too much away... The second... that he really *does* have some form of psychic power and somehow genuinely plucked that address from the ether. Either way, he got us to the boy. I say there's no reason to suppose we can't use him to do it again.'

Chad considered the idea. It wasn't one he relished... but had little in the way of an alternative. 'A point well put,' he finally conceded. 'It certainly makes more sense than just sitting here.'

Bob belched his appreciation of the compliment.

'So... do we assume he lives at the same address?'

'Family home... lived there since he was a boy,' said Bob. 'There's good reason to believe he still does.'

'It *was* a door slam from falling down,' Chad reminded him. 'And he certainly could've afforded a new one by now, given his phenomenal success.'

Bob wasn't so sure. 'Twenty-three plays in five years? I hardly reckon he'll have had time to consider a move.'

Chad nodded. 'I'll buy that.'

'What about security? He's bound to have professional protection, now he's acquired celebrity status.'

Chad angled his head. 'You reckon? I shouldn't think he bothers, knowing Donald. Besides... they say he still lives as a recluse.'

'Good. That'll make our life easier.'

Chad gazed out of the window and at the regimented lines of fleet cars filling the car park. 'I'll arrange the hire of a vehicle for tomorrow morning... though I can't say I'm looking forward to driving on the wrong side of the road again!'

'At least it'll give us an excuse to escape this dump,' said Bob, pushing away his empty plate. 'D'ya reckon fame's changed him?'

'Donald?'

'Yeah.'

Chad considered the question. 'If he's changed at all, I'm prepared to stake my entire fee for this job that it had nothing to do with fame and *everything* to do with that bizarre light we experienced. We might've *seen* it... but he got *hit* by it! Whatever it was, it altered his life. That's the one thing about this whole affair I *am* certain of!'

*   *   *

'What on earth's happened?' exclaimed Xanthia, tottering her way through the excited crowd to where Norman was standing.

Norman took a moment to survey the chaotic scene of fire engines, firemen, and fire-related paraphernalia, and marvelled at the question. 'There's been a fire,' he said.

'What... at the hotel?'

Norman returned his attention to the blackened, smouldering building in front of them. 'Yes,' he said quietly.

'It's a good job you weren't in there, then,' she gasped, wrapping her arms around him.

'I was! And very nearly didn't make it out!'

'Normy!' She nuzzled him tightly. 'To think I might've lost you!'

'I'm alright,' he reassured her. 'Just a little shocked, that's all. By the time I got to the lifts, they weren't working. I had to use the fire escape. But the last few floors were covered in smoke... and if it hadn't been for one of the fire crew stumbling upon me...'

'Normy!' she squealed, even louder.

'I can't believe Gabriel didn't sense what was going on. He very nearly left me to burn!'

'He turned up, then?'

'That was the problem. It's why I ignored the alarm. I thought he'd triggered it. But *he* knew he hadn't... and yet...'

'Well, you're here now,' she said. 'That's the important fing. Accidents will happen.'

'That's what's curious,' he frowned. 'They don't think it *was* an accident. It seems like someone deliberately started a fire in the basement. More worryingly... I overheard one of the fire crew suggesting someone had poured out an accelerant in the shape of a man's genitals.'

'What are they?'

'A cock and two balls.'

Xanthia giggled.

'It's not funny, Xan! That's *exactly* what happened when my bedsit burnt down... remember? Only then... Satan was behind it.'

A look of puzzlement crossed her face. 'I don't remember it happening at Christmas.'

'That's *Santa*,' he said patiently.

'Oh... right.'

'I think it's everything to do with those dark forces Gabriel's been warning me about. He said they'd be even stronger now. What worries me is that I've got to keep one step ahead of them for the next fourteen days. I don't think they're gonna stop at this. If Gabriel's right, it's only the beginning.' He looked at her troubled expression. 'Maybe it's best if you go back home to France. It's not *you* they're after.'

'I'm not going anywhere without you,' she pouted, pulling tightly into him again. 'They can draw as many Jenny tails as they like! I'm staying here!'

Norman embraced her affectionately. 'In that case... we need to find some alternative accommodation. I just hope some of our belongings have survived.'

'Normy!' she exclaimed, grabbing his arm. 'What about the chequebook? I take it you brought it to England with you?'

Norman patted a small protuberance beneath his cardigan. 'It's alright. I'm not letting *that* out of my sight!' He felt her grip relax. 'Anyway... how's *your* day been?'

The corners of her smile retreated. 'Yeah... good, thanks,' she said a little awkwardly. 'I've been catching up with an old face.'

'Actually... I've met with one myself whilst standing here,' he announced proudly.'

'Really?'

'You know the guy I call *The Provider?* Well... when I knew we were coming to England, I arranged for him to pop by and see me. It's a good job he didn't turn up half an hour earlier!'

'Is that your only friend you sometimes talk about?' she asked.

Norman pictured Gabriel judging his reply. 'Well... more of an *acquaintance*, really,' he admitted. 'In fact... he was once my enemy!'

She looked puzzled.

'I'll explain another time,' he laughed. 'Suffice to say... we have a lot in common and he certainly comes in useful at times... hence his nickname.'

'Maybe I'll get to meet him one day,' she smiled. 'I'd like that. I know so little about your past... other than when we were at school together, of course.'

Norman had always thought it best kept that way. The last thing he wanted was to scare her off. Having firsthand knowledge of him shitting himself was bad enough.

'So... who was the friend *you* saw?' he said, changing the subject.

'Nobody special,' she returned, glancing at the ground.

'Well... we'll get something to eat and you can tell me all about them.'

'There's nothing interesting to tell, really,' she countered hastily. 'I'd much rather hear about your meeting with Gabriel.'

'You might not when you hear what he wants me to do!'

'And did you discover more about him?'

Norman's brow creased. 'Well... as you're about to find out... he certainly has a sense of humour!'

*   *   *

The little village hall at Brookton bristled with anticipation as Julian de Vale stepped onto its quaint, Victorian stage and gratefully acknowledged the enthusiastic reception he was being afforded.

Tickets had sold well, with proceeds going towards the church's restoration fund. This latter fact had caused more than a ripple of controversy, given Julian de Vale was about to communicate with the dead. Not since Bert Brabbington's marrow had been unfairly disqualified at the village fête in 1974 had there been such division amongst the villagers. Had the vicar not duly weighed in with his blessing – pointing out that the evening was "all in good fun" – it seems likely that the dead of Brookton would have to have remained so for that particular Tuesday evening.

'I'm delighted to be invited here tonight,' began Julian in a soft, Lancashire lilt that floated between affability and condescension, 'to share my gift.' He gave a supercilious smile that was better used on a pensioner in a home. 'I hope to be able to bring a little comfort and assurance to those whose loved ones might have recently passed over into spirit,' he announced, clasping his hands together for maximum sincerity. He was aware that certain sections of his audience might be harbouring a little scepticism… though even the hardest cynic could be reduced to tears if he happened to hit upon their deceased loved one's name. 'As you know… I don't charge for my services.' He waited patiently for their polite applause. 'Everything I do here tonight is through love and the wish to unite those now in spirit with those they've left behind. Now… I'll try to get through as many as I can this evening… but please be patient, as they're sometimes a little shy in coming forward.' He smiled gently at his own humour then started pacing around the small stage, his hands still clasped together.

The audience sat transfixed… listening to him breathing deeply, as he inhaled excessively through flared nostrils. Just as a few nervous titters started rippling around the audience, he stopped dead and threw his head back.

'Bless you, my love,' he said, placing a hand to his forehead. 'Okay… is there anyone in the audience who knows an Eileen who's passed into spirit?' He held out his other hand as if to catch a reply. 'Anyone want to take an Eileen?' he persevered

350

against an awkward silence. 'Okay, my love. Forgive me. I'm just getting warmed up. She's telling me it's *Ellen*. Sorry, my love. Anyone want to take an Ellen?'

Two separate hands raised in the audience.

'She says you knew her as Mum.'

One of the hands lowered.

He turned to face the owner of the remaining hand, a middle-aged lady who looked like she was just about to get run over.

'She says you've been baking,' said Julian, his raised eyes indicating he was listening to Ellen at the same time as interpreting her conversation. 'A cake... She says you've been baking a cake.'

The lady in the audience shook her head apologetically.

'What's that, my love,' said Julian, addressing his invisible co-performer. 'Okay, my love... bless you. That's my fault. I'm having a little difficulty tuning in to you. I hear you now... I hear you now. *Cooking!* he nodded heavily. He turned to the audience member again. 'She says you've recently done some *cooking?*'

This time the recipient's head moved in affirmation.

'What am I like?' he said via a self-deprecating chuckle. 'I thought she was demonstrating baking a cake! You're gonna have to be clearer, Ellen, my love. This lot will think I'm simple!' He laughed at his own joke again, with a confidence suggesting that although the audience hadn't joined in with him, Ellen had. 'She says you've been missing her,' he continued, 'and that you're not to. She's very happy where she is and wants you to be the same. You're to get on with your own life and stop worrying.'

The woman in the audience nodded appreciatively, her bottom lip starting to quiver.

'She's got a man standing next to her,' pushed on Julian. 'She's pointing to him and smiling.' He turned to the audience member. 'Is that your father, dear?' he asked gently.

'I bloody hope not!' said the man sitting next to her. 'Otherwise she's in for a shock when we get home!'

349

The audience erupted in laughter.

'I didn't think it was,' said Julian, shaking his head knowingly. 'Oh... he's telling me off. He's saying how *dare* I think he looked old enough!' He paused, as if listening. 'Okay, Ellen... Bless you, my love,' he said, seeming to push her away with one hand and beckon in the mystery gentleman with the other. 'He says his name's...' he paused, as if struggling to hear. 'Jack...? *John*...? Is it John...? Bear with me... *Joe?* It starts with a J though, doesn't it...? He's not being very clear, ladies and gentlemen. Can anyone take that? I've got a Jack, John or Joe... Anyone know a Jack, John or Joe... possibly even a James... who's passed into spirit...? It might not necessarily have been recently.'

A number of hands were raised, many with an underwhelming sense of reluctance. A few of the assembled throng looked at each dubiously.

Julian recognised the moment. It was understandable. He was just getting warmed up and he was asking them to believe in something they didn't normally encounter. He just wished they'd show a little more faith. After all... he wasn't doing this for personal gain, having freely given up his time and only asked for petrol money. If he wasn't genuine, why on earth would he put himself through so much trouble? Surely they didn't think he was a sad individual on some sort of self-satisfying ego trip... making out he was special in a desperate bid to crave their attention? *No matter. The spirits were getting stronger.* 'He's looking for someone called Janet... or Joan. What is it with all these Js! Can anyone take that?'

All but one hand were lowered... and even that one seemed to have its doubts.

'I'm *Jean*,' its owner offered timidly.

'Just a minute, my love,' Julian instructed her. 'Is it *Jean* you're wanting to talk to?' he asked Jack, John, Joe or James. There was another pause. 'It is! Well, why didn't you say so in the first place! Who is he, my love?' he asked Jean.

'I think it might be my late husband, Joe,' came the tentative reply.

'Is she right, Joe?' asked Julian. 'She is! Well... no wonder he's late, my love... he's so bloody vague he was probably indecisive in life!'

Julian might have got a bigger laugh with his quip were it not for the fact that the majority of the audience were starting to feel decidedly uncomfortable.

Julian pressed on undeterred. 'He says he likes the blanket you've been crocheting... reminds him of the one you saw in a shop window in Bude on your last holiday together.'

Jean let out a poignant 'yes,' and placed her hand to her mouth to stop herself blubbing.

'He says you wanted to buy it, but didn't have enough money.'

She nodded as best she could under the emotional circumstances, producing a gasp from the audience.

'Well... he says, at least now you'll always have that memory of him to hold on to whenever you're alone in bed... only, he's told me to tell you that you'll never be alone... as he's always watching over you.'

Jean let out a wracking sob, producing a round of applause and many a tear to well up in eyes other than hers.

'Bless you, Joe,' said Julian quietly, gently pushing him away. 'Okay... Oh dear... I've got a young man here... I think he passed over in pain... Kevin, is it?'

A loud cry from the back of the hall suggested it was.

And so the evening continued. As Julian became more confident with his contacts, the audience sat in stunned amazement as a whole new world was set before them. Even the vicar – who'd made a career out of persuading his parishioners that there was more to life than mere atoms of hydrogen, oxygen, nitrogen, and carbon – marvelled at the fact that he was finally being given proof.

Julian had also been surprised at the ease with which he seemed able to grasp the information being offered. He had good days and bad days, but this was proving to be an *exceptional* one.

'I've got a dark, curly-haired lady... passed over at the age of 57... looking for her second cousin, once removed, Correen,' announced Julian assertively.

Two individuals in the audience raised their hands.

'Who's recently had a baby boy,' he added.

One of the hands lowered.

'She's admiring a blue and white, china teapot you keep on a shelf next to your kitchen sink... and says it reminds her of the time she spent with your mother.'

Correen enthusiastically nodded her understanding of its significance.

'She also has a message for your elder sister... who's a little poorly.'

Correen smiled expectantly.

'She says...' Julian's hands shot up and gripped his head, 'MAY THE BITCH GO RAGE IN HELL!'

There was a collective gasp from the audience.

'Oh... I'm sorry about that, ladies and gentlemen,' said Julian weakly, having trouble retaining his balance. 'I don't know what happened there... I really don't!'

The vicar half-rose, as those nearer than he attended to the sobbing Correen.

'That's never happened before,' said Julian, steadying himself on a small table to his side. 'Clearly that particular entity snuck in as an impostor to make mischief. I do apologise.' He was clearly shaken, but keen not to waste the wave he was currently riding. 'Perhaps we could move on. It'd be a shame to let one malevolent spirit spoil what's been an insightful and rewarding evening for so many. Would you be alright if we did that, Correen, my dear?'

Correen was in no fit state to answer, so the vicar gave his proxy approval instead... mindful that the barometer showing the church fund wasn't going to rise if people demanded their money back.

'Bless you, vicar,' said Julian, hastily beckoning forth the next spirit before anyone objected. 'And who in spirit wishes to make contact?' he asked quickly. His forehead furrowed.

'*Liathese?*' he queried, struggling with the answer. 'Are you sure you've got the right village, let alone century?' he quipped, wishing to make light of his current predicament. 'You *have*. Very well, *Liathese*... what would you like to say?'

Only a very few of the mainly elderly audience had ever considered using the mouth that kissed their loved ones to do what Liathese suggested they should with it.

Julian reeled in horror as the words flew out of his own, unable to control their content or the venom with which they were delivered.

Pandemonium broke out. The vicar rose to his feet and appealed for calm, but Liathese hadn't finished. With Julian unable to close himself down as a conduit, the horrified audience were subjected to a hail of abuse that would forever scar their waking days... not to mention a few of their sleepless nights. Bert Brabbington's marrow paled into insignificance, as the once sleepy village of Brookton forever lost its innocence.

But it wasn't just Brookton's inhabitants that had been violated. Up and down the country, clairvoyants everywhere experienced a surge in malevolent entities hurling obscenities at whoever happened to be listening. And some... the most experienced of them... swore they heard a strange whispering in the background that they'd all initially mistaken for a swarm of flies.

* * *

'You're gonna need this,' laughed Norman lamely, pouring Xanthia another glass of wine. 'Because here's what Gabriel wants me to do!'

Xanthia excitedly put her knife and fork down and prepared herself like a child about to be told a bedtime story.

'Okay... I'm to get permission from all the relevant authorities to allow Stone Deaf Pete and his crew to assemble their ridiculously loud sound system... purely to play back two notes at an excruciating and potentially destructive volume... at...' He paused in order to emphasise the absurdity of the next bit. '*Stonehenge*... during the one time of year when most people want to be there and security is, therefore, at its highest!' He sat back and nodded at the irony.

'That's good,' said Xanthia politely.

'No, it's not!' he exclaimed. 'It's very, very *bad!*'

'Is it?' she groped.

'Yes! Why on *earth* would they agree? What *possible* reason is there for them to allow it?'

Xanthia shook her head... though only because Norman's expression of hopelessness suggested she should.

'I mean... I can't even begin to think of a reason for asking them *myself!*'

'Just tell them you're a DJ,' she said, picking up her cutlery again. 'Say you want to provide free entertainment for everyone who's there.' She continued with the meal, confident of having solved his problem.

'I've already thought of that,' he frowned. 'Even if there was the *remote* possibility they agreed... the minute I started blaring out those tones at the volume required, I'd immediately have the plug pulled! I've looked at it from every angle, Xan. There's just no way I can do it... *especially* if Gabriel's not allowing me to break any laws!'

'Did you tell him it can't be done?'

'Well... *yes*,' he answered uncomfortably, trying to recall exactly how it was he'd allowed himself to be left alone with such a problem.

'And what did he say?'

'He said it *had* to be done.'

'Then one of you is gonna lose,' she pointed out matter-of-factly.

'We're *all* gonna lose!' he cried. 'That's the point! The Universe is gonna come to an end!'

The other people in the restaurant put their polite chatter on hold and turned to examine the couple who they'd already thought of as odd. After all... one rarely saw so much female flesh on display at such an exclusive establishment.

Xanthia smiled back awkwardly, as Norman kept his stare to

himself.

'I don't know why Gabriel wants you to copy Stump's song anyway,' she pouted, as the noise in the restaurant finally picked up again. She wrestled with some peas that were taking advantage of her annoyance. 'He should've got *him* to do it!'

Norman looked at her blankly.

'Well... it would've made far more sense,' she insisted, struggling to complete her task.

'What d'ya mean... *copy Stump's song?*'

'Those notes he wants you to play... they're Stump's!'

'Don't be daft!' he laughed. 'Nobody owns individual notes!'

'No... But they can own the order they're played in!' she insisted.

'Yes... but then you're talking about a tune!'

'Well... it's Stump's tune... He wrote it... exactly as you've been playing it on your computer.'

'I beg your pardon?'

'It's the breakdown section from *Trouzerbulge's* live version of *Sex Wench*. I thought you knew. I thought it was something to do with that fing that was missing last time Gabriel gave you a task. You tried to buy it from Stump... the fing you call the master piece.'

Norman's face creased. 'But the two notes of that song's chorus are arranged in a completely different pattern. It's monotonous, but not that monotonous!'

'It is when they do it live,' she said. 'They get the crowd to sing along half way through... just those two notes... over and over again. It's masturbating.'

'*Mesmerizing?*'

'Yeah... that's the one. It can go on for ages.'

Norman tried to reconcile the chances of such a thing being so. 'That's freaky,' he said, shaking his head.

'Yeah... especially as it's the *exact* same notes,' she added.

'What... as in... *identical?*'

'Does that mean the same?'

He nodded.

'In that case... *Yeah.*'

'But how do you know?'

She wriggled with pride. 'I've got perfect pitch. Stump told me. He could play a note on his guitar and I'd know exactly which one it was. Apparently... not many people can do that. It's quite a gift!'

Norman lent forward and cautiously placed a hand on her arm. 'Are you absolutely sure about this, Xan?' he asked, looking deep into her eyes.

'Of course,' she answered stiffly, annoyed by his doubt.

He wrestled with the coincidence. 'I don't believe it,' he muttered.

'Oh... so now you're calling me a liar!' she blurted out loudly, pulling her arm away and turning her head in a fit of petulance.

The restaurant gave them its attention again.

'It's just an expression,' he whispered, pretending he hadn't noticed everybody's eyes on them. 'You've gotta admit... it's quite a coincidence.'

She pouted in silence.

'Perhaps it's *not* a coincidence!' he suddenly announced. 'Perhaps there's more to Stump's song than meets the eye! I wonder if Gabriel's aware of it.' He gave the matter further consideration. 'Then again... it *could* just be chance.' His shoulders dropped. 'Oh, I dunno. What the hell d'ya think it's all about?'

'I dunno either. But I'd much prefer to listen to Stump's version than yours,' she sulked, not sure whether to forgive him. 'Are we buying a pudding?'

Her words caused an idea to explode in front of him like a magnificent firework. 'Oh... Xan! You're beautiful!' he exclaimed. 'You've just given me a brilliant idea! If you're right about this, I'll buy the whole bloody *restaurant* for you!'

She looked at him confused.

'You may just have solved the first of my many problems!'

'I have?'

'Yes... If we got *Trouzerbulge* to play at Stonehenge and perform *Sex Wench* instead of those artificial tones, there'd at least be a genuine reason not to stop the performance... and for us being there in the first place!'

'They always wanted to play next to the stones,' she said. 'It was at the top of Stump's bucket list.'

'Even better!' Norman exclaimed. 'So why didn't they?'

Xanthia ran her tongue over her teeth. 'They couldn't get permission,' she said, pricking his enthusiasm.

Norman sunk into his chair like a deflated balloon. 'Mind you... I hardly think Stump would agree to help me out, even if such a thing *were* possible,' he sighed.

'I don't see why not,' she said. 'He did last time.'

'That was before I stole his girlfriend,' he reminded her. 'And even if he would... it doesn't take me any nearer to making it actually happen!' He sank even lower.

'So, what are you gonna do? Give up?'

Norman didn't answer.

'That's the trouble with you, Norman Penkridge,' she chided him. 'You've lost your fight. You have everything a man could ever want and yet you seem to have lost your purpose. The only time I ever see you excited these days is when you buy another painting! What happened to the man who stole me away in the first place and beat the Devil at his own game? He was driven to succeed, even though it meant risking his life. That's what I found attractive. Because... let's face it, Normy...' She nodded at him awkwardly.

'What are you saying?'

'Nothing,' she said, twiddling her hair.

'Xan?'

'Forget it.'

'I don't want to! Are you saying you don't love me anymore?'

'Of course I do,' she replied... though not nearly as enthusiastically as he would have liked. 'It's just that...'

'What?'

She looked at him uncomfortably. 'Well... you can be a little... *boring*... at times.'

'But I've given you everything you want!' he protested loudly.

'Not *everything*.'

'What else *is* there?'

'Let's just drop it.' She picked up the menu and flicked quickly to desserts.

'No... come on,' he insisted, leaning forward. 'What else is there?'

Xanthia knew she was about to cross a line... but tottered over it anyway. '*Excitement*,' she said quietly, pretending to study the ice creams.

Norman slumped back.

There was a loud *"ouch"* from the other diners. Even the maître d' joined in.

'But I've taken you around the world!' he protested. 'We've gazed in awe together at the ceiling of the Sistine Chapel in Rome... held hands and tossed coins into the Trevi Fountain... marvelled at the scale of Picasso's Guernica in Madrid... shared in the delights of the Louvre in Paris... Guggenheim in New York... Hermitage in Saint Petersburg! There's not a major piece of art in the world I haven't taken you to see!'

'You've taken me *with* you,' she corrected him.

'It's the same thing!'

'No, it's not,' she said firmly. 'It's not the same fing at all. They were places *you* wanted to visit to see your statues and paintings. You've never once asked me where *I* would like to go. Even living in France was *your* idea.'

'But I thought you liked to travel!'

'I like being with you,' she said. 'And I know all that stuff makes you happy.'

'Okay. So where would *you* like to go... when all this is over?'

'See... you're doing it again!'

'What?'

'You shouldn't have to ask me.'

Norman threw his hands up in exasperation. 'Well... how *else* am I supposed to know?'

'If you don't know that, then there's no point in this conversation,' she said, shaking her head.

'Alright... what about Stump?' he challenged her, his tone

changing.

'What about him?'

'Didn't *he* take you with him when he toured?'

'Some of the time.'

'Then, what's the difference? I can't believe *he* ever changed his plans to work around you.'

Xanthia gave him a look that suggested not only was he wrong... she was about to tell him *how* wrong.

'Stump may have sold his soul to the Devil,' she said through narrowed eyes, 'but at least he still has one!'

The restaurant winced.

'I'll tell you the difference between you and him... seeing as you've asked.'

Norman prepared himself for a full frontal assault.

But it didn't come.

Her face softened as she drew on a memory. 'He and I hadn't been going out long. It was just a matter of weeks... and we didn't know each other that well. He had to go and play in Italy... and asked if I'd like to go with him. I said *yes*... and we ended up staying in a place called Como. I remember it because it's easy to spell. There's a lake there... and he took me for a walk along it one evening. I couldn't believe how beautiful it was... with these mountains all around it and the water as calm as the sky it was reflecting. I told him I thought it was the most magical place I'd ever seen. So... the next night he suggested we do exactly the same fing... except, this time, there was a table and two chairs down by the water... and a waiter dressed in white standing beside them. There were candles and everyfing... with a bottle of champagne cooling in a silver bucket placed in the water. He'd arranged it all! We had a meal under the stars as the water lapped gently at our feet.' She stopped... her eyes glazed by the memory. 'It's the most romantic fing anyone's ever done for me.'

There was a sigh from the other diners.

'You told me *that* was when I refused to have sex with you when you were comatose,' pointed out Norman. 'Remember... when the Devil said I could?'

'I lied,' she shrugged. 'I didn't wanna hurt your feelings.'

'Well… they're not feeling too good, right now,' he sniffed, trying to maintain his composure. 'This hasn't been my best day, Xan. I've come close to being burnt alive… and now *this*…'

'You *did* ask,' she pointed out.

'I just didn't expect that answer,' he said, turning his head away. 'I'm sorry, Xan. I guess I'm still the failure I always was… Pooey Penkridge, who shat himself in class and watched as his mother took what was left of the steaming turd away in a paper bag!'

A couple of the diners put their spoons down.

'I'm still him… no matter how I dress it up. For all my trying to be cultured, I'm still apparently crapping all over the place!'

The rest of the diners abandoned their cutlery.

'Which doesn't bode well for the fate of the Universe!' he added.

Xanthia leant forward and pulled his head back by the chin. 'Don't look like that. *I* haven't given up on you… so don't give up on yourself. Gabriel obviously finks you're worth it too. You need to seize the moment and make this fing happen. You've only failed when you stop trying. The world is relying on you, Normy… so don't let it down. And if that's not enough to fire you up… I'm relying on you too!'

Norman looked at her through glistening eyes. She'd been constantly surprising him recently. Maybe he'd underestimated her all these years. Perhaps she wasn't the naive, childlike person he assumed her to be. 'I do love you,' he said passionately.

'I fink I'll have a chocolate sundae,' she said awkwardly, turning her attention back to the menu. 'It says here it comes wiv a big, pink wafer on top.'

*   *   *

Worker One watched the stone they'd transported being hauled into its upright position, completing a circle of other such stones that had all made an identical journey.

338

A shout of jubilation rang out from the assembled throng as the man with the antler headdress threw up his arms in exaltation and shouted something important to the sky. No one knew exactly *who* it was he was talking to... but that's what made him special.

Worker One made a comment in passing that such trust could be open to abuse. After all, he pointed out... the man with antlers on his head only had antlers on his head because a previous man with antlers on his head had passed those antlers on. For all they knew, he could be making the whole thing up.

Worker Three stared at him in amazement. What had gotten into Worker One lately? Why couldn't he just accept that the fact the arrangement had worked for generations clearly proved it was the right one? The logic was indisputable. Things only went wrong when the gods were displeased... and that's precisely when the man with antlers on his head came into his own. He had proved he had the ability to communicate with those deities by intervening and sorting out those awkward situations.

Admittedly – Worker Three conceded – it had taken him a harrowing four complete cycles of the seasons to put an end to the recent spell of bad harvests they'd been enforced to endure... but he'd got there in the end. Only half the community had starved to death. He'd clearly managed to save the rest.

Worker Two asked if they could stop referring to the man with antlers on his head as "the man with antlers on his head", as he had an official title and they should show him some respect. Furthermore... how on earth could Worker One possibly hope to comprehend the inner workings of the gods when he wasn't a high priest?

Worker One said that, as both their arguments were based on circular reasoning, he couldn't accept them. But as Worker Two and Worker Three weren't as clever as Worker One, they didn't know what he meant.

Worker One explained that with circular reasoning, whilst the components of the argument might appear logically valid because, if the premises are true, the conclusion must be true... the reasoning had no value because the conclusion was dependent on at least one of the premises. But as Worker Two and Worker Three weren't as clever as Worker One, they *still* didn't know what he was talking about.

Worker Two accused Worker One of always thinking he was better than everybody else.

Worker One responded by pointing out that at least he didn't feel the need the wear antlers on his head to make the point.

Worker Two said that his argument was probably one of those circular things.

At that point, Worker One realised he really belonged somewhere else.

The assembled throng congratulated each other that at least their back-breaking and dangerous work was done. They could now return to their villages and spend time with their families. That was... once they'd witnessed the magic that the man with the antlers on his head had promised would happen once the circle was completed.

They waited patiently.

The "high priest" – as Worker Two preferred to call him – continued with his incantations. It had been on his insistence that the special bluestones had been brought from a land far away... insisting they possessed special properties. They certainly looked nice.

The excitement that had been building to fever pitch began to level off as the incantations continued without so much as a puff of smoke. Even the high priest looked anxious as the only thing his incantations were producing was a sore throat.

Just as the assembled throng was becoming restless and their mood looking like it might turn nasty, he fell into a convenient trance that caused him to stop his wailing. With his head lolling from side to side, he seemed to be wrestling with a concept that only *he* would be able to understand.

The assembled throng looked on expectantly... grateful that he was wearing his antlers.

After a short while, he froze... his eyes opening as wide as was possible without them falling out.

The gods had spoken.

They wanted *another* circle of stones to complement the existing one... only this time, they needed to be... bigger.

How much bigger? the assembled throng enquired.

Quite a bit bigger, the priest confided.

The assembled throng asked him to be more specific.

Imagine there was a unit of size equivalent to roughly one of your feet, the priest instructed them. Well... imagine about six of those placed side by side. That would be their width.

The assembled throng groaned.

The priest informed them that it wasn't as bad as it sounded. He had some good news for them. They only needed to be half of that in depth.

The assembled throng agreed that this was, indeed, good news.

There was just one other thing, the priest added. He'd just been informed by the gods of a new law they'd decreed which stated that bad news would always follow good news unless it was requested the other way around.

The assembled throng asked him what the bad news was.

He told them.

The answer produced a gasp. *How* high? Was he having a laugh?

He hadn't finished...

Lintels? What the hell were *THEY?*

The priest translated his vision.

The assembled throng's eyes became wider than his. Didn't he know the crane hadn't been invented yet?

Oh... and had he mentioned the horseshoe of five trilithons needed to top the whole thing off? He *hadn't?* Okay... he'd explain about that bit later.

Worker Three dropped his shoulders and conceded that Worker One was right. Perhaps the antlers *had* been a bad idea.

* * *

Chad recalled the drive leading to Donald's house as being untidy. He hadn't remembered it being oppressive. But as he and Bob passed beneath the canopy of neglected trees – carefully negotiating the numerous potholes and uncleared casualties of the wind – he noted the atmosphere had changed. What little sunlight made it through fell unconvincingly on a dank carpet of moss and rotting leaves, merely highlighting the gloom into which they were being drawn.

He marvelled at the fact Donald's literary success had not produced a single gardener or groundsman... let alone an attempt to overhaul the crumbling property to which the drive eventually led.

The house itself clung precariously to its air of grandeur, though only through the suggestion of better years. Even the large fountain that once impressed visitors hadn't *quite* given up... still able to hold a gaze with its intricate, ornamental stonework just visible between the resident weeds and rusting pipework. But any memories of splashing water were only triggered when it rained.

'It's not gonna smell any sweeter inside, is it?' Bob moaned, recalling their previous visits.

'God forbid he risks this dump's structural integrity by opening a window!' laughed Chad. He thought he caught something moving behind one of them, but it was difficult to tell, given the layers of grime that had been allowed to obscure their purpose.

The front entrance hadn't experienced much love either. The bell that Bob had pulled from the cracked masonry on his first visit five years earlier still lay rusting on the floor, leaving Chad to announce their presence on a large, brass door-knocker cast in the shape of an ironing board.

'He ain't gonna answer it,' said Bob, stepping back to survey other options.

'I guess we can hardly blame him. The last time he had contact with us, it was of the physical kind. We're gonna have to win his trust back... and that ain't gonna be easy.' Chad bent down and placed his mouth as close to the rusty letter box as was prudent, before prising it open with his fingers. 'Donald... It's Chad Cheadle and Bob Papadopoulos,' he hollered into it. 'Remember us? The Americans? I know we didn't exactly see eye to eye the last time we met, but that was an unfortunate misunderstanding. It's a long story... and we'd like to have a chance to explain it to you in the hope you'll accept our sincerest apologies!'

The invitation failed to illicit a response.

Bob shook his head.

Chad changed tack. 'We were also wondering, Donald... if there's any chance you've been hearing those voices again? Only... we've obtained reliable intelligence that something untoward is about to go down, and we thought they may have been trying to warn you like they did the last time.'

After a short wait, he thought he detected something moving behind the door.

'Donald? Is that you? Are you there?'

'We *know* you're there!' shouted Bob over him and earning a look of reproach.

'I reckon we may be able to help each other,' continued Chad diplomatically. 'But not through a letter box.'

After a brief silence, a guarded voice announced itself from the other side. 'If you move well away from the door, I might consider opening it.'

Chad nodded positively. 'You got it, Donald!' He immediately stepped back, signalling for Bob to do the same. 'We'll stand as far away as you like!' he shouted, continuing to orchestrate their retreat.

As both men drew level with the ornamental fountain, they stopped and waited... the sound of sliding bolts just audible from behind the large, dark oak door.

'We're here to help, Donald,' affirmed Chad, as it opened slightly.

'Stay where you are,' instructed the voice.

Chad raised his hands to show compliance and watched as Donald finally emerged, his eyes blinking at the novelty of sunlight. His hair was unkempt, his face littered with stubble, his expression that of a worried man. He looked drawn and barely able to support himself.

'Jeez, Donald,' drawled Bob. 'You look like you need a holiday!'

'Weymouth must wait,' he replied weakly. 'They've come back again. There's much to do... and I fear time is running out.'

Chad and Bob looked at each other.

Chad was about to ask him to elaborate, when Donald suddenly appeared to take umbrage with himself.

'I DON'T DOUBT YOU MISS IT... BUT IF YOU THINK I'M PLANTING MY DECKCHAIR ANYWHERE NEAR GRIMSBY, YOU'VE GOT ANOTHER THING COMING! WEYMOUTH IT'LL MOST DEFINITELY BE!'

'Time until what?' Chad pressed, when Donald was done.

Donald bowed his head and gave a half-hearted smile. 'For that, you will have to wait... along with the rest of the world.'

Bob squinted.

'That's the point, Donald,' said Chad. 'It's precisely why we've come to see you. We can't *afford* to wait. We know something's afoot involving those who messed with the paintings you originally tried to warn us about. Now... if you're saying you're in possession of information that could help us make sense of what's going on, you might be able to help us prevent something similar occurring.'

'I'm working on it,' said Donald. 'I haven't slept for two days. They won't leave me alone. The amount of spiritual traffic is unprecedented! But that's alright... because I need them now!'

'You mean the voices? Is it *them* who've been keeping you awake?'

'I've been keeping *myself* awake,' he answered wearily. 'I need to finish something... and they're helping me. Well... some of them!'

'Okay... if that's the case... would they also be interested in helping *us*?' Chad exchanged a glance with his partner.

'Yeah,' joined in Bob. 'How about doing that trance thing

332

you did last time I was here? D'ya remember… it got us that all-important address?'

'You mean the address to which you went intending to kill that poor boy?' Donald reminded him sternly.

'We weren't gonna *kill* him,' Bob scoffed.

'You said you were going to stop him. Eliminate the problem, if my memory serves me correctly!'

'You overreacted,' said Bob. 'We had to put an end to what he was doing… that's all. You saw how he ended up fucking the whole world's economy!'

'Would you kindly moderate your language,' said Donald indignantly. 'There are ladies present.'

Bob looked towards the house.

'In the afterlife,' elaborated Donald, giving a sympathetic tut to any who might be listening in.

'Okay… I'm sorry.' Bob raised a hand in apology to keep him on side. 'But you saw what he did, all the same.'

'I saw no such thing!' protested Donald. 'I merely saw a young man in a humble bedsit.'

'And an explosion… of sorts,' added Chad. 'Which wasn't so humble.'

Donald looked at him differently.

'Yeah,' continued Chad, 'you saw that too, didn't you?'

'I saw a flash of light… yes,' admitted Donald stiffly. 'And I tried to save a life, rather than trying to take one.'

'But you saw it, all the same,' pressed Chad. 'And you *know* it wasn't like anything else you've ever seen. So… if that's the case… what d'ya reckon it was? And what do your voices say happened in that room that day?'

'I thought you didn't believe I could communicate with the spirit world,' Donald challenged him. 'It was only your partner here who finally grasped *that* particular nettle. It's a shame you didn't believe me in the first place. Had you done so, you may have got what you wanted before the situation became so desperate you were prepared to resort to violence.'

'Then help us now,' reasoned Chad. 'We're here because we believe you can. There's no advantage in us arguing anymore.

331

We're in the same boat once again. We need to stop whatever's being planned before it's too late. People could get hurt... *Innocent* people.'

Donald allowed himself something as close to a smile as he could muster. 'Are you *sure* you have reliable intelligence?' he asked. 'Only... it doesn't sound very much like it to me!'

'What do you know, Donald?' demanded Bob, his frustration rising.

'I know the aggrieved won't be made of flesh and blood,' he answered enigmatically.

'And what's that supposed to mean?'

'It means that any action being planned is against something *far* more durable.'

'*Durable?*'

'As in... made of stone. That much, I'm pretty certain of.'

'Are we talking *buildings?*'

'One might assume,' said Donald.

'A *government* building?' asked Bob.

'The Houses of Parliament, perhaps?' suggested Chad keenly.

Donald shrugged. 'All I'm being told at the moment is that the stones hold knowledge of some kind.'

'A museum!' exclaimed Bob. 'They're planning an attack on a museum! Are they back to stealing works of art?'

'Your guess is as good as mine,' Donald sighed. 'Now... if you gentlemen will excuse me... I think I've said too much.'

'You haven't said enough!' countered Bob angrily. 'And what's with the *guessing?*'

'It's a reasonable question, Donald,' cut in Chad civilly. 'Surely your voices are capable of telling you when and where this event might occur?'

'Eventually,' answered Donald.

'What... they're treating this as a *game?*' exclaimed Bob.

'I assure you they take it very seriously,' returned Donald indignantly.

'What we don't understand is... why can't they tell you *exactly* what you need to know?' persevered Chad.

'It's not like picking up television signals, dear boy!' scoffed

Donald. 'It's a question of interpretation. Sometimes they come through loud and clear. But when the spirit world is in the excitable state it appears to be at the moment, things can get extremely muddled. I've never known so much activity... and not all of it good. That's what's been adding to my problems. They're not all on our side. I believe there's a lot of misinformation being fed to me from entities whose only purpose seems to be to muddy the waters.'

'Why would they be bothering to do that?'

'I think you'll find the answer lies in what it is I'm being warned about in the first place,' said Donald darkly. 'There's a lot of bad energy flowing around us at the moment. It seems intent on keeping me from knowing the truth... yet doesn't want to stop me altogether. Most extraordinary!'

'So how can we be sure the information about stones is correct?' asked Chad.

'I'm trusting to my muse for that,' replied Donald. 'It's above mere voices. It's what inspires me to write my plays. I'm using it as a guide to sort the wheat from the chaff. It can't be fooled. It's as if it has a direct line to the fundamental truth. It won't allow me to write anything that isn't so. That's why I've decided to make my next play about the warnings.'

'That's pretty smart thinking!' acknowledged Chad. 'So... can we read what you've written so far?'

'Absolutely not!' said Donald firmly. 'I can't risk losing my muse by breaking my writing rituals. You'll have to wait for the play's performance. I'll arrange for you to attend the premiere, if it helps.'

'And when will that be?'

'Depends on how many interruptions I get before I'm allowed to finish it,' Donald offered dryly.

'Well... can we at least know what it's about?'

'I told you... stones,' answered Donald, vexed.

'That's as far as you've got?'

Donald nodded.

'I reckon we're wasting our time,' said Bob, placing a hand on his partner's shoulder. 'And more to the point... we're wasting *his*. Let's allow him to finish and trust he keeps his word. Looks like you may be getting me in a theatre after all.'

'It better be sooner rather than later,' groaned Chad, sweeping his hair back in frustration. 'Let's hope you're as prolific in your writing as you've been up to now, Donald!'

'I KNOW!' the playwright shouted. 'I HEARD YOU THE FIRST TIME!'

Chad frowned.

'Whitebait,' explained Bob.

'He says you've not been telling me everything. He's asking if you're still working for your government.'

Chad glanced at his partner awkwardly. 'Let's just say... we have ourselves a new client.' Donald concentrated intently. 'He says your client may not be who you think he is,' he passed on.

'I *don't* know who he is,' confessed Chad. 'All I *do* know is... he's on our side.'

'I'm just the messenger,' Donald shrugged. 'Now, gentlemen... are we done? It's time I returned to my writing.' He looked anxiously at the decrepit building behind him. 'Assuming they let me, that is.'

Chad raised his hand. 'Just one thing, Donald... before you go. Does wanting to produce an incredibly loud sound mean anything to you and your muse?'

Donald's expression instantly changed. 'Do you mean like a trumpet?'

'Not exactly a trumpet... no.'

'Then... like voices?'

'Not them, either. More like an annoying car alarm going off.'

'WHEN YE HEAR THE SOUND OF THE TRUMPET, ALL THE PEOPLE SHALL SHOUT WITH A GREAT SHOUT... AND THE WALL OF THE CITY SHALL FALL DOWN FLAT!'

'I beg your pardon?'

'It's from the bible... Joshua, Chapter six, verse five. It's been stuck in my head for days. But I don't know why!'

'Could Penkridge be looking to take out a whole city?'

gasped Bob. 'Is *that* what they're trying to tell you?'

'I've no idea. But Joshua certainly succeeded.'

'He brought down the walls,' nodded Chad.

'He did indeed,' smiled Donald thinly.

'They're definitely developing some kinda sonic weapon!' Bob exclaimed. 'That's what they were attempting in France!'

'They'd have to vastly reduce its size, if it were to be a practical one,' figured Chad.

'Perhaps that's what they're doing right now!'

They both looked at each other.

'I really *must* go,' said Donald, feeling excluded from the conversation and nervously checking behind himself again.

'Don't let us stop you,' nodded Chad, his thoughts elsewhere. 'The sooner you get your play finished, the sooner we'll understand what's going on.'

'Once more unto the breach, dear friends, once more,' Donald sighed. He turned and shuffled back into the house.

Bob waited for the sound of bolts scraping against the door to finish before speaking. 'We'll break in through a window. It shouldn't be too hard to locate his manuscript. The man's gotta sleep *sometime*.'

'Not your best idea,' Chad advised.

'*What?*'

'We take one step inside that place and he's gonna know about it. The last thing we want is to lose his trust again.'

'How the hell's he gonna know? We're the best in the business... remember?'

'He's got half the spirit world conversing with him,' said Chad. 'You don't reckon one of them is gonna alert him?'

Bob stared at his partner in astonishment. 'I don't believe this conversion. If you'd told me five years ago that...'

'Yeah, yeah, yeah,' Chad dismissed him briskly. 'So I happen to believe that such a thing *may* be possible these days. I'm not saying it sits easy with me. But isn't that why we're here? We either believe that man can help us or we don't. *That's* where my logic kicks in. So... let's stick our address through his letterbox and hope he keeps his word!'

'You're not seriously suggesting we wait until opening night to find out what it's all about... are you?'

'Hell, no! But we gotta give him the chance to get on with the thing uninterrupted.'

'So what are we gonna do in the meantime?'

'The only other avenue that's open to us... Investigate another familiar name,' said Chad, with a wink.

*　　*　　*

'Sharky...! Where's my bloody sandwich!'

A beer belly on legs waddled into the room carrying a silver tray and an expression of having heard it all before. 'Don't panic, boss,' he growled, laying the tray on the lap of the man doing the shouting.

'Have you cut off the crusts?'

'Yes, boss.'

'And scraped the cucumber?'

'As always.'

'Organic?'

'Apparently.'

'What d'ya mean... *apparently?*'

'It said so on the cardboard sign in the greengrocer's.'

'What... it said *apparently* organic?'

'No... it said organic.'

'Well it's fucking organic, then... isn't it?'

Sharky gave the matter some thought. 'Apparently,' he conceded, with little emotion.

'Jesus!' seethed Stump. 'And I take it you've used margarine... not butter?'

'Only the best,' replied Sharky, visualising the claim on the lid of the tub.

Stump lifted the top slice of bread and examined the sandwich's contents. 'Is that salt!' he exclaimed, with a look of abject horror.

'As if, boss,' answered Sharky, shaking his head.

'Then, what's all that white stuff sprinkled on it?'

'The usual for your cucumber sandwiches,' said Sharky defensively.

'What?'

'Amphetamine.'

Stump clicked his fingers and pointed at the answer. 'You're right. Well done.'

Sharky stared at him. 'Well... aren't you gonna eat it?'

'Nah,' said Stump, replacing the bread apathetically. 'I'm not hungry anymore.'

Sharky removed the tray without batting an eyelid. 'You know you've got visitors coming shortly, boss.'

'Yeah... hardly likely to forget *those* two, am I?'

'D'ya want me to run you a bath?'

Stump pulled back his silk kimono and sniffed an armpit. 'I think I'll get away with it. I just need to get dressed. But I'll tell you what you can do... Stick some of that *salt* in the dips I'll ask you to bring towards the end of our meeting.' He grinned at the thought.

Sharky snorted his appreciation of the humour and waddled out of the room with the same fatalistic approach to travel as he'd waddled in with.

Fingers interlaced, Stump stretched his arms and puffed out his cheeks. The next hour and however long it took was going to be extremely interesting. The last time he'd seen the man he was going to be spending it with, that individual had been clutching his eye whilst trying to drag two large, pink suitcases to a waiting taxi. Now he was coming back to ask for a favour.

Stump picked up the shotgun that was resting against the *chaise longue* and took aim through an open window at a gigantic wicker elephant standing in the garden. *People were strange*, he mused, as he discharged the first of its two barrels.

'I still don't know how you managed to get him to agree to this meeting,' said Norman, as he recognised the drive into which they'd just turned.

It was very hard not to, given the large, fibreglass statue of Marilyn Monroe under which they were about to pass. Not that Norman had seen that particular *objet d'art* before. It was more a *flavour* you got as you entered through the gates of *Soddem Hall*.

As they were driven beneath the recently commissioned legs straddling the drive, Norman chanced a curious peek upwards... and wished he hadn't. That was obviously one secret Marilyn's biographers had *never* stumbled upon.

'I told you,' chewed Xanthia, her gum masticated at a slightly higher rate, as once familiar surroundings refreshed her memory, 'you can do anyfink you want, if you put your mind to it.'

'Any... *thing*... Xanthia!'

'Same fing,' she huffed.

'I was under the impression that if he ever saw me again, he'd kill me!' said Norman, deciding to keep his curiosity to himself as they passed under a statue of Margaret Thatcher.

'Oh... Stump's just a big softy at heart,' she returned. 'He just doesn't... *think*... before he acts.'

'That's what's worrying me,' he said, as a plastic skeleton with a macabre grin – suspended from a decorative lamppost – caught his eye. 'I don't think the man's ever grown up.'

Xanthia smiled. 'Nah... he hasn't, has he?' she said warmly.

'I mean... who goes to the trouble of placing a sign saying "public urinal" next to a perfectly good swimming pool?'

'I remember when he stole that,' she giggled. 'We'd been to a fancy dress party and he was dressed as the Queen.'

'And what did you go as?'

She gave the matter some thought. 'Dunno... although I fink I was attached to him the whole evening by a lead.'

'Then you would have been a Corgi,' he pointed out sweetly.

'Nah...' she said, shaking her head. 'I remember now... He said I represented the working class.'

Norman continued staring out of the window. 'And then you've got that huge, pointless pile of sticks over there,' he said, surveying the lawn. 'I mean... what's the idea behind that?'

'I fink it used to be an elephant,' she shrugged.

He sighed heavily. 'I just hope he feels the same way about

Satan and wanting to get one over on him as he did when we first met.'

As he spoke, a large bang sounded from one of the rooms of the building they were approaching... and what had once been an ornamental dovecot... wasn't.

Soddem Hall was as imposing as Norman had remembered it. But, though once being the proud home of aristocracy, it was now forced to endure humilities that other stately homes would have crumbled at. Where once the union flag had fluttered majestically above the jagged, gothic roof line, an oversized set of underpants now cocked a snook at the colonial past and served as a warning of the dangers of egalitarianism.

The butler's attire had changed considerably too. As Sharky made himself known at the front entrance, Norman marvelled that a t-shirt could be asked to stretch so much... yet a pair of jeans afforded such ridiculous room to accommodate a single crotch.

Sharky nodded his acknowledgement of their arrival and gave Xanthia an empathetic look as they stepped from the car.

'Sharky,' she greeted him uncomfortably.

'Xan,' he replied back.

'Just like the old days,' she tried, forcing a smile.

'Not really,' he said, faithful to his master.

'So is the old fart ready to see us?' she asked, ignoring the slight.

'He's in the drawing room. I'll take you in.'

They followed their waddling guide through the main hall – past other curious *objets d'art* and abused suits of armour suffering the disturbed humour of their owner. Xanthia walked unfazed; blind to it all through a combination of familiarity and an intellect that struggled with irony. Norman's eyes were more occupied with scanning the numerous paintings that had presumably come with the house... though the portraits might have retained their value a little more if they hadn't had to suffer the same – if graffitied – indignities as the suits of armour. It was as if Stump had purposely gone out of his way to hurt the building's history.

'Hiya, Honey,' she sang, as they entered a magnificent drawing room that had been largely spared such pain.

Norman felt her familiarity sting.

'Hiya, Babe,' Stump replied, turning from the window through which he'd been observing their arrival. The light behind caused his heavily backcombed hair to resemble a halo. 'So, we meet again,' he addressed Norman directly, his hands remaining in the pockets of his torn designer jeans. The top half of his body was attired in an open military jacket – curiously suited to the room in which they were standing – his bare chest covered by a selection of chains and pendants.

'It was good of you to see us,' offered Norman awkwardly. 'I mean... given the circumstances.'

Stump snorted away the attempt at appeasement. 'And what circumstances would they be?' he asked, not caring to wait for an answer. 'Let me see, now... Oh, yes... I remember. I put everything on the line to help you out with a certain and not insignificant problem... and you repaid me by stealing my girlfriend.' He paused so that even Xanthia could appreciate the irony. 'Yes, you're right... it *was* good of me to see you... given the circumstances.'

It was much the reaction Norman had expected. But at least Stump's hands were still wedged in pockets and not heading towards his face.

'I have to admit... you're looking good on the theft, though,' commented Stump, leaning forward and examining Norman's teeth. 'Crime obviously *does* pay. Did *she* get you to fix those?'

'Veneers,' offered Norman.

'Yeah... so I assumed. But can they do the same with personalities?'

'Stump!' Xanthia admonished him. 'We haven't come here for a fight.'

'More's the pity,' he replied, keeping his gaze firmly fixed on Norman. 'So... if not for a fight... why *are* you here?'

'We need your help again,' said Norman, cutting straight to the point.

Stump took a moment to digest the answer... then broke

into an uncontrolled fit of laughter. 'And *then* what are you gonna steal from me...? *Sharky?*'

'We've got the same problem we had last time,' said Norman, battling on.

'No... you haven't,' Stump corrected him firmly, his humour gone. 'Last time... you hadn't pissed me off!'

'Everything's about to come to an end,' chimed in Xanthia. 'Norman's seen Gabriel again. He's told him that we're heading for "almost Reading".'

'Armageddon,' Norman corrected her.

'Yeah... that place. And we fink you may be able to help us put a stop to it.'

'You wanna use my song again?'

'Kinda,' she said.

'It's a little more complicated than that, this time,' cut in Norman.

'I didn't think it was *that* straight forward *last* time!' Stump exclaimed. 'What could possibly make using my song more difficult?'

'We need you to perform it,' said Xanthia. 'We want you to do a concert for us.'

Stump tilted his head to one side as he took in the request. 'What... you want me to reform the band?'

'*Reform?*' queried Norman, shooting a look at Xanthia. 'I wasn't aware you'd split up!'

'We haven't... officially. Bands of our age never do... they just kinda... *disintegrate*. We haven't played live for years now. I'm not even sure if the other members are capable of it.'

'They have to be!' insisted Norman. 'This'll be the most important gig you'll ever do!'

'Can't say it doesn't sound interesting,' reflected Stump. 'But it's not just up to me. A lot of it depends on what planet those other guys are currently inhabiting.'

'But you can make 'em!' said Xanthia. 'It's *your* band!'

'*They* wouldn't want to hear you say that,' Stump laughed.

'But you're not averse to it in principal?' Norman pushed him.

'I'm not averse to reforming the band... no,' Stump clarified. 'Whether I wanna bother doing so for *you* is another matter.'

'It's not for me,' said Norman. 'It's for the whole of humanity.'

'I thought we'd already saved 'em?' said Stump, scratching his head.

'We merely bought ourselves a little time,' explained Norman. 'And now it's about to run out.'

Stump nodded his understanding of the problem. 'Oh, well,' he sighed, turning back to the window. 'It was good while it lasted.'

'This isn't a *joke!*' Norman exclaimed, shocked by his flippancy. 'You *know* what's lurking out there beyond people's normal perception. You've experienced it!'

'Indeed I have,' agreed Stump. 'I've tasted and smelt it all... from every angle and every state of mind. I've done everything I ever wanted to do... and more. There's nothing left that interests me. I've sucked on the marrow of life... and now all that remains are dry bones. I'll still keep sucking those, of course. It's my addictive personality. It's not in my nature to stop. But it's why I don't care if the whole fuckin' thing comes to an end.'

'You don't mean that,' said Xanthia softly, taking a step nearer him.

'Sorry if it hurts, Babe... but I do.'

'We're talking about the end of everything!' cried Norman. 'Not just you, me, Xan and this place... but *everything!*'

'Apparently, that's more than you fink,' said Xanthia.

'She's right,' said Norman. 'We're talking *everything*... as in... the reason for it all existing in the first place!'

'I understood it the first time,' said Stump, turning to face Norman again. 'And I don't mean what you said just now. I was aware of the implications of everything ceasing to be the first time you persuaded me to help you. That's the trouble when you look and act like I do. People think you're stupid. It's as if there's a direct correlation between the length of your hair multiplied by the depth of your depravity... and one's intellect.

Well... you can take it from me, there ain't.'

'I've never thought of you as stupid,' said Norman, trying appeasement again.

'Yes, you have,' said Stump. 'You stole my girl.'

'But that doesn't mean I thought you were stupid,' Norman protested.

'Not so!' Stump fixed him with a stare that cut right through. 'You must have thought I was stupid enough for such an action not to hurt me.'

His words stopped Norman in his tracks. Denial would not only have been pointless... it would have been dishonest.

'It's wrong to distil a man's history and think you know him at any given moment,' continued Stump. 'I'm not a pantomime character, even if I look and behave like one to most people. I do have desires and feelings... just like everybody else.'

'Not *quite* like everybody else,' Xanthia reminded him coyly.

'I'm talking about my inner feelings, Babe. The deepest ones of all... The ones that no amount of drugs and bravado can mask.'

'Then... I'm truly sorry if I hurt you,' said Norman, moved by Stump's candour. 'I guess I didn't think it was wrong because it's what I thought Xanthia wanted.'

'Oh... I *see*,' drawled Stump slowly, with a worrying degree of sarcasm. 'It was only ever about what *Xanthia* wanted... was it?'

'More or less,' said Norman. 'I mean... I'm not denying it worked out pretty well for *me*. But I've only ever ultimately wanted what was best for her.'

'That's very admirable,' said Stump, with a less obvious tinge of sarcasm. 'And is that still the case?'

'Of course!'

Stump looked at Xanthia. 'Then I'll hold you to that someday.'

'There ain't gonna be any other days if you don't help us,' she pointed out.

'I told you... I got it the first time,' said Stump. 'You see... what you failed to appreciate when I last helped you stop the destruction of absolutely everything, was the huge personal sacrifice I made.'

'How could it have cost you anything?' exclaimed Norman. 'You *gained* something! Revenge! You saw it as a way to get your own back on the Devil for persuading you to sell your soul. You said so yourself!'

'You really have underestimated my intelligence,' said Stump. 'And I've clearly *overestimated* yours. Think about it... because I certainly have. When I finally die, I'm going to be rotting in hell for the rest of eternity. That was the deal. All of it now... with payment deferred. And even if you've only got a basic grasp of maths... eternity is a bloody long time to be rotting for.'

Xanthia took his word for it.

'So... if you look at it from my point of view... the end of absolutely everything... eternity included... sounds like an excellent way out of a very sticky predicament... wouldn't you say?'

Norman realised he *had* underestimated the man in front of him. 'I appreciate it would be a sacrifice,' he said slowly.

'Too bloody right!'

They looked at each other in silence.

Norman knew it wasn't only Stump he was staring at... but defeat. It seemed cold, emotionless and final. How could he have been so stupid? He'd allowed himself to be fooled into believing he had a chance to achieve what he'd always known was impossible. How had a logical mind such as his ever thought that Xanthia... precious as she was to him... could be capable of finding a solution to his problem? And he'd only got himself to blame for his failure. He'd gotten lucky the first time around, managing to temporarily soften the heart of a man whose soul was owned lock, stock and barrel by his and mankind's greatest enemy. And by way of thanks, he'd trampled on that heart by only seeing the needs of his own. And now he had to pay the price. Even though that enemy wasn't physically in the room, Norman heard him laughing in the same guttural voice that still gave him nightmares.

'I guess our business is done,' said Stump, shrugging nonchalantly.

Norman guessed it was. There was such finality in his manner. He turned to Xanthia.

'Not quite,' she said.

Stump looked at her quizzically.

'You were wrong,' she addressed him.

'Babe?'

'About what you said.'

'Which bit?'

'The bit about you having done everything you ever wanted to.'

Stump snorted his rejection of her claim. 'I have! I've lived faster and more passionately than anyone else on this planet! I'm famous for it! Why on earth d'ya think the Devil himself showed an interested in me? We're kindred spirits. I'm selfishness incarnate!'

'But you still haven't done it all,' she insisted.

'What's there left to do?' he asked, finally removing his hands from his pockets and stretching them out widely.

'Stonehenge,' she said softly.

As Stump stood with his arms outstretched – the halo of his hair framing his head – Norman realised he might be looking at his saviour after all.

'What about it?'

'You've never played there,' she answered.

Stump considered the fact.

'It was one of your biggest dreams to perform in front of it.'

'I know it was,' he said, chastened by the reminder. 'So what?'

'Well… that's where Norman wants you to play. In front of the stones. So… what if he could make it happen for you?'

Stump's head jerked back. 'That'd be impossible!' he scoffed. 'Even with all *his* money.'

'But what if he could?'

Stump looked at Norman with incredulity. 'Is that what you're throwing me, here? A chance to play at Stonehenge?'

'That's *precisely* why we're here,' said Norman, unsure as to whether Stump had grasped the connection between the fulfilment of his ultimate wish and eternity being reinstated.

'Is he serious?' Stump asked Xanthia.

'Deadly,' she replied.

Stump gave an appreciative whistle. 'Now, that really *would* be worth reforming for.' His expression changed to that of a man contemplating the accomplishment of a long-held dream. 'I've dreamt of playing in front of those stones for as long as I can remember. But it's actually more than a dream. I've always considered it my *destiny!*'

'Perhaps, that's because it *is*,' said Norman deeply.

'*Man!*' cooed Stump, drinking in the prospect.

Norman could scarcely believe the sudden turnaround in his fortune. 'So... does that mean you're with us?'

'You get me permission to play at Stonehenge... and I'll guarantee you *Trouzerbulge's* greatest show *ever*,' Stump asserted.

'And the rest of the band?' asked Xanthia.

'Don't worry about them, Babe,' he grinned. 'I'll make sure they *have* to do it!' He clapped his hands like a Roman emperor and shouted Sharky's name. 'We have much to discuss. I'll get us something to eat.'

Sharky made an appearance.

'Things have changed. Our guests will be staying a little longer than anticipated,' Stump instructed him. 'So, how about you go and fetch those dips we were talking about earlier!' he added, with a wink.

*   *   *

'When you said "investigate another familiar name", I assumed legs would be attached to it,' frowned Bob, marvelling at the strange particles floating in the pint of beer he was about to sample. 'Maybe even a face?'

'Templar Resources,' affirmed Chad, joining him at the table and tossing a packet of crisps onto its sticky surface. 'It's the company Penkridge told you he was gonna use to purchase the Van Gogh. He called it a holding company. But it also cropped up in our original investigation... though at the time, merely as a catalyst for connecting the temple at Arwan El Kahab to that London art gallery we had under surveillance.'

'Yeah... I remember.'

'But now it seems it might have a far bigger role to play in all this, being part of Penkridge's financial arrangements. And, if that's the case... it could be our best way of disrupting him.'

Bob withdrew his lips from the froth they were about to investigate.

'And before you say "I told you so", continued Chad speedily, 'I concede that you and our mystery benefactor were probably right... Interrupting Penkridge's finance could be the easiest way of stopping him doing whatever it is he's up to.'

'I'll take that as the nearest thing to an apology I'm likely to get,' said Bob, reinvestigating the froth. 'Had you followed my advice in the first place, we could've saved ourselves a visit to that screwball Donald!'

'Not so. I'll throw you another bone for your ego... You were right to suggest we see him. We still need whatever information he can give us. Restricting Penkridge's spending power might give our client the result he's after... but it won't give me my answers.'

'*Our* answers,' Bob reminded him.

'Just chew on your bone.'

Bob shook his head. 'So... how exactly do you propose we do it? I mean... we can't simply walk into his bank and politely request they close the account.'

Chad leant forward on his stool. 'How well do you know Lenny Tenko?'

'You mean... the IT whizz back at Langley?'

Chad nodded.

'I've had the occasional beer with him,' shrugged Bob. 'Why?'

'What's he like?'

Bob blew out his lips. 'He's okay, I suppose... A bit weird...

as in... rather anal. But that applies to *most* of the guys in his department.'

'Married?'

'Surprisingly.'

'Kids?'

'Three... I think.'

Chad leant back again. 'So, he'll have a mortgage and all the other financial burdens that go with it.'

'Where are we going with this?' squinted Bob, carefully placing his glass on the table.

'He helped us on that Mexican drug cartel case... remember?'

'Yeah... I think that was the first time I met him.'

'We got him to hack into their computers in order to ascertain how they were laundering their money.'

'With surprising ease, if I recall.'

'There you go! So... what if you persuade Lenny to join your inner circle and ask him to get us inside Templar Resources' bank account?'

'It ain't gonna happen,' said Bob firmly. 'Lenny's not someone I could approach with something like that.'

'We could get our mystery benefactor to make it worth his while.'

'I told you... it ain't gonna happen... Lenny would never be swayed by money.'

'Girls, then?'

Bob smiled. 'Hardly... He's born again. Believe me... he won't be doing *anything* outside of the Agency that troubles his conscience.'

Chad tossed the beermat he'd been toying with onto the table.

'Mind you,' added Bob, with a grin, 'we could always have a word with Donald and see if we can get him to pre-book Lenny a place in Heaven!'

Chad ignored the quip. 'And the other guys in IT?'

Bob considered their options. 'Lenny's the only one I know well enough to chance a conversation like that without the risk of being ratted on.'

314

Chad frowned. 'There's gotta be *someone* out there who can help us access that account.'

'Well... you let me know when you finally work out who,' said Bob, taking the opportunity to reclaim his pint.

He'd barely made inroads into it when a voice interrupted them from behind.

'Excuse me.'

Turning in unison, they saw a young man leaning over from the table behind. He was dressed in a blue and red t-shirt with the word *SUPERGEEK* plastered across its front in superhero fashion... his Achilles heel clearly acne, not kryptonite.

'I couldn't help hear you talking,' he said, in a manner somewhere between an apology and enthusiasm.

'Then you'd do well to go back to your drink and forget everything you heard, kid,' Bob advised him firmly, turning his back on the interloper.

'I didn't mean to listen in,' the young man persisted, disregarding the warning. 'It was just that I heard the name *Penkridge* and it got my attention... especially as you then went on to suggest hacking a bank account.'

'What of it?' asked Chad, looking around himself awkwardly, having realised how carefree they'd been with their conversation.

'Would it be *Norman* Penkridge you were referring to?'

Bob spun around aggressively. 'Look... kid!'

Chad quickly placed a hand on his partner's arm. 'You know him?'

'I know *of* him.'

Chad hesitated. 'What if it was?'

'You want him stopped from doing something?'

Neither man responded.

'And you need a bank account hacked in order to do it,' Supergeek reminded them. 'Well... I'm your man!'

Chad and Bob looked at each other... and then at the talking infestation of pimples.

'I appreciate the offer,' said Chad politely, 'but you're outta your depth on this one. I suggest you take my colleague's advice

313

and get back to whatever it was you were doing.'

'Okay,' said Supergeek, with an unconvincing shrug. 'If that's what you *really* want. But, if you're declining my offer... the only *other* person I'd recommend that comes remotely near me in ability is Penkridge himself! But I doubt he's gonna want to hack his own account!' He looked at them smugly.

'How come you know so much about him?' asked Chad, unsettled by the coincidence.

'Who doesn't?' responded Supergeek. 'He's a legend in the world of coding. They say he was so ahead of the game at university that the lecturers used to ask *him* for advice.'

'And what kinda coding did he specialise in?' pressed Chad, seizing the opportunity to fill in some blanks.

Supergeek looked at him in bemusement. '*All* of it!'

'He's *that* good, eh?' said Bob.

'Yeah... but not as good as me!' The sudden rancour in Supergeek's delivery took them by surprise.

'I feel a rivalry creeping in here,' Chad prodded.

'You could say that,' said Supergeek guardedly.

Bob gave the key in Supergeek's back another tweak. 'You don't like him, then?'

'I *loathe* him,' said Supergeek, burdening the verb with as much venom as possible.

'Okay... you've got ten seconds to explain yourself, kid,' announced Bob sharply, 'Beyond that... we're outta here!'

Supergeek nodded. 'It's fairly simple. Code geniuses like us inhabit a pretty niche community. It's our entire life. We take it extremely seriously. You get a lot of respect within that community for the skills you have... but woe betide if you try and put yourself above everybody else.'

'And that's what you reckon Penkridge has done?'

'I *know* he's done it... which is why it was *me* who fired the first shot across his bow.'

'How so?'

'I proved he's not as good as he thinks he is. I beat him at *Cortex Destroyer!*' Supergeek nodded smugly and waited for the plaudits to rain.

'What the fuck's that?' exclaimed Bob.

'Only one of the most intense, interactive forum games you can ever take part in!' retorted Supergeek, staggered at another human being's ignorance of the fact. 'But, to this day, he doesn't know who his vanquisher was. I kept my identity hidden. I logged on as *Ultimate and Unbeatable Supreme Cyber Warrior 2*. After an epic and exhausting battle lasting many weeks, I finally managed to deplete him of his intergalactic mind juice.'

'That must've hurt!' winced Bob.

'Big time!' smirked Supergeek, failing to spot the sarcasm.

'And what did Norman Penkridge choose to call himself?' prompted Chad, mining for further clues.

'*Ultimate and Unbeatable Supreme Cyber Warrior 1*,' came the extremely bitter reply.

'I did wonder,' muttered Bob.

'But we all knew it was *him*,' snorted Supergeek with rising disdain. 'Because it's a...'

'Pretty niche community,' finished Chad for him. 'Yeah... we got that bit.'

'Sure... But he's now made himself unwelcome in it. His arrogance in assuming he could automatically claim that number one position was just the *start* of his downfall. He pushed too far. He began to think he was better than the community itself.'

'What makes you say that?'

'He abandoned it,' answered Supergeek... *AKA Ultimate and Unbeatable Supreme Cyber Warrior 2*.

'You mean... he eventually managed to get out of his bedroom,' clarified Bob.

'He sold out. He went to France. He lives there now with that celebrity page three model. They say he's worth millions.'

'We know,' nodded Chad.

'That was another line he crossed. It's reckoned he used his hacking skills for purely personal gain. That puts him in a different category, as far as the coding community's concerned.'

'But you offered to hack him for us!' pointed out Bob.

'Not for money!' insisted Supergeek... *AKA Ultimate and*

Unbeatable Supreme Cyber Warrior 2. 'Making a global corporation look foolish is something to be proud of. It shows they're not all that... and that you've demonstrated your intellectual superiority over them. But being motivated to hack in order to steal money is an entirely different ballgame... especially to purists like me. All you've done is show you're as greedy as they are!'

'We're not sure he *has* hacked,' said Chad. 'You can have that one for free... though we've long suspected he's involved in *something* illegal.'

Supergeek... *AKA Ultimate and Unbeatable Supreme Cyber Warrior 2* looked at them animatedly. 'Are you CIA?'

'Shouldn't you be worried if we are?' asked Chad.

Supergeek... *AKA Ultimate and Unbeatable Supreme Cyber Warrior 2* gave it scant thought. 'Nah... I know how to cover my tracks,' he boasted. '*Ultimate and Unbeatable Supreme Cyber Warrior 2* isn't my *real* name.'

'You don't say!' smirked Bob.

'We didn't really believe you were Supergeek either,' said Chad, acknowledging the t-shirt. 'They don't seem to have phone boxes in this country anymore... which would put you at a considerable disadvantage.'

Supergeek... *AKA Ultimate and Unbeatable Supreme Cyber Warrior 2* struggled with the humour. 'I just used that online gaming tag to make a point to Penkridge. My real friends know me as...' He delayed the revelation to increase its impact. '*The Megabyte Master.*'

'You have *friends?*' said Bob, raising his eyebrows.

'It's a virtual community,' explained the Megabyte Master... alias Supergeek... *AKA Ultimate and Unbeatable Supreme Cyber Warrior 2*. 'We only ever meet in cyberspace.'

'I can see why,' Bob nodded.

'Don't let appearances fool you!' retaliated the Megabyte Master sharply. 'If you wanna nail Penkridge... I'm your man!' He extended an unhygienic, nail-bitten hand... which remained extended. 'I would relish the opportunity of doing battle with my arch-nemesis again!'

'This ain't a computer game, kid,' returned Bob.

'It's *all* a game in our business,' the Megabyte Master scoffed. 'It doesn't matter if you're programming an interactive car chase or hijacking someone's social network account... it's about the challenge of coming up with the right code and proving you're smarter than everybody else.'

'And you really reckon you're smarter than *him?*'

'Penkridge?' sneered the Megabyte Master immaturely. 'Just give me the chance to prove it!'

Chad assessed the situation. 'So let's get this straight... You're saying you could get us into this Templar Resources' bank account?' he clarified, lowering his voice.

'I could get you into *anywhere*,' said the Megabyte Master, with an arrogant... if slightly unsanitary... grin.

Chad pulled a ten pound note from his pocket and stuffed it into the outstretched hand. 'Go get yourself a drink. I need to speak with my colleague here.'

The Megabyte Master examined the offering and quickly did as instructed.

'You're not seriously suggesting we use this kid?' hissed Bob, watching as he made his way towards the bar.

'Why not? If he can do what he says he can, we'll be halfway to solving our problem.'

'But he's just some random kid who's accosted us in a bar!'

'Which makes him the perfect candidate for the job!' Chad smiled. 'No connection... no names... no trace.'

Bob shook his head. 'I can't say I'm comfortable with it.'

'Do we really have an alternative?'

On cue, Bob's phone vibrated in his pocket. Retrieving it, he keenly studied the message on its screen. 'We may just have!' he beamed broadly. 'Seems our inner circle's finally come good! They've given us the hotel Penkridge used his credit card to book a room at!'

Chad slapped the table. 'This is turning out to be our day!' he grinned. 'Now we know where he is, we can use the kid to cut off Penkridge's funds and exploit the turmoil it'll cause to flush out his little secret!'

They sat in self-absorbed silence, contemplating the prospect, until the Megabyte Master returned.

'I assumed you meant for me to keep the change,' he smirked, having availed himself of a couple of packets of crisps and a bag of nuts in the process.

'Of course,' Chad conceded diplomatically.

'Good. So... do I get my day of reckoning with Penkridge?'

Bob looked at Chad and acknowledged the decision had already been made.

'You do,' affirmed Chad. 'But we're only looking to *block* the Templar Resources account. We want it temporarily frozen. We're not asking you to steal from it. Understand?'

'I told you... I'm a purist,' replied the Megabyte Master. 'That's what makes me better than him. That's why I'll beat him!'

'We'll still pay you, of course,' confirmed Bob, figuring no one was *that* pure.

'There's no need,' the Megabyte Master surprised him. 'My offer of help's not about money. It's about Penkridge being forced to concede that the title of *Ultimate and Unbeatable Supreme Cyber Warrior 1* should've belonged to *me,* if it belonged to anybody.' There was a sudden look in his eyes that might've scared a prospective mother-in-law.

'You *really* don't like him, do you?' observed Bob.

'I detest him,' spat the Megabyte Master, his nostrils flaring. 'I can't believe fate's finally given me the chance to do something about it.'

Chad winced at the use of the *F* word... but its presence couldn't be argued with in this particular instance.

'You don't know what this means to me!' continued the Megabyte Master, wiping a sweaty palm on his t-shirt.

'I reckon we do,' said Bob caustically. 'A little more real than depleting someone's intergalactic mind juice.'

'Yeah... I guess it is. So when do I get started?'

'As soon as you like,' said Chad. 'How long d'ya reckon it'll take?'

'Depends how good his bank's firewall is,' the Megabyte

Master shrugged. 'But I've never encountered one yet I couldn't crack! How do I contact you when I'm done?'

'You don't,' said Bob firmly. 'We contact *you*. Now... if you'll excuse us... we have a location we need to check out.'

The Megabyte Master pointed at their half empty glasses. 'But you haven't finished your drinks!'

'I've always made it a rule in life never to drink anything the same temperature as the room I'm in,' said Bob.

'Write your contact details on this,' said Chad, handing over a beermat. 'We'll be in touch.'

The traffic in their favour, it took just under half an hour for Chad and Bob to find themselves standing outside the hotel Norman had checked in to.

'Not quite what I was expecting!' said Chad, staring silently at the building's facade.

The smart security boarding hid most of the damage, but the tell-tale scorch marks on the masonry gave the game away.

'I doubt we'll find him inside,' remarked Bob.

'I'm beginning to wonder if we were meant to find him at all,' Chad sighed wearily.

*　　*　　*

Life, as Norman was about to discover, hangs by a thread so fine, it is a wonder it hangs at all. Such are the odds of it not doing so, even if you avoid all risks in the hope of keeping that thread intact, it does not follow that some other event, completely out of your control, won't cut across your path and cause it to snap.

The first part of his journey back from *Soddem Hall* was as unorthodox as the hours that had preceded it. Having spent an inordinate amount of time thanking Stump for his astonishing dips – and the even tastier chocolate brownies that had followed them – he'd enthusiastically strapped himself into the back seat of the car in the belief it was a spaceship ready to assist his leaving the planet... the superhuman abilities he'd suddenly acquired being needed elsewhere.

It was only as the effects of Stump's hospitality began to wear off, and the vehicle had remained stubbornly attached to the A354, that normal service resumed.

Though not *entirely*.

Falling from such a heightened sense of euphoria, the reality that greeted him on his return felt heavier and more cumbersome than he remembered it. Believing there was nothing in the Universe that couldn't be achieved had come as welcome news, given what it was expecting of him. But now the warm, positive glow that had wrapped itself around his thoughts had evaporated, the stark reminder of what lay ahead stared back at him, cold and unmoving.

A freak deterioration in the weather didn't help matters. Reminiscent of the bizarre personal climatic system that seemed to have attached itself to him in France, the car found itself driving through rain so fierce, it threatened to bring them to a standstill. But it was blue, flashing lights on the road ahead that finally did that.

A flustered, rain-sodden policeman informed them through the driver's window that carnage on the road ahead meant they would need to take a detour if they wished to continue their journey. Following his shouted instructions, they found themselves taking a smaller road that cut through dense woodland... the crowded trees on either side only adding to the smothering sense of oppression that had fallen with the rain. Just as Norman thought his spirits couldn't sink any lower, a small bird – mistiming its attempt to find sanctuary from the downpour – found itself mortally acquainted with the car's windscreen. As the unfortunate creature twitched in its death throes, the driver assisted its demise with a diplomatic flick of the windscreen wipers.

Xanthia's initial shriek did little for Norman's nerves. But it was to prove merely a vocal warm up for what was to follow. No sooner had Norman's heartbeat deemed it safe to return to normal, than the driver suddenly and without warning hit the brakes. The car swerved dramatically before veering violently away to the right. Striking the raised grass verge, but refusing to alter its trajectory, it flipped itself over in a continuing roll as the tyres bid *adieu* to the road.

Norman – unsure as to whether his tumbling senses were for real or one final hurrah from Stump's dips – shut his eyes in the hope it was the latter. But Xanthia's all-too-real screams put paid to that.

He waited for the inevitable... the sickening impact of solid wood against hurtling metal. He wondered if death would permit him to register the actual moment. Surrendering to fate... a curious thing happened. Rather than feeling the need to vent his terror, an unexpected calm befell him. As time appeared to slow into an ever-spiralling vortex mirroring the cars motion, he suddenly found himself reliving moments from his life...

...being small enough to be bathed in the kitchen sink by his mother...

...the comforting taste of rusks and milk...

...his first day at school...

...small wooden chairs...

...sitting in class...

...an enormous feeling of embarrassment...

...watching his faeces being placed in a bag...

...the burning humiliation...

...taunts from his peer group...

...being shunned...

...his parents' consternation at his withdrawal from normal life...

...being shunned...

...his parents' reluctant acceptance of his withdrawal from normal life...

...being shunned...

...his first computer...

...the excitement of discovering something non-judgemental...

...his obsession with programming...

...his parents' apathy towards his withdrawal from normal life...

...setting eyes upon a picture of Xanthia...

...his first orgasm (self-inflicted) thereafter...

...university...

...Armageddon Terrace...

...failure...

...Armageddon Terrace...

...his *own* apathy towards his withdrawal from normal life...

...Gabriel...

As his thoughts alighted upon the Archangel, it suddenly felt as if someone had put their arms around him and given him the biggest hug imaginable. His spinning world became an irrelevance. It didn't matter anymore. An incredible peace descended with the knowledge he no longer had to worry about the future.

He waited for the sudden ending.

...the sound of shattering glass...

...the rolling car's loss of momentum...

...the sideways pull of gravity...

...the smell of petrol mingling with damp vegetation...

...his heart pounding in his chest...

...the realisation that time was as it should be.

Thinking his ordeal was over, the car teased him with one final groan from its traumatised skin as it slowly fell back on its roof.

'Everyone alright?' groaned the driver, after a short silence. Norman didn't answer.

He could hear Xanthia crying.

'It was a soddin' great big stag!' the driver exclaimed. 'As big as a bleedin' 'ouse! Stepped out right in front of me in the rain! Just stood there... turned its 'ead and stared... like we didn't exist... If I didn't know better, I'd swear it'd done so on purpose!'

Norman fumbled for his lap belt, his hands shaking uncontrollably. It was as if they were detached from his brain. Shock... they would tell him later.

'I hope you believe it wasn't my fault, sir!' whimpered the driver. 'There was nothing I could do... Honest!'

'It's okay,' quivered Norman. 'I believe you. Very strange things are happening to me at the moment.'

'God bless you, sir!' the driver thanked him.

'He may well just have done,' answered Norman beneath his breath.

After a bit of a struggle, he managed to release the lap belt's clasp... gravity dropping him awkwardly on his head.

Xanthia's crying had turned into a quiet moan.

'It's alright Xan,' he comforted her. 'Everything's gonna be alright.'

'Unless the car explodes before we get out,' said the driver, from his upside-down position.

'You're fired,' said Norman.

It seemed an age before the emergency services arrived... though hardly surprising, given their rural location and the fact dripping petrol makes every second seem like an eternity when unable to escape from it. But as the rescue crews efficiently went about their business, their professionalism ensured all three occupants of the car were released and dispatched to hospital without having been *flambéed*.

As they waited to be examined, the police took the opportunity to breathalyse the driver on account of the fact deer had never been spotted anywhere near that vicinity... and that his language towards Norman, whilst both were being cut free from the wreckage, had grown increasingly un-chauffeur-like. But he steadfastly maintained his version of events... and his driving licence... as the test returned a negative result.

Having been assessed, all three were detained in hospital overnight... though purely as a precaution. With injuries amounting to nothing more than superficial cuts and bruises, the paramedics treating them at the scene had described their escape as a "miracle", when seeing the state of the vehicle from which they'd been pulled.

Assigned to separate wards, Norman was forced to wait

until morning before being reunited with Xanthia. But as they waited in the reception area for a replacement car to take them home, she appeared distant... using repeated readings of the leaflet she'd been given – on what to do if certain symptoms ensued – as an excuse not to engage in proper conversation.

The subsequent journey back to London was undertaken in similar silence, causing Norman to sink even further into a dark mood of introspection.

The negative feelings that were beating him about the head had little to do with the problems of getting permission for Stump to perform in front of Stonehenge, or whether the rest of *Trouzerbulge* were capable of doing so. It was the change in Xanthia that troubled him most. But not the one that had kept her face glued to the window, her interest more in what was occurring beyond the glass than in front of it. It was the change in her that had occurred *before* the accident that caused him his greatest consternation. Much like the transformation he'd witnessed when Deaf Pete and the sound crew had visited them in France, she'd been revitalised by the return to her old home... that new spirit all the more conspicuous by its absence now she was being driven away from it... a fact his plummeting disposition magnified to an unhealthy degree.

Having blossomed in the sunnier climes of her former life, she was now wilting.

Perhaps she *too* had experienced life flashing before her, as the car had somersaulted its way towards an anticipated death... coming to the conclusion that she preferred the way it used to be.

He could hardly compete with that... though God knows he'd tried. But for all the places he'd taken her and gifts he'd lavished on her, he wasn't Stump.

And therein lay the problem.

He'd ignored the embrace Stump had given her as they'd said their goodbyes, pretending not to notice how long the clinch had lasted. Besides... he'd had a rocket to catch.

Given what she'd just been through, he certainly wasn't going to bring it up now, in the car.

That would be extremely foolish.

'You still love him, don't you?' he blurted, less than half a mile later.

Xanthia simply looked at him, shook her head, and looked away.

That went well, he thought.

It was two o'clock in the afternoon by the time the car finally pulled up outside their hotel.

A doorman, attired in top hat and matching jacket, dutifully opened the door.

'You go in,' Norman instructed her. 'I've got an important appointment at the bank. I need to arrange a rather large transfer of funds if we're to stand any chance of having *Trouzerbulge* perform at Stonehenge.'

'Okay,' she shrugged.

'I promise I'll be as quick as I can. It shouldn't take long.'

'Whatever.'

Norman felt awkward.

'I'm sorry about the question earlier. I think I must've bumped my head harder than I thought!'

She smiled politely. 'It doesn't matter.'

Norman knew otherwise.

'Oh... by the way,' she said, with a little more animation.

'Yes?' he responded expectantly.

'I take it you've got the chequebook?'

'Er... yeah... Why?'

'For the bank?'

'Safe and sound,' he said, patting an area close to his stomach. 'The consequences of losing that don't bear thinking about!'

Xanthia put her hand on his and gave it a jaded pat. 'Then, make sure you don't!' She kissed him about a foot from his lips and wriggled herself free of the back seat.

As the car pulled away, he definitely knew she wasn't herself... watching as she walked into the hotel's foyer without stopping to flirt with the gawping bellboys.

Worker Three shouted above the melee and appealed for calm. The assembled throng would get nowhere if they all yelled at once.

The antlers on the head of the man with antlers on his head were starting to look like a dangerous liability. His revelation that they needed to quarry and transport an even *larger* circle of stones than the previous one hadn't gone down at all well.

The assembled throng didn't want to anger the gods... but wasn't it reasonable to expect a little compassion from them occasionally?

The man with antlers on his head bravely stood his ground. It wasn't for them to suggest how the gods should behave. It was the other way around... and as their high priest, he warned them of the horrific consequences that might befall the community if the gods got angry.

The assembled throng certainly didn't want that... but they still weren't happy.

Worker One had stayed well out of it, preferring to contemplate the relevance of the antlers. What was so significant about *that* particular mode of headwear, he wondered. Was it their shape... or their position on the head... or the fact a deer featured somewhere in the equation? If that particular animal possessed special, spiritual properties... how come the gods allowed them to be eaten? More to the point... if deer were *that* tuned in to what was going on, how come they were caught out by a simple bow and arrow in the first place?

Perhaps it was something to do with a particular animal's body part, he concluded... which begged yet another question...

How many attempts had there been in the past to find the most efficient item to wear to communicate with the gods before it was decided antlers were as good as it got? Had... for instance... anyone experimented with underpants made from a cow's udders... or a necklace constructed from dried goats' testicles? If they had, he doubted either would've looked any more ridiculous.

He put this last question to Worker Two, standing next to him.

Worker Two looked at him in disgust and said there was a word for Worker One... It was just a shame that, just like the crane, it hadn't been thought of yet.

Unperturbed, Worker One continued his musings. It certainly made sense to wear the item on the head, he concluded... if only to make the individual stand out from the crowd and look as important as possible.

It was as he was pondering something shaped suspiciously like a mitre that he caught the high priest staring at him.

Although he had serious doubts as to whether the man was as well-connected with the gods as his headwear claimed, Worker One found the stare unnerving. There was definitely a power in *claiming* to know something... especially if it couldn't be disproved.

The high priest was obviously thinking the same thing.

Could *now* be the time to put forward his concept of a single deity, Worker One deliberated. It would certainly prove a crowd-pleaser if he offered the notion that his single god might not expect them to go to all the trouble of carting yet *more* stones over ridiculous distances.

He slowly raised his hand... much to Worker Three's abject horror, who recognised a familiar glint in Worker One's eyes.

The high priest puffed himself up, trying to appear as important as his antlers suggested he was. He recognised that glint too... though it looked to him like a dangerous lack of deference.

Worker One knew he must tread carefully. Those making up the assembled throng might not be as open to change as he was. After all... their blind acceptance of the antlers meant they were undoubtedly stupid.

He began cautiously by asking whether it was *remotely* possible that the dimensions for the new stones had been misheard. He figured that if he gave the priest a convenient way out of the mounting hostility surrounding his pronouncement, it might be enthusiastically grabbed, so as to avoid further confrontation. It would also prove to Worker One that the priest was making it up as he went along.

He carefully set his trap.

Could the new stones required actually be *smaller* than the ones already in place? Had the priest simply misunderstood this new dimension that was supposed to resemble a foot? What if the gods had meant it to resemble a *toe?* It was an easy mistake to make, given one was part of the other... especially for entities who probably had no need of feet.

There was a gasp of collective fear from the assembled throng as the suggestion hung heretically in the air.

But the high priest remained calm. He knew he had the dread of the masses to fall back on.

The dimensions were *exactly* as the gods had instructed. He'd *said* so, hadn't he?

Worker One realised the futility of trying to explain circular reasoning to *this* lot, and admonished himself for thinking that a man with antlers on his head could ever admit he'd made a mistake. His word had to be absolute and without question. After all... faith relied on the infallibility of instructions claimed to have been imparted from on high. Determined not to be outsmarted, he tried a different approach.

It hadn't been suggested *where* the new stones were to come from, he pointed out. Everyone had merely assumed that they were to be quarried from the same stone as the smaller ones... hence their current consternation. But surely this might not be the case? Hadn't they simply jumped the gun? For all they knew, these new and considerably larger stones could be brought from somewhere nearer... say... just down the road. Wasn't that the case?

The assembled throng liked Worker One's reasoning... a fact not lost on the high priest standing very much alone in their midst.

The high priest kept his cool. You didn't get to wear antlers on your head without knowing a thing or two about the importance of theatre. Conceding that it was a fair point, he solemnly announced that the gods would need to be consulted... the decision being theirs and theirs alone.

Worker One regarded this as extremely convenient.

The priest called for a chicken.

Amid a few flying feathers, one was duly submitted.

Following the necessary incantations... and more flying feathers... the chicken was ceremoniously dispatched to cross the road in the afterlife and send back the gods' reply via his entrails.

The assembled throng waited with bated breath.

Keeping them guessing, the priest took his time as he rummaged around in the warm viscera.

Worker One watched impassively. If they were so important an aid in communicating with the gods... how come he didn't wear *those* on his head?

Finally... the priest made a dramatic gesture, as a length of steaming colon and what had once been an anus finally provided the answer.

Just down the road!

The assembled throng erupted in a tumultuous cheer and rejoiced in the magnanimity of the gods... seemingly happy to forget the enormity of the task still ahead of them.

The priest declared his difficult work was done. He would return when the stones were complete and demonstrate the magic power that they would bring. He appreciated that it might take many years. So... in the meantime... the assembled throng were to bring him regular offerings to the gods in the form of food, drink, and the occasional virgin daughter who... he assured them... would be safely returned once the gods had pleasured themselves via his own body.

Still elated by their reduced workload, the assembled throng considered it a good deal.

Worker One considered it an absolute liberty... but decided to keep quiet for now. He'd scored his first victory.

Next stop... monotheism.

*　*　*

'Is this it?' exclaimed Bob, his incredulity stretched by the Victorian, red-brick, semi-detached house in front of him.

'You didn't *really* think the Megabyte Master's "command centre" was going to prove worthy of a James Bond set, did you?' asked Chad, with matching disbelief.

'I know… But are we *sure* about this?'

'You have a better option?'

'Nope. But as far as I'm concerned, the kid's just some spotty loser who's combined a rarely-leaves-his-bedroom mentality with one helluva grudge.'

'You think *Penkridge* is the epitome of an international mastermind? They all look that way, these days. A suit and maturity's a thing of the past. These kids are breaking into the world's most sophisticated internet sites whilst they're barely out of kindergarten! They've grown up on it. It's in their DNA. Besides… his ordinariness makes him perfect for the job. We're not recruiting him. We merely need him to do one thing. After that, he'll melt back into obscurity.'

'If you say so.' Bob gave the offending Victorian frontage another disdainful look. 'Guess I should ring the bell.'

'In the absence of a rock face to abseil down, I'd say that's a pretty good idea,' Chad smiled.

Bob forced one back.

A strangled, electronic rendition of *Greensleeves* – courtesy of a standard, black and white push button – was followed by the whir of a not-so-standard camera, attached to the too-standard-for-Bob's-liking brickwork above, homing in on them.

As both men awkwardly pretended it hadn't, the door opened to reveal a plump woman in her mid-forties who – from the state of her apron – had been in the middle of doing some baking.

'Sorry. I don't believe in God,' she said bluntly.

'Neither do I,' affirmed Chad.

She raised her eyebrows. 'That's unusual. Cos doesn't that mean you're now gonna have to tell me we're *both* going to hell?'

'I'm of the belief we're probably there already,' muttered Bob, under his breath.

'We're not here to convert you,' said Chad.

'In that case... I've got a perfectly good vacuum cleaner, thank you!' she announced.

'Then, that's where we *do* differ,' he smiled engagingly. 'This is gonna sound very strange, but...'

'You're Americans, aren't you?' she butted in.

'Yes, ma'am.'

'Is it about solar power, then?'

Chad failed to see the connection.

'We're here to see the Megabyte Master,' said Bob, putting her out of her misery... and feeling rather silly uttering such a phrase at his age.

Surprisingly, she didn't seem fazed, though a light dusting of flour on her brow cracked slightly. 'He's not in any trouble, is he?'

'Are we talking mentally?' Bob asked, prompting an elbow in the ribs from his partner.

The camera moved again.

'He's upstairs,' she said, turning. 'You'd better come in. And wipe your feet... I was lying about the vacuum cleaner.'

Accepting the invitation, they did as they were told and waited as she yelled up a flight of stairs.

'Kevin! There are two American gentlemen here to see you!'

'Thanks a lot, mum!' came a petulant and muffled reply. 'You've just gone and blown my anonymity!'

'They're standing in our hall, looking up at your bedroom door, dear!' she declared in bemusement.

Chad heard the surveillance camera whir again.

'I know!' Kevin shouted back.

'I'll leave you to it,' she smiled, beating a retreat into the kitchen.

Kevin... formerly The Megabyte Master... alias Supergeek... *AKA Ultimate and Unbeatable Supreme Cyber Warrior 2* made an appearance on the landing. 'You'd better come up,' he said. 'I've got something pretty interesting to show you.'

Contrary to Bob's initial misgivings, his "command centre" was surprisingly impressive for a tree-lined, residential street in the suburbs of London. A collection of eight, separate computer screens had been arranged in an arc... two screens high, four screens wide. Whilst seven contained various codes and tables, the eighth showed a picture of the doorstep on which they'd just been standing. Banks of flickering lights and various metal casings littered the space around them. A single, unmade bed hugged the far wall, which was covered in posters advertising computer games... as well as a number featuring a well-endowed female displaying her talents.

Whilst selective squinting might have you believe you *were* in a command centre somewhere, the odour rather gave the game away... leaving Bob to feel that the room's inhabitant needed to change his socks more often.

'It seems I might have underestimated Penkridge's abilities,' the teenager admitted, acknowledging the screens. 'You gentlemen might be too late.'

'What d'ya mean?' frowned Chad, throwing an anxious look at Bob.

'I'll show you.' Kevin settled himself in front of the monitors and attempted unsuccessfully to crack his knuckles. Ignoring his failure, he started typing. 'After a little bit of digging, I managed to locate the account you were interested in. See...' He pointed at one of the screens now displaying a long list of transactions. 'Templar Resources,' he announced proudly.

Chad studied it intently for a while... then shook his head. 'There must be some mistake. This *can't* be it!'

'I don't make mistakes,' said Kevin boldly.

Chad begged to differ. 'From what you're showing me here, I'd say the total of these transactions runs into *billions* of pounds!'

'And dollars... and euros... and yen... and roubles... and shekels... and every currency you could possibly think of,' said Kevin unfazed. 'It gets converted, of course... but it's coming in from all around the world!'

294

'Then, it can't be Penkridge's!' insisted Chad. 'This looks more like the account of a major international conglomerate. His operation ain't *that* big!'

'But he's connected to it,' said Kevin coolly. 'Take a look at this. He pulled up a second list of transactions on another screen. 'I took the liberty of searching for Penkridge's personal account, even though it wasn't part of the original remit. I assumed you'd want me to be as thorough as possible.'

Chad looked at Bob.

'It didn't take long. Here it is... see... Account name... Norman Penkridge... Current address... blah, blah, blah.'

'Yeah... that's definitely his,' confirmed Bob.

'Oh... I know,' said Kevin confidently. 'Not least because it's been receiving funds directly from this Templar Resources account... the very same one you now seem to think has nothing to do with him!'

As he scrolled down to reveal the latest in a long line of transactions, Bob let out a loud whistle.

'You're kiddin' me!' Chad gasped, joining him in deciphering the final figure at the bottom of the screen.

'You can see why I said you gentlemen may be too late!'

'One hundred and twenty-seven million pounds,' mouthed Bob, in a stupor, 'give or take the loose change!'

'One hundred million of which was paid in only yesterday,' pointed out Kevin, highlighting the transaction with his mouse.

'From Templar Resources,' confirmed Chad, studying the screen closely.

'It's been the same since the account was opened. Only... all previous amounts have been for a fraction of that. This last transaction is in a whole new league!'

'Which suggests he could be about to go operational,' said Bob.

Chad stabbed a finger at the screen. 'We need to take this account down immediately... before he gets a chance to utilise the funds.'

'*Ah...*' said Kevin delicately. 'That's where the

"underestimated him" bit comes in, and why I said you may be too late.' He looked at them with a tempered look of admiration. 'He's already anticipated such an action. You see… people think the banks know what they're doing when it comes to keeping their money secure. But they don't! When it comes to cyberspace… where people's hard-earned savings merely reside as lines of code… they're useless!' He skewed his head. 'I suppose you can hardly blame 'em, really… It's not their area of expertise. But they don't try too hard, either. They only do enough to make the customer *think* their money's safe. Anything beyond that would be too expensive and time-consuming, given the hackers are always one step ahead of 'em. It's more economical for them to set aside a small percentage of their vast profits each year to compensate for the occasional fraudster than seriously tackle the problem head on. You'd be *appalled* at how vulnerable their systems are to attack from people like me. But therein lies an irony… Whilst we're looking at Penkridge's bank account, we're not actually *in* it!'

Chad narrowed his eyes. 'I don't follow.'

'Well… having the skills he does, Penkridge was only too aware of his account's vulnerability. From what I can deduce, he's done the bank's job for them. He's gone to extraordinary lengths to protect it with some additional security of his own. In essence… he's hacked his own account and installed a personal firewall around it!'

'But we can *see* it!' insisted Chad.

'Not entirely. What we're looking at is merely his bank statement. Whilst we shouldn't even be doing *that*… the bit of his account I need to access – in order to have control over it – is sitting behind an ingeniously encrypted security cloak. He's programmed it to be impenetrable!'

'Are you telling us you can't get past it?' cut in Bob. 'I thought you said you were better than him?'

'I am,' said Kevin cockily. 'But he's had a massive head start on me, of course. I'm gonna need every trick at my disposal to break his code… and that may take some time.'

'We may not have it,' said Chad.

'Not really my problem,' Kevin shrugged. 'But believe me when I say I'll be working as hard as I can. It's now gotten personal. He's thrown down the gauntlet and issued a challenge. But he'll lose! I'll crack it in the end! In the meantime, I'll just have to keep an eye on his transactions and alert you if anything unusual occurs.'

'What about Templar Resources?' asked Bob.

'Now... that's a completely different story. In its current state on my screen, I could cause havoc with that in a matter of minutes. But the truth is... I like my mum's cooking too much. You were right... that's one heavy-duty organisation we're looking at. If I messed with something *that* size, I'd bring every country's law enforcement agency straight to my doorstep! Besides... as I told you in the pub... I'm only in this to hurt Penkridge.'

'It'd hurt him if you stopped the source of his funds,' Bob tempted him.

'No... the kid's right,' interjected Chad. 'We need to tread extremely carefully. It could be that Templar Resources are just unwitting victims in whatever Penkridge is involved in. The best thing we can do is keep an eye on them for now. They're not our immediate problem. If they *are* in on this... it's more likely Penkridge is working for them, rather than the other way around. In that case, we're looking at a completely different ballgame.'

'Whatever the connection, they're definitely more than just a holding company!' pointed out Bob.

'Exactly... and while their account remains open to scrutiny, it could provide us with further clues.'

'Why don't I simply stop his *future* funding from them?' suggested Kevin brightly. 'It'd be incredibly easy, seeing as how he's been resorting to a rather old-fashioned method of transfer.'

'How d'ya mean?'

'Well... take a look at these payments.' Kevin ran his finger down the screen. 'They all have the initials CH next to them... See? That means they've been paid by cheque. What's more...

we can see their numbers are sequential... meaning they've been issued from the same chequebook. And seeing as that also means they haven't been used to pay anybody *else*... I'd say Penkridge is in possession of that chequebook and using it to siphon money from Templar Resources.'

'A pretty smart application of logic,' nodded Chad appreciatively.

'And that from the master!' added Bob.

Kevin gave a broad grin. 'So... d'ya want me to cancel it?'

'The chequebook?'

'Yeah.'

'Why not,' said Chad, returning the grin. 'If Penkridge has it legitimately, it might just be seen as an administrative error. But if it's part of his scam, we'll have put serious pressure on him. In the meantime, you can get to work on his personal account.'

'By the way,' said Kevin, 'I must point out the action you're requesting me to perform is completely illegal.'

Bob looked at him incredulously.

'Just make the necessary keystrokes,' directed Chad.

'Okay... Just so long as it's clear I'm acting on *your* instructions.'

'You are.'

Kevin nodded and proceeded to type frantically on the keyboard. After a brief blurring of fingers, he stopped. 'All done!'

'What? As simple as that?'

'When you know how. Whatever's left of that chequebook will be worthless now. He may as well use it to wipe his...'

'One thing,' cut in Bob. 'Are you able to tell us where that last cheque was presented? Given its date, it may help us narrow our search for him.'

Kevin divided a look of disbelief between the two of them. 'You mean... you don't know where he is?'

'Not anymore,' Chad admitted. 'We thought we did... but he's proving to be a slippery customer!'

'Not to mention, lucky one,' added Bob.

'We're assuming he's still somewhere here in London.'

Bob clicked his fingers as a thought struck him. 'Maybe there's something else you can help us with to locate him. We've been awaiting information on the use of his credit card. For reasons that don't concern you, it hasn't been as forthcoming as hoped. Would *you* be able to access those records for us?'

'I don't think much of your support network,' scoffed Kevin. 'It seems like I'm the one doing all the work!'

'Then it'll be all the more rewarding for you when we finally nail our quarry,' said Bob.

Kevin shrugged. 'Shouldn't be too difficult. I doubt he'll have bothered putting his own firewall around *that*.'

'We need to know the last hotel it was used in,' said Chad.

'And how do I let you know when I find the answer?'

'I take it you have a social network account?'

'Of course!'

'Then, you can leave a message for us on that.'

'Only if it's a coded one for us to meet again,' said Kevin. 'That kinda information needs to be passed on by mouth. I'm not gonna post anything that might incriminate me!'

'You're in the wrong job, kid,' said Bob. 'Have you ever thought of crossing over?'

'Not bloody likely!' Kevin snorted. 'I just hope you guys put a good word in for me, if I ever upset your country's law enforcement agencies!'

'That's not likely, either,' said Chad. 'We're strictly undercover on this one.'

'Yeah... of course you are!' Kevin sneered unpleasantly. 'About as undercover as my bedroom!'

'What's that supposed to mean?' demanded Bob.

'What... you hadn't noticed?' Kevin teased. 'Professionals like you? I *am* surprised. Aren't you supposed to be the clever ones? I told you... we coders get our kicks from proving we're smarter than everybody else... and the smarter the opposition think they are, the bigger the kick!' With a single click of the mouse, he changed the image on the screen showing his doorstep to one of the three of them standing in the room.

Chad and Bob threw panicked glances towards a small camera attached to the top of Kevin's wardrobe.

'As I'm sure you've already gathered... this footage and the conversation we've just had has been recorded onto my hard drive. Not that you should be too concerned about my use of the term *opposition* earlier. That applies purely to Penkridge, of course. But one can't be too careful these days. As you'll appreciate... it never hurts to have a little insurance when you're doing something you shouldn't. Now... I think that'll guarantee your cooperation, should I get into any trouble. In fact... I think that'll guarantee your cooperation full stop!'

Chad and Bob looked at each other with alarm.

'Melt back into obscurity, eh?' muttered Bob.

'So... I guess that makes us a team now!' Kevin smirked, a whole new edge to his voice.

*　　*　　*

'I told you it was a mistake!' shouted Bob angrily, scurrying along the street clutching the small bag of homemade cakes Kevin's mum had insisted they take with them. 'What the *hell* were we thinking?'

'That's what the hell was *I* thinking,' said Chad. 'It's the first rule of not getting caught... Make sure you're not being watched! Jeez... I'm so ring-rusty! I wouldn't have made such a beginner's mistake a few years ago.'

'I tried to warn you,' said Bob.

'And you weren't the only one. The little shit inferred *himself* he was a genius. Perhaps I should've taken him at his word and proceeded with a little more caution!'

'No perhaps about it!' smarted Bob. 'The guy's a liability... not least because he's also a friggin' loony! Did you happen to notice the posters covering his walls?'

'Ironically, those I *did* spot! So... he's a little too obsessed with computer games. That's the least of our worries right now!'

'I'm talking about those *others*... the ones of that babe displaying her two best assets.' Bob tried to mime his point without dropping the bag of cakes. 'It's been bugging me where I'd seen those beauties before!'

'Given your choice of reading material, that could be in any toilet on this planet,' said Chad, failing to see where the conversation was headed.

'Well... I now know the answer. And let me put it this way... The last time I saw 'em, I was unable to do anything about it because I needed both hands to cling to the tree I was hiding in!'

Chad shot him a sideways glance. '*Penkridge's* girl?'

'The very same,' nodded Bob.

'But what of it? I understand she used to be extremely popular over here a few years back.'

'And I can see why. But don't you think it slightly odd?'

'He's an acned adolescent. It's part of his rites of passage. *You* should appreciate that... given you don't ever appear to have stopped going through 'em!'

'It's bad enough you've given up applying logic to your thinking,' returned Bob. 'But what happened to your belief in a connection beyond coincidence?'

Chad stopped dead. It was a phrase he hadn't heard for some time... let alone considered. 'You don't reckon it *is* coincidence?'

'What if it's not?' Bob gave him a hard stare. 'What if his obsession with Penkridge is more serious than he's admitting to? What if it's about more than beating him at computer games or hacking? That's Penkridge's girl he's got plastered all over his walls. I'd say young Kevin back there actually wants to *be* Penkridge... in which case, we've just gone and saddled ourselves to something slightly more unstable than an acned adolescent!'

'Are you serious?'

'Deadly... As I reckon *he* could be.'

'So what if he is that obsessed?' Chad shrugged. 'As long as he is, he'll keep working for us until we achieve what we need.'

'Or are we now working for him… until *we* achieve what *he* needs?' suggested Bob. 'He's got us over a barrel. God knows the damage he could do if he ever finds reason to release that recording of us, encouraging him to break the law, to a wider world!'

* * *

Peter Snogden-Lambert squared up the few papers that were on his desk and set his pen to one side, allowing a jaunty enough angle to suggest work just completed. It was, of course, a lie… but his three o'clock appointment wouldn't know that.

Or would they?

The angle of the pen suddenly didn't look jaunty enough.

Or was it too jaunty?

By way of a compromise, he made an infinitesimal adjustment, then glanced anxiously at the clock on the wall.

One minute past three.

His appointment clearly didn't understand punctuality.

Not that it made any difference, being his only appointment of the day. It was the *principle* that mattered.

He drummed his fingers impatiently on the desk.

If he was being honest… it was his only appointment since *his* appointment, having been in the job only a couple of days. But that wasn't the point. Sure… he'd had visitors… a few of the ancillary workers having stuck their head through the door to introduce themselves and wish him luck.

If anyone had asked, Snogden-Lambert would have felt compelled to quickly point out that they'd stuck their heads through the door metaphorically, of course… unlike a previous appointment in a previous job who'd ended up sticking *his* through a radiator grill.

He glanced at the clock again.

Still one minute past three.

Perhaps the papers on his desk gave the wrong impression. Surely they should suggest work in *progress*?

He spread them out and uncapped his pen.

Better.

The hands on the clock moved to two minutes past three.

Now his appointment was *definitely* taking liberties.

Drumming his fingers on the desk again, he only stopped when he realised it was hurting him.

'Relax, Peter,' he muttered. 'Remember what your therapist told you... Nothing matters but your well-being.' He repeated the phrase a few times in his head and began to feel better for it.

As a series of deep breaths added to his increasing sense of calm, the hand of the clock cruelly moved again.

'What the *hell* is he playing at?' he yelled, before thrusting a knuckle between his teeth to achieve what the mantra had failed to do.

He'd only managed to let out a few whimpers before a knock on the door snapped him from his torment. Making a hasty grab for his pen, he pulled one of the sheets of paper in front of him and pretended to be in the process of writing. 'Come in!' he called out boldly.

The door opened.

'Mr Snogden-Lambert?' enquired his three o'clock appointment.

'Exactly as it says on the door,' replied Snogden-Lambert, a split second before he wished he hadn't. Would his appointment now think he had an issue with his name being on it? 'Not that I have an issue with it,' he added quickly. 'I'm just saying... that's my name...' He noticed his appointment looking at him oddly. 'On... the door,' he felt compelled to finish.

'Then I'm definitely in the right place,' smiled his appointment diplomatically.

'Not that there are too many places like this!' parried Snogden-Lambert civilly.

'No... indeed. It's quite impressive.'

'Mr Penkridge, I assume?'

'Yes... and I'm sorry if I'm a little late.'

'*Oh*... are you?' Snogden-Lambert feigned surprise with a telegraphed glance towards the clock. 'I've been so busy, I hadn't noticed.'

'Those stones must keep you on your feet,' joked Norman, trusting the remark wouldn't be seen as facetious.

He'd got that bit wrong.

'You'd be *amazed* at the trouble they can cause,' said Snogden-Lambert fractiously. 'It's not that easy, I can assure you! We get every wacko and space cadet down here believing they hold some personal and deeper meaning for them... though they don't ever seem to know exactly *what*.'

'I was under the impression you'd only just taken over,' said Norman, with surprise.

Snogden-Lambert realised he'd been caught building his part. 'Let's just say... I've heard stories,' he admitted, not wishing to dig a deeper hole. 'I've been doing a lot of reading up on the site as part of my therap...' He stopped himself before the spade hit the ground again. 'My... *training*,' he corrected himself sheepishly. 'Apparently, we attract them all... though I'm assured the majority are genuine tourists and history lovers, of course... fascinated at being in such close proximity to this wonderful, ancient site.'

'Although I understand you can't get right up to the stones anymore without an appointment,' checked Norman.

'God forbid!' exclaimed Snogden-Lambert in horror. 'No... We keep it tightly controlled these days. The stones are too precious. You'd be *amazed* at what some people want to do around them.'

'Really?' squeaked Norman.

'Oh, yes,' said Snogden-Lambert, with renewed authority. 'As an internationally recognised archaeological superstar, Stonehenge is at the top of most people's list when it comes to promoting harebrained schemes that would benefit from such an illustrious connection. We have to be incredibly robust with anyone wanting to associate themselves with this unique site.'

Norman smiled awkwardly. 'Of course.'

'So...' Snogden-Lambert placed his pen neatly on the desk. 'What can I do for you, Mr Penkridge?'

'I was hoping it might be the other way around,' Norman

replied, trusting this tactic would take him out of the *harebrained promotions* category. 'I don't know if you're aware of my history... but I've been fortunate enough – in recent years – to be able to engage in a number of philanthropic ventures, due to my financial situation... mostly within the art world.'

'I have to confess to having done a little research on you before our meeting,' admitted Snogden-Lambert smugly. 'Your name is well-known in circles within which I have been known to move. Your love of the arts is well documented... though I was under the impression it manifested itself more in the *buying* of art.' Snogden-Lambert gave the sort of angled look that was the polite way of saying "I think you might be lying".

'I prefer to keep my philanthropic excursions hush-hush,' countered Norman, placing a finger to his lips... mainly to hide the need to swallow his discomfort.

'*Oh...* I understand,' nodded Snogden-Lambert furiously, as if the secret had been divulged as a privilege.

'Having realised that's where my true destiny lies, I am now looking to spread my wings and indulge in two further passions of mine... music and archaeology... in the hope that both may benefit from my own good fortune.'

'Interesting,' said Snogden-Lambert, continuing his nodding.

'My idea is to raise what I believe are much needed funds for the maintenance of this extremely important site – as well as the archaeological community in general – by promoting a concert to celebrate this wonderful symbol of our country's heritage.'

Snogden-Lambert stopped his nodding... mainly because his neck was beginning to hurt... and stared Norman straight in the eye.

Norman resisted the urge to swallow again. Did the man in front of him realise that his reaction to what he'd just heard would determine the fate of the entire Universe?

Snogden-Lambert put his finger tips together and lent forward, his elbows firmly on the desk. 'Bravo!'

Norman wasn't sure if Snogden-Lambert was sarcastically

applauding sheer audacity – having seen right through him – or genuinely endorsing his plans. 'You *approve?*' he tiptoed.

'I most certainly do!' announced Snogden-Lambert, with the enthusiasm of a man who'd just seen a passport back to his former life. If he ensured he received some credit for the financial rewards that followed, his rehabilitation would be complete. He'd no longer be seen as a charitable case... a pariah to be pitied... a washed up failure no longer capable of great things. 'As you rightly point out, Mr Penkridge,' he fawned, 'such funds are much needed. Your admirable efforts will be greatly appreciated by all who come to benefit.' He meant *himself*, of course.

Norman couldn't believe his ears. He'd asked the question but hadn't expected such an easy answer. Having feared the problem for so long, he now felt a little shell-shocked. 'Great!' he stammered, raising his hands in surprise. 'Then we can start organising this thing right away!'

'Tell me... what kind of programme did you have in mind?' enquired Snogden-Lambert. 'A celebration of music by the great English masters, perhaps? After all... there's nothing that represents England's heritage more than this circle of marvellous stones. Such a thing would be wonderfully appropriate... don't you think?'

Norman braced himself for the next bit. Perhaps he'd been a little hasty in thinking it was a done deal. 'I was thinking of celebrating the music of Trou*zer*bulge,' he braved... stressing the middle syllable of the band's name as heavily as he could, in order to disguise its crude and puerile connotation.

Snogden-Lambert appeared to be running the name over in his mind. 'Trou*zer*bulge?' he enquired. 'Is he Czechoslovakian? I don't believe I know his work.'

Norman counted himself lucky for that. 'No,' he replied innocently. 'British.'

'Well, I never,' remarked Snogden-Lambert. 'Is he contemporary?'

'Very.'

'Then, I should think it'll make for a most interesting

occasion,' approved Snogden-Lambert.

'It'll definitely be that,' said Norman, looking at the floor.

'And when were you thinking of holding this concert, Mr Penkridge?'

In his excitement over Snogden-Lambert's cooperation, he'd completely forgotten about the final hurdle. It was as high as it had ever been. He hadn't crossed the finishing line yet. Taking a deep breath, he went for it. 'I was thinking we could start it on the night of the twentieth of June… and run it through into the morning of the twenty-first,' he ventured, waiting for the tirade of objections.

'The summer solstice,' remarked Snogden-Lambert, giving a sharp nod. 'How appropriate! I think that's a *splendid* idea!'

Norman wondered if he might be dreaming. He took a moment to check the situation before allowing himself the luxury of a smile. That was it… He'd done it! He was going to save the Universe after all… and it couldn't have been easier! Why on earth had he been so worried?

'And *where* were you thinking of holding this concert?'

'As close to the actual stones as possible,' replied Norman, with a confidence born of knowing that the man in front of him had proved himself to be extremely pliable… not to mention gullible.

Snogden-Lambert gave the matter some thought. 'Yes, that would make sense,' he concurred. 'In which case… I think we're talking Amesbury.'

'I beg your pardon?'

'Amesbury. It a small town about two miles from here. I'm sure it'll afford you all the facilities and infrastructure you'll need. If not, you're probably looking at Salisbury or Devizes.'

Norman faced the realisation that his final hurdle had been clipped. It was teetering precariously and about to come crashing to the ground. 'No, no!' he protested. 'I think you've misunderstood! I was looking to hold the concert… *here*.'

Snogden-Lambert stared at him in disbelief. '*Here?* At *Stonehenge?*' He snorted, barely able to believe what he'd heard. 'My dear Mr Penkridge… I'm afraid that would be *completely* out of the question!'

'Why?' asked Norman lamely.

'Because we're an international heritage site. We couldn't allow this area to be swamped by men and machinery... let alone a crowd of what I assume you hope would be many thousands. It'd be impossible!'

'What if it were a small crowd?' tried Norman, in desperation. 'Select... a few wealthy individuals... extremely well-behaved!'

'I'm sure they would be. But hardly appropriate, given this is a monument of the people... don't you think? Besides... your wishing to hold it over the summer solstice completely rules *that* possibility out, even if it were one we could consider in the first place. We attract our largest attendance at that particular time; something which can be a logistical and security headache. I'm not looking forward to my first time in charge on that day as it is! I certainly wouldn't want to do anything that *increased* that burden!'

'It *has* to be here!' insisted Norman, wondering if it was too early in the negotiation to mention the destruction of the Universe.

'Not even if the fate of the entire planet were at stake,' smiled Snogden-Lambert, putting paid to *that* particular avenue. 'I'm afraid you've had yourself a wasted journey, Mister Penkridge.' He rose from his chair. 'Though, I'd be happy to take you on a personal tour of the stones and our visitor centre, if you'd like. I'm more than happy to endorse your worthy project, wherever you end up having it. The benefit to us is obvious, of course. I'm just sorry it can't be here.'

'I'll make it worth your while,' said Norman, making a fist... as if to hold on to an imaginary rein attached to the *extremely* slim possibility of convincing the man in front of him to change his mind.

'I'm sure it would be worth our while *wherever* you hold it,' said Snogden-Lambert, nonplussed.

'No... not *your* while,' said Norman, acknowledging what was a short distance away outside the window. '*Your* while.' He drew the penultimate word out and gazed at Snogden-Lambert intently.

'*My* while?' asked Snogden-Lambert, confused.

'As in... Peter Snogden-Lambert... the name on the door.'

Snogden-Lambert's mood instantly changed. 'Am I understanding you correctly, Penkridge? Are you... *bribing* me?'

'Yes!' nodded Norman enthusiastically. 'Yes, I am!'

Snogden-Lambert seemed unsure as to how to act. He'd offended people in his office before... and look what *that* had led to! Unhappy memories came flooding back. 'I'm deeply offended,' he said, as politely as he could. He didn't want to risk causing offence of his own and antagonising the young, deluded man in front of him. 'I think it best we forget this conversation ever happened and let sleeping dogs lie,' he proposed, nervously scanning the view outside his window for the comforting sign of a high visibility jacket denoting security personnel.

'I'm talking *very* worth your while,' continued Norman, realising that if a line had been crossed, he had nothing to lose by pushing on further.

'I appreciate you're an extremely wealthy man,' responded Snogden-Lambert carefully. 'But I have been given something that your money cannot buy. *Trust.* There are those who have shown considerable faith in me at a time in my life when I probably least deserve it. If you think you can simply come in here and buy my loyalty, you do not understand what it means to be called Peter Snogden-Lambert.'

'I do actually,' said Norman, fixing him with a stare he knew Gabriel wouldn't approve of. 'You see... I did a little research of my own before we met.'

Snogden-Lambert twitched.

'Precisely,' said Norman. 'I'd say your debt to the art world is considerable, given you seem to have deprived it of one of its greatest paintings.'

The twitch was replaced by a sickening squeal and a knuckle in the mouth.

'What I'm offering you is a chance to atone for such a

heinous crime against culture by giving it back more than you took.'

Snogden-Lambert slowly lowered himself back into his chair.

'I understand your loyalty towards those who gave you this position of trust. It's extremely admirable. So, what better way to repay them than by showing you had the brilliance of mind to conceive an event that will net them...' Norman plucked a figure from the air, appreciating its size was immaterial, given his chequebook, '...two hundred and fifty million pounds!'

Snogden-Lambert made a noise Norman had never heard before.

'Yes... you heard right. Quarter of a *billion* pounds... paid to whichever cultural causes *you* personally deem fit. It won't be just a *door* your name will be on. Once it's been associated with such a large gift, I'm sure they'll have entire *buildings* named after you!'

Snogden-Lambert made the noise again.

'And to make that decision even easier... the concert won't be publicised. For those who want to know... it's simply a small event to mark the rising of the solstice sun. Any music will be limited to the hour before that happens and a few minutes after. That way, it won't draw any bigger crowd than you normally get. Furthermore... it'll be *your* idea... *your* vision. *You'll* take all the credit. I'll simply be the mystery benefactor you approached to finance your brilliant scheme... so impressed with your genius, imagination and foresight that I felt compelled to donate this vast sum towards it in your honour. Your name will reverberate throughout the cultural establishment for decades to come.'

'*Peter Snogden-Lambert,*' drooled the owner of it slowly.

'Sounds even better with a *Sir* in front of it, don't you think?' suggested Norman, looking to push more of the right buttons. 'I'm sure a quarter of a billion pounds will garner much appreciation from a certain *elite* section of society.' He turned his head and acknowledged a picture of the Queen that was hanging on the office wall.

Snogden-Lambert thrust his knuckle between his teeth again. 'I'd still need to get the necessary permissions,' he dribbled.

'I'm sure it can be done,' said Norman.

'I mean... it's not just down to me.'

'But you'll take all the glory. I'll see to that.'

'I'll need to run it by various committees.'

'I'm sure the individuals on them will be hard-pushed to vote against such a huge donation towards this country's heritage.'

'Contemporary, classical music, you say?'

'I'd stick to that description, if I were you,' advised Norman.

Snogden-Lambert gazed at a thought that had him kneeling on a cushion, awaiting a much-dreamed-of moment... one that would leave him requiring a longer nameplate for his door. Those that had doubted and mocked him would eat their words... for not *all* his friends and former colleagues had been so sympathetic to his plight. They knew who they were... and would certainly know it now! Talking of which... what of Mrs Snogden-Lambert? How would her bridge set react now? He pictured his estranged wife furiously cursing herself for having passed up the chance of becoming *Lady* Snogden-Lambert. The thought amused him, until his mind strayed further. What of Joan Fanshawe-Whittingham, his former personal assistant? Would she consider having that title in front of her *own* name worth forgetting his behaviour on the stretcher?

A heavy frown interrupted the romance, as the reason for him having been on it in the first place flooded back.

Oh, sweet revenge!

There was someone else who'd feel the full force of the sword about to be laid upon his shoulders.

Donald Tucker-Jenkins.

That filthy, jumped-up playwright... who'd caused his downfall... would realise he'd been beaten to the title by a better man.

He breathed heavily, as he pictured his nemesis. *He* might have thought it funny to masquerade as a tramp... presumably in order to try out some plot for one of his sordid, little plays. But Donald Tucker-Jenkins wouldn't be laughing much longer. It was Sir Peter Snogden-Lambert who'd have the final one of those!

* * *

'Ladies and Gentlemen... I *must* have silence... *please!*' Miriam Prudenberry raised her voice as loud as a woman of her age, upbringing, and loose-fitting dentures could, so as to bring order to the emergency meeting she'd called for the *Clairvoyants, Readers and Psychics of London Association*.

'Chance would be a fine thing!' yelled back one of those on the end of her request.

'Thank you, Doug. But I'll have you know I've been drafted in to bolster the alto section of the Thikston Women's Institute Choir for their performance of John Rutter's *Magnificat* a week next Sunday... and I'll be *buggered* if I'm going to ruin my voice keeping order here today!'

Her request finally brought calm to those facing the table she was standing behind. Alongside her sat a woman sporting a rainbow-coloured headscarf wrapped around a hairdo once fashionable at Woodstock and who projected a persona that suggested the only music *she* listened to was played on panpipes or a didgeridoo.

'I'm going to give Doris, on my left, the floor and ask that you listen carefully to what she has to say. I know a number of you here today opposed the inclusion of Tarot and palm readers into our association last month. But I think the information Doris has to impart vindicates having them on board. They're clearly encountering the same issues as the rest of us.'

The lady in the headscarf lent in close and whispered something in Miriam's ear.

'I'm sorry... I wasn't told,' Miriam announced stiffly. 'Right... I do beg your pardon. Having recently changed her name for whatever reason, we will now be hearing from...' She looked to the woman for confirmation. '*Serenity?*'

Serenity nodded and rose to address the meeting.

'Love and light to you all,' she started, drawing a large heart shape in the air with her hands. 'I'll keep this short… though I can't promise it'll be sweet. I know there is much to discuss here today and that what I'm about to say is just a small part of the strangeness we've all been experiencing lately. It is, however, hugely significant in my opinion, as the cards never lie.'

Not everyone in the room agreed, but Serenity was politely allowed her moment.

She used part of it to take a deep breath, so as to calm herself and build some tension. 'I'm here today to tell you about the inordinate occurrence of a particular card that has started presenting itself during Tarot readings up and down the country. I've been receiving communications, as spokesperson for the wider Tarot community, from many who are worried by this sudden phenomenon.'

'Just one second, Doris,' Miriam interrupted.

'Serenity,' she was corrected.

'Yes… *that* one. Are we talking communications from the living or the dead?'

Serenity looked at her nonplussed. 'The living, of course! I'm talking about fellow practitioners.'

'Okay, dear. I just wanted to clear that one up. Carry on!'

Serenity attempted to re-establish the tension by facially steeling herself for her next revelation. 'The card to which I refer is no less than… the Ten of Swords, ladies and gentlemen!'

There were a few sympathetic murmurs from those in the know… along with various shrugs, blank faces and a couple of purposely loud tuts from those who weren't.

'For any of you not familiar with the craft,' she expanded, her voice quavering, 'the Ten of Swords is the most destructive card that can be drawn from the pack!' She grasped the Eye of Horus amulet hanging around her neck and muttered a brief incantation to herself, before continuing nervously. 'It presages a period of utter devastation... and can be seen as symbolising death more than the Death card itself!'

To many in the room, death was not a problem. Dealing every day with those who'd experienced it, such a thing was no more than a one-way door they could converse through and would eventually have to use themselves. Utter devastation, on the other hand...

'The thing is... I've yet to encounter a single reader of the Tarot who *hasn't* turned this card over in nearly every reading they've given in the last few days. As I'm sure you'll appreciate... such an occurrence is unheard of... the chances of it happening being astronomically remote. But the portents don't stop there! The Tower card – which represents sudden change and abandonment of the past – as well as the Devil card, are *also* appearing with worryingly high frequency. Not only is having to give such negative readings *extremely* bad for repeat business... I believe we are standing on the brink of something truly awful!' She rapidly drew her heart shape in the air, mouthed *thank you*, and quickly sat herself down.

'Well... there you have it,' said Miriam, rising to her feet again. 'And I think we all share *Serenity's* concern, given what's been going on during our own dealings with the spirit world.'

'They're not even allowing me to sleep at night!' said a voice from the floor. 'I've tried shutting myself down, but it's like they've got a foot in the door. They're no respecter of pyjamas!'

'You should worry!' said another. 'I tried to whisper sweet nothings to my wife the other night and ended up getting my face slapped after what came out of my mouth!'

'It's only a question of time until the press pick up on it,' said another. 'And then we'll be a laughing stock!'

'You mean... more than usual,' added another caustically.

The following hour and a half was spent swapping harrowing accounts of unwanted spiritual activity, until Miriam Prudenberry glanced at the clock on the wall and drew the discussion to a close.

'Well... I'm not sure we've resolved anything,' she said. 'But at least we know we're not all going mad.' She looked at the faces looking at hers. 'At least, not individually. Now... before I officially end this meeting... is there anything anyone wants to raise under *any other business?*'

A lady in horn-rimmed glasses and matching nose raised her hand.

'Yes, Margery?'

Margery coughed awkwardly, as if not wanting to make a fuss, but feeling it might be necessary. 'It's about our recent change of acronym,' she squirmed.

* * *

'Jesus... Waggy... It's in fuckin' G!' shouted Stump at his bandmate, who was struggling to hold a bass guitar and remain upright at the same time.

'Okay, Stump,' mumbled Waggy, through a chemically induced haze. 'Go easy with me. It's been a while.'

'But it's *always* been in fuckin' G! How long have we been playing *Bend Over Barbara?*'

'I think it's the alliteration that's confused him,' said a cadaverous figure, a V-shaped guitar around his neck threatening to drag him to the ground. 'He was trying to play it in B.'

'Well... he's gonna be fucked when we get to *Wet Willie Winkie*, then!' barked Stump aggressively. 'There ain't such a note!'

'I'm sure I could find it, if I look far enough up my fretboard,' drawled Waggy, somewhere other than his presence suggested.

'I don't believe this!' Stump groaned, pushing the tangle of sweat-matted hair back from his forehead. 'We've been given the chance to play in front of the most famous Neolithic monument in the world... and you can't concentrate long enough to sort out your musical fuckin' alphabet!'

'Alright, Stump,' chipped in the drummer. 'We're all a little rusty. You know Waggy'll get it in the end.'

'He fuckin' *will* get it in the end,' insisted Stump. Cos I'll shove this bloody mic stand right up it if he doesn't!'

'Whoa, whoa, whoa!' yelled the guitarist, waving his arms through a haze of smoke and alcohol fumes. 'This ain't getting us nowhere.'

'*Anywhere!*' said Stump, gritting his teeth. 'This ain't getting us *anywhere*! Ain't getting us nowhere means it *is* getting us *somewhere*. And it *AIN'T!* You know how I hate double negatives!'

'Oooh… sorry, Lord Byron!' cooed the guitarist, grinning at the others.

'And less of your facetiousness, Fungus. Words are extremely important to a verbal aesthete like me. I challenge you to find any double negatives in *my* lyrics.'

'Perish the thought… They're too bleedin' full of smutty innuendos to leave room for anything else!' retorted the guitarist.

The argument was brought to an abrupt halt by the deafening crash of a cymbal.

'Why do we always descend to this level when we get together?' shouted the drummer, slamming his sticks down on his snare drum. 'It never used to be this way in the early days!'

'That was before some of us developed egos,' winked Fungus.

'Surely it should be… *is not* getting us anywhere,' Waggy mumbled, with half-open eyes.

The others stared at him blankly.

'What Stump said earlier,' he slurred, his thoughts struggling to keep pace. '*Ain't* should be *is not*… if we're bothering to be *literally* correct, that is.'

'Okay, you cocky shite,' Stump rounded on the swaying bass player angrily. 'Try this one for size… Given your mouth is as disconnected from your brain as your fuckin' fingers… and your speech is as sloppy as your playing… did you mean literally as in… a literal manner or sense… or were you trying to be extra clever by referring to it as in… a *literary* sense… *actually* meaning to say *literarily* correct?'

Waggy lurched unsteadily and blew out his cheeks.

'Give him a break,' winced Fungus. 'He doesn't currently

know a B from a G!'

Stump placed a foot on his monitor and slouched in frustration. 'I dunno why I bother! It's not as if I couldn't be focusing on a solo career right at this moment!'

'Oh... here we go again!' groaned the drummer, throwing his head back in anticipation of a familiar rant.

'Well... you tell me why not!' shouted Stump irritably.

'Because you ain't *Trouzerbulge*,' the drummer yelled back. 'Not on your own, you ain't.'

'*Are not*,' Waggy belched.

'Oh... so people are coming to see *you* are they... bongo boy?' sneered Stump childishly. 'I don't think so... seeing as you're stuck at the fuckin' back and don't even play *notes!*'

'They come because they wanna see us *all*,' countered the drummer. 'That's why you're having to suck in that huge ego of yours and suffer our double negatives!'

'If it wasn't for me, we wouldn't be here at all!' bellowed Stump.

'And if it wasn't for *us*, you wouldn't have anything to squawk over!' retorted the drummer.

'*Squawk?*'

'Oh... come on! Guys! Guys! Give it a break!' pleaded Fungus, putting his guitar down. 'This is getting us nowhere... or ain't getting us anywhere! If we're gonna do this thing at all, let's just bury the hatchet for the time it takes and concentrate solely on the music. We're gonna be playing in front of a sacred site. So let's treat this thing with the respect it deserves.'

'Concentrate seems a good idea to me,' said Stump, glowering at Waggy, whose confused lips were now wrestling with the introduction of the wrong end of a cigarette.

'This could be huge for us,' said Fungus. 'Playing Stonehenge at the summer solstice is gonna be one of *the* musical events of the decade. It'll cement our legendary status... not to mention increase sales of our back catalogue!'

'Precisely,' agreed Stump. 'Which is why we can't afford to mess this one up. The eyes of the world are gonna be upon us.'

'And those of the aliens who built it,' added Waggy blearily.

Fungus saluted the idea by giving him the sign of the horns.

Waggy belched a late full stop to the end of his sentence.

'Alright... at least we're all agreed on that,' said the drummer. 'So... a question... Given the importance of the site, how exactly did this Penkridge fella manage it? I mean... if you'd asked me a few days ago, I wouldn't have given him a cat in hell's chance of getting permission for us to play there.'

'He hasn't yet,' admitted Stump, taking his eyes elsewhere.

'*What!*' The drummer stood up in horror. 'No permission? Then, what the bleedin' hell are we all doing here?'

'Making sure we're ready when he does!' replied Stump defiantly.

'And what makes you so sure he's gonna succeed?' snorted Fungus, sharing a look of solidarity with the drummer.

'Listen. If someone as square and geeky as *that* kid can steal Xanthia away from *me*... I believe he can do anything he says he can!'

There was silence in the room.

'Fair point,' conceded the drummer, readying his sticks.

Fungus shouldered his guitar.

'Okay... *Bend Over Barbara*... in G... after four... One, two, three...'

'Did I ever meet this Barbara?' interjected Waggy unsteadily.

'We all did... *remember?*' said Fungus.

Waggy furiously rubbed his nose. 'In that case... anyone got any blow before we start again? It might help me recall the incident... not to mention the song.'

'Sorry, mate,' grimaced Fungus, shaking his head. 'I ain't got none.'

'FOR *FUCK'S* SAKE!' wailed Stump.

* * *

Gabriel had been right. Dark things indeed were beginning to materialise. But whilst Norman believed the stag in the road to be no accident – much like the fire at his hotel – the demons he feared most were those now materialising from within.

Ironically, Gabriel's reappearance had been the catalyst for their stirring. His disappointment at Norman and his use of the chequebook had turned suppressed feelings of guilt into far more destructive ones of failure.

Guilt he could live with. Sure... it made him feel ugly inside. But that was nothing compared to what he'd always experienced on the *outside*. Failure, on the other hand, was something he thought he'd consigned to the past.

And now its bedfellows were awakening too. Old feelings of inadequacy and exclusion were threatening to haunt him, released from their slumber by the one person who'd helped put them to sleep in the first place... Xanthia. Her continued indifference towards him had clouded his newfound sense of who he was. For the first time in a long while, he no longer felt in control.

To make matters worse, a positive decision from Snogden-Lambert's superiors looked less likely the more time passed. His optimism had been naive. Norman pictured the rejection being politely prepared by those less gullible than a man whose mental fragility had been taken advantage of. It felt like he was simply waiting to be put out of his misery.

Comforting himself with the fact there was nothing more he could do about it, he'd told himself the fate of the Universe was now in the hands of the gods... until he remembered it wasn't. It was in *his*... which brought him full circle.

Maintaining her air of detachment, Xanthia had taken herself off to be pummelled by the hotel's masseur... a square-jawed Adonis named Brad, whose arms were thicker than Norman's legs. Imagining her moaning in ecstasy at the touch of Brad's powerful hands, he'd attempted to drown out the thought by switching on the television and watching the news. But as an item on unexplained crop failures around the world had been followed by an even more depressing one about a sudden global rise in suicide rates, he'd decided to go for a walk, lest he added to the alarming statistics.

If hoping fresh air would clear his head, the smell of traffic fumes refused to play ball. And rather than reaffirming his identity by reacquainting himself with London streets, the sight of busy pedestrians skilfully avoiding his meandering passage merely highlighted his lack of direction and sense of isolation.

A stray dog, taking a keen interest in him, seemed scant consolation.

Passing an advert in a travel agent's window, he stopped. It showed a group of young people jumping in the air and enjoying it ludicrously more than the activity warranted.

Were they really that happy?

Comparing the manufactured image of fun in the sun with the one he'd tried to create for himself and Xanthia in France, it suddenly struck him that his own was equally as fraudulent.

The dog – now joined by another – barked in agreement.

The irony hit home that the very privileges he'd surrounded himself with – in an attempt to reinvent himself and become part of normal society – had merely ensured his exclusion from it. Secrecy concerning the acquisition of his wealth made that all but impossible.

Had Xanthia now realised it too? Was that why she was keeping her distance? Was she working out how best to extricate herself from an unhealthy situation?

Frantic barking from behind alerted him to the fact his canine stalkers had inexplicably grown into a pack... its attention on him.

Sensibly moving on, his thoughts focused on Xanthia. Had she been just another prop in his reinvention? Appreciating her beauty for most of his adolescent life, had he used his good fortune to capture and possess it, much like he had the paintings on his walls? In achieving that goal, had he weaned her away from her comfort zone... selfishly ignoring the fact that as the colour increased in his world, it had slowly drained from hers? Is that what she'd been trying to tell him in the restaurant the other night?

Her words had stung more than he knew she realised. He'd worked extremely hard over the past few years not to feel unworthy of her attention or inadequate in her presence. But those feelings had returned... the car accident dredging up memories of character traits he thought he'd buried forever.

The trouble with burying things is that they still exist to be dug up... and the spade had cut the turf when she'd called him *boring* and said her life lacked excitement.

This to the man who'd been called upon to save the Universe not once... but TWICE! How ironic was that!

Rubbing salt into the wound, she'd cited Stump as an example of how he could improve himself... the antidote to her boredom apparently a hedonistic lover and unstable romantic... the antithesis of himself. How could someone who once sought solace in the infallibility of circuit boards ever hope to compete with that? Stump was everything he wasn't... passionate, dangerous, and exciting. Much like his dips, in fact.

Catching his reflection in the window of a crowded wine bar, he momentarily stopped and wondered what those on the other side saw when looking back at him. Was the only thing with which he could impress them, his wealth? Without his paintings around him, was he just a faceless nonentity?

Another spade struck the soil as he realised no one *was* looking back at him... except the dogs, who were now baring their teeth and salivating.

Concerned for his safety, he pressed swiftly on, hoping to outpace their interest.

Eventually, he found himself entering familiar territory. Setting out without a destination, he'd instinctively headed in the direction of his old bedsit. Memories of his solitary existence there came flooding back.

Surely the decisions he'd made since escaping it couldn't be *that* wrong? Had you told him back then he'd be with the girl of his dreams and rich beyond his wildest ones, he'd have assumed you were either mad or a pretty lousy clairvoyant. Even his hopes of becoming a celebrated computer games programmer hadn't seen him envisaging *that* level of success.

Spikey!

The little metal aardvark jumped from a forgotten corner of those memories, taking him completely by surprise. It had been a while since he'd thought about him. Once upon a time that would have seemed unimaginable. They were going to live the dream together... the indefatigable aardvark bouncing his way to fame whilst Norman basked in the rewards it brought. But he'd shamelessly abandoned his two-dimensional cavorting companion, without a second thought, once a three-dimensional one had entered his life.

The guilt returned... though curiously accompanied by a warm surge of nostalgia.

Having spent the last five years trying to disassociate himself from everything to do with his past, this new emotion puzzled him. He'd always viewed his time in the bedsit as one of loneliness, despair, and very little else. If he ever looked back on those times, he did so as if viewing them in black and white...

...and yet... now...

Trying to figure out his conflicting emotions, he suddenly came upon a wide, intersecting pavement that prevented further progress in the direction he'd been travelling. Eight busy lanes of assorted vehicles making their way to and from Marble Arch provided a daunting wall of traffic in front of him.

A hasty glance behind revealed that, far from losing interest, the dogs had spread out on either side, in what looked like an attempt to encircle him.

He was trapped.

Determined not to panic, he wondered what Stump would do in his predicament. After all... given Xanthia believed he was so wonderful, he'd clearly have the perfect answer... wouldn't he?

The advance of the dogs suggested he'd better discover it quickly.

Picturing himself in the wild man's boots, he imagined Xanthia looking on adoringly... expecting him to do something dashing and outrageous.

That *something*, when it came, surprised even himself.

Throwing caution to the wind and thumbing his nose at the risk, he launched himself from the pavement on a reckless dash across the competing lanes of traffic, much to the consternation of the startled motorists.

The dogs seemed astonished too.

Dancing to the sound of screeching tyres and angry car horns, he jigged and weaved his way through the mechanical minefield until reaching the far side in a breathless but triumphant state. His pumping adrenalin – coupled with the fact he was still alive – caused him to burst out laughing.

He threw his head back and yelled at the top of his voice. 'Spikey! You'd have been proud of that manoeuvre!'

A young mother – struggling with a pushchair and hand-holding infant – tutted her disapproval and pulled the child a little closer as she passed.

But at least she'd noticed him!

Reinvigorated by his act of spontaneity, and freed from the threat of the dogs, he carried on with a lighter step through the ornate, metal gate that welcomed visitors into the green tranquillity of Hyde Park... the Bayswater Road away to his right and his old stomping ground close by.

Not that he'd done much stomping in it... *unlike Spikey*.

Further thoughts of the metal-one made him realise just how much he'd missed the little aardvark... vowing to dust off the necessary codes when he finally had some time and resurrect his old jumping friend again... just for fun.

And that's when the truth hit him.

His idea of fun would forever be what most people considered boring and insular. That was the *true* Norman. Whether it was computer programming or being obsessive about his collection of art... that's who he was. Try as he might, he would never come close to being anything like Stump or the kind of person he assumed Xanthia would want to spend the rest of her life with. Using Gabriel's gift to try and make it otherwise had only proven him a charlatan.

Now he was paying the price.

His adrenalin giving way to a stitch, his smile disappeared.

If the walk had achieved anything, it had shown him that the one thing you could never get away from was yourself.

Which led to a sobering thought. If his past decision-making had proven to be so bad, what hope the fate of the Universe? Having been placed in his hands, that burden was his and his alone. Gabriel had warned him from the outset that there'd be no outside help. The choices he was currently making would determine if it actually continued to exist! So what if he got *those* decisions wrong? Given his abysmal track record, how could he be sure he was taking the right paths?

Just as the thought occurred, he found himself coming upon a spot overlooking the Serpentine he would visit in the past whenever life crowded in too much and needed sorting.

He'd been there many times.

A lady – floating indifferently between her sixties and seventies – was sitting alone on his favourite bench. She looked at him and smiled.

'Mind if I join you?' he asked.

'Feel free, darlin',' she cackled back, moving her handbag so as to accommodate him.

He nodded his appreciation and sat beside her... watching as the ducks, coots, and moorhens paddled one way and then the other on the water in front of them... some breaking off to scout for bread being thrown... the others chasing manically when it was.

'Helps put things in perspective, don't it?' she said, as if reading his mind.

'I used to come here a lot,' he replied.

'Moved away, did you?'

'In many senses.'

'Sometimes it's good to go back,' she counselled. 'Helps you evaluate whether the journey you've taken has been in the right direction.'

'That's very profound,' he said, hearing the echo of previous thoughts.

'Not really, dearie... Just common sense.'

He sighed.

'Things not how you'd like 'em to be?' she asked.

Norman didn't answer.

'Sorry,' she apologised quickly. 'I didn't mean to be nosey.'

'It's alright,' he said, alleviating her embarrassment with a thin smile. 'It's not your asking... I just don't know if I have the answer.'

'I think you'd be surprised at how many people would tell you that, if only they were honest enough,' she laughed. 'We all go about thinking we're supposed to know what we're doing... but we don't really. Most of us put on a front and just pretend. I think your honesty's very refreshing, young man. The fact you know you don't know what you're supposed to know means you probably know more than you think you do... if that makes any sense!'

'Perfect sense, actually,' he nodded.

'So where are you now?' she asked, folding her arms and giving herself a hug.

'The South of France,' said Norman, conjuring up a picture of the view from his lounge and wishing he could be there at that precise moment.

'Oh... *very* nice,' she sung.

'It is,' he reminisced.

'But what I meant was... where are *you* now?'

Norman looked at her directly.

'And don't say... *at a crossroad*, darlin'' she smiled. 'There's no such thing.'

'I'm sorry... I don't follow.'

'Well... people always say they're standing at a crossroad when facing a major dilemma, don't they? But that's just daft. A crossroad gives you three choices... assuming you can't go backwards... which is clearly wrong. And if the dilemma is *that* bad, one of those options shouldn't be to carry straight on! It also suggests a drastic change in direction... and life ain't always like that. Sometimes it only requires a minor alteration.'

Norman reflected on her points. 'Perhaps it's more like a roundabout,' he suggested. 'Multiple routes to take... but if you can't decide, you end up going round and round in circles and getting nowhere!'

The lady looked at him askance. 'Goodness me! No wonder you've had to come and sit on this bench, young man. Life's *much* easier than that!'

'It doesn't feel like it at the moment,' he admitted.

'Maybe not. But that's because you haven't considered forks.'

'I beg your pardon?'

'Forks in the road, dearie... as opposed to crossroads.' She carefully smoothed out her skirt and crossed her ankles contentedly. 'That's all problems ever are... forks.'

'But that would suggest I only ever have two choices... wouldn't it?'

'It would... and you do. You can either do something or not. Simple, ain't it! Makes you wonder why people think life's so complicated.' Her attention turned to a squirrel scrambling its way up the trunk of a nearby tree.

'But it *is* complicated!' Norman insisted. 'Especially mine, right now!'

She looked at him again. 'I told you... that's because you haven't considered your forks. Most people don't. They go through life blindly making it up as they go along. Little wonder they get themselves into such a mess! But no matter how complicated it can seem, life's nothing more than a string of simple choices. We make 'em every time we have a thought. I mean... do I sit here continuing to talk to you... or do I come up with an excuse to be elsewhere and leave you to work out whatever it is you need to for yourself? If I decide to stay... do I tell you to pull yourself together... or try and understand your problems? They're all forks needing a considered approach as to which way to go. The secret is to break it down to the smallest one... cos the smaller the fork, the smaller the dilemma... and the smaller the dilemma, the easier it is to resolve. See how it works?' Her expression changed. 'That don't mean you can leave any to chance,' she cautioned sternly. 'The decision you take at every one determines the next fork you'll encounter. But this is the best bit...' Her maternal manner returning, she hugged her bosom excitedly. 'It's *you* who chooses which way to go. So, unlike what most people tend to think... your fate's entirely in your own hands. It's *you* who are in charge!'

She rummaged in her handbag and pulled out some bread she'd been saving for the ducks.

'You make it sound a bit like computer programming,' said Norman, warming to the similarities.

'I'll have to take your word for that, darlin'' she chuckled. 'I'm a little behind the times when it comes to that sort of thing!'

'It's just solving a particular problem by making a string of binary choices,' explained Norman. 'I'm actually very good at it.'

'Well... in that case... you shouldn't have a problem working out which forks to take! Getting to where you need to be should be easy for someone like you!'

She threw the bread with impressive accuracy, causing a flurry of activity on the water.

'But knowing how to get somewhere isn't the same as knowing which way to go,' pointed out Norman. 'And that's precisely my problem! How do I decide which forks to take if I'm unsure what I want my future to be?'

'Oh, no, dearie... you misunderstand me,' she smiled, tilting her head and appreciating the warmth of the sun. 'I'm not talking about your final *destination*. None of us are smart enough to calculate in advance the millions of forks that will eventually take us there! That would be impossible! No... I'm talking about an *ideal*... cos that's all you can ever hope to aim for. But if you use it as your guide every time you encounter an individual fork, that final destination will logically turn out to be your *ideal* one! So... instead of causing doubt and fear, think of each fork encountered as another exciting opportunity to move you further towards it!'

Norman looked puzzled. 'An *ideal*? That sounds a little vague. What exactly do you mean?'

She turned to face him, her eyes twinkling. 'It's nothing more than the way you wish to be,' she answered. 'Your most important destination ain't a big house or fancy possessions with which to fill it. It's who you end up *being*... the person that looks back at you from the mirror.'

'This is rather unsettling,' said Norman, turning away

uncomfortably.

'*Really*, my love? Why's that?'

'You've hit upon everything I've been worrying about recently! It's uncanny!'

'Maybe not *that* uncanny,' she corrected him. 'I think you'll find it's what most people worry about at some point in their lives. But like I said… that's because they tend to make it up as they go along. Trust me… Determine your ideal and the forks will sort themselves!'

Norman *did* trust her. Her words were warm and comforting, giving him a welcome sense of hope. But something still puzzled him.

'If I've lost my way, how do I know what my ideal *is*?'

The lady looked bemused. 'What… you tellin' me you don't know whether you want to be a good or bad person… selfish or unselfish… positive or negative? That's all those things are, dearie… Forks! You only have two blinkin' options each time you encounter one. It's not *that* difficult! Always take the one that best suits the type of person you wish to be and you'll never go wrong.'

'But can it *really* be that simple?' he asked, desperate to hear that it was.

'It is, if you see acceptance of the fact as just another fork to be approached positively!' she smiled.

Norman allowed a broad grin to redesign his face. Apart from his recent flirt with death-by-traffic, it was a while since *that* had happened. 'You're very good, you know!' he complimented her.

'See… you just took the right direction there!' she chortled. 'And that's another thing… The way you approach your forks can be contagious… for good *or* ill. You were positive, just then… and people like to hear positive things said about 'em. It makes 'em feel better… and more likely to approach their *own* forks in a similar manner. It's not unlike ripples on that pond.' She nodded towards the water. 'The effect gets multiplied. And if we all approached our forks positively, who *knows* what could be achieved in this world!'

She clasped her hands together and smiled at the birds going about their paddling.

'I wish I'd met you here some years ago,' he said, mesmerised by her contented manner. 'I think we could've had some interesting chats on this bench!'

'I'm just saying it as it is,' she shrugged. 'Nothing that good ol' common sense couldn't tell you.'

'Maybe that's why it strikes a chord,' he smiled.

'I always think that's when you know something's right. So...' She brushed her skirt nonchalantly. 'You haven't answered my question.'

'I beg your pardon?'

'I asked you where you were... remember?'

'Oh, yes... you did,' he nodded. 'And I have to confess... I would not only have said at a crossroad... I'd have probably pictured something more akin to Spaghetti Junction! I just hope it's not too late to untangle the mess I've made of all my *past* forks!'

'It's never too late for that, dearie. Just so long as you remember... it's not the forks themselves that are the problem... it's how you choose to approach them that *really* matters.' She smiled and looked up at the sky. 'Now, I think I'm gonna make that excuse and leave. It must be getting late.'

'Thank you,' said Norman, as she struggled to her feet.

'You're welcome, darlin'. I reckon you'll be alright now.'

Norman wanted to tell her that he would do everything in his power to make sure she was too... that he would succeed in his task and guarantee her a future... that she'd be able to watch the birds on the water for many years to come.

'That's a nice thought,' she said, tottering away.

Norman was startled. '*Pardon?*'

The lady gently raised her hand as a parting gesture and continued walking.

'It *was* only a thought,' he called out after her.

She didn't answer.

'*Gabriel?*' he sung tentatively.

Again... there was no reply.

'It *is* you... isn't it?' he said a little more firmly. He quickly looked around himself, then sprinted after her.

'Anything the matter, lovey?' she asked, continuing her progress, whilst maintaining the same look of contentment on her face.

'Is that you, Gabriel?' he asked, awkwardly.

'That's a *man's* name,' she remarked.

'It's an angel's name,' responded Norman, looking for a reaction.

'*Archangel...* dearie,' she corrected him.

Her manner suggested he was right. But he could hardly tackle an old lady to the ground.

That gave him an idea.

What if he tried to see if she were solid?

'Best not,' she said sweetly. 'We were getting on so well. It'd be a shame to spoil it.'

'I know you're him!' he insisted. 'You're reading my mind!'

'It's a gift, dearie. I've always had it.'

'Gabriel!'

The woman finally stopped. 'Would you rather I was him?' she asked. 'Only... you seemed quite happy to listen to what I had to say and take my advice. If you're saying you're actually in touch with such a lofty, spiritual being as an *Archangel*, surely you wouldn't have needed to seek out that bench in the first place.'

'Your advice was... *different*,' he stuttered.

'No,' said the woman firmly. 'Your *listening* was different. You didn't see me as a challenge to your beliefs or someone to mentally spar with. You judged me only on what I said... not on what you expected to hear or hoped to gain. Perhaps you should do the same with your Gabriel. Perhaps you might *then* be truly able to get to know him.' She paused. 'I've enjoyed our... *chat*,' she said, with a twinkle in her eye.

Norman felt unsure as to what to do next.

'It's another of those forks. You need to approach it with a positive mind... remember? Go home to those that love you,' she advised him, 'and listen to them in the same way you listened to me. And one final piece of advice... Don't make the mistake of using your prejudices and expectations to misinterpret what is being said. It's possible to think too much, sometimes. Our thoughts can trip us up.'

As the thought of tripping entered his consciousness, he shot a reflex look towards her feet.

The woman quickly retracted them under her long skirt.

Were they brogues she was wearing?

'Like I said... don't read too much into everything,' she remarked.

Norman's shoulders dropped. 'Okay... I get the message. But if you're not Gabriel... though I strongly suspect you are... you're definitely an angel.'

'That's a lovely thought, dearie. See... you've just approached another fork in a positive manner. Keep that going and who knows what you'll achieve!'

'Just one thing before you go,' he said, stalling her departure. 'Did *I* imagine you like this... or was it your idea?'

'Now... how do you think an angel would answer that?'

'Dunno.'

'That's probably because of your not listening to them properly. I'm sure an angel would tell you that both are possible at the same time... wouldn't they?'

'That's the bit I have trouble with,' he admitted.

'Then keep listening. Because I think you'll find angels come in many guises.'

With that, she toddled off... Norman staying put until she'd disappeared out of sight... the path becoming obscured by bushes.

As he turned to go home, a car alarm sounded in the direction of where he'd last seen her.

*   *   *

Having inserted the plastic key card into the slot above the door handle, Norman entered his hotel suite with a far better head than the one with which he'd left it.

257

'Is that you, Norman?' sung Xanthia's voice from the bathroom.

He popped his head around the door and decided to apply his new knowledge of forks. 'Good massage?' he asked positively.

'He was the best,' she cooed, responding to his amicability. 'He reached areas I didn't know I had!'

'I know the feeling!' he smiled.

She looked at him for a brief second, as if trying to work out why that should be... then gave up. 'I'm just rounding it off with a nice, relaxing bath.'

'I can see.'

'Did you go far?' she asked, only her head visible above a huge pile of bubbles threatening to spill over onto the marble floor.

He smiled again. 'You could say that. It's been quite a journey!'

She blew some of the foam away. 'Someone called for you while you were out.'

'In person?'

'By phone.' She struggled to recall the message. 'Peter...' She struggled even more with the next bit. '*Kiss a sheep, Bert?*'

'Snogden-Lambert.'

'That's the one! He wants you to call him. Says he may be able to get an agreement... but with conditioner.'

'That's what you put on your hair, Xan. I think he probably said... *conditions*.'

'I thought it was strange!' she exclaimed.

'Did he say anything else?'

'Yes.'

Norman waited.

'*Well?*'

Xanthia frowned at the curtness of his follow up. As far as she was concerned, she'd answered the question perfectly.

'What else did he say, Xan?'

She looked at him nonplussed. 'He said... *goodbye*.'

Norman nodded. 'I'll call him back.'

Snogden-Lambert was in an extremely jovial mood as he answered the phone. What Norman didn't know was that he'd been practising lifting the receiver for the majority of that afternoon and addressing himself as Sir Peter... trying to do so as nonchalantly as possible whilst still getting the point across.

'You wanted to speak to me,' prompted Norman.

'Indeed I did... or should I say... indeed I do!' replied Snogden-Lambert playfully. 'It seems we might be tantalisingly close to getting permission for your concert to go ahead, Mr Penkridge!'

Whilst delighted it wasn't the rejection he'd been expecting, it still wasn't the positive decision Norman needed.

'*Close?*'

'Well... *closer*, Mister Penkridge.'

'Please... call me Norman.'

'Peter,' said Snogden-Lambert.

'No... *Norman*.'

'Yes... That's my name!'

'You're Norman *too?*'

'No... Peter.'

'Is this a bad line?' asked Norman, pointlessly taking a moment to stare into the end of the receiver. 'My name's not Peter... it's NORMAN!'

'Yes, I know. I meant... you can call *me* Peter.'

'Right,' said Norman, wondering how that had gotten to be so difficult and hoping it wasn't a sign of things to come. 'Though I'm sure that's soon to be... *Sir* Peter,' he offered, keen to maintain Snogden-Lambert's motivation.

He heard the same strange squeal Snogden-Lambert had given in his office.

'Your offer has certainly caused quite a stir!' said Snogden-Lambert, once he'd removed his hand from his mouth. 'It appears the size of your generosity might have softened even the hardest of our potential objectors.'

'I was hoping that'd be the case,' said Norman, relieved.

'But we still have a *little* way to go,' Snogden-Lambert

cautioned. 'There's some concern at just how close to the stones you wish to have the performance.'

'As near as possible,' interjected Norman hastily. 'That's the whole point of it.'

'I assumed as much. So... moving swiftly to the next question that's been raised... Will this be an entirely *acoustic* concert?'

'No,' said Norman cautiously. 'There will be some amplification involved.'

'*Ah...*' said Snogden-Lambert slowly, his voice changing. 'We rather feared that might be the case.' He gave an exploratory chuckle. 'It's been suggested by some of those potential objectors that the vibrations from any electronic speakers you intend using may pose a threat to the stability of the structure.' Quickly adding as an aside... 'You have to bear in mind that there are a number of rather old fuddy-duddies on the committees involved. However... I've assured them that such a concern is completely ridiculous. But I have to ask the question... This isn't going to be a *loud* concert, is it... Norman?'

Norman considered his next response extremely carefully. He was aware of Gabriel's warning about breaking any laws... and he assumed that included not giving a dishonest statement during what might be seen as contractual negotiations. 'I guarantee that it'll be an appropriate volume for the occasion,' he said firmly.

'Splendid!' remarked Snogden-Lambert, relieved to find no nasty obstacles blocking the way to his knighthood. 'That's what I thought. Now... the *other* question that's arisen concerns the choice of music you've proposed. I do happen to know that the current chairman of one of the committees involved is particularly partial to Sibelius. Now... whilst I'm sure this Trou*zer*bulge fellow is extremely good – given your desire to bring his music to the attention of a wider public – might you also consider the inclusion of a few *other* composers in your programme? It may help sway any stragglers to our cause.'

Norman found himself facing a rather critical fork much sooner than expected. Allowing others to steer him along the wrong path could prove fatal. He recalled the old lady's advice about fate being in his own hands and that it wasn't the forks themselves that were the problem, but the way you chose to approach them.

He put her words into action.

'I'm afraid that's not an option,' he said assertively. 'If those who make the decision want my money, they must allow me my artistic freedom. If the chairman... or whoever... wishes to turn down two hundred and fifty million pounds because of a lack of Sibelius on the programme, I guess they'll have to explain their decision to the wider community who would have benefited.' The words having left his mouth with surprising ease, he felt good.

'Of course,' fawned Snogden-Lambert quickly, as if the suggestion hadn't come from *his* lips. 'I totally understand your position.'

'I have an idea, though.' Norman sensed an olive branch might be a good way to stop those more inquisitive committee members from investigating the true source of his music. 'In order to appease the doubters... I'll personally see to it that *Trouzerbulge* composes a special anthem for Stonehenge... which will receive its premiere at the concert.'

'Oh, I say!' squealed Snogden-Lambert with delight. 'What a *wonderful* idea! Yes... that should definitely take care of the stragglers!'

'Now... I have a question of my own,' said Norman, taking further control. 'I take it you haven't mentioned me by name during your discussions?'

'No, no, no!' confirmed Snogden-Lambert feverishly. 'As far as everybody is concerned, your wish to remain anonymous is understandable and will be fully respected.' He suddenly went quiet.

'Is there another problem?' Norman sensed there might be.

'On that point...' tiptoed Snogden-Lambert awkwardly, 'it has been *suggested* by a few... given the vast amount of money that's been offered... that this whole idea may be either some sort of practical joke... or...' At this point, his delivery became even more contorted by embarrassment. 'It has been *intimated*,' he tried again, with increased discomfort, 'that I am... completely deluded and might have made the whole thing up!'

'I guess you can hardly blame them,' said Norman. 'I'm sure they're thinking it's too good to be true.'

'They may well be,' said Snogden-Lambert with heavy indignation. 'But I take slurs on my mental well-being *extremely* seriously!'

'Well... given your past history... I suppose that's understandable,' said Norman, thinking he was helping.

Snogden-Lambert was horrified. 'Mr Penkridge! I can assure you that I am perfectly balanced and sane! My previous assault on a senior member of the Catholic church... and my destruction of a Turner masterpiece... were nothing more than unfortunate misunderstandings. The fact that I subsequently became prone to crying in public...'

'And drinking,' Norman reminded him.

'... and drinking... have absolutely *nothing* to do with my state of mind now.'

'It really doesn't matter,' said Norman. 'The fact is... they're wrong and you're one-hundred-percent right. Mine is a *genuine* offer.'

'As I have told them,' said Snogden-Lambert, calming himself down. 'However...' His awkwardness returned. 'The nub of it is... I...' He hastily retracted his use of the personal pronoun. 'That is... *those doubters*... will only be convinced of the sincerity of this offer if they see it... *in the bank*... as it were.'

'You mean, they want the money up front,' clarified Norman bluntly.

'*Yes*,' whispered Snogden-Lambert.

'Well... no problem. I'll have a personal cheque couriered over to you immediately. I take it that will suffice?'

'A personal cheque?' gasped Snogden-Lambert.

'Yes... At least you'll have physical proof of my sincerity.'

'But... I'm talking the whole amount... Two hundred and fifty million pounds!'

'I assumed you were.'

'But... *I* assumed you'd be needing to talk to a host of sponsors... not to mention make arrangements concerning the movement of your own personal finances!'

'No need,' said Norman. 'I'll write it now.'

'*Now?*'

'Yes.'

'Well I never!' choked Snogden-Lambert.

'Let's just hope it does the trick.'

'I think you'll find it'll definitely do that!' Snogden-Lambert wheezed.

The rest of the call consisted of Norman trying to end it as quickly as possible before Snogden-Lambert's sycophantic eulogising curled his toes permanently.

'Goodbye... *Sir Peter*,' he finally managed, leaving one last reminder that failure wasn't an option.

'Everything okay?' asked Xanthia, as he replaced the receiver. She was standing in the doorway, her skin glistening wet... her body wrapped in a towel.

'I think so,' he smiled awkwardly... desperately trying not to look at her as if – radiating beauty and framed by the doorway – she was one of his paintings.

* * *

'I've got him!' beamed Kevin cockily.

Chad put a hurried finger to his lips and acknowledged the other patrons enjoying their drinks around them in the crowded pub. 'Not so loud,' he glowered.

'Sorry!' Kevin grinned, without appearing to mean it. 'The Savoy! Penkridge used his credit card to book one of their most expensive suites! I hacked their internal system and got his room number. He's staying there with Xanthia!'

'You mean... the girl you've got plastered all over your bedroom walls,' said Bob, fishing for a reaction.

'Yeah,' replied Kevin, somewhat awkwardly.

'Good work,' said Chad, gifting him an easy out. 'We'll take it from here.'

Kevin sat upright. 'No... I don't think so! I told you before... we're a team now. I wanna be involved in *everything*. If Penkridge is gonna be brought down to size, I wanna be there when he is. I want him to know it's *me* who beat him!'

Chad swapped a look with Bob. 'It's just not that simple. We're highly trained in covert surveillance. It's not something that warrants interested bystanders tagging along.'

'I think you'll find I'm more than an interested bystander now!' said Kevin forcefully. 'And I don't intend to merely *tag along*. I'm an intrinsic member of this team! You can teach me your skills, if you're that worried.'

Chad shot another look at Bob. 'Getting access to those rooms is a risk,' he said, biting his lip. 'Your being involved would only increase it. If you *really* want to see Penkridge beaten, you must let us get on with our job and accept we know what we're doing.'

'You didn't know what you were doing when you allowed yourselves to be filmed in my bedroom!' Kevin retorted. 'Your *training* didn't prevent you from compromising yourselves by vastly underestimating the calibre of the person you were dealing with! That's hardly filled me with confidence! Besides... if it wasn't for me, you wouldn't have Penkridge's current location.'

'But we do now,' pointed out Bob.

'And access to his bank account?' sneered Kevin.

'Kevin's right,' cut in Chad, giving his partner a further look suggesting they play along for only as long as necessary.

Interpreting it perfectly, Bob took a deep breath. 'I guess we *could* use a little help, now you mention it.' He relaxed his scowl. 'Maybe an extra pair of eyes might come in useful.'

'Good!' swaggered Kevin, pleased with their contrition. 'Now... I guess it shouldn't be *too* difficult to plant a series of listening devices in their rooms. I suppose we pose as hotel staff or maintenance men.'

'Something like that,' said Chad, biting his lip again.

'Well... now the game can *really* commence!' Kevin announced excitedly. 'I think that calls for a drink!' He put his hand out for some money. 'Shall I get them in?'

*   *   *

Donald's hands trembled. 'REALLY?' he gasped. 'AM I HEARING THAT RIGHT?'

It was a little hard to tell, given his current surroundings. But that suited him fine. In an attempt to reduce his sensitivity to an increasingly intrusive spirit world, he'd cocooned himself in a makeshift, metal bunker... constructing it from sheets of corrugated iron and whatever other metal items the house and gardens could afford to give up without having anything collapse. Tin foil was no longer an option. It wasn't that he didn't think he could survive another attack of whispering, should it come. If that was to be his future, he didn't want to. But he *had* to finish his grand opus before it finished him... and for that, he needed to be selective about who was getting through to him.

With the oppressive atmosphere that had driven him from his study having failed to vacate the house, he'd opted to construct his chamber in the World War Two bomb shelter his father had had sunk into the ground between the tennis court and croquet lawn. Bostock Tucker-Jenkins had deemed it his patriotic duty to prevent the Germans from disrupting the supply of quality, British ironing boards during the hostilities. Ensuring they didn't succeed in dropping a doodlebug on the head of the industry's most radical innovator... and the rest of his family, of course... he'd had the shelter built to his exacting specifications. Use of the cellar had been totally out of the question, given that's where he stored his wine.

'WAIT A MINUTE... TRY THIS!' Reaching up above his head, Donald gingerly laced his hand through the tangle of scrap above him and wound down the window on the passenger door of a 1965 Hillman Imp.

He asked the question again.

'WELL, I NEVER!' he exclaimed, as the original answer was confirmed. '*THOSE* STONES!' Rubbing his stubble frantically, he considered its implications. 'WELL... THAT EXPLAINS AN AWFUL LOT!' Crumpling the paper he'd been doodling on into a ball, he tossed it on the floor to join the others and started scribbling furiously on a fresh piece. It was as if a dam had burst, a flood of creativity pouring out onto the blank canvas in front of him. 'THAT'S IT! I SEE IT ALL NOW!' he exclaimed excitedly. 'WELL... *MOST* OF IT, ANYWAY!'

That had always been Donald's Achilles' heel. But relieved at finally being able to meet his deadline, he conveniently chose to ignore the missing gaps as his creative muse took hold.

What Donald failed to appreciate, in his rapture, was that it was being just that... *creative*. After all... Romeo and Juliet was ultimately a warning about the dangerous and destructive consequences of bigotry. But its writer had deemed it necessary to throw in a Veronese balcony, a few soppy love scenes, and a rather uncomfortable twist, in order to make it more palatable to the paying Elizabethan public.

Donald's muse – being well acquainted with the bard – was no stranger to poetic licence.

What emerged from beneath the writer's pen was the story of an ancient Briton, seeking spiritual answers within a tribal community that had become locked in generations of ritual and superstition. As the hero of Donald's play struggles against the supposed wisdom of the day, his questioning becomes analogous to the battle between logic and faith... science and religion.

Taking on board Donald's final revelation, his muse had set it in the gently sloping hills of Salisbury Plain, directing the cast to construct a replica of Stonehenge onstage as a representation of their character's initial willingness to believe in a higher power.

But as Donald's hero questions the validity of the monument, he sets about orchestrating its downfall at the risk of causing his own. In a final, dramatic scene, he summons a group of likeminded individuals to attack the monument by making a great noise, hoping to topple the stones and bring about its destruction.

Before the result is known, the curtain falls.

As the house lights wait to rise, a voice asks the audience to consider whether their modern-day assumptions that the attempt was futile are correct... or whether the ruined remains, visible today, suggest the play's hero actually succeeded.

The final sentence committed to ink, Donald leant back as far as the clutter around him allowed... emotionally exhausted, but artistically triumphant.

'I think it's my finest,' he announced to whichever spirits had managed to penetrate his inner sanctum. 'So, maybe that means it's my last.'

Wearily shuffling the numerous pages of writing together, he carefully placed a fresh piece of paper on top of them.

In one last effort for the day, he wrote on it in large, bold letters...

... AN ENGLISH JERICHO.

*   *   *

Norman took a steadying breath before pushing the heavy, soundproofed door and venturing into the inner sanctum that was *Trouzerbulge's* rehearsal room. Having done so, he rather wished he didn't need to take another, as the stench of warm sweat, cigarettes, and stale beer kicked at his senses. Stump was waiting for him... sat on a couch at the far end, his knees tight up against his chest, a cigarette paper delicately balanced on them. He was alone.

'Ah... Mr Penkridge!' he announced theatrically, but without a smile. He continued crumbling a small, brown lump of dope along a line of tobacco running the length of the paper.

Norman felt uncomfortable not having Xanthia for support, but he'd insisted on making the journey alone. To his surprise, she hadn't asked the reason why... which was just as well, given jealously was an extremely unattractive trait to admit to.

'Do we have our permission yet?' asked Stump coolly, rolling the cigarette paper and running it smoothly across his tongue.

'Not yet,' Norman admitted awkwardly.

'Well... I bloody hope all this ain't for nothing!' Stump drew Norman's attention to the massive array of equipment set up around them. 'I've given the boys in the band my word you'll come good on this. You better not let me down!'

'I wouldn't worry if I do,' countered Norman. 'Any troubles you have with them will pale into insignificance if we fail.'

'Fail at *what*, though?' Stump scowled, lighting the end of his spliff. 'I mean... what on earth has *Trouzerbulge* playing at Stonehenge got to do with saving the bloody Universe? How does that one work?'

'It's not you, *per se*,' said Norman. 'It's just the notes I need you to play.'

'Oh... thanks!' Stump frowned. 'That's done my ego a *world* of good!'

'I'm afraid it gets worse. It's only the monotonous two that repeat themselves in your live version of *Sex Wench* I'm ultimately after.'

'*That* song again,' the singer nodded.

'Yeah... it's certainly proving very popular.'

'... and less of the *monotonous*, if you don't mind!'

'My apologies. But they *are* extremely important. I need you to keep playing them for as long as possible.'

'And why's that?'

Norman looked sheepishly at his inquisitor. 'I don't know.'

Stump squinted. 'You don't know?'

'Gabriel won't give me any more information. He says there are forces trying to stop me... and the least I know, the better.'

'I always thought that of Xan,' Stump grinned, blowing a long stream of smoke out towards Norman and following it with a not-so-friendly stare. 'Which, in her case... was just as well.' He took another drag and winced, as the heat of it caught his lungs. 'How is she, by the way?'

'She's alright,' answered Norman indifferently, not wanting to make her the topic of conversation.

'She *is*, isn't she?' said Stump, maintaining his stare.

Norman was determined to change the subject. 'Talking of

forces out to stop me... have you had any encounters with Satan since that incident in your room?'

'You mean that little red fella with the funny horns?' Stump considered the question, holding a cloud of smoke in his mouth. 'Not in person,' he finally replied, dissipating it with his words. 'Though I constantly see him in virtually everyone I have contact with. Whether it's the mean-spirited look of little ol' ladies judging me on my clothes and hair... or wealthy geeks abusing my trust and stealing my girlfriend... he always pops up and makes an appearance somewhere.'

Norman wasn't sure how to respond. He'd misjudged Stump... and he knew it. Whilst the man's outer persona perfectly matched his reputation, he clearly had a deeper grasp of things, which Norman was beginning to admire. 'Very profound,' he said, unable to come back with anything of his own.

'Very *true*,' Stump corrected him.

'So... how are the rehearsals going?'

'Like they always do. Complete chaos and anarchy at the beginning... but we always get there in the end. It's just a question of us remembering how good we used to be and carrying on until the magic clicks. It always does... eventually. The only trouble is... there ain't the hunger there used to be. I see it in everybody's eyes.' Stump flicked some fallen ash from his knees. 'It gets harder every time. Our songs were always about expressing our carnal desires... so it becomes a bit of a pantomime when those desires start to focus on fine wines and antiques... Not that I've *entirely* given up on the sex.'

'I was always a big fan,' admitted Norman, hoping it might ease the tension between them.

'Who *doesn't* love sex?'

'I meant... of the band,'

Stump jerked his head. '*Really?* You surprise me! A clean living boy like you! Still... it didn't stop you from...'

'Can we leave that subject alone,' cut in Norman. He wondered if he'd ever stop their conversations drifting back to Xanthia. 'I'm not proud of what I did... but I'm not ashamed of it either. Xanthia's a free spirit.'

'She's certainly *that!*' Stump goaded him with a wink.

Norman ignored it. 'There's something I need to ask you... a final request. It's to do with getting permission for the concert to go ahead.'

Stump's raised eyebrows signalled for Norman to continue.

'I've promised you'll compose an anthem for Stonehenge.'

The eyebrows rose further. 'That was very generous of you,' said Stump facetiously. 'Anything else you want me to do for you?'

'I know... but I thought it might help oil a few wheels.'

'You mean... touch the parts money can't buy.'

'Precisely.'

'Sounds like we're back to Xanthia again,' Stump smirked.

'I take it it's not a problem?'

Stump taunted him with a moment's deliberation. 'Not for a genius like me,' he finally said.

'Thank you.'

'You're welcome.'

Norman waited whilst Stump pondered the proposition. 'It doesn't have to be anything special. It's simply to fulfil my side of the bargain.'

Far from providing encouragement, the comment tore Stump from his thoughts. 'I don't believe it! Did you *really* just say that?' He stared at Norman incredulously. 'That's the trouble with you business types. You're all the fuckin' same! You haven't a soddin' clue when it comes to understanding the artistic mind. You *think* you do... buying your expensive paintings and showing off someone else's blood, sweat and genius on your walls. But they're not *you*. They're what you aspire to be but could never achieve! On the other hand... a creative like me actually *lives* the dream... interprets the truth... tells it like it is, in a way others would love to if they only had the balls and imagination. You might like to pretend you're an aesthete, but that lie is exposed when you assume artists might *remotely* entertain creating something that... quote... *doesn't have to be anything special!* You see... that's the *real* difference between you and me, Penkridge. Not that one's good for Xanthia whilst the other ain't. It's that you have to buy other people's emotion to try and understand it... while I get out there and create so much of it, I'm able to share it with the rest of the world. So take it from me... if I'm gonna compose an anthem for Stonehenge, I'll make sure it's something *more* than special... *Understood?*'

'I didn't mean to offend. I was just saying...'

'Whatever,' nodded Stump, his point made.

Norman took a deep breath. 'You're right. I know I'll never be creative. It's why I've had to ask you to help me out. And to confirm you're appraisal of me... even *that* idea was triggered by Xanthia.'

His contrition seemed to appease the man in front of him. 'Okay... this anthem... I think I may have the first two lines.'

Norman was astonished at the speed of Stump's creative process. It astounded him that someone could pluck something completely original out of the air with such ease and confidence. He hadn't just underestimated the man in front of him... he'd *vastly* underestimated him. 'Am I allowed to ask what they are?' he pushed, hoping the result of that magical process might be revealed to him there and then.

'Yeah... alright. I'll graciously bestow that honour on you.' Stump cleared his throat.

Norman waited in awe and anticipation.

'*I took my baby to the stones... She let me rock and roll her bones.*'

Norman blinked. 'It's not *quite* what I had in mind,' he said delicately.

'What's wrong with it?'

'Nothing... except... it doesn't always have to be about sex.'

'It's not... I've also got rock and roll in there. All I need to do is mention drugs and I've hit the jackpot.'

'Alright, then... it doesn't have to be about *those* three things.'

Stump looked confused. 'What the hell *else* is there to write about?'

'Love?'

He laughed out loud. 'Do me a favour!'

'You don't have to keep up the rock and roll pretence with me,' said Norman. 'We're alone now. Xanthia told me you're a romantic.'

'Oh... *did* she?'

'Yes... She said you once set a table and chairs up on the shore of Lake Como and wined and dined her by candlelight. That's *incredibly* romantic!'

Stump took a second to recall the incident. 'Well... it was romantic for *her*... but I only did it to impress. We hadn't actually shagged at that point and I was getting a bit frustrated at her holding out on me for so long. So I paid some local geezer to fix it up. Not that I can take any credit for the idea. It was actually our tour manager's. He used to do it all the time. But it definitely worked. Xanthia was *very* grateful that night! Girls like that sort of thing. You gotta go through the motions to pretend you care.'

'But she believed you!'

'Of course she did! They all do. I'm extremely good at switching on the charm when it's needed!'

Norman looked at him aghast.

'What?' Stump snorted. 'You don't actually *believe* in all that romantic crap, do you?'

Norman didn't answer. He was thinking of his conversation with Xanthia in the restaurant and how *she* believed in it.

'Man... you really *are* weird!' Stump laughed, stubbing out the end of his joint on the arm of the couch. 'You're too soft.' He jumped to his feet.

As he did so, the door to the rehearsal room swung open.

'Waggy... my main man!' he shouted loudly. 'Yet again... you've managed to wake up one more time than you've fallen asleep! I am impressed! Quite an achievement, given your chemical intake yesterday!'

'Stump,' acknowledged the new arrival lazily, giving Norman a cursory glance.

'This is Norman Penkridge,' said Stump. 'And he believes in love!'

'Very funny,' mumbled Waggy, making for a flight case that was doubling as a drinks cabinet.

'See!' said Stump, addressing Norman. 'You're definitely on your own with *that* peculiarity!'

'I've always been on my own,' said Norman defensively. 'And I might not be creative like you... but at least I'm happy to think as an individual and not play to the crowd. *You* might think softness translates as weakness, but at least I'd never do anything that would cause Xanthia pain if she found out the truth.'

Stump dismissed the jibe. 'Waggy... I'm writing an anthem for Stonehenge. What d'ya think of this... *I took my baby to the stones... She let me rock and roll her bones?*'

'Mega,' drawled Waggy, popping some brightly coloured pills into his mouth. 'But if you don't mind me saying so... I think you need to get something about drugs in there.'

'Told you,' grinned Stump triumphantly.

* * *

Peter Snogden-Lambert drank in the moment and repeated his name confidently in his head. It was easy. Finally... he could own it with pride.

He'd lost count of the number of people coming up to him that afternoon, accompanying *theirs* with a firm handshake, words of praise, and the occasional slap on the back. It was in stark contrast to the past few years when... in best-forgotten moments when he'd lost it completely... the slap had been aimed at his face.

Their attitude towards him had changed. He could now look them firmly in the eye, knowing that when they stared back, it was no longer with a hidden agenda. He was one of them again... the prodigal son returned.

It had absolutely everything to do with the large, cardboard cheque he was holding... like a drowning man clutching a floatation device... a long row of noughts barely able to fit in the amount box. His own initiative; he'd had Norman's cheque reproduced in promotional size for the benefit of the photo-hungry journalists at the press conference he'd arranged... carefully ensuring the account holder's name had been suitably pixelated, of course. Not that the name *Templar Resources* would've given him away.

The pixelation proved as big a story for the media as the amount itself. Descending upon Stonehenge *en masse*, they were desperate to unmask the mystery benefactor who'd donated a quarter of a billion pounds to the nation's heritage. Eager to wring the mystery name from Snogden-Lambert's lips, they'd begged, cajoled, flattered and praised him... reinforcing his newfound sense of importance.

But those lips had remained sealed.

Not that it took much effort on his part. He was only too pleased to comply with Norman's request that he alone be the focus for the media's attention. If they were after a name to heap plaudits upon, he was happy for them to use his!

His rehabilitation was complete. In the morning, he would feature on the front page of every newspaper. Those who had deserted him in his hour of need... Mrs Snogden-Lambert included... would be choking on their cornflakes as they read the headlines and realised their colossal mistake.

His grin was in danger of becoming permanent, as the photographers snapped away. The jumbo cheque he was refusing to let go of guaranteed him pride of place amongst a long row of similarly smiling dignitaries... the iconic image of the stones mere bit-players in the background.

'Well done, Peter, old boy!' voiced one of those smiles, after the final shutter had clicked. 'It's been suggested by many that you're wasted out here in the provinces... and I have to say, I wholeheartedly agree! Not that it isn't an important position, mind. But a man of your calibre should be exploited to the maximum back in London. We need that vision of yours to help secure this country's heritage. Perhaps you'd consider something grander to sink your teeth into, once you've seen this thing through. We should talk.'

'I'd be delighted to,' smarmed Snogden-Lambert, happy not

to let go of the hand not letting go of his.

'Are you a golfer, Peter?'

'I have to confess... I've not always had the time,' came the smart reply.

'I understand! Very diplomatic! I should think whacking a little white ball about would fail to stimulate a brilliant mind like yours!'

Snogden-Lambert replied by shrugging modestly. He certainly wasn't going to object.

'But you don't want to be all work and no play, Peter. I think you've given enough of yourself to deserve a little *me time*. Give me a call when the dust has settled and we'll sort something out.'

Five years had personally been enough "me time" for Snogden-Lambert. But he agreed all the same. 'We'll definitely get something in the diary,' he promised... wondering if he should now let go of the other person's hand.

The rest of the afternoon continued in much a similar vein. As praise for his shrewdness and fundraising brilliance gushed from all quarters, Snogden-Lambert happily obliged by building his part. Towards the end of the day, one might have been forgiven for thinking he'd actually built Stonehenge himself.

Nobody objected. His skill had bequeathed the Nation a rare opportunity to secure its treasured heritage sites for many a year to come. And for that, they and the Nation would be forever grateful.

Snogden-Lambert went to bed that night an extremely happy man. As he turned and looked at the half of the mattress Mrs Snogden-Lambert used to occupy...

...*though strictly speaking, it was more than half*...

...he pictured Joan Fanshawe-Whittingham occupying it instead.

He blushed at the thought... though it didn't stop him exploring the fantasy further.

Or should that be... Lady Joan Snogden-Lambert?

Emboldened by the day's events... not to mention the four glasses of *Dom Pérignon Vintage* previously quaffed... he vowed to discover where she was now living and call her in the morning. Unless it was Timbuktu, she couldn't fail to have heard news of his remarkable triumph.

He speculated about what she'd be thinking. No doubt, it would be remorse at having failed to see beyond the tormented mind on the stretcher and the foam coming out of his mouth. She would be forgiven, of course... much the same way she would forgive him the uncharitable words that had accompanied it.

He tried not to think of what lay beyond her industrial strength brassiere, lest it stopped him from sleeping.

As tiredness finally smothered the dying embers of his excitement... his thoughts drifting towards the abstract... the final thing he remembered pondering was whether she might wish to keep a part of her old identity and be known as Lady Snogden-Lambert-Fanshawe-Whittingham when they were married.

He would, of course, have to reciprocate.

That night – fuelled by a brutal chilli dip and particularly pungent *Pont l'Évêque* chanced during the press conference – he dreamt that, whilst shopping naked in his local home improvement store, he was caught ineptly shoplifting an *extremely* long nameplate.

*   *   *

'I can't believe I've pulled it off!' exclaimed Norman, staring at the newspapers scattered across the bed... the announcement of his planned mystery concert and its financial benefit to the nation blazoned across their pages.

MYSTERY MILLIONAIRE MAKES STONEHENGE SING FOR ITS SUPPER, shouted one of the headlines.

'See... I never doubted you would,' said Xanthia, propped up beside him.

Norman looked at her lovingly... then braved a kiss on the wall of lacquer supporting her hair. 'You're right... you didn't,' he smiled.

Taking that fork returned an affectionate squeeze of his arm.

'*What's* he pulled off?' hissed Bob, from a room just down the corridor.

Kevin sniggered.

Chad shrugged and pushed the headphones harder to his ears. Xanthia had insisted on watching a children's cartoon on the television, and the extraneous noise was making it difficult to follow their conversation. 'Perhaps he's managed to downsize his equipment.'

Kevin sniggered again.

'You mean... made his weapon smaller?' asked Bob.

Tears appeared in Kevin's eyes.

'Looks like we're gonna create quite a stir with this!' said Norman. 'The whole country's gonna know about it!'

'He has! He's actually achieved it!' exclaimed Bob.

'Things are about to get busy,' said Norman. 'We need to start concentrating on logistics.'

'Sounds like we've got to them just in time!' returned Chad.

Xanthia was trying to work out what *concentrating on logistics* meant.

'So... why don't we do something crazy before we have to tackle the *serious* stuff?' Norman suggested, desperate to give Stump a run for his money in the spontaneity stakes.

'Really?' she squealed, jumping up onto her knees and bouncing on the bed. 'Like what?'

Whilst delighted at her reaction, Norman realised getting it was the easy part. He fought to maintain an expression of impending excitement. 'I don't know,' he finally admitted, through a frozen grin.

Xanthia's shoulders dropped.

'No... wait! I've got it!' he exclaimed hastily, desperately wondering what Stump would have suggested. 'Let's create havoc at...'

She waited expectantly... like those in the nearby room.

As much as he wished it to be so, he wasn't Stump. '… the *zoo!*' he finally announced.

'The *zoo?*' she choked.

'The *zoo?*' mouthed Chad.

'Sounds like they're looking to do a trial run,' said Bob. 'Are there significant stone buildings at London Zoo?'

'Dunno,' shrugged Chad. 'Perhaps we should ask our mystery benefactor. He seems pretty partial to such places.'

Sensing Xanthia's disappointment, Norman tried again. 'No, wait a minute… not the zoo… How about something… of historic importance?'

'Like what?' she asked, getting ready to bounce again.

Headphones were pushed even tighter.

'The *Tower of London?*' tried Norman.

'Shit!' grimaced Bob. 'Did he just say what I thought he did?'

'I'm not sure,' answered Chad. 'Someone in the background was loudly boasting to be smarter than the average bear.'

'They're going for an internationally recognised landmark! That place is gonna be packed solid with tourists this time of year! Hell… this is *serious!*'

A series of violent cartoon explosions followed by a loud yelp suggested the ursine hubris had been premature.

Xanthia remained unimpressed. 'Oh yeah… we'll *really* be painting the town red!' she offered sarcastically above it.

'What was that?' struggled Chad.

'Something about… making the town… *red*… I think.'

Chad rubbed his chin anxiously.

'Surely they can't be thinking of causing mass bloodshed… *can* they?' exclaimed Bob.

'Hadn't we better alert the authorities?' chipped in Kevin.

'Not yet,' Chad waved down their concern. 'Something's not right here. These people aren't *terrorists!* You don't go from messing about with paintings to suddenly massacring innocent people!'

'They've got the crown jewels there,' said Norman in an attempt to entice her.

Chad's eyebrows shot up.

Xanthia's shot down. 'What... d'ya mean... men's private parts?'

Kevin snorted.

'No... the most famous set of jewels in the world!' explained Norman. 'They're *astronomically* valuable!'

'That's it!' exclaimed Chad, thumping the table. 'They're going for a heist! *That's* what this has all been about! Donald's assumption about stones was only *half* correct. They're looking to steal *precious* stones! Their sonic device is perfect! If they switch it on, it'll clear the area in an instant! No one would be able to get *close* with that amount of volume blasting through the air! Anyone prepared in advance and wearing suitable ear protection would have the whole place to themselves for as long as they kept the noise going!'

'Holy moly!' wheezed Bob. 'That's friggin' *brilliant!* Finally... everything makes sense!'

'So... *now* do we go to the police?' asked Kevin impatiently.

'No way,' said Chad firmly. 'This is precisely the chance we've been waiting for to rectify a long-standing injustice... and an unfettered Penkridge is our key to doing that.'

'But surely you intend to stop him?' Kevin exclaimed.

'Of course! But we need to catch him in the act. That's where we failed previously and got hung out to dry because of it. Now things are different. We *know* what he's up to... and we'll be waiting for him. He ain't gonna get away with it this time... and it'll be us who get to grab all the glory!'

'I take it by *us* you mean the *three* of us,' said Kevin forcefully. 'I told you before... I wanna be there when he's brought down. I wanna see Penkridge's face when I stare him in the eyes and tell him it was *Ultimate and Unbeatable Supreme Cyber Warrior 2* that did it.'

'You can tell him what you like,' said Bob. 'But I reckon you'll find that'll be the *least* of his worries!'

'You can say that again!' grinned Chad. 'It's been a long time coming... but revenge is sweet. There's no *way* we're gonna be made to look like idiots *this* time!'

*   *   *

Snogden-Lambert gingerly lifted the receiver to his ear and stared nervously at the phone's keypad. Despite his brain instructing his finger to dial the number he'd just scribbled on the pad in front of him, it refused to budge.

He chastised his offending *digitus secundus* for letting the *old* Snogden-Lambert get the better of it.

It wasn't listening.

The standoff between man and appendage was only broken when a continuous tone notified him that the phone had had enough of their silliness.

Replacing the receiver, he bit hard on his lip.

'What's the worst that can happen?' he asked himself. It was a curious question really... given he'd spent the last half-hour running every conceivable scenario for *that* through his head.

The night before, it had all seemed so easy... buoyed by too much alcohol and the buzz of approbation still ringing in his ears. But things were different now. The cold reality of morning had brought his doubts back into focus.

Determined to regain his courage, he grabbed one of the many newspapers littering his desk and opened it to a double-page spread showing him holding the giant cheque. Above him read the caption: *STONE-HENGE ME! IT'S QUARTER OF A BILLION QUID!*

His confidence surged back as he saw his name in print and recalled the plaudits that had been showered upon him.

Pressing the receiver firmly to his ear, he stabbed at the keypad before his finger had time to object.

There followed an anxious wait.

Finally... his heart released itself from the starting blocks. 'Oh... hello Joan... It's me.'

There was a silence.

'ME...!' he repeated, a little louder.

'Peter.'

His mouth felt dry.

'Peter Snogden-Lambert...

234

Yes... quite a surprise, I'm sure...

No, no... I'm not in any trouble! I was just sitting here reminiscing and I thought... I know what... why don't I give Joan a ring and see how she's doing? So... how are you doing, Joan?'

He listened awhile.

'That's good... That's good...

No... you're right... it *wasn't* easy tracking you down. I hadn't realised you'd moved. I had to call a joint acquaintance of ours to get your new number.

Oh, don't worry. I'm sure you had a lot on your mind...

Yes... I've heard it's a lovely part of the country...

No... nowhere near. It's alright... you won't be needing to take out a restraining order!'

Snogden-Lambert snorted at his own quip. Women liked a man with humour. He'd read that in one of Mrs Snogden-Lambert's ladies' magazines.

'No... I was joking, actually! I'm fully recovered now... Haven't you heard?'

His shoulders dropped.

'Really? I *am* surprised... I take it you haven't read the papers, then?'

His shoulders dropped even more.

'No... neither do I, normally... Quite full of rubbish... I agree... It's just that...

Yes... apart from the crosswords, of course...

Me too... The cryptic clues...

No, no... never won a thing. Joan... But that's not why I'm calling. I wonder... have you watched the television...?

Well... *any* television...

You haven't... So you haven't seen the news...?

No, I understood that... I meant, on the television...

Oh, right...

No, no... As I said before, I'm not in any trouble. In fact... far from it. Things have been going extremely well for me recently. I've had a bit of good fortune and I thought I'd like to share it with you.'

He winced.

'I think she's fine. We haven't spoken for a short while.'

He paused.

'We're no longer together.'

There was a longer pause.

'She left me...

Yes... it was quite a surprise for me too...!

No... that's *not* the good fortune I was referring to...

Yes... of course I'll miss her pies...

I'm sure you do, Joan. I'm sure you do. I'll get her to send you the recipe next time I speak to her. Perhaps I could have your address?'

Snogden-Lambert clenched his fist.

'Oh...'

He unclenched it.

'Yes... Okay. I'm sure that's a better idea. She's still on our old number. I'm sure she'd love to hear from you...

Well... when I said she left me, I meant... it was me who had to leave...

Yes... It *is* a lovely house, isn't it...?

You're right... Very spacious...

I do miss it, Joan. I do... Look, Joan... I was wondering... are you ever up this way...

Of course... I didn't say, did I? Silly me... Wiltshire...

Yes... quite a change from London, I agree... Though I expect I'll be going back there soon...

No, no... I'm on permanent release now... It's just that I'm expecting a bit of a promotion, if truth be told. Probably something with an even higher status than my old job!'

He laughed awkwardly.

'Good lord, no! I'm not on any medication! It's all for real...!

Totally understandable, Joan... totally understandable! I don't blame you. I was quite surprised myself. You never know...'

He screwed his face up tightly.

'I might be in need of a personal assistant again...!

No, no!' he said, shaking his head wildly. 'I realise that... I'm sure it gives you the time to do those things you've always wanted to...

Yes... I'm sure it is... It sounds idyllic. It's just that... if you ever feel like a change of scenery, you know where I am...

Of course... I didn't tell you that bit either, did I...? Stonehenge.'

He laughed again.

'No... I haven't become a hippy!'

He stopped laughing.

'Sorry... I thought you were joking. No... Actually, I'm in charge of it...

'Yes... *really!*'

He frowned.

'No, you'd be surprised, Joan. We get all sorts here. It's not *that* easy. But like I say... if you ever...

You *did?* A few years ago? Well... I suppose if you've seen it once...'

Snogden-Lambert realised he was fighting a losing battle.

'Look, Joan... I won't say any more... but see if you can get hold of a copy of today's newspaper...

No, it's nothing to do with the crossword... I'd just like you to see it... that's all.'

Things hadn't gone as he'd envisaged.

'I'd better go now, Joan... These stones don't look after themselves...

No, *really*, Joan... They don't...!

Yes... it's been great hearing your voice too... Does that mean...?'

Snogden-Lambert suddenly lost what little nerve he had left.

'Oh... nothing Joan... I must dash. Things to do and all that. Well... enjoy that beautiful scenery and... look after yourself...

I will... Bye now...

Bye.'

He gently put the receiver down.

You could have heard a pin drop.

'BOLLOCKS!'

231

'Why's he wearing those funny clothes?' asked Xanthia.

'He's a Beefeater,' answered Norman, waiting for her to ask how he knew the man wasn't a vegetarian.

'How do you feat bees?' she surprised him.

Norman was used to it. 'Look at the ravens,' he distracted her. 'They say that if those birds ever leave the Tower of London, the whole country will descend into ruin.'

'How do they know?' she frowned.

'Pardon?'

'How do they know that if those birds ever leave the Tower of London the whole country will descend into ruin? I mean… surely they'd only know that if they did… and *it* did? But they haven't!'

Norman accepted she had a valid point. 'They clip their wings to prevent it,' he said lamely.

'Complete waste of time, if you ask me,' she pouted, moving on.

'Two adults and a child,' said Bob, through the small hole in the kiosk.

'I think you mean… three adults,' said the girl, without a smile. It was the seventh such quip she'd received that morning… and it still hadn't gotten any funnier.

'That's debatable,' said Bob, looking at Kevin and paying.

Chad was anxiously scouting the grounds ahead, keen not to lose sight of their quarry.

'I could've gone online and got us a discount code,' pointed out Kevin.

Bob pulled him through the turnstile.

'I'm going to have to leave you,' said Norman, fidgeting awkwardly.

'What… you dumping me?' exclaimed Xanthia.

'No… to take a pee. I'm bursting! I need to find the toilets.'

'Did they *have* toilets in the olden days?' she asked.

He looked at her askance.

'Well, don't be long,' she huffed. 'I don't like the way those ravens are looking at me.'

Norman would normally have told her not to be so silly. But he had to concede she had a point. The birds were staring at the two of them with a quiet, black menace. He recalled his incident with the dogs.

'I'll be as quick as I can,' he promised.

'They're splitting up!' exclaimed Bob, as Norman headed back towards them.

'Maybe we should do the same,' Kevin suggested eagerly. '*I'll* follow Penkridge.'

Bob quickly grabbed him by his jacket and turned them both to face the opposite direction. 'You stay with me,' he hissed, keeping his head down. 'Chad can check him out.'

'He'll be scouting the place,' said Kevin.

'He'll already know this place back to front,' returned Bob. 'You don't undertake an operation of this calibre without meticulous planning. They'll have done the same for whatever their other target was at London Zoo.'

'I'll wait 'til he's gone by, then follow him,' Chad whispered.

Bob strengthened his grip on Kevin's jacket as their target passed them. As soon as a suitable distance allowed, Chad moved off.

'They must've secreted their equipment nearby,' said Bob, scanning the buildings around them. 'Though without knowing how small they've managed to reduce it to, it could be disguised as anything and be anywhere!'

'I assume when you say *equipment*, you mean *weapon?*' said Kevin.

Bob nodded dismissively.

'But they can't *seriously* think they're gonna get away with this?' insisted Kevin. 'The place where they keep the jewels is heavily alarmed. The minute they attempt to smash the glass, the door is gonna automatically lock shut. They'll be trapped inside!'

'Like I said... this will have been meticulously planned. They'll have already thought of a way around that. They're not idiots!'

'But have *you* thought of how we're gonna combat this sonic weapon of theirs?'

Bob produced an expensive-looking pair of earplugs from his pocket, leaving Kevin to stare at them blankly.

'What's the matter?' asked Bob, feigning incredulity. 'Don't tell me you didn't think to bring any?'

Kevin snorted his annoyance.

'Shame,' said Bob. 'I guess that means you'll just have to vacate the area, along with everybody else, when the action starts.'

Kevin looked at him defiantly. 'Not necessarily,' he sneered.

As Bob waited for elucidation, Kevin suddenly took off on his heels.

'*Now* what's he doing?' Bob cried.

Having covered the ground between him and his target in an adrenalin-fuelled time, a number of tourists screamed as Kevin made a crude, passing grab for Xanthia's bag. Being looped around her arm, the rest of her body went with it.

'Thief!' she screamed, as she found herself wrestling with her attacker on the ground.

The startled tourists got out their cameras.

Just as Kevin managed to prise the bag away from her, his attempt to escape was thwarted by a large pike spearing a leg of his jeans.

'Stay where you are, sonny!' barked its owner, his military training finally being put to use, after years of being gawped at by tourists and asked the same bloody question about the ravens.

'He tried to steal my bag!' shouted Xanthia, grabbing it back and struggling to right herself on her stilettos.

'I know. I saw it, madam,' said the Beefeater.

'*She's* the thief... not me!' yelled Kevin, pointing at the bag. 'They're going to steal the crown jewels!'

'Not whilst I'm here, sonny,' said the Beefeater, with a firm jaw.

'Ask her!' shouted Kevin. 'Ask her to open her bag! She's got a weapon inside it!'

There was a gasp from the small crowd that had gathered.

'*Very* creative,' remarked the Beefeater.

A number of his colleagues arrived to offer their assistance.

'You alright, Tony?' asked one.

'All under control,' he reported. 'The kid here tried to nick this lady's handbag. Now he's trying to make out she's got a weapon inside. I've heard some excuses in my time!'

'Well, that one's easily tested,' said one of his colleagues, turning to Xanthia and smiling. 'Would you mind opening your bag, ma'am? Then we can dispel the ridiculous accusation and cart this young bugger off!'

Xanthia gladly did as was requested.

Kevin peered intently as the bag's contents were exposed. 'How big is this thing?' he shouted towards the crowd.

There was no reply.

Xanthia held up a lipstick.

'She's gonna detonate it!' screamed Kevin, clutching his ears.

The Beefeaters looked at one another and shook their heads.

'I think you'd better come with us, sonny.'

'Wait!' said Kevin desperately. 'I'm not working alone!'

'Your type rarely do,' said the Beefeater. 'Is this a confession?'

'I'm helping the CIA! She's part of a sophisticated team! They were originally going to target London Zoo, but changed their minds! They're after the crown jewels!'

'Can't say I blame them,' smirked one of the Beefeaters. 'They're not only more valuable than an elephant... they're a lot easier to conceal!'

'I'm serious!' insisted Kevin. 'You can ask that guy over there! He pointed to where Bob had been standing.

Only... he wasn't.

'Bit ironic really,' said the largest Beefeater, as he yanked Kevin to his feet by his collar. 'In days gone by, you'd probably have been dragged off to the tower!'

'Penkridge was simply taking a pee?' queried Bob, dodging oncoming tourists as he and Chad beat a hasty retreat along the pedestrianised walkway that skirted the Thames and took visitors to and from the attraction.

'Nothing more!' yelled back Chad. 'And I reckon that's *all* he'll be doing at the Tower today, now he knows they've been rumbled!'

'So, *now* what?'

'We ditch the kid,' cried Chad. 'You were right from the start. He's a liability!'

Bob brought himself close to his partner's shoulder. 'Don't forget... we still need him to block a certain bank account.'

'Oh... don't worry. He'll be doing that regardless! He'll hate Penkridge more than ever now!'

'Not to mention us!' wheezed Bob. 'Aren't you forgetting one thing? He's got the whole of our conversation, instructing him to commit computer fraud, sitting on his computer. I doubt he's gonna take rejection too kindly. He could make things *extremely* uncomfortable for us if he decides to use it!'

'Not if we get to that recording before he does,' said Chad, with grim determination. 'Seeing as how he's gonna be spending the next few hours doing quite a bit of explaining, I suggest we make a beeline for his mom's place and see if we can get ourselves invited in for some more of her cakes!'

*   *   *

'Can I get you anything for it?' asked Norman.

Xanthia was sitting on the edge of the bed, examining the graze on her elbow.

'Nah... I'm fine, really,' she pouted. 'It was just a bit of a shock... that's all.'

'You can say that again!'

Xanthia looked at him strangely. 'I'm fine, really... It was just a bit of a shock... that's all,' she repeated slowly and deliberately, her eyes searching his as to why.

'I wish I'd been there,' he said. 'At least I could've done something to protect you!'

She dropped her eyes and said nothing. She didn't need to. He assumed it meant she didn't believe he would've been capable of doing anything remotely heroic. Instead, she was probably conjuring up an image of Stump intervening on her behalf... no doubt getting a round of applause from the tourists, once he'd had the assailant begging for mercy. But he could hardly tell her that such a scenario would only have occurred had Stump arranged for "some local geezer" to set the whole thing up as a stunt, in order to get her into bed.

'He was persistent... I'll give him that!' she said.

'Stump?' asked Norman awkwardly, his thoughts having drifted.

'What?' Xanthia looked at him with even more confusion.

'Nothing,' he said quickly, realising his mistake.

'I was talking about the *thief*. He was persistent.'

'*Insistent*,' Norman corrected her automatically. It had become a habit over the years. 'You're right... But from what you tell me, those excuses of his were pretty pathetic... if not comical!'

'No... *persistent*,' she maintained, with a frown. 'He'd obviously followed me from the hotel.'

Norman stared at her blankly. 'What on earth makes you think that?'

'I dunno... My brain, I guess,' she shrugged.

'Okay... *Why* do you think that?'

Xanthia was beginning to wonder why she was being required to repeat everything she said, when her brain finally caught up. 'Oh, I see... Because it's true! He was in the foyer last night. I remember seeing him.'

'Are you sure?'

'Positive! He was standing near the lifts, trying not to be seen. But I noticed him, cos he kept looking at me after we came out from dinner. I thought he was alerting the paparazzi... cos he immediately got on his phone and kept staring at me suspiciously.'

'It must've been someone else,' reasoned Norman.

'No, it was definitely me... cos I had my red dress on... and I remember catching sight of myself in a mirror.'

'I meant... *he* must've been someone else.'

'How can he be two different people?' she scoffed. 'Norman... you're being very strange today! I fink you're starting to lose it! Anyway... there was only one of him because he wore the same t-shirt. I remember noticing it because it said *Supergeek*... and I thought of you!'

Norman's face fell.

'Have I said something wrong?' she asked.

'No, no... I've just thought of something odd.' He stood awhile, assembling his thoughts. 'There's something else not quite right, here!'

She looked at him expectantly.

'You said earlier... he told those Beefeaters we were originally planning on going to the zoo!'

'Yes... that's the bit he *didn't* lie about,' she pouted, re-examining her wound.

'But the thing is... how did he know?' Norman considered his own question... then quickly put a finger to his lips.

'Oh, good!' she clapped. 'Are we gonna play charades?'

He shook his head wildly.

'Okay... that means no,' she squealed excitedly, forgetting about her elbow.

Norman stuck his finger in the air, then dashed across to the writing desk to grab a pencil and a small pad of paper.

'Is it a book?' she asked, as he furiously scribbled on it.

He shook his head again and showed her what he'd written.

I THINK THIS ROOM IS BUGGED. WE NEED TO PACK OUR THINGS AND LEAVE!

Xanthia snatched the pad from him and wrote on it herself. WEAR TWO?

ANYWHERE! he wrote back, imploring her with his eyes to trust him.

'Just so long as it's not the zoo!' she said aloud.

* * *

'What time do you call this?' asked Kevin's mum, as his face appeared around the kitchen door.

'Sorry, mum. It's been a really difficult day!'

'I said you'd be back *hours* ago,' she tutted.

'*Said...?*' he queried. 'To who?'

'*Whom*,' she corrected him.

'To *whom* did you say I'd be back?' he asked impatiently.

'The two American gentlemen who've called round to see you again. They've been waiting ages. Are you sure they're not trying to sell us solar power?'

'Waiting?'

'In your bedroom.'

'My *bedroom!*' he exclaimed in horror.

'Well... I could hardly let them into the sitting room, could I? It's a mess. Which is ironic, if you think about it, given I originally thought they were trying to sell me a vacuum cleaner.'

Kevin *hadn't* thought about it. He'd shot from the room instead and bolted up the stairs.

'Ah... The Megabyte Master. Good to see you!' came the greeting, as he swung open his bedroom door to find his two visitors loitering in front of his computer. It had been delivered in a tone suggesting tables were about to be turned.

He fought to keep his cool, inwardly seething at their intrusion into his private domain.

'They let you out, then,' grinned Bob, relishing the shift in power.

'They had no choice,' said Kevin defiantly. 'Those idiot Beefeaters forgot to ask the alleged victim to accompany them to the police station so as to make a statement. In the absence of a witness... and unable to find any stolen property on my person... they were forced to release me without charge.'

'You were lucky, then,' said Chad.

Kevin clearly didn't think so.

'As were we!' Bob smiled.

223

'I think my partner's referring to the fact we've taken the opportunity to turn a negative situation into a positive one, searching your hard drive for any incriminating evidence you had on us,' explained Chad. 'Being the genius you tell us you are, you'll notice I used the past tense just then.'

'Not genius enough to bother protecting it with a password, though,' Bob smirked.

Kevin bit his lip.

'In other words... we won't be buying the drinks anymore,' Bob added.

Chad's countenance darkened 'Not that there's anything positive in the fact you blew our chance of catching Penkridge and his accomplices in the act by your act of reckless stupidity!'

'I reckoned they were gonna detonate that sound device you said they had!' insisted Kevin.

'Oh... d'ya mean the sound rig the size of a house that you somehow thought was hidden in his girlfriend's handbag?' exclaimed Bob.

'You said they'd managed to make it smaller!'

'You really expect us to believe you thought it was *that* much smaller?' scoffed Chad. 'We were talking about a *reasonable* reduction in size... enough to secrete its components in various locations around a considerable target area!'

'How was I to know?' objected Kevin.

'Because... according to you... you're *smarter* than us,' said Bob, fixing him with a glare.

'And... for a few unguarded moments on my part... you were,' Chad conceded. 'But the incriminating video you had of us wasn't the *only* thing we found when examining your computer.'

Kevin's breathing changed.

'Very interesting,' added Bob, with a wink. 'But in your defence... Xanthia's a very attractive girl... clearly deserving her own special folder. You couldn't possibly be expected to have enough bedroom wall space to cope with all *those* images!'

'I wonder what Penkridge would make of your obsession?' threw in Chad.

'Who cares?' retorted Kevin.

'We reckon *he* might,' said Bob. 'Whilst I'm sure he's come to terms with there being numerous individuals coveting what he has... I reckon he'd take umbrage at one of them being *you*.'

'What are you talking about?' Kevin frowned.

'Perhaps it would be appropriate if *I* explained,' said Chad, suggesting the tables were about to be turned yet again. 'As my partner here will verify... I've never had a problem with coincidences. Far from being blinded by the usual prejudice against them in our profession, I've always preferred to wait until I find that one piece of evidence putting improbability beyond doubt. Take this current situation, for instance... Whilst ordinarily, I'd have thought the chances of someone overhearing a private conversation in a bar, latching on to the subject's name and knowing them, would be pretty remote... I accept it's possible. And that's what you hoped we'd think.'

Kevin didn't respond.

'Then I ask myself... what are the chances of that person hating the subject of the conversation so much that they immediately offer their assistance for free, thereby solving the very dilemma being discussed?'

'You didn't *have* to accept my help,' Kevin sneered. 'You could've turned it down!'

'Which was my partner's gut reaction. But I've been a little ring-rusty lately... and you were very persistent. So, against his better judgement, you persuaded me that such a thing needn't be cause for suspicion.' He turned and looked at Bob. 'But now I've stumbled across the one thing that *can't* be ignored... a connection beyond coincidence.'

'Hip friggin' hooray!' hollered Bob. 'Welcome back, buddy!'

Chad acknowledged the sentiment with a gracious nod. 'And it's by far the most interesting part.'

'It might be interesting to you,' snorted Kevin, 'but this whole thing's starting to bore me! I want you outta my room now or I'm calling the police!' He turned towards the door.

Bob grabbed his arm and swung him around roughly. 'I've told you before, kid... this *ain't* one of your computer games!

You don't just get to switch off or press pause when you feel like it! You wanted to play with the big boys... Well... now you've gotta accept their rules.'

'Mum!' yelled Kevin, at the top of his voice.

'That's a good idea,' said Chad calmly. 'Why don't we get her up here? I'm sure she'll be interested in some of those *other* photos we came across when trawling your hard drive.'

'Kevin! Is everything alright up there?' came a concerned voice from downstairs.

Kevin froze. 'It's okay, mum,' he shouted back, looking at the other two. 'I think I've sorted it now!'

There was the sound mum's are expected to make when called to the stairs unnecessarily... Kevin only releasing his breath when the absence of any further mumbling suggested she'd returned to the kitchen.

'And talking of *other* photos... there's one in particular that caught our eye.'

Keeping his grip on Kevin, Bob stretched over to the mouse. 'Shall I do the honours?'

Chad nodded.

A photo downloaded from a smartphone appeared on one of the screens. It was of a hotel being consumed by fire.

'Recognise it?'

'Sure... It's one of many I've taken recently,' said Kevin nonchalantly.

'We recognised it too,' said Bob. 'Which could be considered odd... given we're relative strangers to your city. But that's because we stood in an identical position to where it was taken, shortly after meeting you. Only... *we* didn't see any flames.'

'For a very good reason,' contributed Chad. 'They'd been extinguished the day before.'

'That's approximately only twenty-four hours before our paths crossed,' added Bob, 'in case the point ain't getting through.'

'What point?' said Kevin dismissively. 'I happened to be passing a fire at a major hotel and took a picture. There were loads of people doing exactly the same thing that day. It's no big deal.'

'It is when you factor in that this is the hotel Penkridge booked himself into, before you allegedly knew that fact,' said Chad.

Kevin tried not to look worried. 'So what?' he sneered.

'So... we reckon you're a red herring.'

'A *what*? Now you guys have *really* lost it!'

'Far from it,' responded Chad. 'We've *found* it... that all-important connection beyond coincidence. It proves beyond reasonable doubt our meeting didn't happen by chance. You *knew* where we'd be drinking and choreographed a meeting with us!'

'And how could I have *possibly* known?'

'The answer to that question is why you've managed to get away with your subterfuge for so long. You're right... How *could* you have known? But it came to me as soon as I saw this photograph.'

Kevin looked at them both uneasily.

'You know Penkridge. In fact... you know him so well, you were standing right next to him when you took this photo! Far from being an enemy, he's your friend! That's why you played him at *Cortex Destroyer. Ultimate and Unbeatable Supreme Cyber Warriors 1 and 2* are buddies... hence the matching tags. Like you kept telling us... it's a pretty niche community!'

'But for all those aliases you use to make yourself appear more important than you are, there's only *one* name he uses for you,' said Bob.

Chad fixed Kevin firmly in the eye. '*The Provider.*'

'He knew we were onto him in France and would follow him to England,' said Bob. 'But he didn't know who we were. So he did a little surveillance of his own. It wouldn't have been difficult for a man of his skills to hack the airline's booking system, once he'd landed, and identify two American males turning up at a small, provincial airport together and booking a last-minute flight, identical to his.'

'Far from us following *him*... it's him who's been following *us!*' said Chad. 'Which is where *you* came in. He called you and asked for your help. He might even have got you to hack the booking system yourself. You trailed us from the airport. It's how you knew which hotel we were staying in and where we'd be drinking. You ingratiated yourself as soon as the opportunity arose, in order to discover what we were up to.'

'Penkridge also knew he'd let slip the name *Templar Resources*,' took over Bob, 'He realised it was a huge mistake and that we'd be looking to investigate them. It was only a question of time before we found out for ourselves that he was using a single chequebook to transfer enormous sums of money from their account to his.'

'So he got you to get in first and pretend you'd cancelled it. He needed us to assume we'd neutralised that part of his operation. But our initial request to have his personal account compromised had caused you to panic. So you made us believe you'd encountered problems accessing it. It also threw you when we requested you hack his credit card to find out where he was staying. Though you played for time, you knew you'd have to offer up the answer sooner or later if you weren't to blow your cover. The trouble is… in your misguided arrogance, you vastly underestimated our *own* skills. Having finally conceded his whereabouts, you didn't reckon on us getting our surveillance position up and running so quickly.'

'That's why you ran at Xanthia today,' said Bob. 'You *knew* she couldn't possibly have a weapon in her bag. You were trying to warn him and any nearby accomplices that their plans had been rumbled. You'd been unable to do so whilst with us and were desperate to stop 'em before they incriminated themselves. That girl doesn't seem to know what's going on at the best of times… so wouldn't have had a clue who you were. It was perfect! You knew she couldn't give the game away by recognising you!'

Kevin shrugged himself free of Bob's grip and looked at them both contemptuously. He gave a slow, sarcastic handclap. 'Bravo! With logic like that, you should've both been coders.'

'From the two examples I've come across so far, I'm glad we're not!' returned Bob.

'So where do we go from here? I mean... you can't keep me prisoner in my bedroom forever!'

'We don't need to,' said Chad.

'We could *kill* you,' Bob suggested.

Kevin's eyes widened, having failed to consider that as an option.

'But it wouldn't make any difference,' said Chad, much to the teenager's relief. 'Penkridge already knows we're onto him. Killing you would only upset your mum.'

'*Possibly*,' added Bob.

'We'll leave you to fester in the knowledge you failed this particular game and that you're nowhere near as smart as you thought you were.'

'So... given you're not even worthy of being classed a threat anymore, you're free to go,' grinned Bob.

'Although, technically... it's *us* who now have to leave.'

'It's been real,' Bob gloated, as he made his way towards the door.

Chad gave Kevin one last, lingering look. 'Which is ultimately why you failed,' he added profoundly.

*   *   *

'Ladies and gentlemen... if I could have your attention, please!' The assistant director clapped his hands, bringing to an end the buzz of excitement from the actors and actresses who'd assembled for the first day of rehearsals. 'I know this has all been incredibly short notice... but as you will be only too aware... Mr Tucker-Jenkins is working at quite a pace these days!'

There was an appreciative round of applause as the fact was professionally acknowledged.

'What your agents might *not* have told you, however... given we have all been sworn to absolute secrecy on this, his latest play... is that he is going to direct this one himself.'

There was a collective gasp of amazement.

'Yes... I thought that might please you!'

The buzz reignited, as the cast congratulated one another on the honour about to be bestowed upon their careers.

'Please! Please!' shouted the assistant director, appealing for quiet. 'I know how thrilled you all must be. It will, indeed, be an exceptional privilege to be directly privy to the great man's thoughts, as we undertake this most magnificent work of his. I should add... for those who've expressed surprise at the provincial theatre we find ourselves standing in and the incredibly short time we have in which to rehearse... that Mr Tucker-Jenkins fully intends this production to transfer to a more suitable venue once one becomes available. But he is determined to see it premiered here on the eve of this year's summer solstice. I'm sure, having read the play, you will all fully appreciate the reason why!'

Another round of applause demonstrated they did.

'So... without further ado... I would like to introduce you to the play's esteemed author... and our director... Mr Donald Tucker-Jenkins.'

Those usually accustomed to being on the receiving end of applause, gave it in abundance as the great man's entrance from the wings was anticipated.

On cue, Donald appeared stage left, shuffling his way towards the centre.

The applause dipped considerably as focus switched to the unconventional attire in which he'd chosen to undertake his directorial debut.

Donald's foil turban had become legendary, given its previous outing... the mark of a true genius, many had accepted. It would probably even feature on the Paris and Milan catwalks during next season's collections. But the deep-sea diver's helmet and requisite accoutrements took everyone by surprise... Not least Donald... who was finding progress harder than anticipated, given the lack of deep-sea available at that particular location.

The assistant director pretended not to notice... an Oscar-winning performance in itself.

Those around him didn't know whether they were expected

216

to do the same… their skills at improvisation being sorely stretched.

Donald continued his laboured entrance, completely oblivious to the hanging mouths around him.

'I think I might need a chair,' he announced breathlessly, as he finally reached centre stage and swung open the small window on the front of his helmet.

More hands were clapped as one was called for and duly placed behind his teetering frame.

'That's better,' he sighed, taking the considerable weight from his feet. 'I could have done with one of these on the bus.'

Glances were exchanged.

Donald placed his gloved hands on his knees. 'Now… I feel it only fair to warn everyone here that some of you may not make it to the opening night.'

If those assembled considered this a declaration of his intention to be a harsh director, they were in for an even greater shock.

'There are rather unpleasant elements surrounding us that may try to kill you, in order to prevent you performing my play. Though I'm sure you'll all appreciate… professional as you undoubtedly are… whatever happens, the show must go on!'

The adage was met with stunned silence.

'I trust you therefore all have understudies?'

The assistant director nodded slowly.

'Good… Whilst I will be guided by only those voices in my head that I trust, it is highly likely that others will attempt to subvert what it is we are attempting to say with this work. So… please bear with me if I seem slightly *distracted* at any point during our time together.'

One of the more sensitive actresses stifled a sob, as the clash between the great man's genius and the price he appeared to have paid for it caused her emotions to overflow.

Such was the esteem Donald was held in, the thought of ridicule never entered the minds of the others. They all inwardly vowed to use their training to connect with his personal suffering and use what they were experiencing as artistic inspiration and motivation for the great masterpiece they were about to undertake... along with any subsequent cameo roles they might be offered in which they were required to play a nutter.

'The words I have written are a humble attempt to warn of an imminent and potentially catastrophic danger,' he announced grandly. 'You must use your performances to take from the page what has been given to me and shout it powerfully, so that all of humanity will clearly understand the message. That immense responsibility is in your hands. You must treat it as a gift and use it to its fullest.'

As pre-production pep talks went, it certainly ranked alongside the best of them.

The thought of death forgotten, a slow handclap started... gradually morphing into tumultuous applause as Donald nodded, as best he could, his appreciation of their reverence.

As it reached its zenith, Donald suddenly put his hands to his helmet and seemed to be in some discomfort.

'Are you alright?' asked the assistant director, with appropriate concern. 'Should we be operating some sort of pump?'

'The theatre ghost,' said Donald, his eyes widening.

'Yes?'

'I believe he's been inhabiting this building for quite some time.'

'That'll be old Tommy Grumblestone,' said one of the actors, stepping forward with a keenness to please. 'They say he regularly trod these boards when the theatre was first built, some one hundred and fifty years ago! He's purported to still walk the backstage area, refusing to leave what he regards as his home.'

'That'll be him,' said Donald matter-of-factly.

'Are you sensing him?' fawned the actor, drinking in a moment he hoped to recount at future dinner parties.

'Not anymore,' said Donald. 'He just told me he didn't want to be here, given what's about to come our way... and could I therefore announce to his adoring public... Tommy has *finally* left the building.'

* * *

Worker Two stared at the three small stones on the ground and wrestled with the conundrum they posed.

He wasn't alone. A small group of fellow workers had been doing exactly the same thing for most of the sun's trajectory across the sky. But he was determined to be the one that came up with the answer Worker Three had been seeking when placing them on the ground. As far as Worker Two was concerned, he'd never get a better chance to upstage Worker One... his nemesis having taken himself off that day to indulge in one of his increasingly reflective moods.

He'd been doing a lot of that recently. In Worker Two's opinion, the respect Worker One was being shown for considerably reducing everyone's workload had completely gone to his head and given him a misplaced sense of importance.

The stones being stared at were roughly the same shape and proportions as the much larger ones they were supposed to represent... oblong in shape, with one approximately half the length of the remaining two. According to Worker Three... the longest two needed to be raised into an upright position, whilst the third – to everyone's consternation – had to be placed on top.

Much head-shaking had accompanied the problem.

Given the size and weight of their real counterparts, the first bit looked difficult enough.

As for the *second* bit!

It just couldn't be done, the group decided, as the light began casting longer shadows behind the stones.

Worker Three reminded them that failure wasn't an option. It simply *had* to be done. The gods had decreed it so.

Tired thoughts turned to the power of the gods and the damage they might inflict if unappeased.

It was then that Worker Two had his flash of inspiration. At least, he assumed that's what it was. He'd never had one before and it felt quite strange. It was as if the gods had whispered the answer in his ear without him hearing any words.

He stepped forward.

Worker One wasn't the only one capable of reducing their workload, he proudly announced. He had the answer... and it was obvious, when you knew how. The solution had been staring them in the face all the time, but it had clearly taken a genius like him to see it.

The group looked at him expectantly.

He knelt down confidently in front of the stones.

If the gods had requested the task be done, it was because they considered it possible... he informed their open mouths. And they considered it possible because they wouldn't encounter any problems doing it themselves. After all... gods could do anything... that's why they were gods.

The mouths remained open.

Worker Two then unleashed the clever bit. So, why didn't they ask the *god of all things made of stone* to get together with the *god of whatever it was around them that filled in the gaps between everything else and allow them to simply float the stones through whatever it was around them that filled in the gaps between everything else?*

Worker Two demonstrated his brilliant idea by using what fingers he had left to gently raise the two longest stones into an upright position. Then – his expression promising the best bit was yet to come – he delicately placed the final stone between his thumb and solitary fourth finger and slowly lifted it upwards until it was perfectly aligned with the tops of the other two. As breaths were held, he moved it horizontally until it was hovering above them... then gradually lowered it until it sat securely in place. The task achieved, he released his rudimentary grip and drew his hand away in a self-congratulatory flourish.

The group slowly turned their heads to face him... then looked at him as if he were mad.

So he was suggesting they used... *magic...?* the group

clarified.

Worker Two ran his solution to the problem through his head one more time.

In a nutshell... *yes*, he conceded.

The group looked at him as if he were even madder than they'd *first* thought.

It was then that a lone figure shuffled out from the group. He had a Neanderthal brow and sunken eyes that suggested a quiet but resigned sadness.

He informed them in a painfully slow delivery that Worker Two – whilst clearly an idiot – had given him an idea.

Was he *sure*...? the group asked.

In a cavernous voice that conjured up an image of tar dripping off a log, he put forward his idea.

Rather than trouble the gods... why didn't they get a giant to lift the full-sized stones up for them? Though – in the interest of safety – preferably one with a full complement of fingers.

There was a stunned silence.

Did he *know* of any such giants...? the group enquired.

Only a sleeping one... he announced, without emotion.

Really...?

He returned a lumbering nod.

And where might they find this helpful fellow?

That was easy. They simply had to follow the river downstream until they came to the valley of plentiful deer... head towards the place where the sun got swallowed... then bypass the hills that looked like witches tits, using the chalk pathway that led around them. If they carried on this path far enough, they would eventually come to a large mound of earth where the giant was said to sleep.

How would they know it was the correct mound of earth, if the giant wasn't there?

That *too* was easy. The mound went by the name of *The Sleeping Giant,* on account of the fact it resembled a sleeping giant. All they had to do was wake it up.

The *giant?*

The mound.

So it was simply a pile of earth... the group pointed out.

Not according to the locals who'd named it... came the bemused reply.

Worker Two – sensing the group's incredulity – employed a tactic that would be copied for many generations to come. Seeing a chance to redeem himself and shift attention away from his own shortcomings, he rounded on the lubberly one, loudly ridiculing his suggestion. Was he *serious?* he snorted theatrically.

The lubberly one's eyes retreated even deeper in pain beneath his Neanderthal brow, as he felt the sting of Worker Two's vitriol. Such mockery *still* hurt... even though he was used to it.

The group joined Worker Two's look of derision.

Emboldened by their support, Worker Two unleashed maximum scorn on his cowering victim. What on earth would happen if the giant became angry at being awoken and turned out to be an evil one? The bumbling idiot clearly hadn't thought things through!

The group nodded in unanimous agreement.

It was then that Worker One made an appearance.

Worker Two – sensing his own ascendancy within the group – realised he'd been gifted the perfect weapon with which to knock Worker One from his pedestal and demonstrate to those assembled that he was not as clever as they thought he was.

Kicking the three small stones over with his foot, he challenged Worker One to find a solution to the problem he now knew was impossible to solve without making yourself look stupid.

Worker One asked for clarification on what is was that had to be done.

Worker Two gleefully repeated the problem.

Worker One pursed his lips in thought... then shrugged. He announced that – as far as he could see – the easiest way of raising the two largest stones would be to taper them slightly... thus making them heavier at the bottom than the top. This would mean that when they were hanging over the pit that would need to be dug to stand them up in, it would take less effort to do so. That effort would be reduced further still if they used something he'd been working on called an A-frame lever. He'd explain that bit later.

The group looked at him in awe and admiration.

Unperturbed, Worker Two unleashed his killer punch.

And the *third* stone?

Worker One instantly cracked Worker Two's smug expression by informing him that *that* was the easiest part.

It *was?*

Of course! All they had to do was surround the upright stones with a ramp of earth and haul the remaining one to the top. From there it could easily be secured in place. He suggested a little dimple joint might do the trick. All that then had to be done was remove the earth and... *ta-dah*... they would have the structure they required.

The group looked at him in stunned silence.

Was there anything else they needed to know, Worker One enquired? Only... he had some more thinking to do.

Worker Two would have shaken his head, had he not been concentrating so hard on not crying.

It was as Worker One was walking away from the group that a thought suddenly struck him. It was brilliant and clear... and its implications left him feeling breathless. He'd seen the way the others had looked at him in amazement when he'd suggested the ramp of earth as a solution. It wasn't just because it solved their problem... it was because it was so simple and glaringly obvious once envisaged. What had seemed impossible one moment... only achievable through an act of magic or a miracle... instantly became possible without having to resort to either. But, to future unenlightened visitors to the completed structure – without the benefit of knowing about the ramp of earth – it would seem as if something supernatural had occurred. So... what if there were other ramps of earth – metaphorically speaking – that could solve similarly perplexing questions and did away with the need for magic or divine intervention to explain the currently unexplainable?

As it quickly gathered pace, the developing thought sent a shiver down his spine. For example... what if there were a metaphorical ramp of earth that explained the diversity of wildlife... the bright flecks of light in the night sky... or the creation of the very ground he was walking on? Wouldn't that be amazing? Forget monotheism... If you could discover *those* ramps, it would do away with the need for any god at all!

The thought both excited and shocked him.

And the more he examined it, the more it seemed plausible.

His head started spinning with the implications.

It was too exciting an idea to ignore. He needed to discuss it with someone... and there was only one person qualified enough to hear it... and he'd been putting off a showdown with *him* long enough.

Worker One drew a deep breath.

It was time he paid a visit to the man with antlers on his head.

*　　*　　*

'What is it with these flies?' said Norman testily, shooing a swarm away from his head. 'They've been plaguing us ever since we arrived!'

'Yes... they seem to have taken over the place,' tutted Snogden-Lambert, joining in the swatting. 'I'm wondering if it's got something to do with an atmospheric change. Visitors are complaining they can no longer pick up mobile signals at this site. I'm sure it's connected.' He brushed a couple of the buzzing nuisances from his nose. 'I hope that isn't going to be a problem for you,' he added anxiously.

'We'll manage,' said Norman. 'I'm just pleased to be here. It's such an impressive sight, close up.'

'My previous boyfriend reckoned it was a teleport for aliens,' chewed Xanthia, as she and her jaw considered the breathtaking monument in front of them.

Snogden-Lambert smiled politely, but deemed it prudent

not to comment.

'It's incredible to think they transported these stones from so far away,' remarked Norman, admiring the massive lintels still in place and shaking his head with respect.

'Not if they had a spaceship,' she pointed out.

'Whilst it's true the bluestones making up the inner circle are thought to have come from the Preseli Hills in Wales, one hundred and fifty miles away... many people assume this is also the case with the larger sarsens. It isn't.' clarified Snogden-Lambert, having memorised the brochure on sale in the visitor centre. '*They* were probably brought from nearby.'

'From a shop?' enquired Xanthia, her eyebrows creased.

'*Brought*,' said Snogden-Lambert, heavily rolling the r.

'It's still an astonishing feat, though,' Norman marvelled, taking another swipe at the incessant flies.

'It certainly is.' Snogden-Lambert desperately tried to recall the next bit. 'The sad thing is, mankind will never *really* know the true purpose of it all. Whilst archaeologists around the world continue to build their careers on supposition and conjecture, the truth will forever remain shrouded in mystery.'

'Perhaps they should have a chat with my ex, then,' suggested Xanthia helpfully.

'Perhaps they should,' Snogden-Lambert conceded, with a smile just a facial tic away from a wince.

'And you say there's absolutely no problem with us erecting the stage in front of the actual monument,' clarified Norman, still scarcely able to believe his luck.

'As long as you stay outside our spanking new boundary fence, your generous donation has seen to it that you can,' replied Snogden-Lambert obligingly.

'Talking of which... I assume the cheque's been banked.'

'It went in a couple of days ago,' confirmed Snogden-Lambert. 'I'm told it will take a few more to clear, given the added security checks one of *that* size necessitates... but I'm sure there won't be a problem with it clearing.'

'If there's one thing I can guarantee in this world, it's that!' Norman grinned.

Snogden-Lambert returned the smile... though more through relief than acknowledgement. The thought *had* crossed his mind.

'In which case, I'll get my production team down to recce the site as soon as possible. I take it that's alright with you?'

Snogden-Lambert put his hands in the air. 'You do whatever you have to,' he smarmed. 'You must treat this as your second home... which I believe is closer to the truth now!'

'Until the concert takes place,' confirmed Norman. 'We've found a small pub down the road that does accommodation... *The Druid's Fluid.* It's very pleasant... and much safer than London.'

'*Safer?*' queried Snogden-Lambert.

'I mean... it makes it easier to come here without getting delayed in traffic,' Norman quickly back-pedalled.

'I'm not sure it's *that* safe,' pouted Xanthia. 'The landlord told us a ghost lives there!'

'You mean Seth Broadstock?' Snogden-Lambert laughed.

She frowned. 'He didn't tell us its name.'

'I meant the landlord. I hear he's a bit of a character... always pulling people's legs. I suppose his stories are good for business... especially when you consider some of the fruitcakes we get down here.' He fought an urge to glance at Xanthia. 'He'll even have you believe the stone lintel above his inglenook fireplace originates from here!'

'That can't be true,' pointed out Xanthia. 'It must've originated from those Elvis Presley hills.'

Snogden-Lambert inwardly conceded she had a point... though he'd still debate her on the teleport for aliens.

'Just one thing...' said Norman. 'If anyone should come here asking for us, I'd appreciate it if you didn't say where we're staying... even if they claim to know us.'

Snogden-Lambert tapped the side of his nose. 'Mum's the word. I guess you're worried the press will be trying to unmask you now the story's hit the headlines?'

'Something like that,' answered Norman, deciding it best not to bother the man in front of him with the possibility of *dark forces* or a visit to his attraction from the Prince of Darkness himself. His nerves seemed fragile enough as it was. 'I'll have my people call you. I suggest we use a password to ensure you don't speak to anyone who isn't who they say they are.'

'Good idea,' nodded Snogden-Lambert, brushing another fly from his nose. 'Those journalists can be quite devious. Do you have one in mind?'

'Yes,' said Norman. 'I'll tell my team to identify themselves by using the word *Spikey*.'

'None other shall pass!' exclaimed Snogden-Lambert pompously.

'Then, I think that's us done here,' Norman announced, pleased to leave the flies to themselves. 'I guess that allows us the rest of the day to see if we can catch a glimpse of the *Druid's Fluid's* ghost!'

Xanthia didn't appreciate the humour.

Snogden-Lambert did... and thought he'd match it. 'Well... when you see old Seth again, tell him that if he insists on claiming that lintel comes from here, Peter Snogden-Lambert says he bloody well wants it back!'

Xanthia looked at him aghast. 'But won't that mean his chimney will fall down?'

*   *   *

The actors onstage were doing their best to follow Donald's directions.

It wasn't proving easy.

It had become increasingly difficult for them to work out who the great man was talking to. Even if he aimed the opening of his helmet towards them and looked directly into their eyes, it didn't necessarily follow that what came out of his mouth was meant for their consumption.

To add to the confusion, Whitebait appeared to have taken up the role of assistant director... much to the annoyance of the *real* assistant director.

The real assistant director had found himself in something

of a quandary. He'd never believed in the afterlife... let alone the fact you might be able to talk with someone who lived there. So the fact he was now having to compete with what he regarded as a figment of Donald's imagination was taking some delicate diplomacy on his part. It had been made all the more difficult by the fact his respect for the man doing the imagining knew no bounds.

The actors could only sympathise as they watched his tortured attempts to put Whitebait in his place... which... according to him... didn't actually exist.

A feat in itself.

The scene they were currently working on was one in which the hero of the play approaches the shaman of the tribe undertaking the colossal task of building Stonehenge.

'You have to get inside your character's frustration,' Donald instructed the actor playing the lead role. 'You have to imagine the potpourri of emotions swirling around our hero's head.'

The actor nodded.

'IT'S A MIXTURE OF DRIED FLOWERS, HERBS AND SPICES USED TO GIVE A GENTLE FRAGRANCE TO A ROOM.'

The actor nodded again.

'I WAS USING IT IN THE CONTEXT OF A MISCELLANEOUS COLLECTION, YOU IMBECILE!' Donald shouted.

The actor winced... then nodded for a third time.

'Not you,' said Donald politely, acknowledging the colour the man's cheeks had turned.

'WELL... I SHOULDN'T THINK THEY *DID* HAVE IT BACK IN YOUR DAY... ESPECIALLY NOT IN *GRIMSBY!*'

The actor looked to the assistant director for guidance... who gave an advisory nod that they should both be patient and let the great man sort his demons.

'ELITIST, MY ARSE!' yelled Donald, in the middle of his sorting.

'Alan was wondering whether his character should show his inner turmoil by adopting a slightly tortured gait at this point in the play,' coughed the assistant director, against his own advice. 'I personally think this would be a marvellous idea.'

'ACTUALLY... THAT'S WHERE YOU'RE COMPLETELY WRONG!' bellowed Donald defiantly.

The assistant director withdrew his wringing hands.

'Not you, either,' Donald tutted, giving the poor man a sideways glance. 'I WOULD SAY IT WOULD COME IN *EXTREMELY* USEFUL, IN YOUR CASE! WHY DON'T YOU TRY SOME?'

As he spoke, one of the female members of the cast, who had just excused herself for a toilet break, slid apologetically back onto her chair.

Donald acknowledged her return with a nod of his head. 'THAT SHOULD GET RID OF THAT AWFUL SMELL OF FISH THAT ALWAYS SEEMS TO EMANATE FROM YOU!' he shouted.

The young girl, tears welling in her eyes, rapidly excused herself for another one.

'*Now* where's she going?' said Donald, in frustration.

'I wonder if *Whitebait* would agree with Alan regarding the gait?' asked the assistant director, seeking to intervene and move things on.

'I doubt it,' said Donald. 'He rarely agrees with *anyone!*'

'Might we ask him?'

'If you like,' Donald shrugged.

There was an awkward silence.

'Well?' said Donald.

There was a further awkward silence.

'I'm not saying well to *him*,' said Donald. 'I'm saying it to *you!*'

'Are you speaking to me?' squeaked the assistant director.

'YES!' said Donald testily. 'It's *your* question... *You* ask him!'

The assistant director looked around sheepishly... then cleared his throat. 'Whitebait?' he ventured with acute embarrassment.

Those around him lowered their eyes.

'He says... *what?*' said Donald, interpreting the trawlerman's sullenness.

The assistant director looked at Donald and – for the briefest of seconds – wondered whether the playwright was playing a game with him... and that he was fully aware Whitebait didn't exist.

Donald – for his part – wondered why the man was looking at him in such a strange way. 'Well... get on with it, man!' he instructed.

'I was wondering,' tiptoed the assistant director awkwardly, 'whether you think Alan here...' he pointed timidly at the cringing thespian, 'should adopt a drooped gait when conveying to the audience his character's anguish?'

Breaths were held as Whitebait's answer was eagerly awaited.

'HE'S NOT TALKING ABOUT BROKEN HINGES, YOU MORON! HE MEANS GAIT... AS IN A PERSON'S MANNER OF WALKING!' Donald sighed loudly in frustration. '*YES*... THAT'S RIGHT... *ALAN*... THE ONE THAT ACTS GAY... BUT CLEARLY ISN'T!'

Alan raised his previously lowered eyes to the ceiling... though momentarily allowing them to investigate the expression of one of the actresses sitting opposite him.

'OF COURSE HE FANCIES HER. YOU CAN SEE IT WHEN HIS AURA INTERTWINES WITH HERS! IT'S JUST A GOOD JOB HER HUSBAND CAN'T... GIVEN *HE'S* THE ACTOR SITTING NEXT TO HIM!'

The assistant director stood up quickly and clapped his hands. 'Perhaps we should do this as a one on one,' he said hastily. 'Just our hero and the shaman!'

Alan thought that was a good idea too.

'Whitebait agrees,' concurred Donald... then creased his brow at what he assumed to be the pronouncement of a caveat from his spirit guide. His eyes widened in horror as he realised the nature of his mistake. 'WHERE?' he shouted nervously, as they darted every which way.

The answer was delivered via a sickening blow to the back of his head, a light from the gantry directly above having plummeted to the ground.

*　　*　　*

Worker One studied the dwelling in front of him.

He found it intriguing. Whilst of the usual circular construction – a wattle and daub wall supporting a conical, thatched roof – it had a certain *je ne sais quoi*. Unlike other buildings of its type, its inhabitant had gone to extraordinary lengths to ensure *this* particular one stood out from the crowd.

The first thing that struck him was the sheer amount of "things" that had been hung on and around it. From grotesque, carved, wooden masks, that grinned with other-worldly menace... to less intimidating artefacts fashioned from feathers that fluttered pointlessly in the wind. Skulls seemed to have featured heavily on the owner's mood board. Whether hanging from twine or impaled on poles stuck into the ground, their sun-bleached grimaces gave the first-time visitor a distinct impression the occupant had an unhealthy association with death.

A magnificent set of antlers having been pegged into the thatch above the entrance, Worker One was in no doubt he'd come to the right place.

Uninviting as it appeared, he'd gone there in a positive state of mind. He was keen to discuss the new ideas that had been filling it of late. Not that he was expecting a warm welcome... which was just as well.

Two acolytes doubling as guards – their considerable biceps smeared in animal fat, so as to make them look even *more* considerable – beckoned him inside... their manner threatening, not friendly.

Dutifully obliging, he found his sight temporarily disadvantaged by the darkness of the hut's interior.

As his eyes grew accustomed to the lack of light, he spotted the man with antlers on his house as well as his head sitting atop an ornate, raised chair that had been generously draped in a disparate collection of animal hides. He had on his head his trademark status symbol... despite the fact Worker One recalled being told it was considered bad luck to wear a hat indoors. Smoke, from a large fire behind, meandered slowly up into the roof, to be consumed by the thatch... a few stray beams of shimmering light slicing their way through it, illuminating the gloom beneath.

The acolytes bluntly instructed Worker One to kneel on the ground immediately in front of the chair. He appreciated this would give the man with antlers on his house as well as his head an unfair psychological advantage. But keen to get the discussion underway – and not having the kind of biceps you bother to smear animal fat on – he dutifully obliged.

A brooding silence hung in the air.

Keen to soften the grim expression on the face now looking down at his, Worker One complimented its owner on his unusual choice of décor. He particularly liked the collection of strung animal bones that jostled with each other in the wind to give a pleasant tinkling sound. Some enterprising soul, he suggested, could do quite well for himself if he manufactured these on a commercial basis. He was sure they would catch on.

The man with antlers on his house as well as his head wasn't impressed by such small talk and got straight down to business.

He pointed out he'd noticed a certain degree of irreverence in Worker One's attitude towards the gods of late and considered it highly inappropriate.

There was a perfectly good reason for that, Worker One pointed out.

And what was that?

He didn't believe in them anymore.

The man with antlers on his house as well as his head became apoplectic with rage. Had Worker One *completely* lost his senses?

Worker One suggested he'd actually *come* to them... and hoped that others might follow, once they heard what he had to say.

Over his dead body!

Whose...? The man with antlers on his house as well as his

head's?

No… Worker One's!

But that was precisely the point, Worker One insisted. The gods weren't going to kill *anyone!* He'd been thinking his thoughts for some time now and nothing untoward had happened to him. Given that… his ability to think them and remain unpunished was proof they didn't exist! Pushing on quickly, he suggested they now examine his *other* ideas and work together to develop a better system with which to understand the world they were living in.

Despite his expression of outrage, the man with antlers on his house as well as his head remained surprisingly calm. There was just one flaw in Worker One's argument, he insisted.

Was there?

Yes.

And what might that be?

Circular reasoning.

The hanging skulls grinned in silence.

Worker One chewed his lip. Did that mean he *was* to be punished?

Correct.

The acolytes grabbed his arms.

By mortals?

On behalf of the gods.

But why?

Because the gods had decreed it.

Said who?

The gods, of course.

He hadn't really got his point across… had he?

*   *   *

On their arrival the previous night, Norman had demanded the best room available at *The Druid's Fluid*. The landlord had duly nodded and offered them the *only* room available.

Xanthia figured there was a very good reason for it being empty. According to the landlord, she could expect to share it

199

with someone who had previously died whilst staying there and never quite got round to handing in their room key.

Part of a sixteenth-century coaching house, its low, timber beamed ceiling; uneven, whitewashed walls, and obligatory four-poster bed would ordinarily have conjured up images of romantic weekends away in the country or highwaymen resting up for the night. But it had made her feel anything *but* romantic... and the thought of robbing a stagecoach had never much appealed.

Her aversion to spending time in it hadn't lessened since returning from the stones. She claimed to be able to feel a presence, even though the deceased cohabitant had so far failed to introduce himself. With Norman insisting it was all in her imagination - the landlord merely pulling her leg – she'd made her annoyance at his flippant dismissal obvious.

'Maybe if there's a ghost, it's friendly,' he suggested, attempting to acknowledge and allay her fears at the same time. 'It doesn't always follow they're nasty and out to scare you.'

'I don't care if it's the ghost of Father Christmas,' she pouted childishly. 'I don't want to come face to face wiv 'im in this room, thank you very much!'

'Technically... Father Christmas isn't a ghost,' he pointed out.

'Duh... I know! I was just using him as the best example of a very nice person. Everyone knows he's not actually dead yet!'

'Perhaps you're just feeling this way because you didn't sleep well last night,' he suggested.

'I certainly didn't! I had one those nasty dreams again... where the monsters I first saw in France were trying to grab me! Only, this time, I was in a television studio.'

'Surreal.'

'No... it was definitely a dream!'

Norman knew what was coming next. 'I guess I didn't help you in them,' he ventured.

'You never do. But I know why that is now.'

'You do?'

'Yes... I always have them when you're asleep!'

198

Norman said nothing.

'I just don't like this place,' she frowned. 'I've had a bad feeling ever since we got here. It's like the atmosphere I felt back home. Everything seems... *troubled*.'

'Maybe it's got something to do with the dark furnishings,' he tried. 'They *are* rather oppressive.'

'No... it's not the furniture. There's definitely something unpleasant in here with us.' She looked around anxiously.

'Well... if the landlord's right and there *is* a ghost, I'll ask Gabriel to have a word and get him to temporarily move out,' he promised.

'The landlord?' she frowned. 'Are we gonna take his room?'

'The ghost. I expect I'll be having a meeting with him soon.'

'I hope not! And how do you know it's a *him*?'

'*Gabriel*,' said Norman, with infinite patience. 'And at least I'll be able to report that everything's running smoothly. You know... I still can't believe it's all going to plan. It seems his faith in me was justified after all.'

'And mine,' she reminded him.

'I've got the stage guys coming down to inspect the site first thing tomorrow. But I can't see there being a problem. As for Stone Deaf Pete and his team... they don't need to be here until the day before the show.'

Xanthia dropped her eyes. 'Which reminds me... Have you heard from Stump?'

'I was gonna mention that. I got a message from him shortly after our meeting with Snogden-Lambert ended, saying that the magic had finally clicked!'

'Brilliant!' She clapped her hands excitedly. 'I can't wait to see them back together again after all these years! It's gonna be awesome!'

'I doubt Snogden-Lambert will think so!' chuckled Norman. 'He's invited a load of guests to the performance. I think they're in for quite a shock!'

'It'll definitely be that!' she exclaimed. 'Knowing Stump, he won't hold back on such a big occasion!'

'I shudder to think how Snogden-Lambert will react. I

reckon he'll be amongst some incredibly important dignitaries when the band take to the stage! Still… at least it'll be too late for him to do anything about it.'

'He asked me if *I'd* ever heard of *Trouzerbulge*,' she giggled.

'And what did you say?'

'I told him the truth. I said I was *Trouzerbulge's* biggest fan.'

'And what did *he* say?'

'He said he was very surprised,' she answered, pausing to recall the look of shock on his face.

'Not as surprised as he's *gonna* be! It doesn't matter what happens after that.' Norman suddenly froze, his expression changed. 'I *assume*,' he added hesitantly.

The thought had just struck him that it *was* only an assumption on his part. He still didn't know why the notes needed to be played at such a specific location… or even why they needed to be played at all. He'd simply done what had been asked of him and become so engrossed in the challenge, he'd failed to think beyond it.

Suddenly… things had changed.

'Are you alright, Normy?' Xanthia asked, as he stared straight through her.

A dog howled in the street below.

'I've done my part,' he muttered.

A fly landed on his shoulder.

'Well… *Trouzerbulge* still have to do the show,' she pointed out.

Another dog answered in the distance.

'Yes. And now I've made sure that's possible, I think I'd finally like to know what's going on.'

'Is that wise?' she cautioned. 'You know what Gabriel told you!'

'I don't see how it makes any difference now,' he said confidently. 'Because of the forks I've cleverly taken, those two notes will be played exactly as instructed!'

Xanthia folded her arms and shivered. 'Is it me… or is it getting cold in here?'

Norman ignored her, his own thoughts channelling his

focus. He was on the cusp of saving the Universe for the second time. That made him a very special person in the history of... well... history. Surely it was time his hard work was rewarded. He'd proven himself more than worthy.

Xanthia let out a shriek, setting the dog in the street below off again. 'Normy! Something just touched me!'

Norman didn't flinch. 'Don't be silly,' he mumbled, as if from a distance. 'There's nothing there.' Having justified Heaven's faith in him, surely it should be trusting him more.

This time – like rain starting to spatter on a pavement – every canine in the neighbourhood began responding to the call.

'Something grabbed my hair... I'm telling you!'

Hadn't the old lady in the park told him to think positively?

A door slammed in the room next to theirs.

'Normy... I'm frightened!' Xanthia started trembling.

The door inexplicably slammed again... louder this time.

Wasn't that old lady Gabriel... trying to give him an important message?

'Norman! You're not listening to me!'

What could be more positive than thinking yourself invincible?

Xanthia let out a whimper. '*You* can, if you like... but I'm not staying here another second!'

Without warning, the quaint, leaded light windows gave up their pretence of charm and violently flew open, taking the curtains with them.

Xanthia shrieked again... much to the delight of the dogs, who could now communicate with her properly.

She ran for the door and struggled with its handle. 'I can't open it!' she cried. 'It's covered in flies!'

She was being ridiculous. Why be scared? If he could save the Universe, he could certainly cope with one pathetic, lost soul.

'Norman! Please!'

Mind you... why should he even have to bother? He had friends in extremely high places who should be sorting that kind of minor problem for him. After all... he'd been doing all the *major* work up until now! Where were they? Why weren't they looking out for him? More to the point... how dare they ignore him!

Xanthia was sobbing like a child.

Norman's hubris finally got the better of him. 'GABRIEL!' he shouted at the top of his voice, summoning the winged-one to his presence.

* * *

'It's begun,' croaked Donald, addressing the circle of worried onlookers staring down at him. 'They've been trying to do it for millennia... but I fear they've finally succeeded!'

'What?' asked one of the actors, nervously looking around the theatre.

'Broken out of the spiritual realm!' announced Donald with apposite theatricality.

'I think we should get him to a hospital,' suggested the assistant director, affectionately cradling Donald's head.

'No time,' said Donald weakly. 'The danger I warned you about has arrived, I'm afraid.'

'It should've had a safety chain attached to it,' remarked a stagehand, examining the shattered remains of the light scattered around Donald's supine body. 'It's supposed to stop this sort of thing happening.'

'Am I bleeding?' asked Donald, attempting to feel the back of his head.

'Thankfully, no,' the assistant director assured him. 'Your diver's helmet prevented that. Thank God you were wearing it! Quite remarkable, really! But I still think we should get you checked over. You've had an extremely nasty blow.'

'We must continue with our rehearsals,' insisted Donald, ignoring him. 'It's a race against time now... and I've an awful feeling things are going to get decidedly uncomfortable from here on in! I don't think even my helmet will help me next time!'

* * *

194

The four-poster bed rocked violently, as if in the grip of an invisible tornado trying to find its way out of the room. Lesser items took to the air, swirling precariously around Norman's head. Xanthia had buried her own in her hands – having slid down the door she'd been unable to open – and now lay crumpled against it in a foetal ball.

The experience wasn't new. Norman had encountered something similar back at Armageddon Terrace, when he'd inadvertently invoked a spiritual paradox.

The thought snapped him back to his senses and produced a far more worrying one.

Had it happened again?

Anxiously examining his chain of thoughts, he got to the bit where he'd yelled Gabriel's name. He'd only summoned him for a little help! *That couldn't prompt another spiritual paradox... could it?*

Despite surface protestations, he knew he'd done so in anger... even though it *was* fuelled by frustration and resentment at being kept in the dark.

Did that count?

Demanding answers was not always a good thing, he'd learnt. Now he was sure he'd get them... for good or bad.

On cue, the signs of an Archangel materialising presented themselves. Phones rang in nearby rooms as the barking dogs increased their frenzy, a car alarm in the street below having raised the bar.

With the whirlwind at its height, Gabriel appeared in all his glory... splendidly robed in white, and shimmering the way Norman always believed a good Archangel should. Much to his relief, there wasn't an inappropriate piece of leatherwear in sight... if you ignored the sandals... which were pointless, given he was hovering in mid-air.

'I'm so sorry,' Norman mouthed above the chaos.

Gabriel looked at him, but said nothing.

He didn't need to. Norman already knew the serious consequences of letting his anger get the better of him.

'Can't you stop this?' he yelled. 'I'm an idiot... a stupid fool! I was wrong! I totally accept that! But Xanthia had nothing to do with it!'

'This isn't of my doing,' said Gabriel, his voice clear in Norman's head, despite the maelstrom around them.

'I didn't *technically* ask to know anything!' shouted Norman desperately.

'You cannot hide the intention of a thought,' returned Gabriel. 'Not least with semantics. Words are but a primitive attempt to translate a thought's power. As with the individual brushstrokes of a painting, they can combine to express an important one. But, just like a painting, they are not the thought itself. Only the artist knows the true nature of what inspired him. So it is when you speak. It is the thought alone that carries the real truth. I warned you the last time you invoked such a storm as this... they cause ripples in the Universe that cannot be stopped. Desire determines their direction... which is why it is important to only produce good and positive ones. Yours were anything but.'

'I know, I know! Forgive me!' begged Norman contritely. 'I accept it's all my fault!'

'Not *all* your fault,' responded Gabriel, much to Norman's surprise. 'You have been goaded by negative forces gathering around you... attracted by whatever negative ripples you initially set in motion. They are unfairly influencing your mood.'

'*Unfairly?*'

'There are limits to tampering with free will. What they are doing is against the laws of spirit. But the order of the Universe is breaking down. The other side are growing bolder and think they can ignore fundamental principles. They taste victory, so believe they'll have no one to answer to. Boundaries are being crossed. It is an extremely dangerous time.'

'Is it Satan who's encouraging them?'

'Lucifer is the force to which they are attracted. As you know... he is no lover of rules.'

'We beat him once... we'll do it again!' said Norman

defiantly.

A sachet of instant coffee struck him on the forehead.

'We *have* to,' warned Gabriel. 'This could be the last crossroad at which any of us stand.'

'Fork!' Norman corrected him, keen to show he'd taken on board the advice given at what he *assumed* had been their last meeting.

'The lesson to which you allude is just one of many you were fortunate enough to be gifted. Regrettably, you have shown an inability to benefit from such high counsel by not putting them all together when needed.'

Given the detritus currently circling his head, Norman thought it foolish to argue.

'That *must* change. Now you have demanded knowledge that will further strengthen our enemies, harnessing the true potential of your mind is the only way we will succeed against them!'

'Giving me that knowledge will create another spiritual paradox!' exclaimed Norman. 'I don't think I could face a second one!'

'The only paradox is that, although wishing Xanthia to be safe, the answers you've demanded will put her in even greater danger. But you *were* warned.'

'I know... and there's nothing I can do about it now! But what about the *spiritual* paradox? I'm not supposed to have information beyond my karmic status! You said it gave my soul an unfair advantage and would compromise the workings of Heaven!'

'Another lesson you were taught but failed to heed. However... *that* paradox has already occurred and there can only be one... which is just as well, given the problems it caused.'

'How could I forget? I also remember the solution. I was to receive the sphere of knowledge to cancel out any spiritual advantage I obtained.'

Gabriel nodded.

'But that's not possible now!' Norman grabbed one of the

191

bed's upright posts to steady himself. 'That ceased to be an option back at Armageddon Terrace when the sphere exploded! Which raises another issue... I've often wondered how that resolved my karmic upper hand. We *didn't* resolve it... did we?'

'It's the reason you are in this room now,' said Gabriel.

'What do you mean?'

'You will understand, once you have the answers you've demanded.'

'But if it's impossible to repeat a spiritual paradox... what's all *this* about?' Norman used his free hand to acknowledge a pair of socks whizzing between the two of them.

'I told you before... this isn't of Heaven's doing.'

'Then who *is* doing it?

'Someone in this room,' answered Gabriel.

'Please don't tell me Satan's about to materialise!'

'It is only his influence that is present. I'm talking of another.'

'Well... you told me *I'm* not the one causing it!'

Gabriel said nothing.

Norman took a second to interpret the silence... then looked at the person cowering against the door. 'Xan?' he said, open mouthed.

*   *   *

The crowd that had gathered for Worker One's execution was considerably larger than normal, reversing a declining interest in such events.

Whilst extremely entertaining for those assembled to witness a person's chest being ceremonially ripped open... let alone a still-beating heart beat even faster as its owner realised it was about to be ripped from its comfort zone... it could sometimes get a little... *samey.*

Some had argued alternative forms of entertainment might reverse the decreasing numbers. The victim could be strangled, for instance... their comically bulging eyes always a source of

190

great amusement... especially for the kids.

Others suggested being burnt alive would prove a crowd-pleaser... not least because people liked to stand and chat around a nice, warm fire afterwards.

One individual had even gone so far as to suggest that it might pull a bigger crowd if they dispensed with the killing altogether and got the chance to watch an inflated pig's bladder being kicked from one end of a specially marked-out field to another. Realising he was mad, he'd been dispatched to the man with antlers on his house as well as his head to be cured of his insanity.

His treatment duly took place in public... being, ironically, well-attended. How the children giggled, as his tongue had lolled and his eyes popped out of his head.

But the considerable crowd attending Worker One's imminent demise felt uncomfortable.

After all... hadn't he been the one whose astute intervention had saved them from having to endure years more hard work than was originally thought necessary?

Hadn't he also been the one who'd solved their building problem with a simple solution that would make them all look like geniuses to future generations?

Hadn't he also been the one – Worker Two interjected opportunely – who'd sacrilegiously proposed doing away with all the gods in favour of just one?

Had he? They hadn't heard about *that* particular idea.

Yes, he had, Worker Two confirmed. Worker Three could bear witness to that.

All heads turned to Worker Three.

Worker Three nodded reluctantly.

All heads then turned to the man with antlers on his house as well as his head.

How did that one work, then?

It couldn't... announced the man with antlers on his house as well as his head, pouring scorn on the notion of doing away with all the gods.

The crowd gasped.

Had they ever heard anything so stupid?

Well... yes... actually. Worker Two had suggested they use magic to build the monument.

Apart from that?

They shook their heads.

Precisely... which was the reason Worker One had to die. His heretical ideas were a danger to them all. They must appease the gods by offering them his heart.

The crowd reluctantly supposed so.

Despite his hands being tightly bound to a large, wooden frame that had them tethered either side of him, Worker One managed to raise a finger.

All heads turned to Worker One's finger... including that of Worker Two, who stared at it enviously.

Why...? Worker One enquired simply.

As punishment... came the answer from the man with antlers on his house as well as his head.

Was that to appease *all* the gods...? Worker One asked.

All of them, the man with antlers on his house as well as his head confirmed.

What... even the *god of new ideas?*

Pardon?

Even the *god of new ideas.*

All heads turned yet again to the man with antlers on his house as well as his head.

Worker One had just made that one up! he insisted.

Worker One stated emphatically that he hadn't. Where did the man with antlers on his house as well as his head think new ideas came from? Surely he wasn't suggesting that such a god didn't exist? That would mean the existence of something that didn't have a god! In which case... *everything* could exist without a god!

The man with antlers on his house as well as his head's head turned to the expectant crowd... whose heads had turned to his.

Well?

Xanthia sat with her hands covering her eyes, not wanting to look at Gabriel. As soon as the idea had registered that it was her causing the commotion in the room, the disturbance had miraculously abated.

'I don't understand!' blurted Norman. 'That's impossible!'

'The impossible is merely the possible viewed from the perspective of ignorance,' pronounced Gabriel.

'Then I really *am* stupid! What's Xanthia got to do with any of this?'

'She has a gift,' said Gabriel. 'Some mortals are sensitive to the vibrations of spirit. She is one of them.'

'You mean... like a *medium?*'

'That is one way the gift is sometimes squandered.'

'But wouldn't she know?'

'She might not be aware of what it is she is experiencing. Does she ever shown signs of confusion?'

'You could say that,' answered Norman diplomatically. 'But why create such a storm? She was frightened of it herself!'

'Much like a troubled adolescent producing the effects of a poltergeist, she worked herself into a self-perpetuating state of mind.'

'But she was fine up until a moment ago!'

'Are you sure?'

'Well... she *did* say something here was making her feel uncomfortable.'

'Understandable,' nodded Gabriel. 'This is currently a place of extreme unpleasantness.'

'Are you referring to the ghost the landlord claims is here?'

'Not directly. But it is why that disturbed soul lingers at this location and what it is they are refusing to let go of.'

Xanthia moaned.

'It is the very edge of the material plane... the point at which you might cross over into the spirit world.'

'Are you telling me that's an *actual* place?' Norman gasped.

'Not ordinarily... But this is no ordinary landscape. It is an

187

area in your physical realm representing a confluence between it and the spiritual one. It has been fashioned by the very nature of its creation. That is why the ancients revered it so.'

'You're gonna have to run that by me again,' said Norman, trying to make sense of everything.

'It is a difficult concept to define in limited dimensions... its truest form beyond your comprehension. Put simply... it is the process behind creation made manifest.' Gabriel noted Norman's pained expression. 'Perhaps it is best to think of it as the scar left by an umbilical cord,' he suggested.

'You mean... Stonehenge is a spiritual... *belly button?*'

Gabriel flinched. 'If that helps. It is why the ancient inhabitants of this area went to such lengths to mark it out. They were acknowledging its importance.'

Norman's brow contorted further. 'But how did they know?'

'They didn't. It was something they *sensed*... much like Xanthia is sensing the negative element of its boundary now.'

'Negative? You mean Stonehenge has a bad side?'

'Such a distinction should not be applied in a permanent sense. It is what is currently drawn to this boundary that is troubling her. She is picking up on the torment of lost souls attracted to its very edge. Without greater faith, they are unable to let go of the physical plane. They have forgotten it is ultimately an illusion and become confused by the state in which they find themselves. It is why they are producing negative energy... much like your previous thoughts. They are angry and scared... only increasing their torment by attracting that energy back.'

'From where?'

'From the other side of the only gateway they believe will allow them to finally cross over... one that has a boundary they can comprehend. That is why they have gravitated towards it.'

'But if it *is* the confluence you spoke about... why don't they simply use it?'

'They are waiting,' said Gabriel.

'For what?'

Xanthia groaned again.

186

'For you,' the Archangel replied.

Norman looked horrified. '*Me?* What have *I* got to do with it?'

'They think you are here to open it.'

'Open it?'

'In a way that will enable them to release their trapped souls.'

'And *am* I?' ventured Norman, wondering if his two loud notes might turn out to be some kind of spiritual key that unlocked a Neolithic version of the pearly gates.

'No!' said Gabriel firmly. '*That* would be catastrophic!'

Now Norman was even *more* confused. 'But surely it would be a *good* thing. Those troubled spirits could pass through... or whatever it is they're supposed to do.'

'It is not the transference of their energy from the physical to the spiritual that concerns us,' said Gabriel. 'For such unsettled energy would be dwarfed by the vastness of the realm into which it became absorbed. It is what would occur if such energy were allowed to flow the *other* way! The mismatch of scale does not bear thinking about!'

Norman sensed a change in the Archangel's demeanour, the light around him struggling to maintain its intensity. 'What *would* occur?' he asked apprehensively.

Gabriel held on to the answer, as if not wishing to make it credible with its disclosure. 'The supremacy of the Antichrist,' he finally relented, his words bringing an instant chill to the room.

Xanthia moaned yet again... only this time, like a wounded animal sensing the inevitable approach of death.

The dogs outside howled in empathy.

'But you said Armageddon was coming anyway,' Norman reminded him, 'back in my garden in France!'

'It is true. The final battle is inevitable. That has always been known. And victory will go to the strongest side. If we were to cause a spiritual portal to open, the bile that would seep out from the lowest levels of the spirit realm and swamp your world would make it impossible for that side to be ours!'

'But *why* is such a thing inevitable?' exclaimed Norman. 'How has this been allowed to happen? I thought God was supposed to be all powerful! Last time, my mission was just a case of making sure man didn't destroy himself before the karmic progression of souls had time to complete itself. Now you say the danger is coming from *your* side!'

'It is a consequence of the gift of free will,' Gabriel explained. 'By the very nature of the love in which it was given, it cannot be taken away. But it has been abused. Now we must reclaim its power to oppose those perverting its use.'

'We're talking Satan again, aren't we!' groaned Norman, nodding his own confirmation.

'It is he who will empower the Antichrist. Lucifer has spent millennia drawing the lowest forms of spirit to his cause, enticing them with the promise of once again being able to experience the illusion of separation... indulge in the hedonism of ego and the fantasy that one soul can dominate another with impunity. Now he seeks to unleash those followers upon your world and put man to his ultimate test. That is how far he has corrupted the mission originally given to him. It is why we must prepare every mortal soul to be able to distinguish the truth from the lies. *That* is why you are here, Norman. It is *you* who must make such a thing possible!'

Norman was struck by a wave of nausea. 'You're giving me the answer to how the spiritual paradox was resolved... aren't you?' he groaned. 'You *still* intend making me the new Saviour, don't you?'

Gabriel remained silent.

Norman fought to control his breathing. 'But how?' he quaked. 'I'm nobody! I've always been nobody! Everything about me is a sham! The wealth I've never deserved is the only thing that makes me visible... and I haven't exactly done the best I could with that! You said so yourself! Without it, I'd walk through life completely unnoticed!'

'Well, believe me... that's about to change,' advised Gabriel. 'Carry yourself with the knowledge that *nobody* is invisible... not in the eyes of the Universe. You are part of it and... as

184

such... equally important as any other part. Now it is time to learn what *truly* makes a man rich. It is the decisions they make that demonstrate the real value they can put upon themselves.'

'You still don't understand,' persisted Norman. 'I can think myself invincible... believe all I want in myself... but why should others? The last time you proposed making me the new Saviour, at least it was with the aid of the sphere of knowledge. But that's impossible now! How on *earth* could I do what you require of me without it?'

Gabriel looked at him awkwardly. 'You are not the only one seeking that answer. That is what those opposing us have been searching for. To complicate matters... they have pieced together clues from the writing of a man who had unwitting access to a part of the original sphere. Such irony only makes it worse. That is why they have gathered here so strongly... knowing you would arrive. They are waiting for the explanation they forced you to demand. It will give them the upper hand.' The Archangel took a moment to reflect on the consequences. 'But it must be so. You have made it thus.' He steeled himself for the outcome.

'Wait!' cried Norman, before Gabriel could utter another word. 'If you *must* give me an explanation... can't it be broken down into instalments, allowing us to play for a little more time?'

Gabriel considered the idea.

'Give me just enough to satisfy the laws of spirit... but leave something out. One important detail. That way they'll *still* have to wait!'

Gabriel's aura brightened. 'There's that logical mind again. There might be hope for us yet!'

'Well?'

Gabriel nodded and drew himself up

'Please!' winced Norman, holding up a hand. 'No more chariots. I've had enough things flying around my head for today! I don't think I could take any more drama. Just give it to me straight.'

'Very well,' Gabriel shrugged. All the same... he paused for dramatic effect. 'We are here to create a *new* sphere of knowledge.'

As the words made their way through the ether, the air on which they travelled shook violently. Xanthia gasped in pain, holding her head even tighter. But Norman was oblivious to it all, his thoughts scrambling to make sense of what he'd just been told.

'How can that be? I thought we'd agreed such a thing was impossible! You told me the painting required to reconstitute the sphere had been destroyed beyond all possible renovation!'

'That is true,' acknowledged Gabriel. 'Converting vibrations of divine inspiration is no longer an option. But there *might* just be another way.'

'*Might?*' gasped Norman. The outcome of his battle with the Antichrist hinging on a mere possibility suddenly made that prospect even *more* terrifying... if such a thing were possible.

'Admittedly, we are pushing at the boundaries of how the material world came into being in the first place,' Gabriel conceded. 'But in doing so, we will seek to exploit the very process of creation and produce a sample of the ultimate power behind it.'

'And how are we gonna do that?' exclaimed Norman, wide-eyed.

'By using the universal truth that the power you call God is in everything... and therefore everything is part of God. The essence of that force is in all that exists... a fact your ancients celebrated. *Their* connection to a higher spirit wasn't blunted by the distraction of material things. That is why they instinctively worshipped gods of stone... of trees... of the earth... of fire and water... and of everything your modern mind regards as inanimate. They may not have understood the true nature of the power behind their beliefs, but they were no different to those who utilise modern religions to express what they are feeling. All such systems are merely coping mechanisms... as my own appearance is to you. They are attempts to understand a fundamental truth, the *real* mechanism for which can never be fully comprehended by your kind. But there is a part that can... and the blueprint for that is nature itself. It is that blueprint we are here to exploit... for it contains the mind of God.' The Archangel paused. 'Think of your mightiest ocean. Despite its power and vastness, you can understand its chemistry by examining a single drop of its water. In essence, that is what we intend to do with the power behind creation. We are going to take a sample of it!'

The windows – that had been quietly minding their own business since the whirlwind abated – slammed violently back into their frames. The air shook angrily and Norman swore he heard the sound of whispering above the baying of the dogs outside.

Gabriel struggled to maintain his presence whilst he waited for the turbulence to subside. 'They are considerably stronger now,' he announced, when it had.

Norman now had more questions than answers. 'How on earth are my two notes gonna help us take the sample we need?'

'The answer should sound familiar to you,' replied Gabriel. 'We are going to utilise the same fundamental power behind *them.*'

Norman stared blankly.

'Frequencies,' Gabriel explained. 'They'll trigger a process that stimulates every other frequency that constitutes this site in the material plane. For all matter is energy vibrating... and energy is the power of spirit. The genome of creativity is the pattern those frequencies make. Once we have highlighted them by increasing their intensity, we will use their combined vibrations to create a substitute sphere of knowledge... for it will be pulsating with the creative thoughts of God!'

Norman's mouth dropped open. 'My two simple notes have the power to do all *that?*'

'It is not the notes alone that contain the power,' said Gabriel. 'It is what they are part of that gives them their potential. It is the same for you. Everything in the Universe is connected. There is no such thing as separation. Even the smallest particle can have the greatest effect, if it finds itself in the right place at the right time. So it is with your two frequencies. If delivered with enough force, they will trigger a disturbance in the atoms of two specific constituents of your earth plane... which, in turn, will do the same to others... and so on, and so on... until an unstoppable chain reaction causes every frequency we require to resonate at a heightened intensity.'

The air pulsated again as if the disruptive energy was feeding on his words.

'These specific constituents you mentioned,' shouted Norman above it. 'I assume they're contained somewhere within the area of Stonehenge.'

'They *are* Stonehenge,' said Gabriel... the revelation causing his image to distort. 'At least... the bluestone from which it has been fashioned. Consisting of plagioclase feldspar and augite, the unique atomic structures of their crystals will resonate in conflict with one another and start the ball rolling.'

A large piece of ceiling plaster fell from between two wooden beams. Fearing the whole roof might come crashing down, Norman took refuge beneath the canopy of the four poster bed.

He needn't have bothered.

The commotion abruptly ceased.

'It is done,' said Gabriel. 'Now they know our plan.'

'All of it?' asked Norman timidly.

'Not quite,' the Archangel winked.

A teacup on a tray in the corner of the room exploded.

'Now you can appreciate why those stones have such significance, and why so much effort was expended to transport and place them in the order in which they stand. They are awaiting you, Norman.'

Norman looked at the Archangel in astonishment. 'But that's impossible! They were put there by primitive man!'

Gabriel winced. 'Be wary of using that term in such a negative sense,' he counselled. 'They had knowledge of things your generation have long since forgotten and would do well to remember.'

'But they couldn't possibly have known what their work would eventually be used for!'

Gabriel smiled. 'Did *you* when you produced your sonic key?'

'Are you telling me you instructed them to build the monument?'

'We didn't have to. No more than you have to instruct a bird to build its nest. It was something they instinctively felt compelled to do... to celebrate the mind of something they knew was beyond them... innately sensing the very materials needed to recreate an accurate simulacrum. Some may have forged their own interpretations as to *why* it needed to be done. But what matters is that they succeeded. We can only hope their instincts as to the placement of the stones were accurate enough to achieve what we are after. *That* is where any doubt lies.'

'Well... they certainly had a few doubts of their own when it came to that positioning!' pointed out Norman. 'The brochure Snogden-Lambert gave me says that archaeologists believe they changed the layout on a number of occasions.'

'They did?' enquired Gabriel, exhibiting surprise.

Norman exhibited his own. 'You mean... you *didn't* know?'

'How could we?'

'By *looking* at it?' suggested Norman facetiously.

'We *cannot*,' said Gabriel. 'It would be too risky. It is so sensitive a boundary, between the realms of the spiritual and the physical, that vibrations from our observation might upset the state of balance and cause the gateway I mentioned to open.'

'So let me get this straight... you're putting all your faith in something you've never seen.' confirmed Norman.

'Strange... wouldn't you say?' said Gabriel, with a wry smile. 'It seems the tables have been completely turned!'

'Norman...! Please make him go away!' Having stirred from her self-imposed exile, Xanthia was still refusing to look at Gabriel.

'It's alright, Xan,' he soothed. 'Gabriel's explained

179

everything. Can you believe it was *you* causing all that commotion?'

'I *don't* believe him!' she pouted.

'Xan!'

'Well... I don't fink he's very nice.'

Norman laughed off her comment. 'He's an Archangel!'

'He doesn't look like one to me,' she pouted.

'She's understandably confused,' intervened Gabriel. 'I think it best she were not here at this moment in time. Her sensitivity to the spirits gathering at this site will complicate your task. You need as few distractions as possible.'

'Gabriel's right,' said Norman, much to Xanthia's consternation. 'Now I know what this is all about, I reckon things are gonna get a helluva lot rougher for me! Perhaps it's safer if you stayed with friends in London until it's all over.'

'But I wanna see *Trouzerbulge* play!' she insisted.

'Okay... then until it's time for them to perform. Trust me. It's for your own good.'

Much to his surprise... and disappointment... Xanthia eagerly nodded in agreement. She pointed at Gabriel. 'Now can he go?'

'I'll let you say your goodbyes,' responded the Archangel, triggering further dog howling and car alarms by obliging her request.

'Are you sure you can trust him?' she asked, once she and Norman were alone.

'Why on earth would you say that?'

She shrugged and turned towards the scattered contents of her suitcase.

'He's on *our* side!' Norman exclaimed, as she started gathering her belongings together. 'Why would you think he's not?'

'Like he said... I feel certain fings.' she muttered... her ensuing silence signifying the conversation was ended.

* * *

178

'Mister Tucker-Jenkins?' coughed the stagehand politely, attempting to get the director's attention.

Having insisted on continuing to work without a visit to the hospital, Donald had been staring at the stage for the last five minutes without uttering a word. The theatre staff had become increasingly concerned, given Whitebait had also adopted an uncharacteristic silence.

'Mister Tucker-Jenkins?' the young man tried again... only this time a little louder.

Much to his relief, Donald broke from his trance and looked up from his director's position in the stalls. 'They're moving,' he mumbled with vacant eyes.

The stagehand took a moment to examine the impressive semi-circle of full-size trilithons surrounding him. 'They look perfectly stable to me,' he declared, somewhat puzzled. 'They're all bolted to steel baseplates, so you needn't worry about them toppling over.'

'I meant the spirits old Tommy Grumblestone warned us about,' muttered Donald darkly. 'The more unpleasant ones that have been consistently plaguing me. They're on the move!'

The assembled actors – who'd been patiently awaiting his direction – stopped their casual conversations.

'Do you mean... they're coming this way?' asked one, stepping forward anxiously.

'That's the weirdest thing,' said Donald, tilting his head. 'They're not!'

The assistant director – keen to get proceedings moving now Donald was back in the land of the living – cautiously offered an opinion. 'Well... that's a good thing... isn't it?'

'YOU CANNOT BE SERIOUS!' Donald shouted, his eyes shooting to the top of his head and causing everyone to jump.

'That's not meant for me... is it?' probed the assistant director, shaking his head diffidently. He looked to the actors for confirmation... most of whom returned awkward shrugs. Donald's frequent outbursts had started playing havoc with his nerves... not to mention self-confidence. Whitebait's interventions increasing in frequency, he'd found himself in the most awkward of positions. He was having to compete with and humour someone he despised and detested, despite not believing they were there in the first place! To make matters worse... his unreserved respect and admiration for the playwright he regarded as the greatest writer since Shakespeare, meant he'd even found himself drifting toward the realms of jealousy, when observing the close bond between literary genius and a disembodied opinion who'd only ever trawled for fish.

'Whitebait informs me that... word seeping through from the other side suggests... they no longer need me,' translated Donald, between grimaces.

'Is that good?' asked another of the actors.

'Only if I want to commit suicide,' Donald answered. 'It all makes sense now! Apparently... far from trying to stop me writing and performing this play, they've been seeking to gain answers from it... much like *I've* been trying to myself! *That's* why they stopped me killing myself!'

'You tried to commit suicide?' gasped the first actor, shocked by such a casual admission.

Donald's expression became even more animated. 'As did those two American gentlemen!'

'What... try to kill themselves?'

'No, you numbskull... Keep up! They were trying to find out what my play was about!' His eyes widened as a thought suddenly struck him. 'You know what that means, don't you?'

'They're plagiarists?' ventured another.

'They're working for the other side!' exclaimed Donald loudly.

The actors turned to the assistant director for help.

'Are we possibly talking about... the *Russians?*' he asked, as confused as everyone else.

'*Russians?* What on *earth* are you talking about, man?' his idol berated him. 'Has everyone gone completely mad? Am I the only sane one here? I'm talking about Hell... the infernal regions of the dead... the abode of the damned... Gehenna...

Tophet... Abaddon... Hades... Do I need to spell it out?'

'It might help,' cringed the assistant director, bending obsequiously.

'Very well!' huffed Donald. 'Don't expect it to be all fluffy clouds and eternal sunshine when you lot finally pop your clogs! Death can be an extremely messy business! Not everyone takes to it. There are those who would rather have things put back as they were. Why do you think they're constantly clinging to *me?*'

The assistant director smiled inanely and shrugged his ignorance.

'Oh... this is ridiculous!' yelled the lead actor, throwing his script to the ground in frustration. 'I've had enough! I don't care how many great plays the man's written... he's a complete and utter lunatic!' He turned to the others for support. 'Are we *really* so desperate for work, we're prepared to stand here and pretend we've suspended our logical faculties in order to put up with this absurd *bullshit?*'

The silence from his cringing colleagues suggested that... apparently... they were.

Not that anyone could blame them. In a profession where asking whether French fries were required filled the gaps between playing King Lear or pretending you were part of a family choosing a sofa in the bank holiday sales, it paid to smile at anyone who could lessen the pain between such demands. On top of which... belief in an afterlife might be regarded as less a leap of faith than the belief you might actually be able to earn a living in such a precarious profession.

'I think we're all a little stressed,' jumped in the assistant director, placing a restraining arm around Alan's unsettled shoulders.

'That's hardly surprising!' tutted Alan, petulantly shaking it off. 'The man's got us even more spooked than if we were rehearsing the *Scottish* play!'

'IT'S THEATRE TALK!' announced Donald loudly. 'HE MEANS *MACBETH!*'

The whole cast groaned.

'Now look what he's done!' cried Alan, throwing his hands up in disbelief. 'We're going to have to leave the theatre and perform the necessary rituals before we can re-enter and continue!'

'Doesn't that rather contradict us having logical faculties?' pointed out one of the actors, whose previous professional engagement had seen him dressed up as an orange mint and having to jump around with similarly attired thespians. For him, putting up with Donald's quirks carried considerably less shame.

'I'm just saying that things have gotten completely out of hand!' opined Alan, sweeping his hair back in exasperation. 'This is a demanding enough part for me as it is! I'm finding it almost impossible to take seriously a man who's dressed so ridiculously and claiming to converse with the dead!'

Much to everyone's surprise, his outburst produced an unexpected outcome.

'Bravo!' exclaimed Donald loudly, standing up and clapping as enthusiastically as his attire allowed.

Those onstage exchanged looks of bemusement.

'That's it!' cried Donald, pointing at Alan excitedly. 'That's *exactly* the attitude I'm after!' He beamed triumphantly.

Alan looked confused. 'I beg your pardon?' he said, the wind sucked from his sails.

'That anger... Your frustration... The belief that you're fighting for the truth, having exposed what you believe to be a sham! That's *precisely* what I've been searching for from your character!'

Alan stared at him in stunned silence.

Jaws dropped.

'Oh... my god!' gasped the assistant director, as a thought struck him like a thunderbolt. 'What utter genius!' he crowed, clasping his hands together and shaking his head in wonderment. 'The man truly is a mind apart from all others! He's been prepared to play a part and suffer our private ridicule... purely to draw the perfect performance out of a single member of his cast!' He spread his arms out in

174

stupefaction. 'He's fooled us all, ladies and gentlemen! Every single one of us! We are not worthy of standing in the same theatre as him... let alone taking his direction on this stage!'

There were increasing murmurs of amazement as the penny the assistant director had thrown into the air dropped. There followed a slow ripple of applause, gradually increasing in intensity, until every member of the cast and crew was vigorously demonstrating their admiration for the man selflessly sporting a deep-sea diver's helmet and matching boots... a chastened Alan included.

Donald nodded his appreciation, embarrassed by such a show of affection.

He was also extremely confused.

'Shall we get back to work?' he suggested, not sure what all the fuss was about. 'We only have a few days left to ensure our message is understood when it's delivered to the public.'

'I am forever in your debt,' said Alan sonorously, placing a hand to his chest and bowing theatrically. 'Please forgive me my appallingly ignorant outburst!'

Donald waved the apology away. 'It's all water under the bridge,' he said. 'I've learnt to grow a very thick skin over the years. I've heard *far* worse!'

Alan smiled appreciatively.

'IT DOESN'T MATTER!' shouted Donald.

Alan smiled appreciatively again.

'IT *REALLY* DOESN'T MATTER!'

Alan wasn't sure he could fake an appreciative smile for a *third* time. It wasn't as if he was taking a curtain call.

'LOOK...JUST LET IT GO, WOULD YOU?' yelled Donald.

The assistant director's head dropped.

'WHO *KNOWS* WHAT HE MEANT BY *PRIVATE RIDICULE!*'

It dropped even further.

'I HAVE ENOUGH TROUBLE READING MY *OWN* MIND!' cried Donald. 'I'M HARDLY LIKELY TO BE ABLE TO READ HIS!'

'Have we all got our scripts, ladies and gentlemen?' shouted the assistant director hastily. 'I think we were looking to do the scene where our hero faces his greatest dilemma!'

*   *   *

Given the unexpected turn of events, Worker One should've been elated. Instead of his heart being removed with the large knife that had been ceremoniously – if a little tactlessly – waved in front of him, it had been the twine binding his hands and feet that had finally felt its keenness. Despite his change of circumstance, he couldn't help thinking he'd jumped from the earthenware cooking pot into the fire.

The noisy crowd surrounding him had taken it upon themselves to forcefully remove the antlers from the man with antlers on his house as well as his head and place them atop his own, signalling their desire to follow *him* from now on.

Whilst flattered... Worker One remonstrated that such an action was no longer necessary. Surely he'd proved the power of the antlers was a fallacy.

The crowd struggled with such a revolutionary concept. How could Worker One communicate with the gods if he didn't have the appropriate headgear?

That was the point... He didn't need them.

What... the antlers? The crowd looked shocked and horrified.

No... the gods.

The crowd went *beyond* shocked and horrified.

Worker One quickly realised that beyond shocked and horrified was a place called *stunned and not quite sure what to do*. Appreciating it was not somewhere people usually hung around for long, he knew they'd soon be reaching a fork in the road offering *acceptance of a bold new idea* or *kill what you do not understand*.

The man with antlers on his house though formerly on his head took advantage of the crowd's consternation. He gloated that he'd been right to warn them about Worker One's outrageous blasphemy... and could he now have his antlers

172

back, please?

The crowd considered their options. Had they made a big mistake believing Worker One could provide a better future?

They sought to clarify his position.

When Worker One said he didn't need the gods... did he mean he only needed the one... or was he proposing they ditched them *altogether*?

The second option delivered with fear in their eyes, Worker One appreciated the crowd wasn't ready for such a theological abstraction. Noting the ceremonial knife still glistening – as it was wildly stabbed in the air by one of those demanding an answer – he further appreciated the one he gave would determine the future location of his vital organs. He needed to tread extremely carefully, if that was to be as close to where they were supposed to be as possible.

Scouring the crowd, he caught Worker Three's imploring eyes returning daggered confirmation of his last thought.

The dilemma facing him couldn't be greater.

Whilst immensely fond of his body parts, he'd been gifted a power that could be used to promote rational thinking and a society based on mutual respect... rather than enforced behaviours centred around inherited and inflexible superstitions. This was his chance to change the world for the better. He couldn't throw it away.

Putting their prejudices aside, Worker One began cautiously... how did the crowd feel about a world where people based their actions on common sense and decency... acting purely out of love for their fellow man because it was the right thing to do... not because of dogma or fear of retribution?

The crowd agreed it sounded good in principle.

... and a world where they didn't feel every thought they had was being judged?

The crowd agreed that also sounded good.

... a world where people could debate ideas freely without worrying about upsetting others... as beliefs would be nothing more than the opinion of the individual?

Logical and fair, they agreed.

... and a world where death was accepted as final... being considered the natural conclusion to a life well lived?

Erm... could he just run that last bit by them again?

He did.

Much as expected... it didn't sound any more appealing the second time around.

Not that they were selfishly considering their *own* mortality... but where did that leave their highly revered, dead ancestors?

Worker One coughed awkwardly. They'd still be dead... only, slightly more so than before.

He wasn't really selling it... was he!

Worker One figured he was probably ahead of his time... which was a shame, given it now looked likely to come to an end.

The crowd had turned.

As the ceremonial knife was quickly passed to the front, a pronouncement was made that Worker One would *have* to die. It seemed the man with antlers on his house though formerly on his head had been right all along.

An angry arm was raised. The blade glinted in the sun.

WAIT!

Worker Three stepped from their midst and pointed out that Worker One hadn't *actually* answered their original question. His eyes fixed imploringly on his colleague, he suggested they allow him one last chance to do so.

The crowd exchanged impatient glances.

Fair enough, they conceded.

When he'd previously said they didn't need gods... had he meant they only needed one... or proposing they ditch them altogether?

Worker One held on to Worker Three's intense stare.

Worker Three closed his eyes and nodded gently.

Well?

Perhaps just one would be okay... he replied stiffly.

The crowd tilted their heads as they considered the possibility.

But a very BIG one... he added quickly, reacting to their indecisiveness.

The crowd warmed to the thought.

And somewhere to go to after they'd died?

Of course. He'd only been pulling their leg about that bit.

It was definitely sounding better.

What's more... they needn't ever live in fear again... for the one god would be a benevolent god and love them all as if they were his own children.

Really? The crowd thought the one god sounded a bit soft. They shifted uneasily.

Worker One cleared his throat. But woe betide anyone who disobeyed him... for he would unleash upon them every punishment and suffering their primitive minds could conceive... and quite a bit they couldn't.

The crowd liked what they were hearing. Suffering was reassuringly familiar... and it was always nice to have boundaries.

Worker One informed them that they could have as many of *those* as they wished. In fact... he'd start drawing up a list. They could even put one day a week aside to lay down their work tools in order to be reminded what those boundaries were.

Could?

MUST! insisted Worker One... getting the hang of things.

A healthy murmur went up from the crowd. They liked the sound of this one god. He was kind, cruel, liberating and controlling... offering something for everyone. What more could they want?

Worker One breathed a sigh of relief.

Now... he just had to figure out what to wear on his head instead of those ridiculous antlers.

*   *   *

Norman had slept badly... though in his mind, he hadn't slept at all. Despite the troubled spirits Gabriel had warned him about

169

having declined to put in a nocturnal appearance, every creak and groan of the building's timbers had prevented his restless brain from switching off.

Being alone hadn't helped. Albeit at his own insistence, Xanthia's readiness to follow his advice and return to London had left him feeling crushed. Her eager compliance and lack of objection only cemented his belief that a rift had opened up between them that – for all the positive forks in the world – could no longer be reversed.

However, the prospect of permanently losing the only girl he'd ever loved hadn't been the main cause of his tossing and turning. Credit for *that* went to the shock revelation that he had – once again – been chosen to become the new Saviour and would receive the sphere of knowledge in due course. What did that mean the future held for him now... assuming he succeeded in providing the Universe with one, of course?

So many thoughts had raced through his mind. Would he be expected to don a robe and sandals and walk amongst the public, making deep and meaningful pronouncements? If that were the case, he made a note to self not to ruin the impact by wearing socks. Perhaps he should think about employing a stylist... and maybe a public relations company to get the ball rolling.

Whatever he did, it wasn't going to be pleasant. He imagined himself being fiercely interrogated during televised debates by the greatest minds in science and philosophy, all attempting to trip him up and expose him as a charlatan. He'd be laughed at... pilloried... persecuted... crucified by a cynical media... his motives questioned... along with his sanity.

And how would it feel to know absolutely everything? Like Gabriel, would he see inside other people's minds? Indeed... would he be able to read Gabriel's?

That'd be interesting!

Was he about to find out what Xanthia *really* thought of him... or more disturbingly... what she thought about Stump?

What of those individuals he'd often wondered about? Would he experience how it felt to be the life and soul of the party... adored... attractive... have numerous friends... siblings... be famous... a parent... female... old... disabled... terminally ill? Would he be able to understand the reasoning of evil men... feel their darkness... anger... insecurity... fear... or even appreciate the pleasure their actions brought them?

Would he discover what came before the big bang... its cause... how infinity worked or didn't? Would he be able to solve the greatest mysteries that science had yet to fathom? Might it enable him to perform acts that seemed miraculous or superhuman, but were mere parlour tricks, given what he would know? If that were the case, would it be alright to use them to convince his doubters?

This last thought triggered another.

What of those who wouldn't need such tricks? What of those who actually *believed* him? Would they hang on his every word... interpret his every move... follow him wherever he went? Veneration was the least he could expect. But might he actually end up being worshipped?

The prospect appalled him...

... and yet.

A brief flicker of vanity was quickly quenched by the thought that whatever status he achieved, he was going to have to do battle for it. Not just with crusty academics or a dismissive and vengeful press, but with no less than the Antichrist himself. If Hitler, Stalin, and all other evil men throughout history, had failed to secure that title, how wicked and depraved would the eventual holder turn out to be?

He figured he'd find out soon enough.

Such thoughts causing turmoil in his head, the sound of a cock crowing had come as a blessed relief. Not wishing to stay in the room any longer than necessary, he decided to embrace the accompanying daylight and take himself off for the briefest of walks and some fresh air.

Not bothering to wash, he threw on yesterday's clothes and headed downstairs.

Exiting the building via a deserted snug that reeked of stale beer and chimney smoke, he found his options limited. The village boasted little more than a collection of houses clinging to an inconsequential B road that seemed not to have woken up with him.

Trusting to instinct, he turned right. But it wasn't long before the quaintly leaning buildings channelling him along the main street gave way to open countryside and he found himself surrounded by hedgerows and not much else. There seemed little point in going further.

It was as he was turning to go back that a figure caught his eye along a low ridge delineating the fields from the sky. The individual appeared to be waving at him.

Shielding his eyes from the rising sun, he tried to ascertain if he knew them... but considered it highly unlikely.

Keen not to delay his return – a meeting with the staging company scheduled in a little under an hour – he ignored the stranger's advances and headed in the direction from which he'd just come. But on reaching the first of the perpendicularly challenged buildings, three dogs of differing breeds – though all of a threatening size – scampered from an abutting alleyway and came to a halt a few yards in front of him. Imperiously blocking his path, the largest bared its teeth and growled menacingly, prompting the others to do the same.

Not again!

As Norman considered crossing the road, they advanced... barking aggressively... their salivating jaws forcing his retreat. To his surprise, no heads popped out of windows to see what all the commotion was about... the only person visible, the stranger on the ridge silently observing his predicament.

Once more, he found himself beyond the village boundary.

He threw out his arms in a gesture of hopelessness to the individual... who beckoned him again.

Realising his options were quickly running out, he braved a narrow gap in the thickset hawthorns to scramble over some barbed wire and into the field beyond. Encouraged by the mystery figure, he made his way up the gentle slope, the sound of the angry dogs decreasing as the wind took over and blew their threat away from him.

Assuming it to be a farmer, he wasn't surprised to come upon an individual attired in a beige, knee-length smock and a rounded, felt hat complementing a set of white whiskers protruding from a ruddy face. He also exuded a strong smell of manure.

The owner of the face seemed less accepting of his appearance, if not the smell.

'You need to get out into the country more, Norman. You'll find things have moved on since Thomas Hardy wrote about it!'

'Gabriel?'

'Yes... but not Oak!'

'I understand... The Archangel.'

Gabriel examined his Wellington boots. 'Hard to believe, I know.'

'But why a meeting like this? I nearly didn't come. Were the dogs your idea?'

Gabriel shook his head. 'Hardly.'

'Then why are you in this field?'

'For the same reason my presence at the stones would destabilise an already precarious balance of energy. Disclosing our plans last night brought far more negative forces to this area than anticipated. This is as close as I dare bring myself. Even the village is now out of bounds for me. I'm afraid you are going to have to face the battle on your own from now on.'

'But you didn't tell the other side everything!'

'It made little difference. Whilst I was hoping to keep one key detail from them until the last moment, that cannot be. Our opponents are growing so rapidly in strength, I will soon be forced to retreat even further from this area. They have left me no choice but to reveal your final instructions, as I may not get another chance.'

'Does that mean it's gonna get even rougher than yesterday?' Norman gulped.

'Considerably,' said Gabriel grimly. 'The clock that started ticking back in France is about to chime. Now the battle *truly* begins.'

Norman looked up at the sky and sought comfort in the fact at least there wasn't a ceiling to fall in on him this time.

'There's always the possibility of being struck by lightning, though... especially up here,' Gabriel warned.

'Thanks!' Norman braced himself for what might follow. 'Well... I guess we better get it over with, then.'

Gabriel nodded solemnly. 'So be it.' He took a moment to look about himself, as if scouting for impending danger. 'The timing of your final task is critical. There is no room for error. You must ensure your two frequencies occur during a precise alignment of the cosmos. The heavens will not wait. Though no discernible pattern for your astronomers to marvel at, the alignment of all matter in the Universe is crucial to our master plan. Therefore you must wait until just before the sun's rays rise above the heel stone – on the morning of the summer solstice – and are about to strike the first of the bluestones, before setting those frequencies in motion. It is *imperative* they are at full strength when the rays finally make contact. The sphere of knowledge will then be brought into being and contained within the ring made by the lintels atop the outer stones. You must ensure you are standing at the exact centre of the monument during this time, in order for it to be bestowed upon you. That is everything you need to know.' The revelation complete, Gabriel looked about himself again... though this time in confusion. The playful sound of a skylark and distant rumblings of a tractor accompanied the faint murmur of traffic from a point somewhere beyond the opposite ridge. Only the slightest breeze ruffled his whiskers. 'That's very odd.' he muttered to himself.

Norman didn't think it odd at all. Instead, his thoughts were on something far more alarming. Having carefully visualised the Archangel's orders, the last image presented something of a dilemma.

'Contained within the *what?*' he asked tentatively.

Gabriel broke from his reflection. 'The ring of lintels atop the outer stones that is there to act as a cradle. It's crucial for containing the sphere as it is being formed.'

Norman ran through the description in his mind one more time, just in case he'd missed something.

He hadn't.

'You need a *complete* ring of stones to contain the sphere?'

'Of course. That is what will shape the energy into a sphere. Anything less would spell disaster!'

Norman looked at the Archangel awkwardly. He was unsure how best to broach the subject.

'Something wrong?'

Norman winced. 'You know you said earlier you couldn't *see* the monument…'

'I'm glad *something* of what I say occasionally gets through,' said Gabriel dryly.

Norman stared at him intently.

Gabriel's whiskers quivered. 'What is that image you're presenting in your mind?'

Norman didn't answer. He knew he didn't have to. He'd telepathically invited Gabriel to take a peek… and the rest was obvious.

'Is that *it?*' cried Gabriel.

Norman telepathically answered that it was.

Gabriel stared at him in stunned silence.

'It's that concept we call time,' Norman explained. 'You'll find it plays havoc with old buildings.'

A sudden gust of wind whipped across the fields, nearly taking him off his feet… though Gabriel's hat remained unmoved.

'So let me get this straight,' said the Archangel, consternation twisting his face. 'You're telling me the image in your mind represents the current condition of the monument known as Stonehenge?'

'I can't believe you didn't know it was a ruin!'

Gabriel's head shot back in anguish, waves of violent energy distorting his image. As Norman looked on transfixed, the figure of the nineteenth-century farmer transformed into a rapid succession of previous interpretations of his vibrations. As everything from Norman's own inept and unflattering attempts... to images of a more exotic and alien nature, flashed in front of him, he started feeling giddy. Just as he was praying it would stop, the more familiar figure of the winged Archangel morphed from what had become a blur. But the look of anguish remained.

'No wonder I didn't sense the other side's fury just now!' he howled. 'They must be rejoicing at our predicament!'

'I know last night you said it was too risky for you to observe the site... but I didn't realise that meant you weren't aware of the state it was in!' gasped Norman.

'How could we be?'

Norman grabbed his head. 'This is crazy! I can't believe we're going to fail through something so obvious! Not after me managing to get us *this* far!'

'*Fail?*' Gabriel flexed his wings. 'Such ripples must not be generated! We must act quickly, if we are to succeed!'

'Succeed?' choked Norman. 'Exactly how do you work *that* one out?'

'We must rectify the situation,' answered Gabriel matter-of-factly.

'*Rectify?*'

'Yes... You must put things right.'

'*Me?*' Norman looked at him, open-mouthed. 'How on *earth* am I supposed to do that?'

'I would have thought it obvious,' said Gabriel. 'You must rebuild Stonehenge before the solstice occurs.'

'WHAT!' The ferocity of Norman's outburst sent a number of scavenging birds scattering into the air.

'You must return it to its original condition.'

'In *four* days?' cried Norman incredulously.

'Your mathematics is correct.'

'I know it is! I'm also pretty good at physics, geography, history and common sense! And for any *one* of those reasons, there's no *way* I could achieve such a thing ... let alone all of them combined! It's absolutely *impossible!*'

'Forks and ripples, Norman... remember?'

Norman scoffed at the reminder. 'Any negative ripples from

me are as *nothing* compared to the tsunami of positivity I'd have to generate in order to rebuild Stonehenge in four days!'

'Then you'd better start making your thoughts as positive as possible!' Gabriel advised.

'*Positive?*' snorted Norman. 'Give me *one* positive I could possibly take from this disastrous situation!'

'Apart from the fact you still have a chance to save the whole of humanity?'

'Yes…' said Norman, slightly more muted. 'Apart from *that*.'

'Well… how about the fact you only have to *repair* the monument, not build it from scratch.'

'Oh!' Norman slapped his forehead sarcastically, 'I didn't think of that! What a *huge* difference *that* makes!'

'You should be aware that sarcasm creates unhelpful ripples too,' pointed out Gabriel. 'Given the gravity of the situation, you would be better setting your mind to working out how the repairs can be achieved in the short time you have left.'

'They can't!' Norman insisted. 'And it's *gravity* that's one of the problems, if you'll excuse the pun! It might not affect *you*… but do you know how much those stones weigh? What you're asking is impossible!'

'Primitive man didn't think so,' Gabriel reminded him. 'And he didn't have your technology.'

'He also didn't have local councils, heritage committees and public opinion to worry about! I couldn't possibly persuade the necessary authorities to allow me to mess with the most famous Neolithic monument in the world!'

'You persuaded them to let you set up your sound equipment. I remember you once telling me *that* was impossible.'

'That's different!'

'Really? Wasn't it achieved by applying your logical mind and finding the right solution?'

'Or maybe I just got lucky!'

'Luck is the Universe blessing the path you have chosen. Do not dismiss it so lightly.' Gabriel stepped closer. 'Weren't you the person who once proved me wrong by locating a missing piece of inspiration the whole of Heaven had been unable to find... simply by breaking the problem down into logical steps? Well... now you must summon that belief in yourself again. It was a belief that got the better of Lucifer... and few mortals can claim *that*. The positive mind is an unstoppable power, Norman. Only its own negative thoughts can defeat it. Now is the time to remember everything I have taught you. Forget nothing! Believe there is magic in your mind and there will be! You, of all people, know that truth!'

Norman could hardly argue. Xanthia alone was testament to that. But whilst the Universe had certainly come up trumps in that instance... this was going to take *some* asking.

'Then ask,' said Gabriel, reading his mind.

Norman realised he had no choice but to humour the Archangel. 'Okay,' he sighed heavily. 'Let's put it to the test. So... breaking it down step by step... must I return *everything* to its original condition in order for the sphere of knowledge to be contained within the stones?'

Gabriel peered at him intently. 'From the image you hold in your mind, it appears it is only the outer ring that presents the problem.'

'You mean... as a group... the heaviest stones of all.'

'Their weight is an irrelevance.'

'Not to me, it's not!'

'As long as they are sturdy enough to keep the sphere contained inside the limits they denote... it *is*. We are simply talking spiritual vibrations.'

'And what about the inner bluestones?'

'The plagioclase feldspar and augite?'

'Yes... those. Not only have they had their positions changed over the years, they're *also* incomplete.'

'It is merely the presence of their *constituents* that matters. I believe enough remain in suitable conjunction with each other to start the chain reaction we require.'

Norman took a moment to process the facts. 'Okay... I need to put some steps in motion.'

'You have a plan?'

'Not in the slightest. I'm talking about ones that'll get me back to the village. I've meetings lined up that require my attendance if we're to still go ahead with this thing... though goodness knows how!'

'It *does* know how,' Gabriel assured him. 'The answer is out there. You just have to draw it towards you.'

Norman smiled weakly and raised his hand in a gesture of parting as he started down the slope.

'Remember...' called out Gabriel after him. 'If it's luck you need... that's simply the Universe approving of the forks you take.'

'Then I'm trusting it to have sorted out those dogs, for starters!' Norman shouted back, striding determinedly to where they'd last threatened him... and hoping its laws had been set in motion.

*   *   *

Bob stretched his limbs as best he could, given the confines of the car in which he was sitting. 'D'ya reckon it's crossed young Kevin's mind that we bugged his room?'

'I certainly hope so,' yawned Chad, freshening his face with a vigorous rub.

'And that we're capable of monitoring every phone and computer communication he makes?'

'Well... we're completely wasting our time sat here if it hasn't!'

Bob sighed heavily. 'Just a shame we haven't.'

'Never underestimate the power of paranoia,' smiled Chad.

Bob held his stomach and groaned.

'Not again!' Chad frowned.

'I blame his mother's baking. I dunno what the *hell* she put in those cakes!'

'It ain't their quality that's the problem... it's the quantity! You didn't have to eat 'em all!'

Bob looked at his partner apologetically. 'I get bored on these stakeouts. It's comfort eating.'

'If you *must* evacuate your bowels again, you'd better be quick! If our target shows, we need to be ready to move!'

'D'ya *really* reckon our bluff will work?'

Chad yawned. 'It has to. Annoying as he is, that little shit in his room is our only chance of finding Penkridge.'

'He'll be taking that bedroom apart looking for bugs as we speak. It's only a question of time before he realises there ain't any!'

'At least it'll keep him occupied.' Chad rested his head against the driver's window. 'Anyway... we have no choice. We gotta stick to our plan. The kid knows Penkridge won't risk staying at the hotel, now he's been compromised. He's gonna be desperate to know how he can help Penkridge out. If he believes he's unable to use any form of communication without us eavesdropping on him, he'll know there's only one way to find out... Sit tight and wait for Penkridge to come to *him*.'

'We could be sat here for weeks!' groaned Bob.

Chad shook his head. 'Penkridge will be desperate to know if his stooge sung like a canary after his arrest. Don't worry. He'll be itching to make contact with his *Provider*.'

Bob placed his hand on his stomach again and winced. 'Talking of little shits... It's no good. I'm gonna have to go back and use the toilet at that café around the corner again. I swear they're gonna ask I start bringing my own toilet roll with me.'

'I think you'll find it's more likely they request you bring air freshener.'

Bob opened the door.

'I guess you might as well get us some coffee while you're at it,' Chad suggested.

'I'll also see if they've got any bacon rolls.'

'In that case... don't forget to wash your hands.'

Bob had just placed a foot on the pavement when Chad's body jerked forward.

'Is that who I think it is?'

A lone figure had just exited the house they'd been observing and was striding purposely in the opposite direction.

'That's Supergeek,' said Bob, quickly yanking his leg back

into the car. 'I'd recognise that scrawny body anywhere! Let's go!'

Chad hesitated.

'C'mon Chad… we'll lose him!'

'What if he's just gone for milk? If we move from here, we could miss out on Penkridge!'

'Are you *serious?* I doubt that kid's ever run an errand for his mom in his life!'

Chad started the engine. 'I'll let you have that one!' He waited until Kevin had reached the end of the street before putting the car in gear.

'You don't reckon we'd be better on foot?' asked Bob, debating whether to fasten his seatbelt or not.

'No point. Like you say… the kid's lazy. He'll be taking a bus.' Chad accelerated towards the junction at which Kevin had just disappeared from view.

When they reached it, Bob shot a restraining hand across his partner's chest, his other indicating a bus stop a short distance away to their right. 'Good call!'

'Game on, asshole!' muttered Chad, observing Kevin heading towards it.

Just as they feared they'd be forced to show their hand by prematurely pulling out into the busy stream of traffic… a car tooting from behind… the sight of an approaching red double-decker bus saved the day.

Maintaining a gap of a few vehicles, they watched as Kevin boarded it.

'Seems promising. He's heading straight into the city,' said Bob, as they shadowed it along its stuttering route.

'Perhaps he'd *already* arranged a rendezvous with Penkridge. Things are looking up!'

Their optimism was short-lived.

The bus had barely gone a mile when – during one of its scheduled stops – their target unexpectedly alighted from its doors.

'*Now* what's he up to?'

Chad had already spotted the answer, having glimpsed the

157

train station across the road. 'Don't let him outta your sight!' he shouted, veering to the kerb.

Bob had already opened the door, incurring the wrath of a passing cyclist.

Kevin having safely made it across the busy road, Bob deflected the abuse of startled motorists with an optimistically extended hand of thanks, as he precariously weaved his way between them.

Ignoring the double yellow lines, Chad abandoned the vehicle to its fate and attempted to replicate his partner's reckless choreography. But the traffic was having none of it... having already suffered one idiot. It forced him to wait until a set of traffic lights came to his rescue. But it had cost him precious time.

Entering the station's bustling concourse, he scanned the faces going about their business in the hope of spotting a familiar one. But to no avail. The morning rush-hour made it impossible... two trains simultaneously standing at different platforms only compounding his problem.

Hastily scouring the large, electronic departure board, he determined that only one was headed for the city and quickly made his way towards it. Not risking the queue for a ticket, he elbowed his way through its boarding passengers, desperate to beat the doors.

Instinctively starting at the rear of the train, he squeezed his way along its corridor, systematically umpiring the heads on either side as he went from carriage to carriage.

It was as he was battling his way through the midsection that he finally saw one he recognised coming the other way.

'You neither!' wheezed Bob.

Chad cursed under his breath. 'Perhaps he queued for a ticket!' Crouching so as to peer through the window, he finally glimpsed the answer. As supposed, their target was strolling away from a ticket machine.

A whistle blew.

'Wrong train!' shouted Chad, attempting to retrace his steps and make for the nearest door. But a young girl struggling with a stroller and clutching a baby blocked his route.

Attempting to give her a hand in order to facilitate his passing, she suddenly reached out and grabbed his arm as the train unexpectedly jerked forward.

'Shit!'

The girl looked at him awkwardly.

'We've blown it!'

As the station platform started passing at an ever-increasing speed, Chad resigned himself to his fate.

'That's that, then!' he grimaced, unclasping the infant's hand from his shirt. 'We're back to square one!'

'Where d'ya reckon he's going?' panted Bob, bending over and placing his hands on his knees to catch his breath.

'In exactly the opposite direction to us!' answered Chad.

'Oh… please no!' groaned Bob quietly.

'Jeez… what the hell's that smell?' Chad looked accusingly at the infant.

'He's innocent,' Bob apologised. 'I *knew* I should've gone earlier.'

'Give me a break!' cried Chad, looking to the carriage ceiling for sympathy.

'I doubt the car's gonna be there when we get back, either,' added Bob.

'Could it get any worse?' Chad moaned, dropping his head.

'Tickets, please!' boomed a voice from the other end of the carriage.

*　　*　　*

'Excuse me… Mister Tucker-Jenkins?'

'*Donald…* please, dear boy.'

The young actor smiled his appreciation. 'Donald… Do you remember when I asked if the spirits moving on and leaving you alone was a *good* thing?'

Donald raised his eyes, searching for the memory. 'I do,' he confirmed, when he'd found it.

'And you replied… *only if I want to commit suicide.*'

Donald nodded.

'Well... things got a little sidetracked after that and you never explained what you meant.'

'About the suicide?'

'About that being the *only* benefit. Because that implies it hasn't changed the level of danger you say the rest of us are facing.'

'Oh... but it *has*,' said Donald brightly.

The actor looked confused.

'It's *much* worse now!' Donald elaborated.

The young man's shocked expression suggested an explanation was necessary.

'Look. It's simple... Since souls first found themselves forced to abandon this world, they've been using people like me to reconnect with it. Up until now, it's been their only bridge. Well... it's not just those who were trying to discover what my play was about that have vacated my head.' He rapped it with his knuckles. 'It's *all* of them... from the mildly troublesome to the downright evil. I've never had so many thoughts to myself.'

'And that's not good?' asked the actor slowly.

'Not for you.'

'But...'

'Think about it,' said Donald. 'They don't need me anymore. They've finally gathered enough collective strength to establish a link to this world directly. Why do you think I warned you all about hell yesterday?'

The actor shook his head.

'Well... it's because they're finally bringing it here to earth!'

* * *

'Stump... it's Norman!'

There was a long pause at the end of the phone, before a disgruntled voice croaked a reply. 'D'ya know what fuckin' time it is?'

'Yes,' said Norman, checking his watch. 'It's three-thirty in the afternoon.'

154

There was another pause.

'Oh... right.'

The addition of some high-pitched moaning in the background suggested Stump wasn't the only one who'd been inconvenienced by the call.

Norman presented his next words delicately. 'I've got a bit of a problem.'

'I know... I've seen you,' came the predictable insult.

'With the gig.'

'You're not phoning up to cancel... are you?' Stump shouted, suddenly demonstrating alertness.

'No... no... nothing like that. Only...'

'Is it the staging guys? I told you... don't take any bullshit from those clambering monkeys! Tell 'em *exactly* how you want it... and don't let 'em blind you with tales of topographical inconsistencies or the fact their forklift's gonna struggle if the fuckin' grass gets wet!'

'The meeting with them went extremely well, thank you. In fact, they're keen to get started. Scaffold Pike sends his regards, by the way.'

The name took a moment to register.

'Oh, yeah... Ol' Pikey... What a wanker!'

Norman thought he'd edit the return salutation, if it was ever enquired about.

'So... what's the problem?'

Norman couldn't think of any way to phrase the answer other than exactly how it was. 'I need to rebuild Stonehenge,' he said bluntly.

'What... you're making a *mock-up?*'

'No... I need to rebuild the original.'

The silence on the end of the phone was much longer than the previous ones. Faint murmuring in the background confirmed Stump's company was female.

'Fair enough,' came the eventual reply.

'*What?*'

'I said... fair enough!'

'That's what I thought!' exclaimed Norman. 'I mean... I've

got to put the original monument back to how it used to be!'

'Yeah… I got it the first time.'

'You're not shocked?'

'Nah… I think it'll look extremely cool! It'll be well impressive!'

'It'll certainly be that!' gasped Norman. 'Especially if I manage to achieve it in the first place! That's why I called. I had to share the burden… and you were the only person I can talk to who'd understand the enormity of it.'

'I shouldn't think Xanthia would be too pleased to hear you say that!' said Stump.

'I've decided to keep her out of it. It's for her own good.'

'Anyway… I don't see why you're worried,' Stump yawned dismissively. 'They've recreated the Great Pyramid and Sphinx in Vegas… and you can float on a gondola around the best bits of Venice, if you get tired of playing the slots. I did it last year. My mate Stevie the Props was responsible for some of the work. He's fuckin' brilliant. He built the Marilyn and Maggie statues at the front of my drive.'

'I remember,' said Norman. 'They're very clever.'

'Yeah… but the bollocks were *my* idea!'

'Extremely lifelike… if I recall.'

'Precisely! Which is why you should give him a call. Mention my name and tell him I said it's urgent!'

'I don't understand.'

'Well… you're not looking to rebuild the original in fuckin' stone… are you?' Stump snorted.

'You mean…'

'Fibreglass,' he elaborated. 'That's what *all* our stage props are made of. It's very versatile… and so is he. If you need something to look real but ain't… Stevie's yer man.'

Norman flashed back to his conversation with Gabriel. The Archangel had definitely stated that the weight of the outer stones was an irrelevance… just so long as they kept the sphere of knowledge contained.

'Is it strong?'

'Fibreglass?'

'Yes.'

'As strong as you want it to be, I suppose.'

Norman considered the idea. 'I think you might have something big!' he said excitedly.

'Xanthia been reminiscing again, has she?'

Norman ignored the comment. 'Stevie the Props, you say?'

'The one and only,' confirmed Stump.

'If you give me his number, I'll call him straight away.'

'No problemo. I'll get Sharky to pass it on to you. I'm a little tied up at the moment!' He shared a whispered joke with his companion... leaving Norman to believe he probably meant *literally*. 'I have to say, though... I'm amazed they've agreed to let you do it,' he added.

'What?'

'Tamper with their precious bleedin' monument.'

Norman's initial enthusiasm faltered, as the reality of his task waved at him from a different angle. 'They haven't,' he admitted uncomfortably.

For the fourth time, a silence hung awkwardly on the other end of the phone.

'I'll give you this,' said Stump eventually. 'You'll certainly have proved your balls are bigger than mine, if you manage to pull *this* one off!'

Norman was thinking much the same thing, as the phone went dead.

He kept the receiver next to his ear, a million thoughts passing between it and the one on the opposite side of his head. But out of all of them, the one that kept coming back, having caught the rock star *in flagrante*, was the realisation that – during the whole of the telephone conversation... and despite her name cropping up – Stump hadn't thought it necessary to send his regards to Xanthia or ask how she was.

*　　*　　*

The night closing in, Worker One was taking comfort from the small fire he'd lit to keep warm. Similar fires were slowly peppering the landscape around him, mirroring the stars in the sky. But Worker One had situated *his* far enough from any other, so as to gain some respite from the incessant questions now being asked him.

Gripping imaginations, his one god idea had surged through the community like wildfire. Keen not to anger their new deity, people were desperate to know where the boundaries lay… and Worker One was the only person who could provide the answers.

Or so he'd assumed.

An approaching figure drew his eyes from the flames.

Recognising from the silhouette of the hand greeting him that it belonged to Worker Two, he politely nodded permission for him to sit. Whilst maintaining a civil smile, he was wary of his guest's motives for seeking out his company. He'd witnessed increasing animosity from Worker Two, ever since the hand doing the greeting had found it even harder to pick its owner's nose.

Worker Two settled himself down, the fire highlighting a mischievous glint in his eyes. He clearly hadn't come to exchange pleasantries. There was something he needed to clarify. He looked about himself nonchalantly, as if hoping a feigned attitude of disinterest might distract the delivery of a trick question.

There was something that was puzzling him, he started. When the one god had spoken to Worker One, had he done so directly?

Worker One immediately saw through the subterfuge. Having been present on the raft when he'd formulated his monotheistic theory, Worker Two knew full well it had been developed through a succession of evolving thoughts. Worker One realised that any contradictions or inconsistencies on his part would be reported back to the community and used as a weapon against him.

Prudently, he suggested that the one god had spoken to him in the language of ideas… and that the ideas placed into his head that day on the raft could therefore be seen as the one

150

god's wishes.

Worker Two nodded appreciatively... a thin smile suggesting that was *exactly* the answer he'd wanted to hear.

Worker One felt discomfort at his confidence.

His smile broadening, Worker Two pointed out that he *too* must have been spoken to by the one god, as he'd also received communication in the form of ideas.

Worker One quickly appreciated the trap he'd fallen into, but knew he couldn't object.

Knowing it too, Worker Two expanded on his own conversation with the one god.

It had apparently centred on the lack of ceremony and religious paraphernalia required to worship the all-powerful one. As many in the community had become unsettled by such a liberal form of veneration, their unease needed rectifying... according to the one god.

A crack from the fire spat its disgust at his meddling.

Worker One merely nodded his understanding. It was important to tread carefully... but he also needed to stand firm. Any attack on his authority was an attack on his future chances of survival. Accordingly, he assured Worker Two that he must have misheard the one god, as such ritualistic trappings *weren't* necessary. After all... hadn't they both communicated with the one god without recourse to them?

Worker Two carefully considered the response. It was a good point, he conceded.

Worker One knew it was. That's why he'd made it.

Worker Two sought clarification that Worker One was saying it was possible to mishear the one god.

Of course... as that's clearly what had happened.

Things now made sense, Worker Two announced boldly. It was Worker *One* who'd misheard the supreme deity... his confusion also causing him to momentarily suggest the possibility of there being *no* gods... *Remember?* Furthermore... such fallibility was proof that the antlers *were* needed to communicate clearly and without mistakes.

Worker One realised he'd underestimated Worker Two.

Worker Two then demonstrated by how much. As Worker One had refused ownership of those antlers, Worker Two had taken possession of them. It was on placing them on his head that he'd received his ideas from the one god. Hadn't he mentioned that bit?

Worker One shifted uncomfortably.

Worker Two stared at him smugly through the flames. According to *his* communications with the one god – which had come through loud and clear – all religious rituals and associated paraphernalia were to be restored... in order to signify the one god's importance and keep the populace suitably subjugated, lest they get ideas above their station. Surely Worker One could appreciate the dangers of *that!*

Worker One weighed up the situation and opted for damage limitation. Was that *all* Worker Two was proposing?

Worker Two replied that he wasn't proposing anything. It was the one god that was doing that.

Of course... But that didn't answer the question.

No... it didn't. And the answer was that the one god had also instructed the tribe to build a large place of worship... to be filled with valuable trinkets that reflected the greatness and magnificence of the one god. Worker Two was expected to reside therein... having food and drink brought to him daily, so that he could continue being a conduit between the one god and his servants.

Servants?

Hadn't Worker One been told that bit, either? Was he *sure* he'd been communicating with the correct one god? Maybe it was further proof that he was either misguided or that *his* one god was an impostor. Not that it mattered. For Worker Two's one god had instructed him to become his sole mouthpiece... meaning that anyone who objected or claimed otherwise would be going against the wishes of the one god.

How very convenient.

Wasn't it... But the wishes of the all-powerful one god could hardly be ignored... could they?

Knowing he couldn't allow Worker Two's assault on his

authority to succeed, Worker One decided attack was the best form of defence. Rising angrily, he loudly berated Worker Two for his false and blasphemous claims, threatening to have the *True* one god remove his remaining fingers if he didn't immediately grovel in front of the fire and apologise. He still felt confident he had the upper-hand, given he knew Worker Two had to be lying about the one god's revelations, as he'd also been lying about them himself! He just had to call Worker Two's bluff.

Unfortunately, he'd failed to consider the possibility that Worker Two was completely deluded... truly believing that any thought that popped into his head had done so courtesy of a higher power.

Ignoring the threat, Worker Two suggested they resolve the matter by asking the tribe to choose which one god they preferred to follow... Worker One's *True* one god or his own *Genuine* one god.

Worker One pointed out that there couldn't be two one gods.

Worker Two responded by saying that there could... as an all-powerful one god would be beyond the laws of mathematics.

It was *then* that Worker One realised Worker Two really *had* gone completely mad.

*   *   *

Snogden-Lambert was surprised to see Norman pacing around the stones... not least because it was half past ten at night and he'd been called from the comfort of his slippers and dressing gown by a concerned security team. Recognising the intruder as previously having had meetings with their boss, they'd thought it prudent to get him over in case things got even more awkward.

'I hate to be a killjoy, Norman,' he sung out, entering the cordoned off area, 'but this part of the site is out of bounds to the public... even during opening hours!'

Norman didn't answer and continued with what he was doing.

'Is that a tape measure?' Snogden-Lambert enquired, shining the torch he'd been handed... though he could clearly see it was.

Norman nodded and scribbled something on a notepad.

'If you're interested in the dimensions, I can let you have a detailed plan of the site first thing in the morning. But I'm afraid I can't allow you to wander around this section. It's not fair on the rest of the public.'

Norman temporarily looked up from what he was doing and gave Snogden-Lambert a cold stare. 'Quarter of a billion pounds says it is.'

Snogden-Lambert felt the awkwardness of the moment put pressure on the back of his neck. It was a familiar pressure he thought he'd finally outsmarted and the reason he'd stopped taking his pills. 'You're putting me in an uncomfortable position. I'd prefer it if we could discuss this over a cup of tea.'

'That's very kind,' said Norman. 'But I'm afraid I don't have time. I desperately need to get these figures to someone for a quote.'

'A *quote?*'

'Yes... Not that price is an obstacle. It's the timescale I'm worried about.'

'Timescale for what?'

'To finish the job.'

'What job?'

'The completion of the monument.'

Snogden-Lambert took a moment to interpret the answer. '*Completion?*' he queried, once he'd failed to do so. 'What on earth do you mean?'

His goal looking hopelessly impossible, Norman had nonetheless decided to take his first, blind steps towards it. Working out exactly what needed to be replaced – should he miraculously be allowed to do so – he trusted his positive ripples to provide that miracle before it was too late. Beating about the bush was pointless. He'd decided to trust Gabriel's assertion that the Universe would provide if he were positive enough.

'Well... it's in a pretty sorry state, wouldn't you say?' Norman offered, unable to elaborate.

'So would you be, after four and half thousand years!' returned Snogden-Lambert smartly.

'Precisely... so I need to tart it up a little.'

'A little?'

'The whole lot. I need it looking as good as new.'

'Oh, please don't do this to me,' pleaded Snogden-Lambert, his knees buckling. 'I gave everyone my personal assurance that you *weren't* mad!'

'And I gave them my cheque.'

'Yes... but it doesn't clear until tomorrow... and I've an awful feeling...'

'*What?*' Norman stopped what he was doing. 'That I'm some kind of loony who gets his kicks from wasting people's time?'

'I didn't say that... But you must admit you're acting very strangely!'

'So would you, if you knew what *I* knew!'

'Are you sure you don't want that cup of tea?' Snogden-Lambert was desperately trying to work out how many of his unused sedatives he had left and whether they were tasteless when dissolved.

'I told you, I...'

'Do you need a hand, sir?' asked a security guard, who'd decided it was time to step into the fray. Only having to deal with visitors espousing peace and love and looking for spiritual connections was all very well... but it had been a while since he'd been involved in a punch up and he quite missed it.

'That depends on our visitor,' said Snogden-Lambert diplomatically. 'I'm sure he doesn't want to bring unnecessary attention to himself.'

Their visitor didn't... and it was with reluctance that he accompanied Snogden-Lambert to his office, the security guard close behind and maintaining an enthusiastically clenched fist... just in case.

Chad stared bitterly into his coffee. 'Well... I hope whoever's availed themselves of our car is making better use of it than *we* did!'

'It sure has proved an expensive day,' agreed Bob, admiring the reflection of his replacement trousers in the café's window. 'Just as well our client's got deep pockets.'

'I'm not sure he'll be wanting to put his hand in them, given our lack of results.' Chad scowled. 'Not only have we failed to compromise Penkridge's operation... we haven't even been able to locate him!'

'So, where does that leave us?'

'Without a paddle,' answered Chad sourly.

'Don't tell me you left *that* in the car!' Bob's attempt to snap his partner from his sullen mood didn't work. 'Okay... then where do we go from here?'

Chad shook his head. 'At the moment, I'm thinking *home*. I'm starting to believe this was all a big mistake.'

'You can't mean that!' scoffed Bob. 'You were desperate for answers... and still are. That'll *never* change. At least you can attempt to do something about it while you're in the game.'

'True. But a lead on Penkridge isn't the only thing we're missing.'

'So... we'll hire another car.'

Chad looked at him irritably. 'I'm talking about backup, Bob. I'm talking about proper intel and everything that goes with it. You know what I mean... ears to the wall... eyes in the sky... boots on the ground. That sort of thing! I remember when we could put in a call and get a trace on a mobile phone halfway around the world within seconds. Now we can't even track a friggin' credit card until it's in danger of expiring!'

'I don't believe it!' Bob grinned. 'You're *actually* missing the Agency!'

'I'm missing being able to do my job properly. When I agreed to take this one, I figured it was gonna be pretty straightforward. We had an identified target and his address. I also hoped your *inner circle* would suck up any risk and provide us with a little more help than it has. After all... we're tying up a shared loose end with this Penkridge guy.' He blew out his cheeks. 'Perhaps we really have bitten off more than we can chew. I'm feeling like we belong with the dinosaurs. Our approach is old school. These kids are running rings around us!'

'You can hardly call their set-up professional!' countered Bob.

'Precisely... That's the problem! Without them having previous form or a recognised *modus operandi*, there's nothing for us to get our teeth into. It's what'll enable 'em to get away with whatever it is they're planning. It worked for Penkridge last time... hiding away in an anonymous, run-down apartment, whilst we ran around looking for an obvious big fish to hook!'

'It's last night's lack of sleep talkin',' said Bob. 'I'm feeling it myself. You're tired, that's all.'

'Yeah... of this goddamn country! What is it with these Brits? Don't they know how it's *supposed* to be done? This is the birthplace of Sherlock Holmes and James Bond! Whatever happened to sophistication?'

'There was nothing unsophisticated about that ball of light we saw when we were over here last time,' Bob baited him.

'Yeah, okay... you're right... I *am* tired. But it don't alter the fact we're clean outta leads.'

'We could stake out Kevin's place again,' Bob suggested.

'No point. We've blown our chance with that one. He can communicate with Penkridge any way he likes now. I doubt he'll be going back home in a hurry.'

'And Donald?'

'I reckon his voices have let him down this time. He knows where we are. His silence says it all.'

'So what now?'

Chad tipped his head back in frustration. 'We pray?'

Bob nearly spat his coffee out. 'Wow! Chad Cheadle finally referencing the metaphysical realm! Perhaps it *is* time you went home!'

'I'll tell you something...' Chad stared at his partner earnestly. 'If such a realm exists... I'd sell my soul to the Devil just to get another lead!'

As the final word left his lips, the door of the café burst open, inflicting a violent gust of wind upon the fixtures and fittings.

The two men instinctively grabbed hold of their drinks, as ketchup sachets, paper napkins, and plastic spoons took to the skies to mingle with the dispersed contents of ashtrays and whatever detritus hadn't yet been cleared from the tables.

'Bloody 'ell!' shouted the café's owner, ducking behind the counter. 'Someone shut the bleedin' door before we all get blown to bits!'

Chad and Bob being his only customers, the latter battled his way towards it and forced it shut with his foot. What was in the air immediately fell to the ground.

'Same again, gents?' asked the proprietor, resurfacing and shrewdly sensing business in the spilt remains of two cappuccinos.

Bob returned to the table. 'What the hell was *that* about?'

Chad didn't answer... his eyes transfixed on the remains of a newspaper that had dropped in his lap.

'Chad?'

'I don't believe it!'

'What?'

He spread the paper out on the table. 'Have you seen what's written here?'

Bob read one of the crumpled headlines. 'You gotta be kiddin' me! One in ten people have claimed to have witnessed some form of paranormal activity in the last two weeks!'

'No... here... this showbiz gossip column. There's a comment about Donald's next play.'

'But he hasn't finished it yet,' frowned Bob.

'According to this, he has! It says an industry insider informed the paper yesterday that he's currently engaged in secret rehearsals at an unspecified theatre... and is preparing to premiere it within days!'

'*Days?*'

'Looks like Donald's been holding out on us!'

'I *told* you we should've broken into that crumbling dump of his and sneaked a peek when we had the chance!' exclaimed Bob.

Chad continued reading. 'Apparently... invitations have already gone out to the great and the good. Those attending have had to sign a confidentiality clause ahead of the performance regarding its location at the request of the playwright himself... who is also rumoured to be directing it.'

'I bet he'll use that as an excuse as to why he hasn't been in touch. He'll say he's been too busy to call!'

'He can say what he likes. We'll definitely be getting in touch with *him!* He gave us his word he'd keep us in the loop!'

'Does it say where these secret rehearsals are taking place?' asked Bob, struggling to read the article from his upside-down position.

Chad looked at him in bemusement.

'Point taken,' acknowledged Bob. 'So how are we gonna track him down if he's had everyone sworn to secrecy? Assuming he'll be putting in some heavy hours directing it, I doubt he'll be staying at home.'

'It shouldn't be too difficult to locate this mystery theatre,' said Chad. 'It's gotta be somewhere in or close to the West End, given his literary status. That narrows our options considerably.'

'What are we waiting for?' said Bob, standing up eagerly.

Chad ripped the article from the paper and joined him.

'You can 'ave 'em for 'alf price!' shouted the café owner, as they headed for the door, 'and I'll even throw in a couple o' biscuits!'

*   *   *

'Okay, Norman. Now... I don't know what all this is about. But given I can't detect alcohol on your breath, I'm assuming it's got something to do with drugs!' Snogden-Lambert shut the office door, affording them the privacy he assumed a more *compos mentis* Norman would want. However, not before whispering a request to the security guard to remain close by on the other side of it... just in case.

Norman didn't much care for such a meeting, but the glare he'd received from the security guard suggested it would be wise to comply. He stared at Snogden-Lambert dispassionately. 'Or maybe I'm just mad.'

Snogden-Lambert's heart sank. The same thought had crossed his mind... but he was being polite. 'Not that I'm condoning their use, but I'd rather it *was* drugs. You won't be the first person caught wandering around these stones at night under the influence of something that chemically enhances their meaning.'

'Believe me,' said Norman, giving a wry smile, 'what this place represents doesn't need enhancing! But, for my purposes, the condition of it *definitely* does.'

Snogden-Lambert signalled for Norman to take a seat. 'That's the bit I'm struggling with,' he tiptoed. 'I'll be honest with you... I don't believe we've ever had anyone ask for their admission fee back because the monument was looking a little... *old*.'

'My problem isn't its age... it's the fact it's incomplete,' returned Norman, knowing any further explanation was impossible.

To his surprise, he didn't need it.

'I understand,' said Snogden-Lambert, nodding his head sympathetically.

Norman stared at him in amazement. 'You *do*?'

'Absolutely! You won't believe the number of times I've driven past that pile of near rubble and thought... Peter... you really must do something about it!'

Norman wondered if Snogden-Lambert was the one who'd been taking drugs... or was the man simply making fun of him?

Snogden-Lambert's studied look of understanding and compassion suggested he wasn't. He *too* had completely lost his marbles at one point in his life and knew what it was like struggling to cope with reality, only for the world to compound the problem by heaping its ridicule upon you. He wasn't going to make the same mistake and increase the anguish of the young man in front of him... not least because he only had to coax him through the next four days and he'd have ticked all the boxes for his knighthood. Permissions had been granted and the cheque banked. It was just a question of covering up the donor's insanity long enough to ensure the concert went ahead. After that, he'd be home and dry. 'One appreciates you want the whole thing looking spic and span for the occasion,' he said, humouring Norman as best he could.

Norman couldn't believe what he was hearing.

Had Gabriel's laws of the Universe finally kicked in? Was this those forks and ripples working?

'I just need the outer ring of sarsens to be complete,' he said cautiously, testing the water.

'Of course you do! Of course you do!' soothed Snogden-Lambert. 'There's nothing worse than an incomplete one.' He tutted and raised his eyes in hammed empathy.

Norman pushed on quickly, in case Snogden-Lambert had a change of heart. 'Imagine everyone's excitement when they get to see Stonehenge as it would have been when first built!' he enthused.

'I can't begin to imagine the reaction!' replied Snogden-Lambert, consoling himself with the fact that – despite the necessary deception – at least he was telling the truth on that one.

'I have to say... you've taken this a lot better than I thought you would!' remarked Norman, flabbergasted.

'I aim to please,' said Snogden-Lambert... meaning *himself*.

'But what about the committees? Aren't you going to have to run it by them first?'

Snogden-Lambert shook his head imperceptibly, pursing his lips in friendly and confident dismissal. 'No, no, no. That's not a problem. *I'm* in charge here. One word from me and they'll do exactly as I say!' To his surprise, he enjoyed the pretence. It felt liberating. He could say anything he liked because it didn't matter!

From the other side of the desk, Norman interpreted Snogden-Lambert's display of megalomania as confirmation of his ripples working. The best thing possible had happened... the man had gone completely mad. He knew he'd flirted with its boundaries... but the thought of a title and the praise he'd been receiving had clearly tipped him over the edge. Not wishing to look a gift horse in the mouth, Norman decided to play along. After all... he only needed to take advantage of Snogden-Lambert's mental decline for four more days. Who cared what repercussions followed after that? When Wiltshire Council – or anyone else who might take offence – realised they had a new Saviour in their midst, everything else would pale into insignificance.

'They're clearly in awe of your shrewd, enterprising attitude!' Norman fawned, encouraging the man's compliance.

Having gotten used to praise and plaudits in the past few days, Snogden-Lambert almost forgot he was playing a game. 'It's a rare gift and I'm blessed,' he nodded enthusiastically.

Norman seized the advantage and threw out some numbers, deciding to put Snogden-Lambert's insanity to a real test. 'Research shows there were originally thirty sarsens supporting an equal number of lintels,' he said. 'That's what we'll need to repair the monument.'

'Thirty *schmirty*,' shrugged Snogden-Lambert nonchalantly, passing it with flying colours. 'You can have as many as you like!' What did he care? *It wasn't as if they were actually going to get built!*

Norman felt a pang of guilt, given the level of Snogden-Lambert's condition.

The man needed professional help...

...but not just yet.

'Thirty will be fine, thanks,' he acknowledged.

'Any particular colour?' enquired Snogden-Lambert, probing the depth of Norman's madness.

'I was thinking they'd really stand out if the whole thing was painted pink,' Norman replied, curious to see how far Snogden-

Lambert could be pushed.

Nutty as a squirrel's winter hoard, assessed Snogden-Lambert. 'I'm sure the ancients would've approved!' he smiled.

Absolute raving fruitcake, determined Norman. 'Will you be wearing your pyjamas to the concert?' he poked, just for his own amusement.

Snogden-Lambert tried not to let his sadness at the young man's condition show. 'Just try and stop me!' he cooperated.

Entertaining as it was, Norman knew Gabriel wouldn't approve of anything approaching ridicule. Quitting whilst ahead, he rose from his chair. 'I'll make the necessary arrangements.' He offered out his hand so as to seal the deal.

'You do exactly what you need to,' said Snogden-Lambert, returning the gesture.

As their hands made contact, something crashed violently against the window.

'Goodness me!' cried Snogden-Lambert. 'Was that another bird?'

'*Another?*'

'Yes... that's the seventh since this morning. Most extraordinary! I don't know what's the matter with them at the moment!'

'You'll probably find it's got something to do with the Devil,' said Norman, forgetting himself for a second.

'Oh... yes... of course!' tutted Snogden-Lambert, no longer shocked at anything that came out of the young man's mouth. 'Then it's a good job we've got double-glazing. That should keep him out!'

Norman looked at the site director and felt pity. 'On second thoughts... I probably won't bother with the pink,' he said, feeling bad about his teasing.

'Shame,' sighed Snogden-Lambert, maintaining the charade. 'It would've stood out well against the grass.'

Norman smiled politely.

They both considered mentioning something about yellow spots... but decided against it.

Snogden-Lambert hoped the young man would now go

back to his hotel and have an extremely long lie down.

Norman had different ideas. 'If you'll excuse me... I've got to finish my quote. Time is running out!'

'Will you be using workers from the local tribes?' asked Snogden-Lambert, giving the pretence one last effort, so as not to unsettle his parting guest.

'*Tragic*,' mumbled Norman, as he hurriedly exited the room.

* * *

Every conceivable space on the hillside had been filled. The surrounding air buzzed with excitement and anticipation. Elders from every tribe for miles around had come to the Place of Important Words to hear Worker One and Worker Two deliver their pronouncements on what the new one god expected of them. Although opinions were divided as to who would triumph in this crucial debate, Worker One seemed to have won the battle for hearts and minds by something approaching a healthy majority. After all... it was *him* who'd outsmarted the priest and *him* who'd solved the problem of how to raise the stones. Worker Two was just an idiot.

Worker One's popularity was affirmed, as he quietly entered a circular area at the foot of the hill, marked out by a ring of carefully placed, white stones. Humbly bowing to those who'd come to hear him, he raised a hand of grateful acknowledgement for the appreciative cheer that rang out in support.

Worker Two was nowhere to be seen. Some in the crowd muttered that he'd taken fright and disappeared before he could be publicly humiliated.

Encouraged by Worker Two's failure to show, Worker One wasted no time in instructing those assembled how the *True* one god expected them to behave. He saw it as the perfect opportunity to create a fairer, more equal society, where peace prevailed and everyone respected each other because... if they didn't... they'd be punished in the most hideous and unimaginable ways by the loving and just *True* one god.

It was simple. So long as they stuck to a basic set of rules which ensured they got on with one another, worked hard and weren't selfish... the *True* one god would reward them with reasonable health and good harvests. That said... if they still got ill and the crops failed, it wasn't the *True* one god's fault. It just meant they hadn't tried hard enough.

Mention of crop failure drew a question from the crowd.

What about seasonal sacrifices? Would they still be required?

Worker One pronounced them a thing of the past. From now on... virgins could sleep soundly in their beds and chickens hang on to their entrails. No one had to die unnecessarily.

The crowd liked what they heard... as did some nearby foraging chickens. Mortality rates were high enough as it was. It had always irked many that the old gods had regularly demanded the demise of someone young and about to contribute a useful existence to society. But as the priests had pointed out... if someone old and redundant had been offered in their place, it wouldn't have been much of a sacrifice... would it?

Worker One having made all the right noises, the consensus was that it would've taken an exceptionally strong, intellectual pitch from Worker Two to have won them over, had he bothered to turn up...

... or some rather nice headwear.

For as soon as Worker One finished speaking, Worker Two made his carefully planned entrance. Far from fleeing the battlefield, he'd ensured his standard towered above his opponent by wearing the very antlers that had bestowed unquestioned authority on past generations of priests.

But he hadn't stopped there.

In addition to appreciating the power of the familiar, Worker Two had embraced the mood for change by having them inlaid with shiny metal and semi-precious stones. Making sure the crowd got the point, he moved his head from side to side... the antlers glinting spectacularly as he strutted in the sunlight.

The entire hill gasped.

The chickens panicked.

Worker Two was promising them the old and new combined. What more could they want?

Not that they had a choice, he pointed out before they could reply. For he immediately laid down the ground rules as given him by the *Genuine* one god... who'd commanded them to obey his every word or suffer the consequences in a never-ending cycle of grotesque punishments.

At least the last bit sounded reassuringly familiar. Did that mean sacrifices were back on the menu again?

No. But having to hand over virgins *was*. He'd get to that bit later.

To prove their loyalty and complete subservience to the *Genuine* one god, they were to construct a hut so magnificent in scale and rich in adornment that the *Genuine* one god would consider it an appropriate place for him to live.

Is that what was going to happen?

Sort of... Worker Two would reside there on his behalf.

In that case... wouldn't the great stone monument they were currently building suffice?

Were they kidding? It didn't even have a roof!

But how would they find the time? Things were difficult as it was, what with this new-fangled farming fad and all that wattle and daubing. To build both at the same time would be impossible!

It was a test of faith, they were told.

But what was the point of having a test if it was impossible to complete?

That was the point of faith, Worker Two instructed them. You were required to trust that what you thought impossible was completely the opposite.

There was an alternative, coughed Worker One respectfully, not wishing to be shut out of the debate.

No there wasn't, announced Worker Two boldly, shutting him out of the debate. Because the *Genuine* one god had decreed that any other beliefs pertaining to a one god were hereby heretical.

The crowd shifted uncomfortably. Didn't that put Worker One at an unfair disadvantage?

He should've thought of that before he stepped into the circle first, Worker Two observed... and less of the backchat, as the genuine one god was judging their every utterance.

The crowd fell silent. That was that, then.

Just as they were considering departing for their various homesteads and relaying the wishes of the *Genuine* one god to their communities, something unexpected happened.

Worker Three stepped into the circle.

The chickens stopped pecking.

Glaring at Worker Two, he pointed out that the self-proclaimed supremacy of Worker Two's *Genuine* one god didn't make Worker One's *True* one god any less real.

So what was he proposing?

That they resolve the issue by worshiping a single one god that sat somewhere between the get-on-with-it-yourself-just-so-long-as-it-is-within-reason benevolence of the *True* one god and the autocratic, absolute dictates of the *Genuine* one god.

Effectively a *third* one god, Worker One pointed out.

If that's what it took, Worker Three replied.

Worker Two protested that such a thing was impossible.

Then he should try using that faith he talked about earlier, Worker Three reminded him.

Seeing Worker Three hadn't been struck by lightning for what had been a heretical viewpoint a few moments earlier, some in the crowd took is as a sign that *his* one god must be authentic.

And so a split occurred.

As the elders returned to their villages, personal preferences ensured the *True* one god, the *Genuine* one god and the *Authentic* one god each found favour with separate tribes... producing a monotheistic society in name only.

*   *   *

133

'Stump suggested I give you a call,' said Norman, the fingers of his left hand crossed so tightly, they were turning white. 'I wish to place a commission for a number of fibreglass structures and understand you're the man I should be talking to.'

'Interesting,' said the voice on the other end of the phone. 'What kind of structures are we talking?'

'I need to recreate the outer ring of stones as would've originally existed at Stonehenge,' Norman replied, his fingers about to snap.

'Are we talking life-size?'

'Yes, we are.'

'Plus lintels?'

'Of course.'

'No problem,' said the voice confidently. 'In fact... as luck would have it... I've still got some designs I could scale up.'

'*Designs?*'

'Yeah... Some geezer needed a rush job of half a dozen uprights and matching tops for a theatre show he's putting on. What are the chances of that? They must suddenly be all the fashion!'

'I guess,' said Norman, figuring another ripple had come to his aid. 'Does that mean you'll be able to deliver them quickly?'

'I'll do my best. How many d'ya need?'

'Well... there were thirty uprights and thirty lintels in the original monument... but some are already in situ.'

'Ah... you've obviously been using a competitor of mine and they've let you down! I won't ask who... but work not up to standard, eh?'

'No... Those that already exist are *extremely* lifelike, as it happens,' said Norman. 'I've calculated I just need fourteen uprights and twenty four lintels to complete it.'

There was a professional intake of breath. 'And where do they need to be delivered to?'

'I'd rather keep that bit secret for now.' Norman replied, feeling it safe enough to uncross his fingers and let the blood flow back. 'But suffice to say... somewhere near Salisbury,'

'Very appropriate!'

'More than you think.'

'And when do you need 'em by?'

'The day after tomorrow,' said Norman, wondering whether he'd been premature with his fingers.

He had.

'Goodbye,' said the voice on the end of the phone.

'Wait!' Norman yelled. 'I've got lots of money!'

'And I've got lots of fibreglass,' said the voice. 'But only one pair of hands! What you're asking for is impossible.'

'The impossible is just the possible viewed from the wrong angle!' said Norman quickly.

'It may well be,' said the voice. 'But mine's the only angle I've got. If you think of another, let me know!'

'Helpers!' said Norman desperately, his body almost lurching into the mouthpiece. 'You could hire lots of helpers!'

The phone went dead.

*   *   *

'This is a list of every theatre and performance venue in London,' said Chad, placing a piece of paper in front of Bob. 'All we gotta do is eliminate those currently advertising shows and then investigate the rest in person. That'll be where Donald's rehearsing.'

'Shouldn't be too difficult,' responded Bob.

*   *   *

'Stevie?'

'Are you the guy that called me a few seconds ago?'

'Yes.'

'Then, it's *Mister the Props* to you.'

'I'm Norman.'

'No… you're a fuckin' insult!'

'I don't understand… I'm offering you work!'

'Then I'll explain. I'm an artist. An extremely good one.

131

You'll find my pieces displayed at some of the most prestigious sites in the world.'

'I know... I've seen Maggie and Marilyn's genitals,' said Norman.

'And Stump's drive,' Stevie the Props conceded, a little less brazenly. 'I was doing him a favour.'

'And I thought I'd be able to do *you* one,' said Norman. 'I'm offering you a chance to have your work exhibited at an *extremely* prestigious site!'

'No,' insisted Stevie the Props again, without bothering to enquire as to where that might be. 'You were offering to have work displayed that had been done by others. *Helpers...* I believe you said.'

'Only so that it could be completed on time!' insisted Norman.

There was what he took to be a sigh of exasperation at the other end of the phone.

'D'ya think when Michael Angelo spent four years on his back painting the ceiling of the Sistine Chapel, the thought didn't occasionally cross his horizontal mind that things might progress a little quicker if he got some *helpers* in?' asked Stevie.

'They mixed his paint,' tried Norman.

'And probably were allowed to dab away at the sky... I'll give you that. But to all intents and purposes, he stuck to his guns and did it all by himself. That's because he was a true genius... a one off... and why he's gone down in history.'

'Lots of the renaissance masters used assistants,' Norman argued. 'And many of them have gone down in history.'

'Oh... we're an art expert now, are we?'

'You could say that,' returned Norman. 'Which is why I would never intentionally insult you. No one appreciates the craft of an artist more than I do. I'm in awe of anyone who can interpret the world through their hands... and you're clearly one of those people. It's small wonder you take such a pride in your work and fight so hard to guard its purity!'

'Flattery... That's a start,' said Stevie, his voice softening.

'Does that mean you're interested?' asked Norman, crossing

his fingers again.

'It makes no difference whether I'm interested or not,' replied Stevie. 'I work alone and always will do. I told you... I'm an artist. I seek to expose greed and hypocrisy through my creativity... to represent honesty and truth in their most aesthetic forms... and am prepared to sacrifice everything by way of my day-to-day suffering to uphold those sacred and immutable principles. So... if that means turning down your commission to maintain my integrity... so be it. As you pointed out... I'll fight to guard the purity of my art.'

'I'll pay you a million pounds per piece,' said Norman bluntly.

There was something approximating a cough at the end of the phone.

'Did you say fourteen uprights and twenty-four lintels?' enquired Stevie the Props, weakly.

'Thirty-eight pieces in total,' confirmed Norman.

'I'll make the necessary calls,' Stevie mumbled, his jaw moving the little his poleaxed brain would allow.

* * *

The room spun. Snogden-Lambert's hands shook uncontrollably. He stared at the piece of paper they were doing their best to keep hold of and tried to focus on the words that were written on it. But they were blurring.

Though of standard office A4 size – a thickness of 120gsm implying importance – the letterheaded, single sheet appeared to exist in a separate dimension to his stapler, pen holder, and the one his brain had happily been inhabiting prior to opening the envelope it had just arrived in.

'Oh, please God... no!' he whimpered.

He felt sick.

MUST TRY HARDER.

Three words flashed mockingly in front of him.

MUST TRY HARDER.

Curiously... they weren't part of the letter.

MUST TRY HARDER.

He always visualised them written in red ink.

MUST TRY HARDER.

Burnt into his consciousness.

MUST TRY HARDER.

Mercilessly taunting him when things went wrong.

MUST TRY HARDER.

They certainly had.

MUST TRY HARDER.

An admonishment from his past, they were so common an assessment of the private education he'd squandered, he'd marvelled that his tutors hadn't had the phrase committed to a rubber stamp, saving them the effort of writing it every time.

MUST TRY HARDER.

It was the story of his life.

He couldn't even argue he'd tried as hard as he could. In truth... he'd only tried as hard as a privileged upbringing had necessitated. After all... why struggle to make business connections when family ones would do? When a succession of socially engineered promotions saw him take charge of a major British art gallery, he'd continued to do as little as was expected and just enough to maintain the salary.

His laziness didn't just pertain to work. Even his love life hadn't been stretched beyond a social convenience. Mrs Snogden-Lambert was his first and only conquest... though hardly a battle he'd had to fight too hard to win. As her love of baking pies also encompassed a love of *eating* them, it had been more a grateful surrender on her part. Even then, it was *she* who'd finally pointed out the futility of their union and actually done something about it.

Perhaps, he mused, MUST TRY HARDER would be stamped on his *decree nisi* when it eventually came through.

They also seemed to be permanently etched into the expression of Miss Winkleman – his much-put-upon therapist – whenever she looked at him... and with good reason. Despite her best efforts, his rehabilitation back into the outside world had nothing to do with him. It only took place when his old boys' network finally decided enough embarrassment had been caused to the school tie. It was *them* who'd pulled strings to get him to where he was currently sat. They'd figured he could hardly mess up a pile of old stones.

MUST TRY HARDER.

And now this!

Just at the moment when another gifted opportunity looked set to crown his return and place him on the pedestal he so richly *didn't* deserve... his dream of being someone important looked set to remain just that, courtesy of two paragraphs of *times new roman*... 12 point.

The first paragraph was innocuous enough. It trusted he was well... then politely informed him that an issue had arisen that required his attention, given it was *"presumably an administrative or clerical error that can be easily rectified".*

It was the second paragraph that caused his tailspin. The trustees of the organisation whose logo sat proudly atop the letter had been informed that *"the cheque presented by Templar Resources for the cultural benefit of the nation"*, had been returned to them with the words *RETURN TO DRAWER* stamped on it. Could he please advise.

As he tried to picture the offending item, the words *MUST TRY HARDER* substituted themselves for the red-inked rejection.

His body wretched, as the memory of his last meeting with Norman came flooding back.

The boy was clearly mad. So why had he accepted the word of a lunatic when it came to guaranteeing the authenticity of such an improbable amount?

How foolish did that make him look?

It was bad enough his previous fall from grace had left him the pariah of the art world and laughing stock of the Home Counties. He'd escaped wider notoriety thanks to the attention the media had on more pressing issues at that time.

But now – Stonehenge a regular homing beacon for the World's press – it would hang like an international millstone around his neck.

He wretched again, as the thought threatened to swamp what little senses hadn't already vacated him.

His sparsely furnished office – provincially safe and benign just over a week earlier – now seemed like a bunker... the door, through which he'd struggled to enter on his first day, promising an even greater battle should he wish to exit.

He didn't.

Trapped in his stupor, he became oblivious to the amount of time spent staring at the letter. Hoping to wake up and find it was all a horrendous dream, he only accepted reality when the alarm clock by his bedside table failed to materialise after an interminably long time.

He finally put the piece of paper down and placed a finger on his stapler.

Leaning forward, he ejected a staple.

'Joan... could you get Mister Penkridge on the line, please?'

Unfortunately... the reality he'd accepted wasn't everyone else's.

The stapler failing to return Joan's voice, he mumbled something about staff taking advantage of extended tea breaks and irritably dialled the number himself. A pre-recorded message greeting him, he left a frantic one of his own requesting that Norman return his call immediately, as there was something extremely important that needed to be discussed.

Replacing the receiver, his eyes shot to the bottom drawer of his filing cabinet. He shook himself from the lure of the siren's voice that was whispering his name from behind a suspension file labelled *Health and Safety*.

It wasn't easy.

She spoke in a sweet Scottish lilt, having spent much of her life in an oak cask north of the border. She promised to take his troubles away... though he knew she would only be the start of them.

In an attempt to take his mind from her, he rocked himself backwards and forwards in his chair. He found it also helped if he hummed... the distraction akin to hearing his mother's heartbeat in the womb. Not that he could recall it… but how he wished he were there now.

He cradled his body and tried to imagine he was.

He couldn't.

Typical.

MUST TRY HARDER.

*　　*　　*

The Reverend Ian Clapp patted the bonnet of his beloved Morris Minor and drew in a breath of resilience.

He would need it.

As part of his work for the wider dioceses, he was the *go to* man when work the church would rather keep under its *own* bonnet needed doing.

He studied the semi-detached house in front of him and marvelled at its ordinariness. Not that he would judge the veracity of its occupant's claim by the innocence of its appearance. He'd come to realise that properties he was sometimes required to visit weren't all suggestive of a horror movie set.

Behind the neat net curtains, he would – no doubt – find a troubled family who'd called for the help of the Church as a last resort, preferring *that* to calling the local psychiatric department. Their concern would pertain to a loved one displaying symptoms that, at best, could be described as uncharacteristic.

At worst, they could be described as demonic.

Not that he'd actually encountered any *real* demons over the years. It usually required suspension of his critical faculties to interpret the affected voice of the patient as a tormentor from Hell, or their actions as anything but a disturbed mind looking for someone else to blame.

But it wasn't his role to judge. If the Church insisted you accept the presence of Heaven and the good its attendants could do for you, you also had to accept what the source of that belief told you lurked at the other end. Hampshire might be a

125

peaceful county, blessed by a level of affluence that made other counties twitch. But having one of the lowest per capita homeless rates didn't exclude its residents from having their bodies squatted in.

As for never actually encountering any demons... he'd never actually encountered God either. It was His *influence* that counted... as much as it could be Satan's that had brought him to his current address.

There were some in the Church who questioned his being there in the first place. His role – though officially sanctioned – sat uneasily with them. Being less open-minded, they believed possession by an evil spirit to be the product of a medieval mind or a very sick modern one. They certainly didn't believe it to be the product of a world that boasted the internet, space travel, and stem cell technology. But, as he would point out in theological debates... that was the very same argument used by atheists against *them*.

If God could move in mysterious ways, so could the Devil. It was simply the Reverend Clapp's job to show love, compassion, and understanding... and, through his guidance, help to put things right.

He set off up the path, admiring the neatly arranged flower borders on either side and smiling as he caught sight of a gnome pushing a wheel barrow across the small front lawn. A flyer in the front window reminded those who cared to know that the local church fête was taking place in a little over four weeks' time.

Before announcing himself at the door, he took a moment to mentally check his toolkit. Though personally believing the healing power of God to be beyond the need for such things, he knew people expected to see the relevant paraphernalia... and far be it from him to disappoint.

First and foremost was the crucifix... standard fare for the exorcist about town. In his case, he'd made sure it was of an impressive enough size to suggest he'd taken the possession seriously. It was also of an impressive enough size so as not to risk – should he ever actually find himself backed into a corner by something terrifying and needing to brandish it as his weapon of choice – encountering the mocking phrase "*is that it?*"

A black, leather doctor's bag also contained a vial of holy water... bible... book of exorcism rites... purple stole – the kissing and donning of which indicated that the pantomime was about to start – and a pack of custard creams. The latter was not so much a weapon against the forces of evil, as an insurance that – having completed the job and been offered a cup of tea by someone for whom stocking the kitchen cupboards had become pretty low priority – you had something to accompany it and round the visit off nicely.

They could all be seen as placebos, of course... the custard creams excepted. But if they did the job, the Reverend Ian Clapp had done his.

The curious thing was... for some peculiar reason, it suddenly needed doing a lot. Whilst demand for his services usually ran to about half a dozen cases a year, he'd had five requests in the last two days, and was looking to squeeze in another appointment that very afternoon.

The custard creams would have to wait.

He rang the doorbell.

Seeing a shape approaching through the frosted, glass panels in front of him, he straightened himself up. A loud *crack* sounded from inside his bag and what appeared to be water seeped from its bottom.

As the door opened, he was greeted by a smell so vile it caused him to gag... accompanied by a low, guttural voice.

'I hope you've come prepared,' it said.

Looking up and seeing what was confronting him, he instinctively flipped the bag's catch and fumbled about inside. His mouth frozen in an expression of disbelief, he pulled out a wooden cross and held it up defiantly in front of him.

'Is that it?' snorted the voice.

The Reverend Ian Clapp gulped... then nodded lamely.

'Oh dear,' it sneered. 'Then you *are* in trouble!'

Over four thousand miles away, Pastor Brad Oakley patted the bonnet of his beloved Buick Convertible and drew in a breath of resilience.

He would need it.

Further still, Shaolin monk Twan Ka Phwi patted the nose of his beloved donkey...

*　　*　　*

Just when Norman thought he'd mastered the art of positive ripples, Snogden-Lambert's frantic message looked like draining the pond.

Returning his call, he'd managed to work out – between slurred renditions of the *Skye Boat Song* and *Donald, Where's yer Troosers?* – that the cheque had bounced.

Assuring Snogden-Lambert that a mistake had clearly been made... a reply had come back via a curious drawl that sounded like... *Yee nay wrong there, laddie!*

Confident of his position, Norman had promised it would turn out to be nothing more than a clerical error and that he'd get it sorted immediately.

The response had been a belch of acknowledgement... followed by an incomplete version of *Green Grow the Rushes O...* the singer having passed out shortly after requesting of the listener, *what was his six O?*

Norman had put the phone down, determined not to let negative ripples contaminate his plans. Against all odds, everything else was going smoothly.

Under normal circumstances, he would've returned to the field outside the village – or one further away, if necessary – and summoned Gabriel for advice. But, much to the consternation of the locals, a virulent swarm of oversized horseflies had descended upon the village that morning, laying siege to its alarmed residents and refusing to disperse. So aggressive were the intruders, its inhabitants were being forced to remain indoors.

Norman suspected that even if he braved the threat, something greater would undoubtedly manifest to stop him.

He was on his own.

Refusing to panic, he resolved to heed Gabriel's advice and use logical thinking to get himself out of the mess.

He began by assuming the issue wasn't with the *Templar Resources* account. Gabriel had given him his word that cheques could be written for unlimited amounts. He'd never had a problem in the past... even having made the previous one out for one hundred million pounds. Though not wishing to let any negative thoughts gain a foothold, he *did* admit quarter of a billion pounds was considerably larger than that... which is when the thought did precisely what he didn't want it to and attracted a far more obvious and worrying one.

All money had to come from *somewhere*.

Not giving the matter much consideration in the past, he'd simply assumed a small group of religiously connected financiers or wealthy individuals had set up the account... its name suggesting Masonic connections. After all, Heaven wouldn't break the law by metaphysically fabricating a balance.

Beyond that, he'd considered it none of his business.

As the years passed and his withdrawals had grown bolder, Gabriel's promise of unlimited funds cemented itself as his default thinking on the subject.

But now, as his logical mind forensically examined the problem, the realisation hit home that it was *impossible* for any bank account to hold an infinite amount of money.

Wasn't it?

That fact led to an even more disturbing conclusion.

Gabriel's promise was a lie!

As this last thought prompted an image of Xanthia questioning whether the Archangel could be trusted, his own concern as to why Gabriel hadn't alerted him to the fire at the hotel, until it was almost too late, resurfaced.

Suddenly, Gabriel didn't seem so gleamingly white.

Was the room exerting its influence again?

He shook the negative intrusions from his head.

121

Gabriel had obviously never envisaged him taking out such a colossal amount of money in one go. After all... why would he? The amount he'd offered Snogden-Lambert had clearly been way too optimistic.

But if that were the case... why hadn't Gabriel said anything? The figure had been plastered all over the media in recent days. Whilst Gabriel might not have been able to see Stonehenge, he could surely read the newspapers!

'STOP IT!' he berated himself.

He wouldn't let the room and whatever had been drawn to it get the better of him a second time. It had already cost him Xanthia. If he didn't trust Gabriel, there was no point in *anything*. The fault *had* to lie elsewhere.

Perhaps the cheque had been blocked for security reasons. Having received two cheques for record amounts in the space of a week, perhaps it was simply a case of a vigilant computer flagging up an irregular and suspicious pattern.

The theory felt plausible... and certainly more palatable.

If the bank were merely being cautious, the situation could be easily verified and rectified.

He stared at his reflection in the dressing table mirror, awaiting the appearance of a smile.

The corners of his mouth remained static... unlike his shoulders, which fell as another thought trumped its predecessor.

If he'd written the cheque from his own personal account, it would simply be a case of calling his account manager and having the matter resolved.

But he hadn't.

Due to the amount involved, he'd done so on an account that was neither in his name nor for which he had authority... let alone knowledge.

His reflection stared back in anguish.

He'd hit a brick wall.

Gabriel would tell him there was no such thing and to think positively... which was rather ironic, given the Archangel wasn't even able to cope with a door. The old lady in the park would suggest he examine his forks.

So he did.

The only positive thing about a brick wall was that it left you with the most basic fork of all. If you weren't going to allow it to stop you, there was no option but to go *through* it.

His reflection slowly raised a grin.

Brick walls weren't a problem if you had the expertise to drill into them!

Grabbing his laptop, he employed the skills for which Heaven had singled him out. Revelling in the challenges of the binary world, he set about hacking the *Templar Resources* account.

The following hours were spent overcoming a predictable string of challenges... methodically working his way through lesser minds' futile attempts at stopping him. Familiar territory, it was something he once did for fun. But *now* he could indulge that pleasure without feeling guilty.

Each step a positive one, the buzz felt incredible. He'd forgotten how stimulating the challenge could be. But nowhere near as exhilarating as when he'd penetrated the final barrier and found himself with the power to access every single piece of information held within the account.

Not that he hadn't considered taking a peek before. In earlier days, curiosity had often thrown up the temptation of discovering who it was that funded his lifestyle. But, instinct telling him Gabriel wouldn't approve, he'd stuck to the position it was none of his business... and certainly hadn't wanted to risk having the chequebook taken away from him.

Now he had a valid reason to at least see how much money was at his disposal.

His hand trembling, he brought up the account's all-important balance on the screen. His heart beating at the back of his throat, his lips attempted to decipher the stupefyingly long row of noughts strewn in front of him. If he'd worried about the amount for which he'd written the cheque, he *needn't* have.

He gave up trying to find out how little it was a problem

before he went cross-eyed.

A thought he could neither categorise as positive nor negative entered his head. Being one of temptation, its polarity was subjective.

Why not use this opportunity to find out who the account's signatories were?

He could finally lift the veil on the enigmatic Templar Resources.

He looked to his reflection in the mirror again, as if seeking his own approval.

It was highly doubtful Gabriel would consider the thought subjective, it warned.

That was the point of it being subjective.

Fair enough. Then, what valid reason would he give for his inquisitiveness?

It was possible they could be contacted to help resolve the problem, given Gabriel could not.

Wasn't that just a convenient excuse?

That depended on your viewpoint.

The subjective defence again... eh?

Yes.

Clever.

Wait a minute!

What?

Who's this argument with?

Yourself.

Really?

Either that or you're going mad.

Or being influenced again?

But you're the one insisting on taking a peek.

Good point.

At that, Norman realised he was merely wasting time. Determined not to be sidetracked further, he set about locating the root of his immediate problem.

The answer – when he eventually found it – came as a massive shock... not least because it was so simple. It was one he hadn't even contemplated.

Much to his consternation, the chequebook Gabriel had gifted him had simply ceased to exist. No record of it could be found... just the past footprint of cheques already cashed.

Reeling from the implications, he took out and examined the genuine article... constantly turning it over in his hand and thumbing its remaining pages, as if confirmation of its physical presence might alter the finding.

It didn't.

Finally deeming such futile actions a positive thought too far, he realised his only option was to rectify the situation himself. Having full access to the account, he just needed to get it to accept that another chequebook existed in place of the original. As long as he ensured it started with the same number as the one he'd written Snogden-Lambert, that cheque would be validated upon re-presenting... along with any subsequent ones. What's more... the bank would surely have to prioritise it, given it would appear the mistake was theirs and the possibility of looming worldwide adverse publicity meant it should clear immediately.

Aware the clock that had started in France was ticking ever louder, he urgently set about his task.

His confidence high – having already defeated those responsible for the site's main security – he found himself tipping a nod of respect to whoever it was who'd devised the additional firewall needing to be cracked in order to put his plan into action. For some reason, they'd gone to extraordinary lengths to stop the very thing he was attempting to... the extra code appearing to have been added as something of an afterthought. But it was extremely effective... of a far more sophisticated nature than anything he'd encountered before. The particular mind responsible was clearly no fool. It knew what it was doing. Curiously... it was if it had pre-empted the exact techniques he might employ to circumnavigate it... always turning out to be one step ahead of him.

Despite relishing the challenge, he thought it odd.

He thought it odder still that... as the light began to fade from the window, and despite his best efforts... he still hadn't managed to get the better of that mind.

*   *   *

Snogden-Lambert breathed as gently as he could. Anything more than the smallest intake of breath caused invisible hammers to strike his already-throbbing cranium without mercy.

Propping himself up in his office chair – a feat in itself – he awaited what he hoped would be his only appointment that morning. He'd already taken the precaution of removing the telephone from its hook and muffling its howling receiver by stuffing it in the filing cabinet... along with an empty bottle of whisky and his socks.

If only he could stop the regular queue of kamikaze birds that were crashing against his window. Some still twitching, their bodies were starting to pile up in a macabre heap beneath its sill.

Despite advertising the fact he'd spent the night on the floor, his unkempt appearance seemed the least of his worries. He was just deciding whether to use his fingers as a comb when the door burst open.

'I promise there's nothing for you to worry about!' blurted his appointment, by way of an edgy introduction.

Whilst preferring a knock, the news came as sweet music to Snogden-Lambert's sensitive ears. Still reeling from yesterday's news, he drank in the relief that it had all been nothing but a ghastly misunderstanding.

'Other than I'm currently two hundred and fifty million pounds short at this precise moment in time,' qualified his wide-eyed appointment.

Snogden-Lambert groaned quietly.

'I've not slept all night,' said Norman, taking a seat without being asked. 'I've been trying to rectify the situation... but it's complicated.'

Snogden-Lambert had feared it would be. Any pity he had left for the young man in front of him evaporated with the confirmation. 'You're mad... aren't you?' he said bluntly, staring Norman in the eye.

'Absolutely bloody furious,' responded Norman, thumping the desk in frustration.

Snogden-Lambert pointed delicately to his head. 'If you don't mind.'

'Sorry.' Norman could see a tough time had been had... which made two of them. Try as he might, he'd been unable to crack the extra security put in place to prevent the issuing of a new chequebook. Time had eventually got the better of him. Frustrated, he'd been forced to call it a day, night, and quite a bit of that morning, in order to make his appointment as promised.

'I meant mad... as in a box of frogs,' explained Snogden-Lambert without emotion.

Norman took a brief moment to study his accuser. The unshaven face and badly creased suit might've been better overlooked if it hadn't been for the Post-it note stuck on his forehead... the words *MUST TRY HARDER* scrawled across it in angry biro. The fumes were a bit of a flag-waver too.

'I guess mad depends on your viewpoint,' said Norman diplomatically.

'Were you trying to punish me?' asked Snogden-Lambert.

'I beg your pardon?'

'Hurt me for the crime I committed against the art world?' It had crossed Snogden-Lambert's floundering mind that the individual pretending to look confused from across his desk had deliberately set him up for the highest possible fall. Perhaps he was more on the psychotic edge of insane. Perhaps he was incredibly clever... and cruel... and had done so in revenge for his own destruction of a much-loved national treasure. After all, his tormentor had built a reputation in the art world for an obsessive love of its greatest works. The Turner certainly ranked amongst those. 'Well, congratulations!' he conceded. 'You couldn't have done a more thorough job. What little reputation I might've hoped to rebuild has been comprehensively annihilated by your twisted scheme! There's no need to continue the pretence further. I admit defeat. You are clearly not *that* insane.'

'I haven't a clue what you're talking about,' responded Norman, shaking his head. 'But that doesn't matter right now. What matters is that the concert goes ahead as planned.'

'Are you serious?' exclaimed Snogden-Lambert indignantly. 'Are you trying to rub my nose in it?'

'It has to!' Norman insisted. 'If you give me time, I'll make sure you get your money. In fact...' He considered the amount of noughts he'd attempted to decipher the previous afternoon. 'I promise to *double* it!'

'Stop this!' cried Snogden-Lambert, rising from his chair unsteadily. 'My nerves are shredded enough! The joke's over!' He pointed at the door. 'This meeting is at an end, Mister Penkridge. Our business is finished. Get out!'

'Oh, but I'm serious!' insisted Norman, clasping his hands together and refusing to budge from his seat. His tired mind scrambled for a solution to his predicament. 'If you *must* know... there's more to this concert than meets the eye!' he blurted.

Snogden-Lambert looked at him impassively.

Norman took a deep breath. 'I know you won't believe me, but I guess I've got nothing to lose now... The fate of the entire Universe is at stake! I've been asked by the Archangel Gabriel to perform a certain piece of music when the sun rises above the heel stone on the twenty-first of June. It'll make me the new Saviour... which means I'll be able to battle the Antichrist and hopefully save us all!'

You could've heard a pin drop.

Snogden-Lambert slowly lowered himself back down into his chair. 'Oh, dear God,' he mumbled to himself. 'It's *far* worse than I thought.'

'Yes, it is!' said Norman excitedly. 'So... you believe me!'

Snogden-Lambert shook his head apologetically.

'I told you, you wouldn't,' groaned Norman, grabbing his.

'I don't know what's more comforting,' reflected Snogden-Lambert philosophically. 'That I *haven't* been the victim of pure malice... or that I've finally met someone who's in need of more psychiatric help than I am!'

'It doesn't have to end like this,' tried Norman desperately.

'Oh... but it does,' declared Snogden-Lambert. 'Your lack of sanity isn't the problem. I was quite happy to overlook that, while it suited me. It's your lack of *money* that's put the noose around my neck.'

'But I *have* money!' insisted Norman. 'Just not as much available cash as I originally offered! But it's okay. If you give me time, I'll be able to write you another cheque!'

Snogden-Lambert shrugged. 'So... I'll be able to cash it *after* you've had your concert, will I?'

'Of course!'

'Provided you win your battle with the Antichrist, I presume?'

Norman skewed his mouth. 'I guess.'

'Well... what's there to worry about, then?'

Norman jumped to his feet. 'So we have a deal?' He stuck out his hand enthusiastically.

Snogden-Lambert squinted at him aggressively. 'Do you *really* think so little of me? Do I honestly come across as *that* gullible?'

Norman thought it best not to answer.

'It's one thing to make a mistake,' asserted Snogden-Lambert. 'It's another to make it twice.'

'But you said you'd researched me. You *know* I'm a wealthy man,' maintained Norman, refusing to give up.

'Clearly not wealthy *enough*,' Snogden-Lambert reminded him.

'That's not strictly true. Look... I can phone my bank right now and have them transfer...' Norman gave the matter some thought, 'something in the region of one hundred million pounds. They'll guarantee it for you on the spot. It'll be in your account this afternoon!' He looked around for a phone.

'It's in the filing cabinet,' said Snogden-Lambert.

'O...kay,' sung Norman slowly.

'Which is where it's staying.'

'But...'

Snogden-Lambert put a hand up to silence him and used the other to scratch his chin theatrically. 'I don't remember the newspaper headlines promising the nation... *something in the region of...* or me offering you a last-minute discount. My extremely-hard-to-convince superiors... and those to whom I gave my word... are expecting the full amount... right down to the very last penny.'

'Then don't tell them you haven't had it all yet,' suggested Norman. 'You told me the other day it was *you* who was in charge here. You said one word from you and the relevant committees would do exactly what you say!'

Snogden-Lambert wriggled uncomfortably. 'I might've overstated that last bit,' he admitted.

'Anyway... the money's immaterial,' said Norman. 'If I can't beat the Antichrist, I doubt there'll be anything to spend it on!'

Snogden-Lambert wagged his finger slowly. '*That's* the bit I think they'll struggle with the most.'

Norman grabbed his head again in frustration. 'This is ridiculous! We're so close! All I need is a little more time to try and hack a particular bank account! If I can trick it into accepting the old cheque as valid, you'll have your money *before* the concert!'

'Why would you need to hack your own bank account?' enquired Snogden-Lambert, confused.

'Not *mine*.'

'Then... *whose?*'

'That's the problem... I don't really know.'

Snogden-Lambert rose quicker than his head would've liked. 'Right... that's it!' he shouted angrily. 'GET OUT! NOW!'

Norman still refused to oblige.

'I'll have you know I've dealt with far bigger men than you,' smouldered Snogden-Lambert, making his way around the desk purposefully. He forcibly grabbed hold of Norman's shoulders and looked around for the nearest radiator grill.

'Wait!' cried Norman, holding on to the desk. 'There might just be another way out!'

'No... there's only the one door, I assure you.' Snogden-Lambert proceeded to drag him and the desk towards it. 'And I should know... because it's got MY BLOODY NAME ON IT!'

'I meant... out of our predicament!'

'La, la, la, la, la,' sang Snogden-Lambert childishly. 'I'm not listening! I'm not listening!'

Norman tried to anchor his feet into the carpet. 'But what about your knighthood?'

'I don't even want my *ordinary* name at the moment, thanks to you,' Snogden-Lambert growled, going for a headlock.

'Why haven't you got any socks on?' gagged Norman, as he found his head thrust downwards. Whilst blindly attempting to grab Snogden-Lambert's ears, he'd heard the best way to disarm an attacker was to say something completely off the wall.

'Because they're next to the phone in a suspension file labelled *miscellaneous*,' answered Snogden-Lambert, as if privy to the same advice.

They both stopped their struggling and drew in deep breaths.

'What... in the *filing cabinet?*' Norman wheezed.

'Yes.'

'*Why?*'

'I have absolutely no idea,' sighed Snogden-Lambert, tightening his grip again.

'Just tell me what I can give you to make you change your mind,' Norman choked.

'My sanity back, for one,' came the answer.

'I don't think that's possible,' ventured Norman bravely.

'Oh... and why's that... you little *shit?*'

The hold tightened even more.

'Because you've got a Post-it note stuck to your forehead?' tried Norman.

Snogden-Lambert froze.

Norman waited expectantly, still forced to stare at his opponent's sockless feet.

He eventually felt the arm around his neck loosen slightly and start shaking.

Snogden-Lambert said nothing.

'Are you crying?' asked Norman, after a few minutes.

* * *

A full cycle of seasons had passed since Worker One's failure to convince the community that worshipping the *True* one god would be its best option. Whilst a small contingent of converts had enthusiastically adopted his rules and pronounced him their spiritual leader, an equally small group had favoured Worker Three's argument for the *Authentic* one god... seeing compromise as the best way out of their dilemma of not offending the other two one gods and sensibly hedging their bets.

The majority, however, had embraced Worker Two's *Genuine* one god. They felt comfortable sticking to familiar ceremonial practices... though their comfort was to be short-lived. The *Genuine* one god's divinely ordained representative on Earth wasted no time in consolidating his position of authority by decreeing that the building of his palatial residency be given immediate priority... which meant all other work ceasing.

Didn't he mean the *Genuine* one god's palatial residency?

If that helped.

It did... but Worker Two's demand produced a split amongst his followers. Some insisted that the ring of stones still be completed, not wishing their previous efforts to go to waste. The man with antlers on his house though formerly on his head was foremost amongst them, arguing that, as the old gods had decreed it, the command shouldn't be ignored.

But those gods didn't exist anymore, he was chastised. You could only have one god now... and at least he had three of them to choose from.

The man with antlers on his house though formerly on his head refused to acquiesce.

A group of staunch *Genuine* one god devotees pronounced it heresy and said he should be put to death.

Followers of the *True* one god disagreed. Killing was now a bad thing. Read the rules.

Their rules, maybe, countered the *Genuine* one god's supporters.

Adherents of the *Authentic* one god couldn't decide *who* was right. Both views were equally worthy... according to their *try-not-to-offend-anyone-especially-if-they're-a-god* principles.

Much to everyone's surprise, the man with antlers on his house though formerly on his head proposed a way out of his own predicament. He suggested a compromise. Given it was incontrovertible that there were *once* many gods... surely the strongest of those gods had been their leader... a *supreme* god, if you like. Assuming the majority didn't think it heresy, he would be prepared to renounce the many gods in favour of that *Supreme* one god... thereby solving their problem and his.

Many supporters of the *Genuine* one god found themselves drawn to the idea. Having chosen their faith because of its connection with the past, they figured a switch to the *Supreme* one god would enable them to embrace it fully.

Worker Two was less impressed. In danger of losing half his congregation... and power... he lambasted the proposal of a fourth one god. If followers of the *True* and *Authentic* one gods joined him and his supporters in a temporary alliance, their combined opposition would be strong enough to stop its creation, he proposed.

But those worshipping the *Authentic* one god found themselves theologically unable to argue against the idea of a further compromise. After all... hadn't that been the foundation of their own religion? Weren't they morally bound to support the creation of such a god as the *Supreme* one god?

Opinions finely balanced, followers of the *True* one god realised their decision was crucial. Being politically advantageous to have their main rival's power reduced, they shrewdly abstained from the debate. Besides... they were already having to deal with three one gods. A *fourth* wouldn't make much difference.

The man with antlers on his house though formerly on his head had won his argument. The *Supreme* one god was now an officially recognised deity.

But hang on...

Some following the debate saw logic in Worker Two's suggestion that joining forces would present the strongest front. Surely then... a one god that combined all three one gods would be the *ultimate* one god... wouldn't it?

Not quite... coughed the man with antlers on his house though formerly on his head.

Oh yes... sorry... they'd forgotten that bit. It was very hard keeping up these days. Surely a one god that combined all *four* one gods would be the *ultimate* one god... wouldn't it?

As some heads nodded, another split looked likely.

In an attempt to prevent yet another one god... and protect their own interests... the majority disagreed.

But those pushing the idea refused to back down. They didn't care they were a minority. It couldn't be considered heresy to have one god representing all the others, as you'd be giving allegiance to all of them at the same time.

In that case, worshipping this *Ultimate* one god would prove extremely difficult... wouldn't it?

The new converts to the *Ultimate* one god considered the question. Granted... it wasn't for the faint-hearted. But that's what made them special.

Special?

Yes... in the eyes of the *Ultimate* one god.

Hang on a second! Where did *that* come from? What made them think they were superior to everybody else? Surely *everyone* was special in the eyes of their own particular one god?

Not necessarily. And besides... they'd thought of it first.

* * *

'I promise I won't tell anyone,' said Norman, as Snogden-

Lambert peeled the Post-it note from his forehead and read it.

'It doesn't matter anymore,' he sighed wearily, collapsing into his chair. 'I'm ruined. You've seen to that. There'll be no more last chances for me now.'

Norman placed a polystyrene cup of water on the desk and stood back respectfully. 'You're not seeing it from the right angle,' he insisted gently. 'We've still got time to make this work.'

'The angle I'm seeing it from is an obtuse one,' answered Snogden-Lambert... rather cleverly, in his opinion. 'As in... it's you who are being obtuse. We had a deal, Mister Penkridge. You gave me your word and I gave you mine... and when a Snogden-Lambert says they'll do something, they do it. That is because a Snogden-Lambert's word is sacrosanct. You... on the other hand... seem to think it's perfectly alright to alter the terms of that agreement and carry on as if everyone else is stupid. Whilst I realise it's because of your barking insanity, I *was* hoping we'd be able to conclude our business before they carted you off somewhere safer.'

'Hang on a second!' objected Norman, stepping forward. 'If any one's gonna be labelled...'

Snogden-Lambert brusquely raised an objecting hand. 'Did you or did you not request putting the monument back to its original condition the other night?'

'Absolutely,' affirmed Norman.

'I rest my case,' Snogden-Lambert nodded.

'I rest *mine!*' countered Norman indignantly. 'You agreed to my request without even asking *why!*'

'I didn't have to,' Snogden-Lambert shrugged. 'And if justification were needed as to why... Well... it's hardly been a hive of activity out there on the repair front, has it?' He looked out of the window, just in time to see a house martin head-butt the glass.

'That's because the stones I need aren't being delivered until tomorrow morning,' explained Norman.

'Of course,' smiled Snogden-Lambert. 'On a wagon pulled by a unicorn, no doubt.' The smile fell. 'It's just a shame my *money* won't be on it!'

'Wait a minute,' said Norman slowly, the penny dropping. 'Did you agree to the restoration because you think... *I'm* mad?'

Snogden-Lambert gave a look that suggested words weren't necessary.

They weren't. Norman suddenly appreciated the fortuitous balance of his circumstances. 'Fair enough,' he said quickly, not wishing to upset the apple cart he'd been gifted and lose any advantage he *did* have. 'So that's why you don't trust me. I get it now.'

Snogden-Lambert gave another look that suggested much the same thing as the first one.

Norman drew a deep breath. 'In that case... I have a solution.' The drawing of an even deeper one suggested it didn't sit easily with him and would involve great pain on his part. 'I'll call my bank immediately and authorise them to transfer every single penny of mine into an account of your choosing. I believe you'll find it's somewhere in the region of one hundred million pounds. You'll be able to verify its transfer for yourself. I'll then have my solicitor arrange for the deeds of my property in France to be signed over to you as a personal gift. If you then wish to bequeath it to the Nation, that's up to you. But I should say... it has a very nice view from the living room.' His breathing became laboured, as he fought with himself to complete the proposal. 'Finally... I'll put a call through to my estate manager and have him arrange for the immediate transportation of every single piece of art I own to this address, in exchange for the remainder of money owed.' He steadied himself... deciding it would be most unbusinesslike to throw up at that point. 'If we act quickly enough, they should be here by tomorrow afternoon. I think you'll find the combined values of those actions will *more* than cover what was originally promised. You can't get a more tangible guarantee than that!' Norman could see the cogs of Snogden-Lambert's mind whirring faster than his face could conceal. Encouraged... he struck while the iron was hot. 'Furthermore... should those artworks not arrive by sundown... you get to keep the money that's transferred, along with the house... the concert will be cancelled and you'll never hear from me again. All I ask in return is that the preparation work for *Trouzerbulge's* performance be allowed to continue in the meantime, and that it will still go ahead as agreed if I succeed in delivering my part of the deal.'

'You're not just talking about constructing a stage, are you?' clarified Snogden-Lambert, slowly.

'No, I'm not.'

'You still want me to believe... even though I've been totally upfront and told you to your face I think you're *completely* mad... that somewhere in the region of thirty sarsen stones will be arriving here tomorrow morning and put in place before that performance?'

'Absolutely!'

Snogden-Lambert considered the unexpected turnaround in his fortune.

'On that last point,' clarified Norman. 'You said earlier the word of a Snogden-Lambert was sacrosanct.'

Snogden-Lambert straightened his back. 'One hundred percent! You have the word of a Snogden-Lambert on that!'

'So you won't attempt to stop the monument being reconstructed tomorrow morning when the stones actually *do* turn up?'

A look of pity returned in Snogden-Lambert's eyes... which Norman realised was a *good* thing.

'Just so long as you accept that... whilst we both know you're clearly certifiably insane... this is what you want and that my conscience can be clear,' Snogden-Lambert confirmed.

Norman stuck out his hand.

'You *are* mad, aren't you?' Snogden-Lambert added cautiously, sticking out his.

'As mad as you want me to be,' smiled Norman... morphing it into an inane grin, so as to cement the deal.

*   *   *

A second cycle of seasons had passed since schisms had complicated the worshipping of a single god. The emergence of an *Ultimate* one god had been confusing enough. What followed would test the patience of a saint... if enough time had passed for one to exist, that is.

A fanatical faction of devotees of the *Genuine* one god – angry at Worker Two's willingness to align himself with the heretical followers of the *True* one god and *Authentic* one god in opposition to the *Supreme* one god – formed their own breakaway sect... worshipping what they insisted was the *Only Genuine* one god. Believing violence should have been used to defend the *Only Genuine* one god's integrity, they branded adherents of the *Genuine* one god as recreants... suggesting their lack of devotion should be punishable by death.

The introduction of a *fifth* one god caused a serious rift amongst followers of the *Ultimate* one god. The "special" ones had founded their religion on the belief that *their* one god was an amalgamation of all the other one gods. Now they faced a dilemma. Did that include the *Only Genuine* one god as well... or should it not be classed as a separate one god?

Followers of the *Only Genuine* one god threatened death to them, their offspring, and whatever descendants escaped the net, for such blasphemy.

A small group believing the *Only Genuine* one god *should* be included in the worship of the *Ultimate* one god suddenly found themselves ostracised. With no choice but to follow their convictions, they formed themselves into disciples of the *Definitive Ultimate* one god...

...which caused a dilemma amongst its new followers.

Should they now include their own *Definitive Ultimate* one god in that amalgamation of one gods?

Fearing they'd created a philosophical paradox, a few salved their consciences by becoming adherents of the *Conditionally Definitive Ultimate* one god.

But those who felt unable to contravene their founding principle pushed ahead as converts to the *Categorically*

Definitive Ultimate one god...

...which caused a dilemma amongst its new followers.

*   *   *

Bill Dribble cut the engine on his *Biggablade X320* and pulled the cap from his head. In thirty-eight years as sexton of Saint Margaret's, he'd never encountered anything like it.

The smell of two-stroke mingling with that of freshly cut grass, he wiped the sweat from the back of his neck using a handkerchief that had seen better days.

As had Bill himself.

Looking around in disbelief, he doubted that *any* Dribbles of Little Sponding had encountered anything like it... and that was an awful lot of Dribbles. Stretching back further than the church records had recorded, the position of sexton had been passed down as a tradition from father to son. Scythes in hand, the Dribbles of Little Sponding had diligently tended the grounds on which the old Norman church had been built, constantly battling the encroaching grass and weeds to ensure they respected those who sought final peace beneath it.

Sadly... that tradition looked like coming to an end. His sperm count living up to the family name, Bill was the last in his line.

Stan Dribble... Bill's father and the first to countenance a petrol mower... once swore he'd caught a strangely attired individual urinating on the gravestone of a previous vicar. His tale curiously echoed that of village folklore, which claimed one of his ancestors had given chase to an imp-like creature caught doing much the same thing upon the church altar... though *that* Dribble had also claimed to have seriously wounded the offender with a well-aimed collection box astutely filled with holy water hastily scooped from the font.

But as each tale had undoubtedly been embellished with every retelling in the village pub... and Stan had also claimed to have single-handedly overrun an entire German machine gun position in the last war – when mother insisted his arched feet had never got him past the training camp at Basingstoke – Bill had always viewed both with a certain degree of scepticism.

However, what lay in front of him was very real.

If father were alive today…

Looking across to where there was concrete proof father *wasn't*… well… stone, at least… he shared his outrage that such a thing could happen.

Strewn across the grounds of the graveyard were the smashed lids of every raised tomb in the care of Saint Margaret's, the insides of the open sarcophagi finally feeling the warmth of the sun after centuries of curiosity. A stone cross, proclaiming the peaceful sleep of a beloved wife, mother, and grandmother, had been callously uprooted and repositioned upside down. Scattered amongst the mayhem were flowers that had been lovingly placed on graves just days before.

But that wasn't the worst of it.

An odour was growing stronger… overpowering that from the sweat of his labour… as if what lay beneath the tombs had finally seeped its way into the air.

Bill Dribble suddenly found himself in shadow. From his perspective, the sun had merely gone behind a cloud.

From the perspective of anyone having bothered to climb the worn, stone steps of the Norman tower and be looking down on him, the shadow had a shape.

'Bloody kids,' he muttered, under his breath.

Only his cap would make it through to the morning, its solitary presence on the newly mown grass finally marking the end of nature's centuries-old battle with the Dribbles of Little Sponding.

*   *   *

It had taken Norman the best part of an hour to convince his estate manager in France that he was not only who he said he was on the phone, but that he hadn't been held to ransom or simply taken leave of his senses.

The facts established, he'd eventually managed to arrange to have every piece of artwork he possessed removed from the house and placed in as many trucks as it would take to transport them to England. A private security firm ensuring their protection – with enough muscle and machinery to start a war – he'd given express orders that the fortified convoy and its team of drivers were not to stop until they'd reached their final destination... refuelling, toilet breaks, and the English Channel excluded.

Should any other obstacles present themselves – dogs, deer, flocks of birds, or anything that might be construed as being suspiciously improbable – they were to plough straight through. He'd take personal responsibility and deal with the consequences afterwards... along with the problem of how he was now going to pay for it all.

Desperately trying not to picture the paintings being taken from the walls, or the rooms he no longer owned stripped of everything he'd lovingly collected over the past five years, he'd attempted to distract himself by dealing with last minute preparations for the concert. But it wasn't until lack of sleep from the night before finally got the better of him that, as evening approached, the pain of losing everything he owned was given some respite.

Surprisingly, he would sleep soundly... a dark, solid, blanket of nothingness finally bringing relief to an exhausted mind.

It was just as well... given what lay ahead.

*   *   *

'Bravo! Bravo! Magnificent!' shouted Donald, enthusiastically applauding the cast onstage. 'You have given my words the crucial breath of life they needed and I will be forever grateful!'

As dress rehearsals went, it couldn't have gone better. Everyone involved... from actors to stagehands... agreed *An English Jericho* would go down in history as Donald's finest achievement... if not theatre's itself.

They also agreed they'd been lucky to have made it to the

end whilst maintaining their own "breath of life". The last few days had turned out to be hell on earth. But then, Donald had always said they would be.

The cast stood in a line, heads bowed... the remaining sarsen uprights that had survived the play's spectacular denouement towering majestically behind... a powerful reminder of the question their performance evoked.

'Tomorrow night the world will get the chance to witness your triumph,' Donald promised. 'And I will have answered my calling.'

The cast remained stooped, their exhausted bodies drained of emotion.

'I'm just so sorry for the personal traumas you've had to endure in order for us to get this far. But let us take comfort from the fact that those who cruelly sought to silence our message will have failed by this time tomorrow night.' He watched proudly as the cast finally stood upright. 'Alan,' he announced, offering out a hand of respect. 'We may not have seen eye to eye in the beginning... but the fact you didn't desert us after that tragic incident involving your parents yesterday morning is testament to your standing as a professional.'

Alan acknowledged the compliment with the briefest of nods, his eyes those of a man who hadn't slept.

'How they both ended up at the bottom of that grain silo, we will never know,' added Donald. 'Especially as they were both retired librarians.' His outstretched hand moved to the woman on Alan's left. 'And Catherine... the loss of your brother in *those* circumstances beggars belief.'

Catherine stifled a sob.

'And so young.'

His adjunct caused the next one to break through.

'Then, of course, we have our dear Rosy,' Donald smiled affectionately as his hand moved yet again. 'Living proof that there *is* a silver lining to every cloud.'

The young girl in question smiled back awkwardly.

'Not so fortunate for the person she was understudying, I grant you... but the chance to finally shine in her own right...

and we will be making a collection for her colleague on opening night.'

The assistant director stepped in before Donald could lower spirits any further. 'Not forgetting our esteemed director and writer of the play himself...' he held out a heavily bandaged arm. 'Donald Tucker-Jenkins.'

The applause that accompanied the credit was muted but respectful. It wasn't that the cast didn't appreciate his talents. It was just that they were too tired and traumatised to give anything more.

Donald modestly waved down the attempt. 'And of course... finally... someone who has helped me enormously during our troubled efforts here... and without whom I could not have reached this point...'

The assistant director bashfully prepared himself, lowering his head as much as the surgical collar around his neck allowed.

'Whitebait!' announced Donald grandly.

Mouths grimaced in sympathy.

'I EXPECT HE PROBABLY IS,' shouted Donald. 'BUT I'M SURE HE'S GOT MORE IMPORTANT THINGS TO THINK ABOUT, GIVEN THE CURRENT STATE OF HIS BICYCLE!'

The assistant director deflected any embarrassment by quickly brandishing the notebook he had in his hand. 'As wonderful as that last rehearsal was... I've got a few quick notes to go through before we call it a day. So, ladies and gentlemen... if you don't mind...'

'Well... at least we know this has to be it,' said Chad, standing back and confirming the name of the theatre as that on the piece of paper in his hand.

'What were the chances it turned out to be the very last one on our list?' moaned Bob. 'I can't believe it's taken us this amount of effort! All I can say is... thank *God* we only had to visit those that *weren't* advertising shows!'

'It's only there at the bottom because I didn't think Donald would opt for somewhere this suburban,' said Chad, looking around with disdain.

A proliferation of cheap, fast-food eateries and charity shops had put paid to any magic the building's facade might once have evoked.

Pressing his face against the glass of the main door, Bob shielded his eyes from the reflected glare of a neon sign shaped like a kebab. 'At least we're not too late. Something's definitely going on inside!' he squinted. 'I can just make out some lights at the far end.'

'Better get this over with, then,' said Chad firmly.

'And if you can just remember to keep your face turned to the audience at that point, your parting line will be given stronger meaning by your expression.' The assistant director turned the page of his notebook and smiled on discovering it was blank. 'Well... I think we've covered everything!' he announced brightly.

'One last thing, if I may,' interrupted Donald stepping forward.

'I don't think it's bolted,' said Bob, rattling the stage door.

Chad clicked the fingers of his outstretched hand and took the credit card that was promptly offered. Sliding it into the gap between the door frame and Yale lock, he gave it a deft flick.

The door popped open.

'I'm gonna teach that wacko a lesson for failing to keep his promise!' said Bob, taking the lead and storming into the building.

'I want you as fresh as possible for tomorrow's premiere, so I need you all to get a good night's sleep,' Donald instructed the cast. 'Though Whitebait informs me that's not going to happen.'

Anxious glances were exchanged.

'And for those of you with cars... may I suggest you drive *extremely* carefully!'

'Can I help you gentlemen?'

Chad and Bob stood in silence as they surveyed the empty theatre.

'I didn't think I'd left the door open,' the caretaker leaning on his broom remarked, a cigarette balancing precariously on his bottom lip.

Bob put out his hands, playing for time. 'We were...'

'...hoping to meet someone here tonight,' finished Chad.

'And who might that be?'

The two Americans looked at each other.

'Maybe we're too late,' said Chad.

'Looks like there's no maybe about it,' commented the caretaker wryly.

'We were expecting to find something special here tonight,' elaborated Bob.

'That's the magic of the theatre,' said the caretaker, releasing one hand from his broom and arcing it through the air dramatically.

Chad studied his list. 'I don't understand. It *had* to be here! This is the last dark theatre in London. We've personally checked every other one!'

The caretaker rescued the cigarette from his lip. 'Checked 'em for what?'

Chad figured further subterfuge was pointless. 'We were hoping to find the playwright Donald Tucker-Jenkins rehearsing his upcoming play here.'

'You mean... the one he's been trying to keep a secret?'

'You know about it?'

'I should think the whole of bloody theatreland knows about it!' laughed the caretaker. 'Despite the confidentiality agreement he's said to have insisted upon... apparently for "Health and Safety" reasons! He should've known there's no such thing as a secret in this business. Too many luvvies liking a good gossip.'

'In that case... you wouldn't happen to know *where* he's been rehearsing it, would you?'

The caretaker took a guarded drag from his cigarette. 'That

depends.'

'On what?'

'On how badly you want to know,' the caretaker replied, looking away to no point in particular.

'How about... *very* badly,' answered Bob.

The caretaker took a sharp intake of breath. 'I wouldn't have been so honest, personally,' he advised. 'You could've got me *much* cheaper.'

'How much do you want?' asked Chad tersely.

The caretaker fiddled with his broom. 'I reckon a pony'll do it.'

'You wanna *horse?*' exclaimed Bob.

'That's twenty-five quid to you.'

'It's yours,' said Chad, reaching for his wallet.

'I take it you don't do receipts?' asked Bob, as the money was handed over.

The caretaker allowed himself a small smile. 'A bit like you gentlemen don't make appointments,' He counted the money and stuffed it in his pocket. 'According to what I've heard, it's a little place called the Tivoli... in Wiltshire.'

'*Wiltshire?*' exclaimed Bob. 'Where the friggin' hell's that?'

'A long way from here,' the caretaker replied. 'I hope you've got a car.'

'Wiltshire... That's an entire state, ain't it?' said Chad.

'County,' nodded the caretaker.

'So... exactly whereabouts in the county?'

The caretaker shrugged. 'If I knew that, I'd have charged you double.'

'We'll find it,' said Chad, turning to leave.

'If you're travelling by car, it'll take at least a couple of hours from here,' the caretaker advised. 'So I doubt you'll be catching Mister Tucker-Jenkins *tonight.*'

'Tomorrow will do,' said Chad determinedly.

'I certainly wouldn't leave it any later,' said the caretaker. Cos I understand that's when he intends premiering it.'

Chad and Bob stared at him in shock.

'I know,' smiled the caretaker. 'I'm going soft in my old age.

I'm giving you that bit for *free*.'

Chad slapped Bob on the back, signalling it was time for them to leave. 'Thanks for the intel,' he called back, as they headed for the exit.

'Used a credit card, did we?' mumbled the caretaker, returning to his sweeping.

'I'm sorry to have kept you and your staff so late, Mister Knight-Lee,' Donald apologised. 'We needed to fine-tune a few last details. I can't afford anything less than perfection tomorrow night.'

The theatre manager wrung his hands obsequiously. 'That is why you have the unequalled reputation you do,' he smarmed. 'And as I've told you before... please do call me Kieran.'

'You'll have the great and the good descending on your theatre tomorrow evening,' Donald pointed out. 'This place will be rammed with critics from all around the world. My agents have seen to that.'

'I still can't believe this is happening to us,' Kieran exclaimed excitedly. 'I keep having to pinch myself! It's such an incredible honour.'

'But one well-deserved,' said Donald. 'You put your faith in me in my hour of need and trusted I would finish writing my play in time.'

Actually, Kieran *hadn't*. But he wasn't going to argue. He was happy to accept Donald's gratitude. 'At least now I know why you chose to premiere it here,' he smiled.

'If it couldn't be in the West End, your close proximity to the stones was the next most appropriate,' nodded Donald. 'It's just a shame we seem to have picked up some unfortunate interference from the area.'

Kieran hadn't a clue what the last comment was supposed to mean. But he'd gotten used to being confused when Donald spoke.

'I think that's what caused the fire in your foyer yesterday,' added Donald ruefully.

Kieran still didn't know what he was talking about... other

95

than the incident itself. He'd never seen so many fire engines. 'Thank goodness someone spotted it in time,' he said. 'We could've lost this whole historic building forever.'

Donald took a cursory glance around him. 'Oh... don't worry,' he said broodingly. 'There's still plenty of time for that.'

*   *   *

Using his knees, Waggy pushed the damp duvet from his sweltering body and felt the heat dissipate... an equally unpleasant cold, clammy sweat instantly replacing it.

The fact it was dark and he wasn't wearing his sunglasses suggested it was going to be a long, restless night. He cursed himself for having taken so much cocaine before going to bed, having assumed the ketamine that followed would counteract its effect.

Perhaps it was the five shots of whisky that had topped it off?

He snorted in its lingering effects and turned over onto his back.

Or maybe it was the excitement of knowing Stonehenge beckoned tomorrow?

Fumbling in the dark for his bedside clock, he struck the button that illuminated its time.

As the announcement of quarter past four in the morning briefly lit the room, a movement slightly away from the foot of the bed caught his attention.

Bleary eyed, he raised his head and peered into the temporary half-light.

He could just make out a curious shape.

Attempting to decipher what it was, a stronger than normal fug in the room caused him to wretch.

Just as his addled brain suggested it might be clothing draped over the wardrobe door, the shape stepped forward.

'Walter William Cuthbertson... otherwise known as Waggy?' it asked, in a deep, gurgling, guttural voice.

His breath on hold, Waggy nodded slowly.

'Well... if you believe a certain adage... I'm the one you're better off knowing than *not* knowing.'

*   *   *

Peter Snogden-Lambert stared in horror as the first of the flatbed trucks started manoeuvring itself into position, readying itself for its unusual cargo to be offloaded. Six giant sarsen stones – securely tethered together – were being reversed towards the outer boundary of the monument... half a dozen similarly laden trucks waiting patiently in line behind.

'I had no idea he intended putting my work *here*,' declared Stevie the Props, shaking his head in disbelief. 'He only gave out the precise location once the convoy had crossed over into the county. When I realised he wasn't joking, I assumed he was mad!'

'Ditto,' groaned Snogden-Lambert, desperately trying to obliterate the image of his handshake with Norman the previous day.

'I can't actually believe someone's given him permission to do this!'

Snogden-Lambert's ensuing silence belied his inner turmoil. He knew the rest of the world would be thinking exactly the same thing... its incredulity foreshadowed by those members of his staff currently watching proceedings and waving their arms at each other in utter bewilderment.

'Talk of the devil.'

'I'm sorry I'm late,' said Norman, out of breath. 'Toads on the road. A whole blanket of the things stretching for as far as the eye could see. I've never seen so many in my life! Still... it makes a change from horseflies. The taxi driver refused to drive over them until I showed him what I intended leaving as a tip.' The corners of his mouth creased awkwardly. 'I've never seen such a sticky mess.'

'You too?' remarked Stevie. 'Must be a plague of 'em. We had to make a detour after they forced the closure of the A303 just outside Thruxton.'

'Good job it wasn't anything worse,' grimaced Norman. 'We

don't have much time as it is. We need to get everything set in position before the music starts.'

Snogden-Lambert whimpered like a wounded animal.

'Four o'clock tomorrow morning, it says here,' said Stevie, reading from his notes.

'At the absolute latest,' Norman confirmed.

'This wasn't meant to happen,' mumbled Snogden-Lambert in a daze.

Norman placed a sympathetic hand on his shoulder. 'I know. But we shook on it... remember?'

Snogden-Lambert twitched at the reminder. Not that he needed one. That handshake was the root of his problems. The dishonour that was inevitably about to fall on his name was as nothing compared to that which would fall on the family one, if he went back on his word.

'The good news is they're only fibreglass,' Norman consoled him. 'They can be taken down as soon as the music finishes.'

It didn't seem to help.

'Talking of which... I've had to add tabs to the bottom of the uprights, so they can be secured to the ground,' explained Stevie. 'It's the only way to stop 'em toppling over if the wind kicks up.'

'Good... because that would spell disaster,' said Norman. 'We need to guarantee the lintels they support stay firmly in place.'

'No problem there,' Stevie said confidently. 'We're using heavy duty bolts to keep everything together. You'd have to experience one hell of a storm to see *those* things dislodged.'

Norman wasn't sure they weren't going to get one. 'As many as you like,' he suggested prudently.

Stevie nodded. 'So... when does the old bugger arrive?'

'I assume you mean Stump?' Norman glanced at his watch... then at a small, black dot, low in the sky, heading erratically towards them. 'I think you'll probably find that's him now,' he said, acknowledging its wayward approach.

They both watched in silence as it drew nearer, until it was finally hovering directly above the stones. Remaining there for a while, it performed a series of unpredictable circling manoeuvres that suggested its pilot was either showing off or had forgotten how to land.

Eventually, through boredom or the reading of a manual, it came to a bumpy rest a short distance from where they were standing.

Its blades grinding to a halt, the doors opened to disgorge not one but two occupants.

Norman's heart sank as he saw who the second one was.

'Xan!' whistled Stevie. 'What are *you* doing here?'

Xanthia waved awkwardly whilst flashing a difficult smile at Norman.

'I thought she'd finished with him,' said Stevie under his breath.

'So did I,' returned Norman under his.

'My destiny!' shouted Stump, facing the stones and raising his hands in the air triumphantly.

'And who might this gentleman be?' asked Snogden-Lambert, trying to regain control of the situation.

'That's Mister Trou*zer*bulge,' said Norman.

'The *composer?*' exclaimed Snogden-Lambert, shooting a horrified glance towards the man's red, leather trousers and what appeared to be a codpiece.

'He'll be performing as well,' explained Norman.

'I somehow imagined an *older* gentleman,' muttered Snogden-Lambert, perplexed.

'I can assure you, he's no spring chicken,' returned Norman loudly, looking pointedly at Xanthia as he made the remark.

'He's no gentlemen either!' laughed Stevie, grabbing Stump's extended hand and doing something with it the Masons would've been proud of. They hugged each other roughly whilst keeping a firm grip.

'Stump gave me a lift,' she said.

'Yes... I can see,' Norman replied.

'He didn't want to use the roads.'

'Toads?'

'No... roads!' she scowled.

'No matter... How are you feeling?'

'Oh, much better now!' she said brightly, before figuring that perhaps she should rein in her enthusiasm a little.

'Well... I gotta hand it you, Norman,' Stump beamed, taking in the frenetic activity on and around the large stage that had been erected in front of the monument. 'You've only *actually* gone and done it!'

Snogden-Lambert coughed loudly.

'Sorry,' apologised Norman, directing Stump's attention towards him. 'This is Peter Snogden-Lambert, the site's director. It's *him* we have to thank for making this whole thing possible.'

Snogden-Lambert extended his hand warily.

Grinning broadly, Stump did the same thing with it that he'd done with Stevie's... before yanking Snogden-Lambert to his bosom. 'Yo! The main man!' he exclaimed, slapping him enthusiastically on the back.

Snogden-Lambert glanced over at Norman, like a startled baby being winded. Finally released from his embarrassment, he returned his collar and tie to where they were supposed to be. 'I understand Norman is an enthusiastic champion of your music,' he said, as cordially as professionalism dictated. 'Whilst I have yet to have the pleasure of hearing your work for myself, I hope our world-renowned setting here will more than do it justice. As you can see from the work currently being undertaken... we've certainly been persuaded to push the boat out for the occasion!'

'It couldn't be better,' said Stump, placing a hand on his heart and bowing graciously.

'I also understand you've composed a special anthem for us,' said Snogden-Lambert, warming to the gesture.

'I have indeed... Do you wanna hear a bit of it now?'

'Xanthia,' interrupted Norman, hastily pushing her towards Snogden-Lambert. 'Why don't you get Peter to show you where the bathroom is? I'm sure you'll be wanting to freshen up after your journey.'

'How remiss of me,' said Snogden-Lambert, glad to be given

an excuse to escape the cruel reality in front of him. 'We'll leave these gentlemen to get on with their preparations. I'm sure they have much to do... and probably better if I'm not reminded of it.'

She linked her arm around his, flirtatiously.

Snogden-Lambert welcomed the advance and threw a hostile look towards Norman. 'Purely temporary, you say?'

'I assure you... it'll all be over by sunrise,' Norman promised.

'Weird bloke,' said Stump, as Snogden-Lambert and Xanthia headed towards a small electric cart used for traversing the site, her stilettos fighting the terrain.

Whilst desperate to quiz him about his being with Xanthia, Norman knew it must wait. 'Trust me,' he said instead. 'That's been the biggest positive the Universe has given us.'

Stump glanced towards the stage. 'So... any of the other guys put in an appearance yet?'

With perfect timing, the sporty roar of a twelve cylinder engine drew their attention to a wedge-shaped, mechanical amalgamation of sex and adolescence kicking up dust along the access road. Ignoring its speed limit and any form of parking etiquette, it swerved to a halt as close to the stones as possible. As its doors rose into the air, two men awkwardly extricated themselves from its unfeasibly low interior.

'Where's Waggy?' yelled Stump, knowing it only had two seats and scanning the road behind for a repeat performance.

'We've got us a bit of a problem,' shouted back Fungus.

Norman's heart skipped a beat.

'He's been arrested,' shouted the other, who Norman recognised as the band's drummer.

Norman heard the words, but his brain wondered whether it was best to pretend it hadn't.

'That's slightly more than a fuckin' *bit!*' yelled Stump, *his* brain having no such doubts. 'What the hell happened?'

They had to wait for the two men to make their way across the grass before getting the answer.

'We got a call on the way down here from his girlfriend. He's been caught trying to score some gear off a couple of undercover cops,' said Fungus. 'Apparently, his usual supplier was unavailable.'

'For fuck's sake!' cried Stump, reeling backwards with the news. 'I fuckin' told him... don't do anything stupid until this gig was outta the way!'

'He might be off his face most of the time,' chipped in the drummer, 'but he's usually really careful about that sort of thing.'

'So why *now* of all times?' wailed Stump.

'That's the weird thing,' said Fungus. 'She swears he told her that he was persuaded to go out at four o'clock this morning to get a little something by a demonic figure who told him it would be the best stuff he'd ever experience!'

'That'd be about right,' said Norman, joining the conversation.

'Don't worry about it,' said Stump, waving away their baffled looks. 'Look... They can't keep him in custody more than twenty-four hours simply for possession. If he was arrested around four this morning, that'll allow just enough time for me to get him here, if I go back and pick him up in the chopper!'

'It's a little more complicated than that,' said Fungus awkwardly. 'They used his arrest as an excuse to search his house. I'll leave it to your imagination as to what other illegal activities they discovered. I don't think he'll be playing the bass for a while.'

Stump dropped down on his haunches and locked his hands behind his head. 'I don't fuckin' believe it!' he yelled into the ground. 'I was so fuckin' close to experiencing my dream! I could've gone to eternal damnation a happy man!'

'You could still play without him,' suggested Norman desperately. 'There aren't any bass frequencies in the notes I need!'

The drummer looked at Norman with disdain. 'Are you for real?'

'Leave it,' said Stump, still holding his head. 'He has his reasons.'

'I don't fuckin' care!' said the drummer aggressively. 'It's bad

88

enough he's insisted on us playing the last song to a click track! But *notes*? What does the pillock think we are... a heavy metal tone generator?'

'Well, actually...' started Norman.

'Leave this to me,' said Stump, getting to his feet and putting a hand against Norman's chest. 'I need time to think.'

'About what?' exclaimed Fungus. 'It's simple, ain't it? Waggy can't do it, so we pull the gig. Granted, it's unfortunate and incredibly bad timing. But it's not the end of the world!'

'Well...' said Norman again.

'Besides... we ain't exactly got no choice,' added the drummer.

'HAVEN'T GOT *ANY* CHOICE!' yelled Stump angrily.

His outburst brought a temporary silence.

He sighed heavily. 'No... you boys are right.' He dropped his head in resignation. 'Without Waggy, the whole thing would be a farce.'

'But you *know* why it has to go ahead!' whispered Norman, frantically pulling him to one side and out of earshot of the others.

'And *you* know the only reason I said I'd do it,' Stump hissed. 'I told you before... my only way out of eternal damnation is for everything not to exist at all. It was purely the chance of playing in front of these stones that made me fall on my sword and forgo such a possibility. Well... now it looks like that chance has gone. You're never gonna persuade the other two to do a show without Waggy. Tell 'em why you *really* need their services and they'll think you're mad! I suggest you take advantage of this situation and the rig you've got assembled here and play those notes you need through your laptop when the time comes.'

'As much as I wish it weren't... that's impossible,' said Norman. 'If *Trouzerbulge* doesn't take the stage at the time agreed, there's no *way* we'll be allowed to remain on site a minute longer! That's an hour before sunrise! I've pushed Snogden-Lambert to his limit... and he didn't have far to go in the first place! He's just *aching* for an excuse to have his security remove me and all this equipment from here as soon as possible without breaking his word. If I break mine first and give him that excuse, we're finished!'

'Then you've settled your own argument,' said Stump philosophically. 'The minute we attempt to play without Waggy, he'll recognise it ain't properly *Trouzerbulge* and pull the plug anyway.'

'I very much doubt he'll know.' Norman looked at Stump awkwardly. 'He thinks he's in for an evening of classical music.'

Stump stared back open-mouthed... and then at the stage. 'I *wondered* what all those fuckin' chairs were doing up there.'

'It's part of the deception,' said Norman sheepishly. 'He'd never have agreed to having *your* kind of music played here. So I've got to keep him in the dark and onside for as long as possible. They're coming off at the very last minute. I never actually confirmed to him what type of music you play. So he can't get me for an assumption on his part. I've always chosen my words carefully... and he'll know it.'

'As do I... now,' said Stump slowly. 'So *that's* why you asked us to keep our appearance here a secret.'

Norman nodded apologetically. 'That... and the issue of not drawing a larger than normal crowd.'

'You really are something else,' said Stump, shaking his head contemptuously. 'You could've at least trusted *me* with that little piece of information.' He gave a withering look before turning his back in disgust.

'I never wanted this responsibility,' Norman insisted. 'All I wanted was to save the Universe and get back to living in it!'

Stump spun around to face him again. 'Call what you do *living?*' he scoffed. 'Xanthia's told me all about your passion for collecting famous works of art. Shame that passion doesn't stretch to anything else!'

'What's she been saying!' said Norman, alarmed.

'Oh, don't worry... any bedroom secrets you two have are safe. I'm not sure I could stomach hearing about *those*. I'm talking about the passion you profess to have for that beloved collection of other people's genius you've chosen to keep hidden behind your walls!'

'What do you mean?'

'I need to explain? Well... okay.' Stump drew his breath like a weapon. 'It's bad enough you've had to buy what buzzes you rather than create it yourself. But I've already attacked you for that. I'm talking about the fact that with all your money... having pleasured yourself with other people's creativity... other people's ingenuity and hard work... you've given *nothing* back in return.'

'That's not true! I've given *some* money... to art charities,' Norman retaliated, though the word *some* sound uncomfortably sparse, even to him.

'Okay. Apart from *that*... how many starving artists have you *directly* supported and encouraged in the last five years?'

Norman couldn't answer, because he hadn't.

'Precisely... Which doesn't say much for the depth of your so-called *passion*, does it? But that should hardly come as a revelation either... given you're a complete fake. You might've fooled Xanthia, but you've never fooled me. You're a pitiful, talentless, monochrome, self-centred fraud!'

The criticism hit home with laser-like precision... not least because Norman couldn't have summed his character up any better himself. Hearing someone else confirm his self-perceived flaws only made them more real.

But Stump wasn't finished.

'You've only ever shown interest in the work of those whose genius has already been recognised. And d'ya wanna know why?'

Norman kept quiet, assuming he was going to be told anyway.

'Because for all your pontificating to Xanthia about your newly found appreciation of great art, you wouldn't *really* recognise what makes something great if it shoved itself up your lily-white arse and waved at you from outta the top of your vacuous head! You only collect what other people have already *confirmed* is great. Cos if that weren't the case, you'd be investing your time and money in those unknowns who possessed the talent you claim to appreciate, so it could be encouraged and enjoyed by the rest of the world! But that would be doing something good for *others!* I reckon you're only doing what you're doing right now just to save your own skin... and because you've been told to!' Stump glared at Norman to let the point sink in, before striding forcefully off.

'Where are you going?' implored Norman, taking off after him like an abandoned child.

'To find that khazi Xanthia was taken too. I'm dying for a dump... and I've too much respect for this sacred edifice to drop my pants and have one here!'

*　　*　　*

Kevin sat on the seat of the *Biggablade X320* and lazily played with its throttle. His feet dangling on either side, he idly kicked at its blood-splattered bodywork. Graveyards weren't his favourite place. Too many dead people. Not that you could see them, of course.

Well... not *all* of them.

He looked over to the thick, rusted cover of the old well and felt immense pride that he'd managed to lift such a heavy object all on his own.

Well... he was *Supergeek*.

Not that *he'd* been responsible for the old man's body he'd dragged there. But it would've been disrespectful to just leave it lying out in the open... especially on such a hot day.

The crows lining the trees delineating the churchyard's perimeter disagreed. Lured by the aroma of putrescine and cadaverine, they'd been looking forward to pecking at the softer bits.

Entrails clearly didn't like direct exposure to the sun. Their pungency hadn't made his task any easier. But then... he'd smelt worse.

Talking of which...

Kevin's thoughts returned to why he was there in the first place. He'd gone to great trouble to get himself to where he was on time. He didn't appreciate having to be kept waiting... no matter *who* it was.

Something caught his attention.

He sniffed his hands and then the air. His eyes watered. It was as if every grave that ever existed had simultaneously released its suppressed stench.

A thin smile crept across his face.

At last.

'You are a wretched disappointment,' croaked a low, guttural voice from behind.

Kevin calmly turned to face his denigrator. 'I managed to stop Penkridge's chequebook,' he countered.

His detractor wasn't impressed. 'You were supposed to stop *him*,' he hissed aggressively, the surrounding trees flinching against the sound.

'It wasn't my fault those two idiot Americans didn't want to work with me!' Kevin insisted.

'They were on your side,' came the burbled reminder.

'Yeah... but they found a picture I took of the fire you told me to start at the hotel and completely got the wrong end of the stick. They actually thought I was his *friend*... someone called *The Provider*. They reckoned he'd had me follow them from the airport and ingratiate myself. I could hardly tell them it was *you* who commanded me to do that, could I!'

'It's immaterial now. Penkridge is dangerously close to achieving the task he has been entrusted with. I've put more obstacles in his way... but he is proving extremely resourceful. We cannot take any further chances. You must kill that loathsome thorn in my side before the sun gets to rise again.'

'And then can I have Xanthia?' asked Kevin. 'You promised me her as well.'

'I've already told you... You can have whatever you desire.'

Kevin grinned at the thought.

'I suggest you leave this place immediately,' came the advice. 'It won't be long before some pathetic soul comes to stand over the putrid remains of a loved one and weep selfishly for their own loss. I doubt even a veil of self-centred tears will cause them to miss such an obvious trail of blood and viscera.'

'He did leave rather a mess,' said Kevin nonchalantly. 'Did *you* kill him?'

'His ancestor saw to that,' came the cold reply. 'They sealed his fate here many centuries ago. I merely took the opportunity to settle an old score. Holy water stings! No one attempts to get the better of me without incurring my vengeance... and that includes Penkridge!'

*   *   *

'I'd give it a while, if I were you,' winced Stump, shutting the toilet door behind him.

Xanthia giggled.

'I must say... I'm impressed you have a pilot's licence, Mister Trou*zer*bulge,' twitched Snogden-Lambert, feeling it prudent to change the topic of conversation, if there had to be any.

'So would I be, if it were true,' Stump laughed.

'Peter... would you mind if I have a few minutes alone with Mister Trou*zer*bulge,' requested Norman anxiously.

Xanthia giggled again.

'I'll be in my office,' said Snogden-Lambert, glad for an excuse to retreat.

'You can't leave me to deal with this alone!' hissed Norman, once Snogden-Lambert had managed to brave it past his nameplate.

'I can do pretty much anything I like,' returned Stump nonchalantly. 'That's what Satan promised me when I sold him my soul... remember?'

'I understand all that,' said Norman dismissively. 'And I understand why you'd be better off if I fail tomorrow. But if you don't want to help *me* find a solution to the problem... then do it for *Xanthia*.'

She cocked her head. 'What's he talking about?'

'Waggy's gone and got himself arrested,' Stump explained. 'But even if *I* would, there's no way the boys will play onstage without him.'

Xanthia looked at Norman, who returned a shrug of hopelessness.

She turned her attention back to Stump. 'Would you go onstage without him for me?' she asked.

'Of course, darlin'' he pouted.

She gave the matter some thought.

It took a while.

'In that case... I fink I have a solution,' she finally announced.

Both men prepared to let her down gently, when whatever came out of her mouth had finished. It was something they'd both grown used to.

'There's a very good tribute band called *Trouzerfudge*,' she started. 'I went to see them once in a pub with a friend. They dress up just like you and play all the songs. They take it very seriously.'

'Which is more than we've ever done,' Stump cackled.

'My point is... why don't you get their bass player to stand in for Waggy? If Fungus and Ritchie go on in their usual state, they might not notice the difference!' She nodded her own full stop and awaited their reaction.

Norman stared at her in stunned silence.

Stump roared with laughter. 'Wouldn't that be a gas?'

'Exactly!' she squealed. 'Normy would get the notes he needs to save the Universe and you'd get to realise your dream!'

'I was joking,' he said, realising she wasn't.

'Well... *I'm* not,' she confirmed. 'You said just now you'd go onstage without Waggy for me. So... that's half the band taken care of. If the others don't see him until they're onstage, we might just get away with it.'

Stump's smile evaporated as the idea slowly sunk in. After allowing it to marinate, he looked across at Norman. 'D'ya think they *wouldn't* notice?'

'Not if we plied them with enough alcohol,' said Norman, his eyes widening at the possibility.

'I dunno,' said Stump slowly, maintaining his gaze.

'Just think,' Xanthia cooed in his ear. 'You'll be up there like the magnificent rock god you are... finally playing in front of Stonehenge... sticking a finger up to that nasty Mister Devil who thought he was cleverer than you.'

'You've always known how to push my buttons,' he muttered slowly, visualising the scenario.

'That's because I've always known what's important to you,' she replied softly, putting a hand on his shoulder.

Stump broke from his trance. 'Okay... If I'm to achieve the biggest "fuck you" in the history of the Universe, how do we get hold of this... what are they called?'

'*Trouzerfudge,*' replied Xanthia excitedly.

'Yeah... them.'

'Leave that to me!' said Norman. 'They're bound to have a website or something. You just need to tell the others that Waggy's managed to arrange bail... though won't be able to get here until the very last minute. Xanthia's right... If we keep those two apart from his doppelganger until they're onstage, we may just pull this thing off!'

'Assuming nothing else goes wrong, of course,' Xanthia reminded him.

'Thanks,' said Norman sardonically. 'Which reminds me...' He looked anxiously at his watch. 'I wonder how my convoy's getting on.'

* * *

Pierre Malair studied the irate man shouting in his face and calmly took a drag of his cigarette. He didn't have a clue what was being said. But if asked to guess, he'd say it probably had something to do with the long line of stationary vehicles that stretched back from the point in the road at which he and a handful of his colleagues were standing. If asked to guess further, he'd suggest the woman and children being heatedly pointed at during the exchange were the man's family, and that they were trying to return home via the terminal behind him and a row of burning tyres. Any words producing spittle were probably threats and, at some point, the validity of his parents' marriage would have been called into question.

The angry man's words finally exhausted, Pierre looked across at the two officers from the local gendarmerie who were leaning on their car.

He shrugged.

After reciprocal drags on their own cigarettes, the officers shrugged back.

That was that, then.

Except… it *wasn't*.

Whilst Pierre had gotten used to deflecting the fiery rants and impassioned pleas of frustrated drivers using nothing more than a downturned mouth to craft a Gallic expression of *c'est la vie*, he was about to discover that it only worked on things that *weren't* made of metal and travelling at high speed.

Thundering up the previously deserted *going-the-other-way* lane came a line of trucks sandwiched between an equally impatient escort.

Pierre's brain rapidly processed the following calculation:

$$\frac{distance\ to\ be\ travelled}{speed\ of\ object} < time\ left\ to\ shrug = merde!$$

It was enough to make your *croissants* uncurl.

Making a hasty dive for the verge, he hoped his fellow protestors were as adept at mental arithmetic as he was.

Such flagrant disregard for the *Entente Cordiale* was down to the man currently instructing the vehicles behind him to ignore the fact they possessed a brake pedal. Ex-SAS officer Chris Issis… affectionately known to his men as "Major Crisis"… was a man for whom danger was an occupational incentive.

Having commandeered the accelerator pedal of the lead vehicle, his foot was flat to the floor. Tasked with ensuring Norman's artworks reached their intended destination as quickly as possible, his mission had already been heavily compromised.

Thirty miles south of Avignon, a group of terrified horses

had inexplicably gotten themselves spooked and broken their fence... choosing the north bound carriageway of the *Autoroute du Soleil* to frustrate those wishing to leave the good weather behind.

It had taken the best part of two hours to round them up and get the traffic moving again. But it was an incident at a fuel stop on the outskirts of Lyon that had put the mission in real jeopardy.

A man claiming 'knowledge of things to come' had suddenly appeared from nowhere and slashed at a number of the convoy's tyres before he could be restrained. Despite the additional delay his actions had caused, "Major Crisis" couldn't help but feel a small amount of professional admiration for the individual... given his *knowledge of things to come* must have included foreseeing the serious kicking he was given whilst the damage was being repaired.

With the English Channel and almost one hundred and fifty clicks still to travel, any further hold-ups would mean the convoy reaching its destination after dark... something he'd been instructed was not an operational option.

Accordingly... neither was joining the back of a long queue of static vehicles.

As the row of burning tyres proved as effective at stopping one hundred and eighty tonnes of speeding machinery as a row of burning tyres, Pierre found himself having to dodge a cascade of smouldering rubber... given a shrug wasn't an advisable course of action against that either.

As "Major Crisis" studied the adrenalin-fuelled remonstrations in his rear view mirror, he hadn't a clue as to what was being said. But he assumed any words producing spittle were probably threats and, at some point, the validity of his parents' marriage had been called into question.

He shrugged.

* * *

Having looked forward to making the call – expecting

incredulity, hysteria, and a suitable amount of fawning gratitude from the other end of the phone – the conversation didn't quite go the way Norman had anticipated.

'Hello... is that Colin Shoesmith?'
'...Yeah.'
'Bass player with the tribute band *Trouzerfudge?*'
'......Yeah.'
'Then... are you currently sitting down, Colin?'
'...........Yeah.'
'Well... I have some news that may possibly make this the best day of your life!'

Colin appeared to be listening.

'My name's Norman Penkridge and I'm staging a secret gig in the early hours of tomorrow morning with *Trouzerbulge*... the *real* band. Unfortunately, Waggy's become unavailable... so we'd like to offer you the chance to stand in for him!'
'............'
'*Colin?*'
CLICK......

Norman's second attempt didn't fare any better.

'Colin... I'm assuming you thought my last call was a wind up. Well... it isn't, I promise! Your services really *are* required by the genuine *Trouzerbulge*.'

There was a brief period of silence before a voice asked, 'is that you Dave?'
'*Pardon?*'
'Dave... you bloody bastard!'
'No... it's not Dave.'
'Alan, then... you cheeky c_'
'NO, I told you... it's Norman Penkridge... and I'm offering you the chance to...'
CLICK......

Norman had anticipated a healthy dose of scepticism. Who wouldn't? You receive a call out of the blue from a complete stranger offering the chance to perform with your idols and live out the ultimate dream.

Unfortunately – if not ironically, given he was in a tribute band – Colin inhabited the real world.

In desperation, Norman tried again.

'Colin-please-don't-put-the-phone-down-on-me-as-this-isn't-a-prank-and-I-really-am-calling-on-behalf-of-*Trouzerbulge*-and-I'll-get-Stump-on-the-line-if-you-need-actual-proof!' he gabbled, as quickly as he could.

The lack of an abrupt dialling tone meant he still had Colin's ear. All he had to do now was get the rest of him.

'I know this sounds unbelievable and probably comes as a shock… but it's a one hundred percent genuine request. The band has an extremely important show in less than twenty-four hours. Though I can't go into details, a serious problem's cropped up concerning Waggy. But the show *must* go on. That's why we'd like you to take his place. I need to fix this urgently and am running out of time… so certainly wouldn't want to waste mine or yours. This isn't a prank call. *Please* believe me!'

'If the boys have put you up to this, you're a dead man… whoever you are,' said Colin warily.

'I promise they haven't,' insisted Norman. 'I don't even know who they are. Just tell me what you need from me to convince you I'm telling the truth.'

'Not the voice of Stump on the end of a phone, for one,' answered Colin. 'Dave… or *Slump,* as he's known onstage… has that down to a tee.'

'Yes, I suppose he would have,' reflected Norman. 'Okay… Then, *what?*'

'Not that I'm saying I believe you… I'm not that much of a mug,' said Colin guardedly. 'But I'll amuse myself by playing along for now… if only to see how far you're prepared to take this.'

'Fair enough. I totally understand.'

'So… if you're telling the truth… how come the band is back

together and playing after such a long absence?'

'It's a very special event,' explained Norman. 'They've agreed to do it as a one-off performance. You could say it's a... *save-the-planet* type of thing.'

'And it's tomorrow morning, you say?'

'The extremely early hours of the morning, if we're being accurate.'

Colin seemed to give the matter some thought. 'That's plausible, I suppose.'

Norman let out a sigh of relief. 'Thank you for believing me.'

'So... *where* are they performing?'

'You might struggle a bit with this one,' admitted Norman.

'Try me.'

'...Stonehenge.'

CLICK......

* * *

A number of harvests had passed since a plethora of *one gods* had been established.

But future harvests looked to be in danger. Religious division had caused social division, as adherents to each faith deemed it necessary to leave their established tribes and group together for protection. Some of the more fanatical sects had taken to employing extreme tactics to push their own beliefs and discourage those they disagreed with. Hut burning had become a particular favourite... followed by the odd walk-by stoning or rotting carcass down a well.

As these new communities looked inward for solace, dialogue between them ceased. Positions became entrenched and the problem exacerbated.

Without a consensus, work on the stone monument had ground to a halt. Only positioning stones for the remaining uprights had been laid out on the grass, and many wondered whether it would *ever* be completed.

The major divisions being bad enough, even opinion within some niche faiths had become factionalised.

It was now possible to be a follower of the *Categorically Definitive Ultimate* one god and find yourself at loggerheads with another of that exact same persuasion. Members of *The Fundamentalist Movement of the Categorically Definitive Ultimate One God* regularly took it upon themselves to harangue fellow adherents on market day by standing on a log and claiming everyone else wasn't worshipping hard enough.

More annoyingly... a splinter group calling itself *The Evangelical Fundamentalist Movement of the Categorically Definitive Ultimate One God* required its members to stand on other people's logs and do much the same thing.

But worse than all of them... members of a further offshoot calling itself *The Extreme Evangelical Fundamentalist Movement of the Categorically Definitive Ultimate One God* weren't beyond knocking on your hut door of a rest-day morning and asking to come inside for a chat.

*   *   *

'If you don't mind me saying so... things are getting outta hand, sir!' The security guard gave a look of professional concern, though skewing his eyebrows in suitable sympathy as he noticed Snogden-Lambert struggling with the statement. Despite his boss's discomfort, he deemed it necessary to elaborate. 'The A303's come to a complete standstill, due to all the rubberneckers and those getting out of their cars to take photos... the car park's full of impromptu visitors... and I've had the police on the phone warning us to expect larger than normal crowds for tonight's solstice celebrations, thanks to the sudden media frenzy.'

'Media frenzy?' Snogden-Lambert's knees weakened in direct proportion to his facial muscles.

The guard looked surprised. 'You mean... nobody's been in touch with you?'

'I wouldn't know,' said Snogden-Lambert faintly. 'I've purposely kept my phone in the filing cabinet all day.'

'*Right,*' the guard said slowly. 'Well... it's gone completely crazy out there. We're all over the radio and telly. Everyone's wondering what's going on here. We're headline news! But then...' He looked at his boss questioningly. 'You must've known we would be.'

Snogden-Lambert didn't answer.

'I'll give you this, though,' said the guard. 'Despite the stink it's causing, those fibreglass replicas look just like the real thing. When it's finished, I personally think it'll look *well* impressive!'

Snogden-Lambert didn't give a damn about how it looked. His only concern was about how *he* would look. 'Did you say *stink?*' he probed nervously.

The guard nodded.

Snogden-Lambert's knees had had enough. 'Do you mind if I sit down?' he asked, as they finally objected to his weight.

The security guard gave a different look of concern and dragged a chair from across the room. 'Here you are, sir. Do you want me to get you a glass of water?'

'You haven't got anything stronger, have you?' requested Snogden-Lambert, without embarrassment.

'We're not allowed alcohol on the premises,' the security guard reminded him. 'And anyway... I'm not sure that's a good idea right now.'

Snogden-Lambert disagreed. He thought it was an *excellent* idea. And besides... it was the only one his tortured mind could come up with. He sighed heavily and looked around the room. It was one he'd only ever popped his head in before. Though smaller than his own, it had a warm, homely feel to it... having been adorned with the sort of personal touches that served to remind the person at work why they were putting in the hours.

'Is this your wife?' he asked, nodding towards a photo in a frame.

'For my sins,' said the security guard awkwardly.

'She has a lovely smile,' said Snogden-Lambert, childishly attempting to replicate it himself.

'Shame she never uses it on me,' returned the guard, unsure as to what was happening. He sniffed for no apparent reason. 'About these expected crowds tonight, sir,' he started.

'Children?'

'I think you'll find they'll be mostly adults, sir.'

'I meant... do *you* have children?'

The security guard chewed his lip. 'Two boys and a girl,' he said measuredly.

'That's very nice.'

'Most of the time.'

Snogden-Lambert sighed wistfully 'Must be a lovely feeling having a family to welcome you home.'

'Not that they'll be seeing much of me in the next twenty-four hours,' said the guard, swiftly grabbing the opportunity to get the conversation back to a matter for which they were both being paid. 'The question is... do we still restrict access to the site by only allowing through a certain number of people... and if so... how do we stop the expected surplus?'

Snogden-Lambert appeared to be considering the problem. Relieved, the security guard awaited the answer... then learnt that appearances can be deceptive.

'Marion left me.'

'Beg your pardon, sir?'

'Marion... my wife. She decided thirty-two years of me doing the right thing wasn't enough to balance out a couple of years of me doing the wrong thing.'

The security guard puffed out his cheeks... and left it at that.

'Mind you... it wasn't as if I really enjoyed the time we *were* together,' Snogden-Lambert reflected, from a greater distance than the chair he was sat on. 'I always felt there was meant to be something better... something...' He paused before correcting himself. '*Someone*... better.'

'Extra security barriers are what we need... and they won't position themselves,' said the guard briskly, pretending to look at his watch. 'Do you want me to call someone on your behalf before I go?'

'You mean Joan?' A sudden glimmer of hope appeared in Snogden-Lambert's eyes.

'I thought you said your wife's name was *Marion*,' said the guard, tilting his head.

'It is,' mumbled Snogden-Lambert, lowering his. 'Forget what I just said.'

'I meant... someone......*else.*'

Snogden-Lambert groaned. 'Like who?'

'A *doctor*... perhaps?'

'Will he make all this go away?' Snogden-Lambert enquired weakly.

'Depends how powerful his sedatives are,' muttered the guard.

Snogden-Lambert looked up at him. 'You know... I envy you,'

The security guard tugged at his collar, as if to release the tension. 'I trust you're not talking about the wife,' he quipped. 'I should warn you... it's a very flattering photograph.'

Snogden-Lambert smiled wanly. 'You have no one causing you any problems... do you?'

'Only the occasional Druid, sir.'

As the guard spoke, there was a thud outside.

'And *those,* of course.'

Snogden-Lambert looked confused.

'Rabbits,' explained the guard. 'For some reason, they keep throwing themselves against the door. Been going on for a couple of days now.'

'Mine's birds... against the window,' said Snogden-Lambert matter-of-factly. 'I'm accumulating quite a collection below the sill.'

The guard scratched his chin. 'That's very strange. The sweet kiosk's been reporting kamikaze squirrels... and we're not exactly surrounded by trees.' He shook his head. 'Must be something to do with the ley lines.'

'Actually... I'm told it's the work of the Devil,' Snogden-Lambert informed him.

'I'm not sure he *actually* exists,' pointed out the guard carefully.

'Oh... he not only exists, I had a conversation with him not more than an hour ago. He's taken the form of a young man out to destroy me.'

'I'll call that doctor,' said the guard, nodding to himself.

*   *   *

'What d'ya mean you've never heard of us!' cried Bob indignantly. He pointed at his face and smartly whipped his finger around its contour. 'This example of gorgeous perfection has been drooled over by more TV viewers in America than you've made mistakes... which is clearly one heck of a lot, Mister Where's-ya-ticket!'

Chad nodded in agreement at the embattled theatre usher and let Bob carry on with his tirade.

'I'll have you know... *Theatre Time with Danny and Crispin...*' He pointed at his face again and sung a huge 'He...*LLO*...... is also syndicated in over twenty-seven other countries.' He looked the usher up and down in disdain. 'Though clearly we need to work a little harder when it comes to reaching out to the people of... *Wiltshire.*'

The usher raised his hands to placate the angry American in front of him. It was an extremely embarrassing situation, given the stares the incident was attracting from the other attendees. 'I'm just following instructions, sir. I've been told it's strictly invite only. We're having to adopt a very rigorous security policy, given the status of tonight's performance.'

'Status?' yelled Bob, disregarding those filing around him with *their* tickets. 'You wanna talk status? Well, let me tell you something... I am *Mister* status in the world of theatre!'

The usher squirmed. 'As I said, sir... I'm just following instructions.'

Bob snorted disparagingly. 'D'ya think Marlon Brando followed instructions? D'ya think the name *Stanislavski* would've tripped off the tongue so easily, if he had? What planet are we on here?' He took an angry breath, then placed his hands on his hips and stared at the floor. 'Danny and I have made a transatlantic crossing at great expense and inconvenience to preview this show to the benefit of its producers. So if you don't want millions of viewers around the world knowing what dumbheads they employ in these backwoods – not to mention one helluva lawsuit slapped upon you and your misguided employers – I suggest you drag your knuckles over to the box office and get them to allocate a couple of seats... *PRONTO!*'

'There's no need for rudeness, sir,' sniffed the usher.

Chad took his cue to intervene. 'You're absolutely right... there isn't.' He stepped between the warring parties and smiled warmly. 'You'll have to forgive Crispin. He's tired from the flight and more used to people asking for his autograph than his exit. As you've probably figured... there's *clearly* been a mix up somewhere betwixt London and Los Angeles.' He raised his eyes in humorous exasperation. 'I can see our tickets sitting on someone's desk unopened, as we speak! Now... I'd hate to have to call upon a personal friendship and drag Donald Tucker-Jenkins himself into this foyer to resolve the matter. I'm sure he's got enough on his mind as it is tonight, without getting involved in such a trivial issue. But if you're *insisting* we spoil that great man's evening...'

'You know Mister Tucker-Jenkins?' clarified the usher, sensing a face-saving escape from his predicament.

'Let's just say... well enough for him to have once lent me a pair of his father's trousers!' fumed Bob from over Chad's shoulder.

'Clearly a close relationship, sir,' nodded the usher.

'It's not what you think,' added Chad.

The usher looked around furtively, telegraphing the fact he was about to do them a huge favour. 'In that case... you gentlemen wait right here. I'll see what can be done. I won't be a minute.'

'I hope all this is worth it,' said Chad, once he'd disappeared. 'The journey to get here was bad enough. I don't think I've ever spent such an excruciating time in a car... and that's saying something, given *our* work history!'

'I'm with you,' agreed Bob. 'First... they get you to drive on the wrong side of the road... and then they tell ya to get off it and find yerself another!'

69

'Along with half the friggin' country it seems.' added Chad. 'Trust Donald to pick the one day they decide to give Stonehenge a face lift and turn the whole area into a people magnet!'

'Especially after *how* many thousands of years without bothering!'

Chad's frown softened. 'Still… I guess we're lucky to have made it here at all. And looking on the bright side… some of tonight's invited guests won't have. I doubt we'll have trouble getting spare seats.'

'We should've dragged Donald out here for real,' said Bob. 'After all… he gave us his word.'

'The fact he never followed through on it means he clearly doesn't want us here,' Chad reminded him. 'His promise of tickets was to get us off his back. He obviously hasn't forgiven us our previous encounters. You've seen the security ringing this place. One word from him and we'll *never* get in!'

'Seems like you gentlemen are in luck,' announced the usher proudly on his return. 'A number of guests have had to cancel due to transport-related issues. I've therefore managed to procure a couple of prime seats for you near the front!'

'*Near* the front?' sneered Bob ungratefully, springing back into character.

'Sorry, sir,' stuttered the usher, his expression of smugness evaporating. 'We're only talking row *five*, though.'

Bob huffed loudly. 'Then… I guess they'll have to do.' He gave an exasperated toss of his head. 'Just don't expect to ask me for an autograph!'

As the *crème de la crème* of the international theatre world settled down in their seats, Kieran Knight-Lee sat proudly at the head of them… the great playwright, and now esteemed director, beside him in the front row. Drinking in the heady buzz of anticipation filling his humble theatre, he deemed it the proudest day of his life.

Ensuring it lived up to the occasion, he'd stuck his neck out and spent next year's allocated budget for new urinals on a swanky red carpet. He assumed his decision would meet with the approval of tonight's distinguished male patrons, given the cracks in the old ones were ideal for target practice.

As the lights dimmed and the curtain opened to reveal three men moving a large block of stone across the stage, he sat back in his seat and prepared for a memorable evening.

It would certainly turn out to be that.

*　　*　　*

'We're losing the light!' declared Norman, looking about anxiously.

'No problem,' returned Stevie the Props calmly. 'I knew we'd be working into the dark, so came prepared. Don't worry. We've got floodlights. You'll have your structure in place before the band goes on. I promise.'

'It's no longer the structure I'm concerned about,' groaned Norman. 'It's my artworks. If they're not here by the time the sun goes down, all this will have been for nothing!'

Stevie hadn't a clue what Norman was talking about. He also didn't care. Things were going perfectly to schedule. He might not have slept for two days, but come four o'clock the following morning... the most unusual commission of his career fulfilled... he'd finally be able to rest his head on his pillow a very rich man.

Norman scanned the A303 for a convoy of trucks. But most of the vehicles clogging it belonged to an unprecedented swarm of solstice celebrants flocking to the stones, along with the inquisitive and the seemingly hostile.

Having abandoned their vehicles on verges, many had made short work of the flimsy wire fence that was supposed to prevent access to the stones by foot across a tempting stretch of grass... much to the consternation of the outnumbered security.

Whilst some of the descending hoards applauded the work being undertaken, an equal number were extremely unhappy that so revered a monument was being tampered with.

Remonstrating noisily with those carrying out the work, they were making an already tense situation more so. It seemed to Norman... the wackier their appearance, the more vociferous the protest. So God help the blood pressure of those he'd just spotted arriving with tambourines, bongos, and footwear that included little, tinkly bells.

The exception to this rule was a man inhabiting a crumpled suit, who'd alighted from his electric buggy and was now approaching with an all too familiar expression of hostility.

'I knew it,' Norman grimaced. 'He's checking his watch!'

'Nine twenty-six,' shouted Snogden-Lambert, his eyes burrowing into Norman's. 'That's when the sun officially sets! If those artworks aren't on site by then, as promised... this whole lot's coming down and I'll have you removed from the site immediately!'

'What's all this about the sun again?' demanded Stevie, looking alarmed.

'I have an agreement with him,' Norman explained. 'But it doesn't affect you.'

'It better not!' exclaimed Stevie. 'I've worked my butt off to meet your punishing schedule! He can do what he likes with the structure... sun or no sun... so long as I get paid!'

'What happened to fighting to guard the purity of your art?' enquired Norman, surprised at the artist's sudden *volte-face*.

'That was a dream I cherished before I sold my soul to you,' responded Stevie coldly.

The phrase and manner of delivery rocked Norman. 'Is that what you think I made you do?'

'What... you mean you were just being altruistic when you offered me such an obscene amount of money for my skills?' Stevie snorted.

The sarcasm stung... especially after Stump's recent tirade.

'There's a greater purpose to all this,' Norman promised. 'You'll understand, come morning.'

'I don't need to understand,' said Stevie, shaking his head. 'I just need an assurance that the value of my soul ain't gonna drop with the sun.'

'Oh... You haven't been paid *either*,' cut in Snogden-Lambert, a mischievous glint in his eyes.

Stevie flashed an alarmed looked at Norman. '*Is* there a problem?'

'There has been for me,' said Snogden-Lambert. 'I'm still waiting for my recompense.' He looked at his watch again. 'Forty-three minutes... That's all you have left!'

'You'd better not be pulling a fast one!' warned Stevie, pointing at Norman as he made his way back to where his team were working. 'Or it won't be *fibreglass* bollocks that are dangling from my next creation!'

Snogden-Lambert treated himself to a smirk. 'Seems like your actions are finally catching up with you,' he declared.

'I'm not beaten yet,' responded Norman.

'Forty-*two* minutes,' said Snogden-Lambert icily.

*   *   *

It was as the curtain opened on the second act that the penny suddenly dropped. Whilst the audience had been enthralled by an intriguing storyline and clever interplay between the various characters onstage, the playwright had been intentionally vague when it came to suggesting a setting for the action. But the sight of seven impressive trilithons almost touching the lighting gantry brought an appreciative gasp from the audience.

Chad grabbed his partner's arm. 'So *that's* why he chose this location!'

Disapproving stares accompanied sharp shushing sounds.

'Donald said the target would be made of stone! Well... we have it now!'

'*Stonehenge?*' returned Bob incredulously

There were more requests for them to hush.

Chad slapped his forehead. 'My God... June twentieth! The day before the summer solstice! We're talking an international media event! With all the hype going on today, that place is gonna be packed tonight!'

'*Please* be quite!' tutted someone from behind.

'Here, here,' voiced another.

'FUCK YOU!' returned Bob defensively. 'We're trying to save lives here!'

'And *we're* trying to watch a play,' trilled a lady indignantly.

The actors on stage appeared temporarily thrown.

'What's going on?' demanded Donald, rising from his seat and turning to face the disturbance.

Kieran Knight-Lee placed a hand to his face as the play ground to a halt.

'What happens to the monument, Donald?' shouted Chad, from a few rows back.

'Watch out... spoiler alert!' cried a wag from the audience.

A ripple of involuntary laughter swept throughout the auditorium.

'This is not a comedy!' Donald bellowed angrily, bringing the levity to an awkward stop. 'Neither is it a pantomime requiring audience participation! It is a stark warning of an imminent cataclysm, the likes of which this planet has never seen! I suggest that everyone in this theatre takes it *EXTREMELY* seriously! Suffice to say... death is no longer the worst fate we have to face!'

Eyes widened in bemusement.

'Furthermore... if you can't appreciate *that*, I respectfully ask you show a little more courtesy for what is the last play I will ever write!'

A gasp of horror replaced the awkward silence.

'It *can't* be!' shrieked someone hysterically.

'Please, no!' implored another.

A clamorous wailing erupted; the anguish becoming contagious.

Donald waved down the protests. 'I appreciate your support, but would much rather it be given to those onstage.'

A smattering of applause competed with the outcry.

'You need to tell us what happens,' shouted Chad above it. 'We may not have time for this theatrical explanation!'

Donald peered into the audience. 'Who *is* that? Do I know you?'

'Not well enough to keep a promise... apparently,' returned Bob.

'That accent... You're from America.'

'And syndicated in over twenty-seven other countries,' shouted the usher helpfully, from his small seat to the side.

Donald's face suddenly dropped. 'I *do* know you, don't I?' He stabbed his finger wildly at where the voices had come from. 'Satan's spawn! Satan's spawn!' he started yelling at the top of his voice.

Chad rose to his feet.

'IT *IS* THEM!' Donald confirmed to his spirit guide. 'WHY DIDN'T YOU TELL ME THEY WERE HERE?'

'Maybe we should take this outside, Donald,' suggested Chad, as a rolled-up programme found the back of his head.

The accuracy of the projectile prompted jeers in the same direction.

'OF COURSE YOU MUST'VE KNOWN! THEY'RE IN LEAGUE WITH BEELZEBUB! SURELY YOU FELT HIS PRESENCE?' Donald raged, to the astonishment of those around him.

The local Chief Superintendent of police – having been invited to sit alongside the mayor and other local dignitaries – decided it was time to intervene. Assuring his fellow guests that he had everything under control, he rose and addressed the baying audience.

'Ladies and gentlemen... can we have a little order, please!'

His request fell on deaf ears... particularly those belonging to Donald, who'd started clambering over the stalls in order to reach the objects of his ire.

'Mister Tucker-Jenkins!' barked the Chief Superintendent. 'Please return to your seat... *immediately!*'

'Not whilst there are potential murderers in this theatre!' Donald shouted back, ignoring the request.

A number of women screamed at the prospect.

'Do you have proof for that accusation?' exclaimed the Chief Superintendent, above the ensuing commotion.

'Not that would hold up in a court of law,' returned Donald

grimly, his flailing torso pushing aside a couple in row C.

As panic took hold, most of the audience left their seats and started heading for the exits.

'Time for us to get outta here!' said Chad, signalling to Bob for them to join the exodus.

'Don't let them leave!' shouted Donald, gesticulating wildly at the doors.

'Stop those men!' yelled the Chief Superintendent... though he didn't know why. He just wished he had a whistle to blow.

'Seems that Mister Tucker-Jenkins really *does* know you two,' growled the usher, blocking Chad and Bob's escape. 'Though I doubt he'll be lending you any more of his father's trousers.' He gave a look of menacing irony. 'Now... what was that you were saying about my knuckles?'

* * *

'Norman... we need to talk,' insisted Xanthia, accosting him as he clambered down from the stage.

Using it as a viewing platform, he'd been scanning the easternmost point of the A303 in the hope of spotting anything remotely resembling a convoy of vehicles.

'Not now, Xan,' he said, shaking his head. 'Can't you see I've got rather a lot on my mind?'

'But you've been avoiding me all day,' she pouted.

He stopped and looked at her wearily. 'Can you blame me?'

'Well, of course I can... it's not *my* fault!' she huffed, folding her arms.

'This time, it may well be,' he replied bluntly.

The uncharacteristic coldness of his reply unsettled her bottom lip. 'Normy... what's wrong?'

He stared at her in amazement. 'Are you *serious?* You can't wait to leave me here on my own... and then when you *do* return, it's with your previous lover!'

Her brow creased. 'But you told me to go!'

'Not to *him!*' Norman exclaimed.

'I *do* have a name,' announced Stump from behind.

Norman spun around.

'So... you've changed your mind.' Stump challenged him.

'Pardon?'

'About only wanting what's best for Xanthia... Remember?'

Norman didn't answer.

'I told you I'd hold you to that one day,' Stump smirked. 'Seems like you really don't want her to have her own mind.'

'What's he talking about?' she asked.

'Nothing you need worry about, darlin'' Stump smarmed. 'It just seems *Normy* has found himself on the horns of a rather awkward dilemma.'

'What's one of them?'

'Well... in his case, it's preaching about the right thing to do... then suddenly finding yourself viewing things from a completely different perspective. It can be quite a rude awakening. But if he's got any sense, he'll be grateful he's learnt that truth is subjective. How something looks depends entirely on who's doing the looking. Claiming to appreciate the work of so many diverse artists, you'd have thought he'd have realised that *long* ago!'

'I still don't know what you're talking about,' she frowned.

'But *he* does,' Stump smiled.

'There's no dilemma,' declared Norman. 'I know what I have to do. It's just a question of taking the correct fork.'

Stump flinched, as if having taken a heavy punch. He looked at Norman peculiarly. 'Now you sound just like my *real* nemesis!'

'What's *that* supposed to mean?'

'Forks!' he exclaimed. 'Exactly what the Devil told me I should break my decisions into, once I'd sold my soul to him.' He scanned the memory. 'The smaller the fork...'

'The smaller the dilemma,' Norman finished.

'Yeah... word for bleedin' word!' mumbled Stump, nonplussed. 'He told me that's the secret. Set yourself an ideal and take the forks that best suit it. That way you get exactly what you want. It certainly worked for me!'

'He wasn't in a... *dress*, was he?' asked Norman charily.

'*What?*'

'The Devil... when he gave you that advice.'

'Are you nuts? He was as you'd imagine him to be... red, horned, and reeking of glorious temptation!'

'Not grey, old, and reeking of lavender water?'

Stump's expression became even more incredulous. 'Have you finally flipped?'

'The honest answer is... I might have,' said Norman, his thoughts flying off in directions he deemed dangerous. 'If I haven't... I should start thinking there's something uncomfortably wrong here!'

'Like w*hat?*' pressed Xanthia.

'It doesn't matter. But one question, Xan... What exactly did you mean the other night when you said that Gabriel didn't look like an Archangel to you?'

She shrugged unconvincingly. '*Did* I say that?'

'Yes... You asked me if I was sure I could trust him. You said you felt certain things and that you didn't think he was very nice.'

'I thought you didn't believe those feelings I got!' she glowered.

'He said himself you were sensitive to such things... so I guess I should.'

'I can't explain it,' she struggled. 'It's just that when I fink of an Archangel, I fink of 'em as being pure and perfect and honest. But when he looks at me, I can tell he's hiding something... and that he's worried I'll find out what it is.'

'This is all very well,' cut in Stump, 'but maybe this should be left for another time. Let's get back to more important issues. What about the bass player? Have you managed to get hold of him?'

Norman's line of thought was severed as he realised he'd omitted Stump from that particular loop. 'Yes,' he blinked. 'But it wasn't easy. He wouldn't believe me. I eventually had to track down the other members of his band and get them to convince him I was for real. His attitude is somewhat different now! He's coming as quickly as he can. He reckons it'll take a couple of hours.'

'And the rest!' snorted Stump. 'Have you *seen* the chaos out there?' He gestured at the queuing traffic in the distance.

'I'm well aware of it,' said Norman. 'But it shouldn't be a problem. He's got a motorbike. I've told him he can use Waggy's equipment.'

'He'll have to,' said Stump. 'We don't want the others getting suspicious.'

'Talking of traffic… all this may be pointless anyway,' Norman declared. 'If my artworks don't arrive in the next fifteen minutes, we won't be allowed to continue.'

'You've bought more paintings?' asked Xanthia, puzzled.

'They're ones I already own… or owned,' Norman corrected himself. 'I've had them transported up from France.'

'How *many* paintings?'

'All of them… and the sculptures. In fact… everything I've ever collected. I had to promise them to Snogden-Lambert in order for things to go ahead.'

'I thought you gave him a cheque,' she frowned.

'It bounced.'

Xanthia looked at him horrified.

'Oh… and he now owns our house,' Norman added. 'I had to sign that over too.'

She was speechless.

'Precisely,' nodded Norman. 'I no longer have any money and all my assets have gone. That should make your choice extremely easy.'

She squinted. '*What* choice?'

He drew a breath. 'The choice between me and Stump… if you hadn't already made it, of course.'

Xanthia looked at Stump.

'It's alright,' said Norman. 'I've known for a while. I also accept I'm never gonna be able to compete with him. The Devil was right about one thing… He's everything I'm not. Wild… Unpredictable… Famous… Cool…'

'Talented,' threw in Stump.

'I prefer… *lucky*,' said Norman, giving him an icy glare.

'Romantic!' cried Xanthia, joining in the game.

Stump gave a smug nod of acceptance.

'Would you be referring to Lake Como?' enquired Norman, maintaining his gaze with Stump.

Stump's cocksure expression immediately changed.

Xanthia clasped her hands together and pulled them tightly to her chest. 'Oh, Normy... it was so special,' she cooed, pirouetting on her heels and caressing the memory again. 'I'll never forget it as long as I live. I wish you could've been there!'

Norman sharpened his stare. 'That might've proved a little *awkward*,' he said measuredly.

Stump's left eyebrow rose uncomfortably, begging Norman's silence.

Norman could hear Xanthia squealing to herself. She always did so when deliriously happy. It had been a while since he'd heard it.

A bead of sweat broke on Stump's forehead.

Norman took a while to savour the panic in his eyes.

Xanthia squealed again.

Stump appeared frozen.

Norman let out a sigh and gave him a small nod. 'Yes, Xan,' he said quietly. 'I'll let you hang on to *romantic*.'

Stump nodded back in gratitude.

'But you're much better than him at computers!' she giggled, continuing the fun.

'I guess that's because I'm a geek,' Norman shrugged. 'So why pretend otherwise?'

'You got us this far,' said Stump appreciatively.

'It might not be far enough,' returned Norman, acknowledging Snogden-Lambert's purposeful stride towards them.

'Leave it to me,' Xanthia whispered. As Snogden-Lambert reached them, she flirtatiously put her arm around him and snuggled in close. 'Peter,' she pouted. 'Normy tells me he's given you all his paintings.'

'That's what he *claimed* was going to happen,' said Snogden-Lambert, brusquely removing the smothering appendage. 'But as we all know with your boyfriend… things are never how he says they are.'

Norman was about to object when Xanthia beat him to it.

'I fink that's a little unfair. Because, as you can see… the traffic is really, really bad at the moment.'

'And who's fault is that?' returned Snogden-Lambert, unmoved.

'Yes, I know… But what I was wondering was… if…'

'Xan,' said Norman quietly. 'You're wasting your time.'

Snogden-Lambert looked at her coldly and confirmed the fact with a sharp nod.

'This doesn't make sense!' said Stump, fronting up to him. 'Why not give Norman a little longer. What's to lose? The music doesn't start 'til four in the morning, so there's still plenty of time. And even if they *don't* turn up by then… big deal! Cos if the show doesn't go ahead, I'm fucked, he's fucked, you're fucked… we're *all* fucked!'

'I don't much care for your language, Mister Trou*zer*bulge,' Snogden-Lambert reprimanded him sharply. 'For your information, this is purely a matter of principle between your patron and me. My stance at least enables me to hold on to some pride… what little I have left. Outside of that… I'm ruined… regardless of what does or does not happen here tonight. Your unhinged supporter has guaranteed that. So… though you find my reasoning disagreeable, it does not matter one jot to me. Protestations are pointless. Whilst you'll forgive me my own unchivalrous language… you can never win against a man who no longer gives a shit!'

Stump looked at Norman. 'That's true,' he nodded.

'Four minutes,' said Snogden-Lambert, looking at his watch.

'There's no way, man,' cried Stump, pointing at the vehicles stuck on the road. 'Not unless those artworks are being carried to the site in backpacks!'

'Then, it's a shame for you they're not,' twitched Snogden-Lambert, trying to stifle a look of glee. 'My head of security informs me that the police have decided to shut off every single approach road within a ten mile radius in order to clear the congestion.'

'Why... has everyone caught the same cold?' asked Xanthia. Norman didn't correct her. He was staring into the east.

'You gotta face it... It's impossible,' Stump winced, placing a heavy hand on his shoulder.

'It won't let me down,' said Norman, his gaze fixed.

'What won't, Normy?' enquired Xanthia.

'The Universe,' said Norman, defiantly. 'It will *always* provide.'

'Then it better hurry up,' pointed out Snogden-Lambert acerbically. 'Because it has precisely...'

*   *   *

'Three minutes!' shouted Bob angrily. 'I'll give you three minutes to get these cuffs off me and place a phone in my hand! I have friends at the US embassy who will see to it you're directing tractors in this godforsaken backwater for the rest of what little career you have left, if you don't!'

'Obtaining... goods... by... deception,' said the desk sergeant, typing the charge on his keyboard.

'Slightly less than being accused of attempted murder, though!' retorted Bob.

'Still a crime... all the same,' replied the desk sergeant calmly.

'So is false imprisonment and harassment,' shouted Bob.

The desk sergeant looked up from his keyboard. 'Do you wish to report a case of that, sir?' he asked sardonically.

'Yes, I friggin' do!' yelled Bob.

'Then I recommend you run it by the duty solicitor first, if you wish to avoid having the charge of *wasting police time* added to your charge sheet.'

'This is wasting *our* time!' said Chad, gesticulating angrily with his shackled hands.

'I completely agree. So I suggest you get your partner here to stop interrupting me while I'm processing this form.' The desk sergeant pecked slowly at his keyboard again. 'Causing... a... public... nuisance.'

'WHAT!' shrieked Bob.

* * *

The spectacle of three Chinook helicopters skilfully landing their suspended payloads outside the visitor centre caused quite a stir amongst the watching crowd.

Having received reports of complete chaos along his remaining route, "Major Crisis" had wasted no time in calling in some favours from his mates at RAF Odiham. Only a few clicks from his point of request and less than forty-five to Stonehenge, he'd arranged a rendezvous *en route*.

The convoy's payload successfully transferred, the final container touched down on its intended target with thirty-two seconds to spare.

"Major Crisis" checked his watch and nodded to himself.

Mission accomplished.

* * *

Worker One sat on an abandoned stone near the centre of the monument, studying the stars in the night sky. Deep in thought, he didn't hear the figure approaching from the dark until the very last moment. Startled, he fumbled for the knife he now kept inside his tunic.

The figure took a step back and asked if that's what things had come to.

Recognising the voice of Worker Three, Worker One sheathed his weapon and replied that he feared it had... and that it was his own fault.

Worker Three acknowledged that life had certainly been easier before Worker One had unleashed the ideas in his head.

Worker One responded that just because the truth was difficult, it didn't mean it should be ignored.

Clambering up to join him, Worker Three asked if they would ever be sure what that truth was.

Worker One stated that it certainly wasn't an infinite list of one gods, for a start. That was even more ridiculous than what he'd been trying to replace.

Worker Three agreed and reminisced about how it used to be. At least there hadn't been competition between the old gods. Their boundaries had been defined. They'd also possessed a presence... be it an angry nudge from the *god of wind* on a stormy day or the approving caress of the sun god on a warm one. You knew where you stood with them.

Worker One chastised himself for not being stronger and pushing the idea of *no* gods. You couldn't have numerous examples of those!

Worker Three pointed out that he wouldn't have got very far doing so when his vital organs were being paraded about on a stick.

Worker One looked up at the stars again and reflected on that prospect. Perhaps it was why people needed gods. Fear of death was assuaged when believing something else lay beyond it.

Eyes widening, Worker Three hoped he wasn't suggesting something *didn't* lie beyond it.

Worker One assured him life would always continue. He just wasn't so arrogant as to think it had to contain *him.*

Worker Three stated that the thought of it *not* containing himself was enough to promise nightmares.

Worker One asked him if he'd been that worried about the situation *before* being born.

Worker Three conceded he had a point. But what, therefore, was the reason for his being born at all?

Worker One puffed out his cheeks. That's the bit he couldn't explain. But like his ramp of earth – which, when no longer visible, would cause people to gaze up at the lintels in awe – there might be metaphorical ramps behind everything else that was held in wonder... including existence itself. Discover *those* ramps and the answer might be obvious.

Discover the one god who devised those other ramps in the first place and that *deity* would be obvious, Worker Three proposed.

That was his point, Worker One insisted. Perhaps that deity didn't exist. Perhaps the master one god everyone was searching for was nothing more than a concept representing the mechanics behind all those individual ramps... a less abstract embodiment of a complex set of connected solutions.

What... like a master plan?

No. Because that implied a planner. More like a master set of rules.

In that case... who came up with those rules?

Worker One puffed out his cheeks again. Perhaps there was one last ramp behind *that* mystery.

And where did *that* ramp come from?

Worker One asked Worker Three to give him a break. He'd only *just* come up with the one made of earth. But given enough time...

Worker Three needed more convincing. So what did that make the stars in the sky?

A pattern made by those rules.

And he himself?

Just another part of that vast pattern.

Worker Three claimed that was even worse than there being nothing after death. Now he felt even *more* insignificant.

Worker One suggested he should feel the opposite. As part of a pattern to be viewed with awe, that made him *very* significant... for it would not be the same one without him.

Worker Three conceded Worker One was extremely clever.

Worker One thanked him and hopped off the stone.

Where was he going?

Worker One replied he'd heard stories from traders that if you travelled far enough, you'd find monuments that knocked theirs into a cocked hat. If that were the case, those who'd built them had also come up with the idea of ramps... only bigger. In which case, they might have bigger answers. He was going to find them.

Acknowledging Worker Three's friendship with a smile, he turned and disappeared into the dark.

Worker Three felt the urge to call out to him. He wanted to

tell him that being clever wasn't the same thing as being wise. Worker One obviously considered it a waste of time, but completing the ring of stones had a significance beyond the structure itself or what it was supposed to achieve when finished. It would stand as a permanent reminder, to all those who came across it, of the extraordinary power of belief. And whether that belief was down to a single god... or a multitude of individual ones... or a series of hidden ramps... it made no difference. The result was the same. Perhaps the master one god would turn out to be a shared consciousness... the impressive ring of stones an eternal reminder of the fact that anything was possible when its power was embraced.

*   *   *

The welcome sight of a Harley-Davidson motorcycle making its way along the ceremonial approach route to the stones brought five hours of purgatory to an end for Norman. Despite the euphoria of seeing his artworks arrive in spectacular fashion, his mood had slowly spiralled downwards, as the passing hours had failed to bring news of the replacement bass player's progress.

Had that news been forthcoming, it would have reported an unnaturally high and improbable stream of incidents that included not one but *two* punctures... an electrical fault resulting in the bike's lights no longer working... a temperamental fuel pipe... seven violent assaults by birds against the rider's visor... eleven kamikaze rabbits... and the final gut-wrenching discovery that the police had closed every approach road in order to prevent any more people accessing the site.

In true Waggy spirit, his doppelganger had refused to lie down. Unperturbed, he'd set about negotiating his way across fields and along bridleways in the dark... doggedly determined not to miss out on the dream of a lifetime. Repeatedly forced to turn back by unaccommodating hedgerows and belligerent fences, he'd experimented with various routes... his determination eventually paying off as he found himself riding along the ancient avenue that once carried worshippers to Stonehenge.

Skirting security and pulling up behind the stage after an excruciating seven hours in the saddle, he dismounted with an unsteadiness Waggy would've considered his trademark.

Norman breathed a massive sigh of relief...

... as did Colin, who removed his helmet.

If Norman's breath could've turned around, apologised to one and all for being totally inappropriate and re-entered his body, it would have done.

'Don't tell me that's him!' exclaimed Stump, standing by Norman's side in eager anticipation. 'He looks more like my fuckin' accountant!'

He did, indeed, bear a closer resemblance to the man whose job it was to cope with Stump's annual lack of paperwork than someone epitomising chemically induced self-destruction.

He didn't sound much like Waggy either.

'Gosh... I've finally made it!' he enthused, his voice more educated than had come across on the phone. 'This is all incredibly surreal! I can't believe it's really happening! My goodness... I've been a fan of *Trouzerbulge* for more years than I care to admit!'

Either the excitement, or sudden attack of night air, had caused his substantial, tortoiseshell glasses to fog over... which didn't help.

'This is actually *the* most amazing thing that has ever happened to me in my entire life!' he babbled.

Watching him meticulously rearranging his helmet hair back into its previously coiffured order, Stump didn't doubt it.

'At first, I was convinced it was a joke!' he continued, wiping his glasses.

'It *is* a joke,' said Stump, his words aimed at Norman. 'A complete and utter farce! The boys would have to be so off their faces to believe this is Waggy they wouldn't even be able to recognise *themselves!*'

'Is there a problem?' asked Colin politely.

'You could say that,' winced Norman. 'We think we might've misunderstood Xanthia. When she said you dress up and play like Waggy... we rather assumed you might *look* like him too.'

'Or anything *remotely* like him,' added Stump caustically.

Colin looked bemused for a few seconds... then recognised their concern. 'You mean *this?*'he laughed, pointing at his face. 'Oh, don't worry! I wear a wig and makeup. You won't recognise me when I've finished!' He patted his backpack. 'It's all in here.'

'In my opinion, the transformation would have to be nothing short of a miracle, mate,' said Stump. 'In which case... you've got just under two hours to perform it!'

'I'll do my best,' smiled Colin graciously.

'Please do!' pleaded Norman. 'There's rather a lot depending on it.'

'Thus far, I've never let anyone down,' Colin assured him.

'AIN'T EVER!' Stump corrected him angrily. 'At least get *that* bit about him right!'

* * *

Snogden-Lambert crouched in his chair, knees tight against his chest, his mouth hanging in a senseless gape.

If ever a moment could be described as *bittersweet*, the one he was currently trying to pretend wasn't happening was it.

Outside his door... its nameplate now an epitaph... the small, tranquil area of English heritage over which he'd been given guardianship was in complete and utter chaos. Hordes of visitors – many of them angry – had been drawn by a media frenzy for which he himself was responsible. Having stood in silent dignity for thousands of years, he'd managed to ensure those proud, original stones were now indistinguishable from the offensive, fibreglass tributes surrounding them... and on the most important day in the site's calendar.

But most damning of all – and to his eternal shame – was the fact he'd managed to fail a simple task so spectacularly in only thirteen days. That particular number had certainly proved unlucky for him.

Such a stain would never be erased. If destroying an artwork of international renown had once sullied his name and momentarily brought the world's spotlight to his door, he trembled at the thought of how bright it was now shining beyond his current one.

That was the bitter.

The sweet belonged to the small collection of artworks being currently displayed in his office – a poignant reminder of his past – and only a small sample of what lay in containers in the car park.

Norman had delivered on his promise. Their value was beyond question. The nation had obtained a rare bequest. But the price paid to achieve it had been beyond money. As far as Snogden-Lambert was concerned, he'd not only sold his own soul... he'd also sold that of Stonehenge itself.

He clutched his knees tighter to feel something other than pain.

What offence had he ever caused the Universe to merit his life disintegrating so rapidly? Why had it been so cruel? How could such a comedy of errors have been allowed to happen yet again?

As a tear hit his cheek, he tried to remember the last time he'd been happy.

It had been a Monday.

His hands twitched.

He'd been conducting Bach's Brandenburg Concerto No. 3 in G major... in his office.

The violins, violas, cello, and double bass were flirting with each other whilst vying for the listener's attention, a busy harpsichord in the background determined not to let them have things all their own way.

His fingers started moving.

The melodies criss-crossed one another in a sublime, precise dance.

He dropped his feet to the ground and motioned for the

violas to stand theirs. They were in danger of deferring to their more famous cousins.

The cellists eyed his hands for their own instructions.

Snogden-Lambert obliged.

Tilting his head back, he drank in the sound.

He was happy again... as he had been on that Monday morning... until...

There was a knock at the door.

...there'd been someone at the door.

He didn't remember Joan saying he had an appointment!

Of course not... She'd been on holiday, visiting her sister in the Isle of Wight.

His hands were busy.

The temp agency had sent that awful Gusset woman.

There was a second knock, only louder and far more urgent.

The woman was useless.

He tutted and moved towards the door.

The musicians would have to cope alone.

He paused in confusion.

But the door had already been opened. Miss Gusset had been standing there.

He took hold of the door handle as if in a dream.

Closely followed by another unwanted interrupter.

The music tripped over itself, crashing to a halt.

Clutching carrier bags.

He yanked the door open.

Donald Tucker-Jenkins!

'So we meet again,' grinned Donald, sticking out a muddy hand in greeting.

'Is this a dream?' asked Snogden-Lambert unsteadily.

'Not unless it's mine!' replied Donald. 'And if it is, I think I'd like to come in!'

Snogden-Lambert instinctively moved out of the way, his mind racing to find solid ground.

'It's been a while... and a lot has happened to me since then,' said Donald, accepting the invite.

'Me too,' muttered Snogden-Lambert vacantly.

'But I guess you've probably heard.'

'Ditto.'

'Though... enough about me. I've come to warn you of an impending danger.'

'I know,' Snogden-Lambert mumbled.

Donald telegraphed his surprise. '*Really?*'

'They're going to steal my paintings,' nodded Snogden-Lambert, accessing a vague memory.

'*Are* they?' Donald looked at the paintings in the room. 'Then, you don't want to leave them lying around like this. Some of these look quite valuable!'

Snogden-Lambert tried to ascertain if the figure in front of him was real or just a figment of his tortured imagination. The last time he'd remembered them meeting, the man's trousers had been stained with urine.

He chanced a quick glance at Donald's crotch.

A large, wet stain greeted his eyes.

Snogden-Lambert felt a perverse sense of relief. It *was* a dream.

'Yes... sorry about that,' said Donald, spotting the peek and disappointing him. 'They've closed all the roads. I had to do the last bit on foot. It wasn't easy in the dark. I had a bit of a tumble in a ditch.'

'What's happening?' groaned Snogden-Lambert, grabbing his head.

'It's what's *going* to happen that you need to be worried about,' replied Donald. 'There are these two American gentlemen. I tried to have them detained. But it seems the local constabulary decided their crimes weren't serious enough to warrant a night in the cells. I suspect they'll be heading this way. They're definitely up to no good.'

'Crimes? Are they thieves?'

'No... but I'm pretty sure they're in league with the Devil.'

It was all too much. Snogden-Lambert let out a wail.

'Steady on, man... there's no need for that! He can only use his influence. It's those that are flesh and blood you want to worry about!'

Snogden-Lambert put out a hand and poked Donald firmly in the chest.

'Is everything alright?' asked Donald, following the finger warily as it was withdrawn.

'As are you... aren't you?'

'What?'

'Flesh and blood.'

'I should jolly well hope so,' replied Donald. 'Whitebait's the only one out of us here who isn't!'

Snogden-Lambert shot a look around the room.

'Don't worry... you can't see him.'

'But I can see *you*,' said Snogden-Lambert, trying to make sense of everything.

'NO... I *DON'T* THINK HE'S OKAY!' shouted Donald.

Snogden-Lambert jumped back in shock. He desperately tried to access the part of his brain that was stubbornly refusing to play ball. 'I remember now... Didn't we fall out?'

'I do believe a headlock was involved somewhere in our previous dealings,' reflected Donald. 'But all water under the bridge now, huh?'

Snogden-Lambert wasn't so sure. Donald's admission had kick-started his memory. The real world was all-too-painfully flooding back. 'I remember now... You ruined my career!' he glowered.

'*Did* I?'

'Yes... I've always reckoned you were trying out some sick plot for one of your plays.' He checked himself. 'You *are* him... aren't you?'

'Yes... I'm me,' confirmed Donald with a smile.

Snogden-Lambert decided he'd aim for the throat.

*   *   *

'Miserable wanker... He might at least have come and said hello!' moaned Fungus, flicking his hair from out of the back of his guitar strap. 'Since when did we sanction this *separate dressing rooms* crap?'

'I reckon he's just embarrassed,' Stump placated him. 'He knows he could've ruined it for everyone. He probably thought it best to keep outta the way.'

'I can't believe they've given him bail!' commented Ritchie, lazily drumming his sticks on the side of a vodka bottle.

There was a smart rap on the portacabin door. 'Three minutes, gentlemen!' shouted Sharky from behind it. 'Your public awaits.'

Despite the level of secrecy employed, word had spread via information coaxed from the crew that *Trouzerbulge* had gotten together and were about to perform. A frenzied rush for the small, unrestricted area between the stage and the stones had ensued by those not fuming at the intrusion... a fairly sizeable crowd now enthusiastically chanting the band's name.

'Let's do it!' yelled Stump, giving the air a motivational punch with his fist.

'And Waggy?'

'He'll meet us by the stage.'

'Precious prick,' muttered Fungus, practising a last pout in the mirror.

Ritchie shouted the obligatory, 'Rock 'n' roll!' as he jumped to his feet and spun his sticks skilfully between his fingers.

With leather trousers straining under the pressure of approaching middle-age, and hair backcombed to hide its cruel advance, the three of them staggered their way out of the portacabin and towards a row of metal steps leading to the stage.

Whilst maintaining the arrogant, *de rigueur* strut of a prima donna flaunting his self-worth, Stump apprehensively scoured the area ahead for signs of Waggy's substitute. To his consternation, Fungus and Ritchie had remained relatively sober and were nowhere near as wasted as he feared they needed to be for the deception to go unnoticed.

But he needn't have worried. On reaching the steps, the door to the nearest portacabin flew open.

'I give you Waggy!' announced Norman proudly... stepping from it and signalling the errant bass player's presence with his hand.

'That's *two* pricks,' mumbled Fungus, ignoring them both.

As Colin's alter ego was revealed, Stump could hardly believe his eyes. The man who had previously resembled his accountant now looked every inch the rock-scarred wastrel he'd come to love and occasionally want to throttle. A tangled mane of hair cleverly hiding the best part of his face, the heavily smudged eye makeup and precariously dangling cigarette, that were as much a part of Waggy's persona as the infamous needle marks on his arms, were all in attendance. With impressive attention to detail, Colin had even replicated the latter... courtesy of a biro.

Norman caught Stump's eye and winked.

'Let's get up there and live this dream!' shouted Stump, turning imperiously and placing a foot on the steps.

*   *   *

It had been a while since Donald had found himself so rudely acquainted with the ground. His recent years as a revered playwright had ensured that kind of thing didn't happen anymore.

Snogden-Lambert didn't care. 'I'd still be in charge of that gallery, if it wasn't for your sick meddling!' he yelled, wrapping his legs around Donald's to prevent him struggling free.

'I think you're missing the point!' returned Donald, doing his best to thwart him. 'There's more at stake tonight than your pride! I fear someone might die!'

'Too bloody right!' cried Snogden-Lambert, tightening his grip.

'What are you doing here anyway?' Donald choked.

'It's my job to make sure this place runs smoothly,' growled Snogden-Lambert.

There was a brief silence before Donald spoke again.

'Whitebait's just asked me if you've stuck your head outside the door recently,' he relayed.

'I'm going to stick yours *through* it!' Snogden-Lambert

screamed.

'I DON'T THINK HE'S BEING IRONIC,' shouted Donald. 'HE HAS HISTORY!'

It was as Snogden-Lambert was about to re-enact it that a loud boom stopped him in his tracks.

'What in God's name was that?' he said, forgetting his struggle and lifting his head.

'E minor, I believe,' answered Donald.

Another boom followed the first... accompanied by an unpleasant rumbling that shook the filing cabinet.

'That doesn't sound like any orchestra *I've* ever heard,' said Snogden-Lambert, scrambling to his feet. 'Especially when you consider the stage is a mile and a half away!'

'I think we finally agree on something,' concurred Donald, relieved his ordeal was over.

The mist through which he was seeing things having just turned even redder, Snogden-Lambert stormed towards the door, its barrier no longer a consideration as he breezed through it.

Scrambling onto his buggy, he proceeded to head at maximum speed towards the offending sound, the rushing night air helping revive his senses.

The scene that eventually greeted him as he pulled up close to the stones was one of total bedlam. Many attendees were vociferously bemoaning the intrusion of noise, shielding their ears with their hands, and expressing astonishment that such an inappropriate thing could be allowed to happen. But others, who welcomed the surprise entertainment, were dancing where they stood... a greater sea of revellers bobbing enthusiastically in front the stage, now brightly lit with pulsating lights.

'Get out of my way!' he screamed, dismounting and tearing through the bemused onlookers as he headed straight for it.

The cacophony of sound was overwhelming.

As he reached the fenced-off backstage compound, a couple of white-robed Druids, carrying important-looking staffs, recognised him from a previous visit.

'This is sacrilegious!' shouted one angrily. He'd been remonstrating with a hastily beckoned crew member, but to no avail. 'This is a blatant rape of Mother Nature! The earth spirits will sense this as an attack on her sanctity and may cease their millennia-old benevolence!'

'GET A LIFE!' screamed Snogden-Lambert, barging past them.

Norman was his next target.

Snogden-Lambert spotted him standing at the bottom of the steps leading up to the stage, quietly watching proceedings from behind.

'This isn't classical music!' he yelled, as he reached him.

'I never said it was,' retorted Norman, having been awaiting the confrontation.

'You *implied* it, then!'

Norman's defence was well-rehearsed. 'No, I didn't! You just *assumed* it would be!'

'In that case... who's this Trou*zer*bulge we talked about?'

'It's the name of the band... and it's *Trouzerbulge*... as in...'

'Yes! Yes! I get it!' fumed Snogden-Lambert. 'A final joke at my expense, no doubt!'

'No one's laughing,' said Norman. 'I meant what I said about saving the Universe. You're gonna see something truly remarkable in just over an hour, and then you'll know I was telling the truth!'

'I don't think I care to wait that long,' growled Snogden-Lambert, eyeing up the steps. He made a move towards them.

'Where are you going?' asked Norman, alarmed.

'To do what I should've done days ago... Put a stop to this farce!'

'You can't!' cried Norman. 'You gave me your word!'

Snogden-Lambert placed a foot on the first step.

'You said a Snogden-Lambert's word was sacrosanct!'

Snogden-Lambert faltered, his other foot struggling to comply with the instruction it had just been given.

'You promised I could play *Trouzerbulge's* music! That's *exactly* what I'm doing!'

'I didn't say you could turn this place into a tacky theme park!' retaliated Snogden-Lambert, frozen by his dilemma.

'I've only done what you said I could. *You* gave me permission to smarten up the site. You even said you thought the ancients would approve if I painted it *pink!*'

'I thought you were mad!'

'It doesn't matter. You gave me your word! And *I'm* sticking precisely to every syllable of our agreement. So I expect you to do the same!'

Snogden-Lambert's tortured expression changed. 'You're right,' he said, as if having undergone an epiphany. 'We *should* stick to every syllable.'

The transformation and fresh glint in his eyes worried Norman.

'It's true, I allowed you to rebuild the monument,' Snogden-Lambert leered. 'But I never said for how *long* it could stay that way.'

'Yes, you did... I mean... well... not *exactly.*' Norman suddenly realised his case wasn't as watertight as he'd thought. 'I assumed we were at least talking the duration of the concert!'

'*Oh...*' said Snogden-Lambert, drawing out the word with teasing malice. '*Now* who's guilty of an assumption?'

'What are you gonna do?' probed Norman nervously.

'Play your game of semantics to its ultimate conclusion,' replied Snogden-Lambert, removing his foot from the steps. 'The concert can continue... and I've allowed you to restore the outer ring of stones to its original condition. That means I've kept my word and the honour of the Snogden-Lamberts. But you'll now excuse me if I personally take them down.'

'*What?*'

The bright yellow tractor had never been driven at such speed. Fitted with a large, metal bucket attached to its front loader, it was more used to pottering around the site and assisting in menial tasks.

People scattered in terror as it thundered across the grass without regard to their safety, its driver viewing his progress

41

through a fog of hate and vitriol.

The overwhelmed security staff looked on in horror as it sped, lights blazing, towards its target... and then in astonishment as they recognised the driver.

Snogden-Lambert braced himself for impact as he singled out a fibreglass replica. When he'd shattered that one into smithereens, he'd plough on through and attack another. That should be enough to bring the entire ring of lintels crashing down.

Norman had given up the chase and could only watch the drama unfold in sheer disbelief. With just over an hour of music to go before the sphere of knowledge needed to be contained within the structure, any damage to it would bring his plan to a catastrophic end. He'd come so far and beaten every obstacle thrown at him. Failure, now, would be the cruellest blow of all.

Black smoke billowed from the tractor's exhaust as Snogden-Lambert forced it through the temporary boundary fence and onto the hallowed grass. Those who had dived out of his way screamed as they awaited the inevitable.

He closed his eyes, his target only feet away. Anticipating some pain when his body encountered the fibreglass debris, he reasoned it would be as nothing compared to that which he'd suffered over the last five years.

It might even prove cathartic.

What he *hadn't* anticipated was the sickening, bone-jarring *thud* as Newton's laws of motion taught him an important lesson.

It wasn't that his body would continue forward at an identical speed, even though the force propelling it had come to a sudden, gut-wrenching halt... or that flesh against metal at high speed was not to be recommended. At least Pierre Malair had done the maths.

The lesson he learned was that he ought to have taken more time to study the monument he'd been in charge of and known which were original stones and which were not.

As the genuine sarsen stood its ground – as it had done for

thousands of years – his teeth attempted to free themselves from his gums... his nose and eyeballs following in sympathy. The impact of the steering wheel forced the air so violently from his lungs it seemed it might never return.

The tractor engine spluttered and stalled, giving one final, agonising jerk as if to punish him for its demise.

Snogden-Lambert's groans would have sounded worryingly terminal to those hurrying to the scene, were it not for the fact they were being drowned out by the caterwauled tale of an extremely accommodating lady from Hamburg.

Struggling to hang on to consciousness, he sensed the consternation around him.

'Is it serious?' asked an onlooker apprehensively.

Perceiving tearful cries of concern from the others, he thanked the maker he was about to meet that his last moments on Earth would be ones where he'd *finally* received some compassion.

'Not really,' came a reply. 'It's a little bit chipped... but at least it's still standing.'

It was the final straw.

Adrenalin surging through his veins – and to the astonishment of every bystander – he hauled his shattered body upright and grabbed a wheel brace from a metal tool box attached to the tractor's wheel arch. His tongue lolling, he staggered forward in excruciating pain and started attacking the stone.

He'd managed to gouge a few flakes from it, before being pulled away and laid on the ground.

'Is that *foam* coming out of his mouth?' someone enquired.

'It's a little hard to tell,' came a reply, 'what with all that blood.'

'We should call the police,' voiced another. 'He's vandalised the monument.'

'I think an ambulance might be more appropriate,' suggested the first. 'I don't think knees are meant to bend that way.'

It was as the stretcher was being loaded into the ambulance

that Snogden-Lambert spotted a familiar face in the crowd. In fact... he'd spotted quite a few; being those belonging to the incredibly important dignitaries he'd invited along to witness his night of triumph.

But the face that caught his attention eclipsed all others. *Surely it was all a dream... wasn't it? It couldn't really be her!* The owner of the face was staring at him in abject pity.

'*Joan?*' he called out feebly.

'Peter,' she mouthed in confirmation.

He managed the closest he could get to a smile without teeth. 'You came!' he gummed. Utilising the only part of his body that still appeared to be working, he wiggled the tip of his left index finger to beckon her forward.

The paramedics paused as they interpreted his last request for a comforting presence.

'I read the newspapers,' she said, hurrying to his side. 'Just like you suggested. It seemed you'd finally found your feet again.' She chanced an ironic glance at his mangled legs. 'I felt very proud. I thought it would be nice to pay you a surprise visit, now things had...' Her brow creased as she glanced over her shoulder at the tractor imbedded in the monument. '...returned to normal.'

'It's not how it looks,' he whimpered.

She didn't answer.

'I've just had a bit of a bad day,' he said, tears welling in his eyes.

'I know,' she nodded gently.

'Bit of an understatement,' a voice joined them. It was Donald's. He winced as he saw the extent of Snogden-Lambert's injuries. 'It doesn't look good, old boy,' he advised. 'ARE THEY COMING TO HELP HIM CROSS OVER?' he shouted insensitively. He waited for a reply before shouting again. 'WHAT DO YOU MEAN, "THEY DON'T WANT HIM"?'

'It was a simple mistake,' groaned Snogden-Lambert. 'One stone was indistinguishable from another.'

'I know,' said Donald brightly. 'You've got to hand it to that

Stevie the Props chap. He certainly knows what he's doing!'

'You *know* him?' exclaimed Snogden-Lambert, his eyes targeting Donald's.

Donald had instantly recognised the artist's handiwork, having commissioned him to produce the set for his play. It was Donald who'd insisted on them looking authentic.

'It was me who suggested he make the stones as realistic as possible,' he confirmed.

'Forgive me, Joan,' said Snogden-Lambert politely, momentarily turning his eyes back towards her. 'It seems I haven't quite finished my breakdown.'

The words that then exited his mouth were not any she'd encountered in a crossword. Such was the shock to her sensibilities, she would never leave Cornwall again.

*　　*　　*

Stone Deaf Pete looked up from his mixing desk. 'I didn't count on there being this amount of people,' he shouted above the cacophony from the band.

'Is that a problem?' Norman yelled back directly in his ear.

'I said... I didn't count on there being this amount of people. Are you sure you still want me to go for broke when we get to the breakdown in *Sex Wench?*'

Norman thought it best to nod.

'Okay,' he shrugged. 'You're the boss!' Stone Deaf Pete presented his thumbs to Speaker Jim, who returned the gesture.

Due to the severe restrictions posed by the site and Norman's desire to get the speakers as close to the stones as possible, the front-of-house mixing desk had been situated to the side of the stage. Curiously... Stone Deaf Pete had commented that he wouldn't have placed it in front of the speakers anyway – given the choice – as he didn't want to damage his hearing.

With the band delivering their uncompromising brand of musical mayhem, Norman watched Xanthia dancing to it on the opposite side of the stage, her eyes focused solely on Stump. He, in turn, was cavorting about like a god... thriving on the adulation of his eager worshippers.

Despite an uncomfortable jealousy, Norman considered the fact that most eyes were on Stump to be a good thing. For no one seemed to have noticed the interloper. *He* was also having the time of his life; struggling to believe he was part of the real thing and that he wouldn't have to put his bass guitar down half way through the set in order for a raffle to be called.

Norman examined his watch against a set list taped to a flight case. They showed fifteen minutes and three songs left to play. Stump had given his word that the two crucial notes would be played at the exact time the sun showed itself above the heel stone... so Norman could only hope his rival in love was better at maths than he was at writing lyrics. Why Amiable Amy gave of herself so freely was not at all clear from the narrative.

Turning his attention back to Xanthia, he felt a sweaty hand on his shoulder. It came attached to Virgin Merv.

'You're needed for a moment, guv'nor,' Virgin Merv blasted in his ear, with breath suggesting a change of name wouldn't be necessary anytime soon. 'There's someone wanting to see you. Says they're a friend of yours.'

Norman looked confused. 'But I'm not expecting anyone,' he shouted back.

Virgin Merv shrugged. 'He said to tell you it's... *The Provider.*'

Norman recoiled in shock. 'What's on earth's *he* doing here?'

'He said he needed to see you.'

'I can't!' exclaimed Norman, looking around anxiously. 'Not right now!'

'He said it was *extremely* urgent,' added Virgin Merv.

Perturbed, Norman reluctantly nodded his acknowledgement and hurriedly proceeded to follow a textbook example of *builder's crack* from the stage.

'Security caught him trying to gain entry to the backstage area and passed him on to us,' explained Virgin Merv, as they made their way swiftly across the grass. 'Although he says he's your friend, we've told him to wait behind one of the portacabins. You can't be too sure these days.'

'He *is* my friend,' confirmed Norman. 'But how did he know about my connection to this event? I never told him!'

'I guess he's gotta be your dealer, with a name like that!' Virgin Merv grinned, sealing the assumption with a wink.

'Certainly not!' Norman glowered. 'He's the nephew of an ironmonger I once upset and who was forced to take over his uncle's shop because of my actions. I felt so guilty, I eventually made peace with him and now put as much of my business his way as I can. That's how he got his name. It's a joke between us. That's all!'

'Well... your *friend's* waiting over there.' Virgin Merv stopped and stabbed an unhygienic finger at an area behind one of the portacabins. 'I'll leave you to it. I'm needed elsewhere.'

Norman nodded his appreciation and carried on alone, trying to figure out how his friend knew where he'd be and what the emergency was. He'd said nothing to him about Stonehenge when they'd last met up outside the burning hotel. Only Xanthia had been privy to Gabriel's revelation that day.

Rounding the corner of the portacabin, he saw someone he took to be a member of security standing with his hands behind his back.

'Where is he?' he asked.

'The Provider?'

'Yes. I was told he was waiting here for me.'

The assumed member of security looked at him strangely. 'Norman Penkridge?'

'Yes... as requested. So where's my friend?'

'*Ultimate and Unbeatable Supreme Cyber Warrior?*'

Norman's head jerked with surprise. 'I *beg* your pardon?'

'I believe you also go by that name,' said the individual, who Norman now realised was too young and slight to have anything to do with security.

'I only ever used that tag once in an online computer game,' he said, looking around and realising he was on his own. 'What exactly is this?'

'Don't you wanna know who *I* am?' asked the stranger.

'Funny… That was *precisely* what my next question was going to be,' Norman countered, glancing at his watch and seeing he only had twelve minutes to go. 'But you'll have to be quick. I've something very important to attend to!'

The stranger didn't appear to be in a hurry. 'My friends know me as… *The Megabyte Master*,' he announced slowly.

'Do they really?' responded Norman indifferently, looking up at the sky and noticing it was starting to lighten.

'But you know me as…' The stranger paused for effect, much to Norman's exasperation. '*Ultimate and Unbeatable Supreme Cyber Warrior 2.*'

Norman took a second to process the information. 'Look,' he said, not sure where the conversation was headed. 'I *don't* know you. I've never seen you before in my life. I was expecting to meet a friend here.'

'I'm definitely not that,' said Kevin.

'No, you're not. Now, if you'll excuse me…'

'I'm your worst enemy,' cut in Kevin, with sudden menace.

Norman instantly appreciated how vulnerable he was. Although the individual in front of him gave puny a bad name, he himself could raise a snigger when removing items of clothing at the beach. 'What's all this about?' he asked uneasily.

'It's about me proving you're not as clever as you think you are,' Kevin answered coldly. 'It was *me* who beat you at *Cortex Destroyer!*'

Norman's brow creased before expanding in misplaced relief. 'Oh… right! I remember now. Well… congratulations.' He looked at Kevin awkwardly. 'Were you expecting a *prize?*'

'Oh… don't worry,' said Kevin through a troubling smirk. 'I've already been promised her!'

Norman looked at him in bewilderment. '*What?*'

'I'm here to stop you.'

Norman assumed he wasn't objecting to the music… which only left one other option. Of all the forces he'd been warned would be rallied against him, he'd assumed they'd take a slightly more impressive and maleficent form than a disgruntled, acned teenager. Then again... the frogs hadn't exactly been capable of putting up a fight. However, Kevin's cocksure manner suggested he had powerful backup close by.

'I take it you're not working alone,' Norman ventured, looking around anxiously.

'You could say... I've been *sent*,' Kevin confirmed.

Norman's blood chilled. 'So I take it you have something to do with...' Not wishing to make his predicament any more real, he hesitated to utter the name he dreaded.

Kevin spared him the agony. 'I think you'll find he has something to do with all of us, at some point in our lives,' he grinned malevolently.

'*Oh my god*,' Norman groaned, having believed he'd already overcome the last of his hurdles.

'Wrong side,' said Kevin coolly. 'But he *is* mine.'

Norman considered his options. The minutes were ticking by and the sun would soon be making an appearance. All he had to do was get himself in position and the job would be done.

He looked for his quickest escape... but Kevin was ahead of him. Moving to one side, the young man blocked the way between the portacabins.

'If you think I've come this far to be stopped by the likes of you, you well underestimate what I've gone through!' growled Norman, dipping his head. 'No matter *who* your boss is!'

'My mum would say it's *whom*,' Kevin taunted him. 'And I beat you at *Cortex Destroyer*... so I'll beat you now.'

'That was just a computer game. *This* is a little more serious!' Norman clenched his fists. 'You might think you're intimidating... but you're nothing more than yet another fork.' With as much force as he could muster, he launched himself at Kevin, who finally took his hands from behind his back.

Norman caught sight of the large kitchen knife too late to stop its impact.

At first, it felt like a stinging punch.

Pulling away, he reeled backwards.

'Mum's gonna wonder where that's gone,' said Kevin, acknowledging the handle protruding from Norman's abdomen.

Norman staggered in reverse until the wall of a portacabin stopped him going further, his eyes bulging in disbelief.

'And don't ever say *just* a computer game,' Kevin admonished him. '*Genuine* computer geeks take that kinda thing *very* seriously.'

Norman gurgled his shock. The initial adrenalin that had numbed the pain was giving way to an excruciating, burning sensation. Unable to believe what was happening, he placed his hands on the knife for confirmation.

Kevin watched impassively as his victim started to slide down the wall of the portacabin, a smeared line of blood recording his descent.

'Okay... I did it!' Kevin shouted proudly into the air. 'Now it's time to grab my prize!'

Though viewing everything through a haze of unreality, Norman was aware of the music having stopped and what sounded like Stump addressing the crowd. Sitting crumpled on the ground, he gasped in short, shallow breaths to avoid antagonising the razor-sharp metal of the knife. He could feel the warm blood soaking into his groin.

Kevin seemed to be waiting for someone.

Norman's head lolled to one side.

As it did, he caught the waft of an unforgettable aroma.

He whimpered.

A greenish cloud materialised a few feet in front of him, its stomach-churning stench having accompanied many a frequent nightmare. As the scaled monstrosity he'd been dreading stepped imperiously from its midst, a huge cheer erupted from the audience.

The Devil grinned... the opening chords to *Sex Wench* shattering the silence.

'I don't think you'll make it,' he drawled. 'Isn't mortality a drag?'

'Gabriel,' cried Norman pathetically.

'Oh... like *he's* gonna come and help!' the Devil sneered.

'I know he will,' gasped Norman, struggling to find enough air to speak. 'I command it!'

The Devil waited for the lack of a response, then threw his head back and roared his ridicule into the brightening sky. 'Oh... he's played you good and proper, hasn't he?'

Undeterred, Norman closed his eyes tightly and summoned help from the Universe with every fibre of his being.

When the lack of any cavalry arriving caused him to open them again, he found the Devil close up in his face, crouched on his haunches. 'You don't get it... do you?' he hissed venomously. 'I told you the last time we met... it's all a *game!*'

Norman mustered enough energy to spit in his face. 'At least I know what side I'd rather be on,' he said defiantly.

'Ah...' sneered the Devil, springing back onto his hoofed feet and licking the offending spittle with relish. 'But do you know what side *he's* on?'

Norman didn't reply.

The Devil cocked his head. 'Do I take that silence to be your answer?'

'I believe in him,' countered Norman, with as much conviction as his pain permitted.

'Well... you *did*,' the Devil clarified. 'Which is why you've got yourself in this mess!' He casually examined his talons. 'But I believe you've recently been having doubts.'

Norman couldn't argue.

'And who can blame you?' The Devil looked about himself sarcastically. 'I mean... where's the winged wonder now? Not exactly flying to your aid... is he?'

'He can't,' struggled Norman. 'I should've remembered that. You know it too.'

'I know a lot of things about him,' the Devil smirked. 'I know he's been playing a double game with you, for a start.'

'Just another of your lies,' winced Norman, trying to stop his head from dropping any further. 'That's all you've got to throw at me.'

The Devil jerked his head back sharply. '*Really?*' He gave an assured smile. 'Well... why don't we examine the facts? Did you know, for instance, that there have been two American gentlemen doing their incompetent best to stop you?'

'Amongst a host of many other things,' Norman mumbled, his loss of blood beginning to tell.

'Ah... but on this occasion, they had nothing to do with *me*. Their hatred of you has been encouraged by another. And would you like to guess who that *other* is?'

Norman's body began to spasm.

'Oh dear,' said the Devil, feigning sympathy. 'Given you appear to have little time left, I'd better give you a clue.' He flapped his arms sarcastically in slow motion.

'Liar,' Norman whispered, fighting to keep his eyes open.

'Apparently not,' sneered the Devil. 'The proof's out there for anyone with hacking skills to see. It's recorded, in that binary code you so love, that they were given a financial incentive to put a stop to your plan... by the very person who claimed he wanted you to succeed! Very *grubby*, wouldn't you agree? Not to mention rather awkward from your point of view.'

'It wouldn't make sense,' Norman croaked. 'You're just trying to summon Gabriel to get him to explain himself. That way his vibrations will unsettle the portal and open it up for you.'

'On the contrary. I thought we'd already established he isn't bothered about you. Believe me... he senses your pain. He just doesn't *care*. You've been played!'

'It's true,' piped up Kevin. 'I've seen the evidence myself... a number of transactions made from the Templar Resources account to a Chad Cheadle and Bob Papadopoulos in America. They've been trying to track you down and stop you. They told me themselves after I infiltrated their scheme. It was *them* who found out you'd be at the Tower of London and took me along as an accomplice. That's why I was able to tackle Xanthia. You see... they already knew in advance you were up to something!'

'And how did they know?' teased the Devil. He slowly flapped his arms again. 'So... *now* what do you think of your precious Gabriel?'

Norman knew from the sheer joy in Kevin's eyes that the revelation had to be true. The doubts Xanthia had expressed over Gabriel came flooding back, along with those he'd tried to ignore himself. An emptiness, so vast it almost stopped his breath, gripped him.

Gabriel had once said he should never feel alone. But with his life ebbing away unnoticed in a cold, remote part of a site where thousands of others were partying no more than a stone's throw from him – oblivious to his fate – he had never felt more so.

What was Gabriel up to? He certainly wasn't on the Devil's side... so whose side was he on? Was the god of wrath that some of the scriptures warned of real? Were fire and brimstone, retribution and genocide the real face of a Supreme Being? Was the medieval mind more attuned to the truth than a modern one? Was this punishment for abusing the chequebook?

'I kept telling you it was a game,' crowed the Devil. 'But you wouldn't listen. The deluded call it *faith*... the promise of something to come in a time to be determined. But I prefer to take my pleasures *now*. Guilt hangs on the framework of time. So without it, there's no right or wrong. There's just being in the moment!'

'Not much of a moment for you now, *Ultimate and Unbeatable Supreme Cyber Warrior*... is it?' joined in Kevin.

Norman closed his eyes.

'An appropriate thing to do,' remarked the Devil, 'Faith blinds you... makes you only see what you want to see. Any who doubt that might like to reflect on the fact they would probably have assumed it was *me* who paid your Americans. It's a fool's comfort blanket... a mirror reflecting one's own warped prejudices and making the pain of having to follow someone else's demands bearable. It's all things to all men. But given all men are fallible... so is faith.'

'I still wouldn't want to be on your side,' mumbled Norman. 'You've wasted your time trying to convert me.'

'*Convert* you?' mocked the Devil. 'Is that what you think I've been doing?' He sneered contemptuously. 'You poor fool! I don't *have* to! The threat you posed is over. You're dying. I've won! There's no reason to persuade you one way or the other. I'm merely letting you know in your final, pathetic moments on this planet that you made the wrong decision when you chose your side. Your agony in that knowledge is purely for my own amusement. It makes no difference if you believe in me or not.' He laughed out loud. 'Don't flatter yourself you're *that* important!'

Norman slowly opened his eyes and blinked away the tears. Unlike his near-death experience in the car, there were no flashing memories from his past. They, at least, might've distracted him from the emptiness. He was getting colder... his lips turning blue... his body growing numb... the only comfort of warmth coming from the blood he could still feel trickling out of him.

Despite his condition, he raised a small, defiant smile. 'When I said you'd wasted your time, I was referring to something else,' he whispered. 'Your hubris has been your undoing.' He slowly turned his wrist and looked at his bloodstained watch. 'I might be dying, but I've still managed to get the better of you by keeping you talking. In three minutes time the sphere of knowledge will be created. It's too late for even *you* to stop that now. I might not receive it, but *someone* closest to the centre of the stones will. You haven't won... you've lost!'

The Devil looked up at the sky. 'I have to agree with you,' he said. 'Someone *will* receive it. You've done well to triumph against everything that's been thrown at you during this task... even by Gabriel. You see... we *would've* made a good team. But, not to worry... I have an extremely keen replacement desperate to step into your shoes.' He turned triumphantly to Kevin. 'NOW!' he commanded him forcefully.

With that, Kevin took off towards the stones.

'You forget... I *own* this tune,' the Devil laughed, cocking an ear to listen to the music. 'And now if you'll excuse me, it's time for me to savour its power!'

'It's loud, but not *that* loud,' shouted Bob, as he and Chad stumbled across the field.

'Be thankful for that!' Chad returned. 'It means we might still be in time to stop whatever it is they're up to!'

'I'm getting too old for this,' Bob panted, eyeing the silhouette of the stones a short distance in front of them.

'Just focus on the goal,' Chad encouraged him. 'Penkridge is within touching distance. And having set this whole thing up, we're gonna make sure he sees it come crashing down!'

Bob struggled to keep up. 'So how do we stop him when he *does* raise the volume?' he wheezed.

Chad gritted his teeth and upped his pace. 'Simple. Pull the plug!'

*   *   *

'You beautiful, gorgeous people!' bellowed Stump above the sound of a thumping, primal drum beat. 'We're not just sharing this solstice... we're sharing the consummation of a long-held dream of mine!'

Fungus and Colin had ceased their playing and were encouraging the audience to raise their hands aloft and clap.

'I've always known this monument was built purely as a venue for *Trouzerbulge!*' Stump crowed.

An enthusiastic cheer acknowledged the idea.

'Apart from it being a teleport for aliens, of course,' he added swiftly. 'So let's make sure we make this historic moment a *really* special one!'

The audience cheered again.

'You all know what's coming next!' he teased.

They did.

'Now it's *your* turn to make some noise!' He struck a side-on pose and pointed at them aggressively. 'ARE YOU READY TO ROCK?' he yelled.

The cheer that answered him eclipsed all others. They

certainly were… but he milked their enthusiasm anyway.

'WE CAN'T HEAR YOU!' he screamed.

Whilst this was only true in Stone Deaf Pete's case, Stump had one eye on the brightening sky, aware it was time to give Norman what he needed.

'I SAID… ARE YOU READY TO ROCK?'

The crowd screamed its readiness back.

'THEN LET'S DO IT!'

It was just two notes… but their inclusion in a *Trouzerbulge* concert had become legendary.

With the air pulsating from the drums, Stump bawled into the microphone as loud as he could to start the anticipated ritual. 'SEX… WENCH… SEX… WENCH.'

Fungus had already made the walk to his amp and turned it up as loud as it could go. Strutting back to his pedal board, he stamped on one of an impressive array of gadgets and wrung the two most famous notes in rock history from his guitar.

The crowd went wild as the wailing tones wrestled with the feedback and momentarily took over from Stump.

The singer glanced across at Stone Deaf Pete and gave his sound engineer a short, sharp nod. 'OKAY, YOU MUVVERS!' he bellowed, on the limit of his vocal chords. 'NOW LET'S *REALLY* MAKE SOME NOISE!'

The audience joined in deliriously as he started shrieking the words *Sex Wench* over and over again into the microphone, the hypnotic rhythm stirring even the most introverted into compliance.

Stone Deaf Pete took his cue and began raising the faders.

*   *   *

The Devil towered over Norman's bloodied body. 'Imagine the new Saviour being on *my* side!' he gloated. 'Can you imagine how delicious that'll make things?'

Norman was now too weak to respond, his spirit all but extinguished. The irony cut deeper than any kitchen knife could. The two notes for which he'd overcome ludicrously

26

implausible odds were finally being played at a rebuilt Stonehenge on the morning of the summer solstice exactly as instructed. He'd achieved the impossible. He could hear them gradually getting louder and knew they'd soon be at a level to trigger the chain reaction that would produce the sphere of knowledge. But it wouldn't be him who received it. It had been gifted to the opposition.

As the numbness that had been slowly creeping in from his hands and feet started shutting him down, he wondered if fate would decree he witness that actual moment.

'It seems young Kevin has finally won his battle with you,' the Devil smirked.

Norman moved his lips, but struggled to get words past them.

'What's that?' simpered the Devil, coming in close to his face. 'An acknowledgement of my pathetic minion's superiority? So... what kind of failed runt does that make *you*?'

Fired by the insult, Norman summoned up the very last of his strength. 'At least I didn't sell my soul,' he whispered almost inaudibly.

The Devil snorted. 'Are you sure about that? Because from where I'm standing... that's *precisely* what you did.' He gave Norman a look that promised the pain of one last irony. 'There's another reason I don't have to convert you. I *already* have! You see... you came over to my way of thinking when you persuaded others to sell theirs. Think about it! Your use of pride, greed, and trickery to tempt all those you needed to help you into abandoning their principles was no different to anything I would've done. You kidded yourself it was for the good... but I doubt they would agree. So... a final lesson before the effort of taking another breath beats you. Morality is subjective. It's all a question of where you're standing when you make a judgement. One man's faith is another man's scorn. One individual's truth is another's derision. Draw a line to establish the average of Man's rectitude and you'll find I'm no further away from it than your winged friend and his accomplices. It's simply a matter of *perspective*.' He raised his head and drank in the approaching light. 'That's the problem with those who preach... They talk so loudly, they fail to hear anything other than their own voice!'

The air began pulsating violently.

Norman's head finally dropped.

*   *   *

'They're going for it!' shouted Chad, above the see-sawing chant. 'They're pushing up the volume!'

Having finally reached the monument's western perimeter, he was frantically scouting for the quickest route to the stage on the opposite side. But the dense crowd jockeying for position to glimpse the first rays of sun looked like making anything with speed impossible.

'There's only one thing for it,' yelled Bob. 'We're gonna have to go straight through the centre of the stones!'

'Then you'd better hope you've still got enough in those legs of yours to outrun security! They ain't gonna like it one bit!' warned Chad.

Bob flinched at the crescendoing noise. 'We don't have a choice! It's now or never! C'mon... let's do this!'

He barged his way through the remaining cordon of bodies and launched himself over the boundary fence before anyone could object. Landing on the hallowed grass, he was immediately spotted by a number of burly gentlemen wearing high-visibility jackets.

'Back off!' he mouthed aggressively, swiping his finger between them and daring their intervention.

To his surprise, the tactic worked. Whether they believed in the half-light he possessed a weapon – or were just tired and wanted to witness the sunrise uninterrupted for themselves – the appearance of Chad landing beside him and offering a similar threat cemented their apathy.

Not waiting for a change of heart, the two intruders struck out for the centre of the stones.

A supportive cheer went up from the onlookers as they

made it past the outer ring of megaliths.

Safely inside, Chad fought the temptation to stop for a brief second and marvel at his surroundings. But forced to skirt a fallen upright that had broken itself on another close to the centre of the monument, they found their progress halted by an individual standing with his back to them. Dwarfed by the inner trilithons, he was referencing his position in relationship to the ring of lintels.

'Security?' yelled Bob, placing his hands over his ears as the level of sound became unbearable.

Chad didn't answer, having been forced to do the same thing.

Contemplating their next move, they became aware of another figure standing to their right. Sensibly wearing ear protectors, he was studying an electronic device in his hand. Chad realised he'd seen him before... having stolen a glimpse of the man's startled face as he'd fallen from a tree in France.

Unperturbed by their presence, Donkey Dave was concentrating on the job he'd been tasked with. He shook his head uneasily, as the meter in front of him failed to register its intended target.

'AND IT CAME TO PASS, WHEN THE PEOPLE HEARD THE SOUND OF THE TRUMPET, AND THE PEOPLE SHOUTED WITH A GREAT SHOUT, THAT THE WALL FELL DOWN FLAT!' bellowed a voice from behind.

Though barely audible over the cacophony coming from the stage, it was delivered with just enough angry force to make the two men turn to confront it.

'AND THE PEOPLE SHALL ASCEND UP EVERY MAN STRAIGHT BEFORE HIM!'

'I think he intends to hit us,' said Bob.

'Donald!' exclaimed Chad. 'Not now!'

Donald raised a fist defiantly.

'We don't have time for this,' yelled Chad, ignoring him and turning back. 'Let's just deal with the immediate threat.' He nodded at the less than impressive figure in front of them inadvertently blocking their way. 'Shouldn't be too much of a problem!' As he spoke, the figure in question spun around. Chad's face fell. 'What the f_'

The figure looked equally shocked.

Chad snorted with disdain. 'Kevin... I suggest you get yerself outta our way! It's not you we're interested in! It's your boss, Penkridge!'

'He's a dead man!' confirmed Bob.

'Funny you should say that,' retorted Kevin, with a smirk.

'The game's over!' Chad shouted.

'Well... it certainly is for *him*,' Kevin sneered. 'But for me... it's just about to begin!'

'You deal with this idiot,' Chad bellowed to his partner. 'I'm going for the power supply!'

Bob grinned at Kevin. 'With the greatest of pleasure!'

'Not so fast!' screamed Donald, hurling himself at Chad's legs, causing the two of them to tumble to the ground.

Leaving his partner to fend for himself, Bob launched himself at their other problem.

Kevin yelped as he was knocked backwards... then launched into what Bob assumed was a string of expletives, as he found himself pinned to the ground. It was hard to tell, given the music had reached its zenith.

Donkey Dave anxiously studied his meter. Sitting at 144 decibels, it was stubbornly refusing to take the final step.

A short distance away, Stone Deaf Pete released a sweaty hand from the master fader he'd been coaxing and wiped it across an equally sweaty brow. He glanced anxiously across to a small device rigged by the side of his desk. Containing an illuminated red light alongside a dormant green one, he'd been waiting on Donkey Dave to send a signal that would change its colour status once their target had been achieved.

Blowing out his cheeks, he turned to Speaker Jim – fretting beside a rack of overworked amplifiers being pushed to their limit – and shook his head.

Speaker Jim dropped his.

They'd done all they could do. Everything was at maximum.

The amplifiers were starting to complain. Stump had done his best and whipped the crowd into a frenzy... but their voices were beginning to tire. There was nothing left in the tank.

Bob the Belly sidled behind the row of portacabins and quickly surveyed his surroundings. Ensuring he was alone, he unzipped his fly and prepared to release the results of that afternoon's intake of lager. As his bladder gave a sigh of relief, he caught sight of a crumpled object lying on the ground a few feet in front of him. Leaning forward to investigate – without splashing his shoes – the simultaneous act of doing so and the shock of what it actually was caused him to fart.

Against the scale of the Universe, the energy of a bottom cough is woefully unimpressive. Unlike the explosion behind a supernova, its effects are extremely limited... and of little interest to scientists... unless they are unfortunate enough to be in the same room when it's unleashed. Whilst true a particularly deadly one can clear a sizeable area – or produce great mirth or protestation in equal measure – its effects are... if you'll excuse the pun... on the *whole*, mercifully short-lived.

On a scale of one to ten, Bob the Belly's ranked formidably high. It had come as quite a shock seeing Norman's bloodied body slumped and lifeless. Not that he needed an excuse to evacuate anything from his orifices... but it certainly helped.

At the same time, an easterly gust of wind caught the sound struggling from the speakers and assisted in its journey towards the stones. As volume is related to the intensity of a sound wave... which is energy carried in distance and time... it helped take Donkey Dave's meter to within a quantum breadth of its target.

But nearly... no matter how microscopically close... is still not quite enough.

So infinitesimally small was that missing final step, the fate of the Universe hung at that precise moment on the existence of just one extra single particle of air.

Or... in Bob the Belly's case... *methane*.

Like the straw that broke the camel's back, it made the difference.

As the sun's rays finally flared over the heel stone and struck the tallest of the bluestones, Donkey Dave's meter registered 145.

At that precise moment, individual atoms within the plagioclase feldspar and augite crystals forming the very tip of the bluestone took their cue. Just as Gabriel predicted, the crystals reacted to the combination of sound wave energy and minute gravitational forces by resonating in conflict with one another. As their jostling increased, the disturbance quickly spread until the whole stone had awoken.

Its molecular structure in flux... a thin, blue light – barely visible to the human eye at first – seeped from its core and hovered like a ghostly mist above the surface. The vibrations gaining strength, the light became bolder... until the whole stone started to shimmer.

Disturbing the air around it, the rapidly pulsating energy assailed a second bluestone, setting an unstoppable chain reaction in motion.

Oblivious to what was occurring, Chad placed Donald in a headlock and dragged him over to where Bob was sitting atop Kevin.

'Grab hold of this idiot too!' he yelled. 'It's imperative I get to that power source before we're all rendered senseless!'

Bob did as instructed... but in shifting his weight to take custody of a flailing Donald, he momentarily lost balance as Kevin fought back.

Taking full advantage, Kevin wriggled free and scrambled to his feet.

Holding on to Donald's belt, Bob snatched at Kevin's trouser leg and hung on grimly.

Free of his human anchor, Chad took a few seconds to orientate himself and locate the stage. As he did so, his attention was stolen by the shimmering bluestones.

'What the...'

No sooner had he spotted them, a third morphed into life. He froze.

'What are ya waiting for?' screamed Bob, his attention focused solely between his hesitant partner and the two individuals trying to escape his clutches.

Chad couldn't answer. Mouth agape, he stood rooted to the spot as a fourth stone joined in the display.

Their oscillating had now become so intense, fingers of vibrant, purple light were shooting off and arcing themselves against the nearest of the giant sarsens. As soon as the larger stones became involved, they too began to transform. The coruscating ripples danced upwards until they found themselves constrained by the lintels. It was then that the most spectacular effect of all occurred. In less than the blink of an eye, the mesmerising light shot out in both directions and travelled around the artificial ring at blistering speed. As the two forces met again, colliding head on, the entire area in-between joined together in a silent, dazzling explosion.

The gathered multitude gasped in awe as a giant ball of light began forming from the centre of the disc... expanding outwards until it was being constrained by the ring of lintels.

Within the ball itself, various-sized strands of multi-coloured light fought and intertwined with each other, some so large they stretched the distance between its bulging poles... others engaging in their choreography on a scale so minute they became lost in the greater scheme of things. Each participating molecule danced with a vibration that, when combined with its neighbours, represented the structure of the Universe, the thoughts of man, and the entire history of everything that had occurred within it... offering a tantalising projection of what might be if things were left unchanged. Every answer ever sought flirted with the causes of that ignorance... bigotry, sociology, psychology, biology, and the sheer enormity of the physical world in which they interacted. From the physicists' Holy Grail of a theory of everything to the reason behind the Mona Lisa's smile... the thoughts of Socrates and Einstein... Mozart and Da Vinci... Descartes and Buddha...

vied for space with the dreams of Alexander the Great and Martin Luther King. Every note of music ever played... picture painted... word spoken... expression of joy and wail of torment... prayer and curse... silently competed with individual life stories... family histories... fossil records... gravitational patterns and a complete plan of each galaxy... all written in a brilliantly dazzling, unfathomable shorthand... so great its intensity, it seemed it would split the monument apart.

Some in the crowd escaped their floundering logic by turning and running. But the majority just stood and gawped... their senses numbed.

Like a one-man-band tumbling down the stairs, *Trouzerbulge's* performance stuttered to an undignified halt... the singing crowd only aware something was occurring behind them by the looks of stupefaction on the musicians' faces.

'Shit... I think the aliens have finally made it through!' drawled Stump uncomfortably into the microphone.

As the audience turned to investigate, their chanting collapsed into a stunned silence.

Curiously... despite the thousands of celebrants gathered for the solstice, not one raised their voice in fear... even amongst those deciding it might be a good idea to flee. There was an inexplicable beauty in the danger and a feeling of something beyond the fear of death.

An eerie, expectant silence befell the entire site, as the pulsating sphere kept the observers guessing as to its next move.

When it came, it was as unexpected and dramatic as its appearance.

In the space of a nanosecond, the sphere condensed to almost nothing and appeared to fall into the centre of the monument.

And that was that.

*   *   *

The flashing blue lights ricocheting off the white portacabin walls were entirely man-made. As a team of medics arrived at the scene, the police immediately started cordoning it off. Whilst word was about to spread backstage that someone had met an untimely demise, the news would be completely swamped by talk of the spectacular appearance of the sphere of knowledge.

Unable to process what had been witnessed, the majority of attendees thought it best to attribute the breathtaking display to *Trouzerbulge's* lighting team and a quantum leap in laser technology. Its equally dramatic disappearance had even brought a staggered round of applause from many in the stunned crowd.

But a few hugged each other deliriously, as years of faith in something beyond the ordinary had finally been rewarded. Their only regret was that the proof had been so fleeting. With the site returned to an unremarkable field in an average landscape – boasting nothing more than an incongruous scattering of silent stones – even Mother Nature seemed less awe-inspiring now.

No longer needing to be restrained, Kevin had taken advantage and scrambled to his feet. Carefully checking his position in relation to the centre of the monument, he'd been agitatedly pacing around in circles.

'A random sum... that'll test it,' he mumbled. 'Okay... What's one hundred and forty-four multiplied by three thousand, seven hundred and ninety-six?' His brow wrestled with the answer. 'Come on! This should be child's play!' He examined the ring of lintels and checked his feet again. 'One hundred and forty-four multiplied by three thousand, seven hundred and ninety-six?' he repeated desperately.

'Five hundred and forty-six thousand, six hundred and twenty-four,' said a voice to his left.

Looking up, his face fell. '*You?*' he exclaimed in horror.

Having sat awhile in stunned silence, Bob finally stood up and brushed the grass from his trousers.

'Whaddya mean it's *Norman* who's died?' cried Stump, as news of Bob the Belly's gruesome discovery fought its way past the ringing in his ears. 'How the hell did *that* happen!'

'It's entirely my fault,' Virgin Merv whimpered.

Stump looked at the distraught crew member aghast. '*You* killed him?'

'I mean… I should never have left him to go alone!'

'Left him to go *where?*'

'To meet somebody called *The Provider*. He said he was a friend.'

'Yeah, *right!*' snorted Sharky. 'His *dealer*, more like!'

'No… It's a joke.'

'What… he *ain't* dead?'

'I meant the name. He's an ironmonger.' Virgin Merv looked at their blank faces. 'It's a long story.'

'He was stabbed by an ironmonger?' frowned Stump, struggling with the narrative.

'They *do* sell knives,' pointed out Sharky.

'I don't believe it!' groaned Kevin.

Bob looked at him calmly.

'I'm telling you,' came the voice to his left. 'One hundred and forty-four multiplied by three thousand, seven hundred and ninety-six is five hundred and forty-six thousand, six hundred and twenty-four.'

Kevin stared at its owner.

Donkey Dave stared back.

'You're kiddin' me!' Kevin yelled. 'It was meant to be *me!*'

'So let me get this straight,' exclaimed Stump. 'Norman's been killed by an ironmonger friend of his who happens to sell knives?'

'Amongst a range of numerous other goods, I expect,' ventured Sharky. 'That's the whole point of 'em.'

'Yeah… The one near me even stocks plumbing equipment,' chipped in Fungus.

'Handsome,' nodded Sharky.

'My missus bought a washing line from ours,' contributed Bob the Belly. 'But I believe they're a dying breed.'

'Washing lines?'

'Ironmongers.'

'Give me a break!' shouted Stump angrily. 'And less of the *dying,* if you don't mind! Show some fuckin' respect for an incredibly courageous friend of mine!'

'It can't be true!' lamented Kevin, staring at Donkey Dave incredulously.

'Irrefutably so,' asserted Donkey Dave. He held up a second device he'd removed from his pocket. 'It says so on my calculator here.'

The implications of him doing so took a moment to sink in.

'Then... *who?*' implored Kevin, once they had.

Donald stepped forward and slowly raised his hands to the heavens. 'AND YE SHALL KNOW THE TRUTH, AND THE TRUTH SHALL MAKE YOU FREE!'

'And who the hell are *you?*' demanded Kevin.

'I could ask the same thing,' Donald huffed.

'You mean... you don't *know?*'

'Who I am?'

'Who *I* am,' Kevin clarified.

'Should I?'

Kevin looked at Bob. '*Whoever* he is... it's definitely not *him.*'

Bob stared back blankly... which suggested to Kevin it also wasn't *him.* The trouble was... he couldn't be sure. The man who'd just prevented him becoming the Antichrist *was* looking a little strange.

From Bob's point of view, it was hardly surprising. His attention finally caught by the spectacular light display, he'd glanced up seconds before it collapsed and headed towards him. Though a fleeting glimpse, he'd felt the same incredible feelings of love and awareness he'd experienced back at Armageddon Terrace five years earlier.

He'd instinctively turned away, fearing it would hit him.

But it hadn't.

Now upright, he was ignoring Kevin's ranting and looking around for an explanation. It was only then that something actually *did* strike him.

'Where's Chad?' he asked.

* * *

'Though extremely close to death, he hasn't passed over yet. His life can still be saved.'

The paramedics looked up and wondered how the person who'd made the announcement had managed to slip unnoticed inside the police cordon.

'You're not supposed to be here,' said one sternly. 'I suggest you leave immediately!'

'You must listen to what I say,' responded the unauthorised visitor calmly.

'I think you'll find it's the other way around!' the paramedic retorted. 'If you don't go now, I'll see to it you're arrested! You're interfering in an *extremely* serious medical emergency... not to mention a crime scene!'

The threat went unheeded.

'The knife has penetrated to a depth of precisely six point two three centimetres, puncturing the omentum and passing between the small and large intestines. The peritoneum has not been breached. The inferior vena cava and abdominal aorta are intact. The individual is in a state of severe hypovolemic shock due to the right gastroepiploic artery having suffered trauma. Due to the amount of O-negative blood that will have been discharged via the wound since the injury occurred, I calculate that if a transfusion is not administered within the next seventeen minutes and twenty-eight seconds, death *will* occur.'

'Are you a doctor?'

'No.'

'I didn't think so. Even the best wouldn't be able to make such a diagnosis! I'm calling the police over!'

'To substantiate my skills... your own stomach currently contains the remains of two rashers of bacon, one fried egg and half a tomato, seventeen chips, three slices of white bread and... a certain quantity of alcohol. I can be more specific about the latter, if you wish.'

The paramedic looked awkwardly at his colleague.

'Your associate's contains a packet of salt and vinegar crisps, and a strong coffee... milk, no sugar... on account of the fact you're not supposed to drink on duty. I'm sure he'll testify I'm right... on both counts. Do you still want to call the police?'

'How on earth do you know all this?' the paramedic stuttered.

'I'm not exactly sure... but I do. What's more... that time has now decreased to sixteen minutes and fifty-five seconds. So I advise you don't waste any more of it.'

The paramedic stared at his colleague again and shook his head. 'If all that's true, there's nothing more we can do here. The nearest hospital is almost thirteen miles away. With the dispersing crowds and congestion on the roads, we'll never make it in time.'

'Nine point four as the crow flies. There's a helicopter available exactly one hundred and ninety-two metres from here which will get you there in time, provided you're airborne within the next five minutes and thirty-six seconds. You'll find the pilot in the portacabin marked *Trouzerbulge*.'

Mouth agape, the paramedic nodded.

'One last thing... You'll need to ignore the fact he's *also* been drinking.'

*   *   *

'You should get some sleep,' suggested the nurse. 'It's been a difficult operation. It could be some time before he regains consciousness. But you needn't worry... we'll look after him. He's safe with us.'

Xanthia smiled sweetly. 'I'd rather wait here with him, if it's all the same to you.'

'I understand,' nodded the nurse. 'Just ring the alarm if you need me.' With that, she left the room.

Xanthia stared at Norman and the mass of tubes and wires attaching his body to a bank of machines monitoring his progress. Leaning forward in her chair, she carefully placed his hand in hers. It felt cold. She gave it a gentle squeeze.

The machine monitoring Norman's heartbeat registered a change.

'*Normy?*'

Norman's lips moved slightly around the small tube in his mouth.

'It's Xan!' she said expectantly. 'You can hear me, can't you?'

After a slight struggle, his eyes opened.

'You're in hospital,' she said, as they fought against the intrusion of the light. 'You're gonna be alright! You were brought here just in time!'

He swallowed awkwardly and tilted his head towards her.

'Hello, babe,' she smiled.

Tears welled in his eyes.

'You're supposed to say... you must be an angel,' she prompted, trying to make light of the situation.

His head recoiled as an expression of angst gripped his face. Her use of the word *angel* had triggered the reason for his predicament.

'Tell everyone I'm sorry, Xan,' he croaked. 'I messed up.'

Rising from her chair, she leaned over him. 'We'll have less of that! You did everything you possibly could.'

'I failed,' he groaned. 'I didn't make it to the centre of the stones!'

'It's nothing to worry about.' She poured a glass of water from the jug on the bedside cabinet. 'Everything's gonna be alright. The most important thing is that you get yourself well again.' She offered it to his lips and encouraged him to take a few sips. 'There... that's better, isn't it?' she said brightly.

He gazed at her and marvelled at her naivety. He thought it best not to tell her what was about to come. He didn't want to cause her any more pain. 'I also owe *you* an apology,' he mumbled.

'I should think so too!' she smiled. 'I've been extremely

'worried about you!'

'For doubting you when you warned me about Gabriel,' he muttered. 'You were right. He's not who we think he is.'

Her expression changed. 'I thought you once told me he's *whoever* we think he is!' She cradled his head and forced him to take a few more sips.

'I saw the Devil again,' he struggled. 'He told me that Gabriel hired people to actually *stop* me!' He waited for her reaction.

There wasn't one.

He assumed either she couldn't process the implications or didn't believe him. 'It wasn't a lie, because he thought I was dying. He had no reason to tell an untruth.' He closed his eyes to block out the enormity of this new reality.

'Things aren't always what they seem,' she comforted him.

'You can say that again!' He paused... expecting her to repeat her comment. In his muddled state, he'd forgotten to avoid using such a phrase in her presence.

'I mean it in relation to Gabriel,' she surprised him. 'We make judgements from an extremely narrow point of view. That's why there's so much conflict in the world. If someone could see the bigger picture, they'd appreciate just how unqualified they were to assume *anything*.'

Norman opened his eyes again.

Xanthia looked at him lovingly.

She never ceased to amaze him. 'That's incredibly profound!' he gawped.

'Gabriel *is* on our side,' she grinned. 'And I have some important information for you.'

'You've seen him?' he said, startled by the news.

'Not quite,' she replied.

*　　*　　*

'Where the friggin' hell have *you* been?' seethed Bob, pointing his watch at Chad in disgust. 'I've been going outta my mind wondering what's happened to you! Trust this freakin' place not to have any cellphone signal! I've spent the whole day

11

wandering backwards and forwards over the entire site looking for you! Word's been going around someone got stabbed this morning. I was beginning to fear it might be *you!*'

Chad calmly raised a hand in acknowledgement of his partner's suffering and sat himself, cross-legged, on the grass.

The stage in the distance was being dismantled and work had already begun on doing the same to the fibreglass megaliths. A sizeable crowd still remained, watching proceedings.

'What the hell happened?' Bob demanded, standing over him. 'Are you *alright?*'

'I'm *more* than alright,' Chad smiled serenely.

'So… are ya just gonna sit there like a demented Buddha or am I gonna get an explanation for your vanishing act?' reacted Bob sharply.

'I'm not sure I can give you one you'd be able to understand,' Chad replied, looking up at him.

'How about… you *try* me!'

Chad shook his head hopelessly. 'It's difficult. It all feels very strange.'

'You're not wrong there!' said Bob facetiously. 'Perhaps you'd care to enlighten me!'

'Enlighten seems an apposite word,' nodded Chad thoughtfully. 'Let's just say… I'm not the man I used to be. I'm suddenly seeing the world in a *completely* different light.'

Bob looked about himself in disbelief. 'I don't believe it! Don't tell me this place has turned you into a friggin' *hippy!*'

Chad chuckled at the irony. 'You clearly didn't experience what I did. Didn't you feel the full beauty of that light?'

'I had my hands full at the time… if you remember,' Bob retorted. 'I was only permitted a glimpse. And yes… for a brief moment, it felt all warm and gooey. But what's *that* gotta do with anything?'

'*Everything!*' Chad grinned. 'I can state as a fact now… there's more to our existence than I ever imagined… and it's beautiful… and it's big… and there's nothing to be frightened of!'

'Far from it, Cheadle. *You're* scaring the crap outta me!'

'Thoughts only appear as demons if you choose to fight them,' Chad counselled. 'That's where I've been going wrong these last years. I now accept it was fate that brought me to these stones.'

'Fate!' spluttered Bob, unable to believe what he was hearing. 'You can't be serious! Isn't that the most obscene F word in your vocabulary?'

'I've just had it massively expanded,' replied Chad. 'And it's enabled me to see that I've been so busy in life analysing the detail... I've completely missed the bigger picture.'

'And what the hell's that?'

'All of this,' Chad beamed, extending his arms and looking about himself in wonder. 'Approaching questions using logic might've once promised the hope of a logical answer... but I now realise I would've been far better off looking for the *beautiful* one!'

* * *

'It's true... Gabriel *did* hire two people to try and stop you,' announced Xanthia. 'Two American gentlemen. But it was for your own good.'

Norman looked at her aghast.

'He knew, the moment he assigned you your task, the other side would be watching your every move.'

'I know. He told me.'

'He also knew they would be stronger and more determined than before.'

'That too.'

'So he needed to come up with a decoy... something to distract their attention.'

Norman would've raised a hand to intervene, had he possessed the strength. He got that Gabriel paying others to work against him would mess with the opposition's head and create a cunning diversion. A little reverse psychology might make them think his plan was *not* to succeed and cause

9

complete confusion. But what if those decoys had actually succeeded in doing what they'd been hired for?

'They threw quite a few spanners in the works,' she continued. 'It was them who initiated the freezing of your finances. They also found out about *The Provider* being your sole friend. That information – when inadvertently passed to the other side – proved to be your downfall. The Devil knew there was no way you would compromise your mission so close to its completion for anything other than a call for help from your one and only friend.' She smiled. 'Excluding me, of course.'

'I rest my case,' Norman flinched. 'It was a massively flawed plan!'

'I thought you told me a few moments ago that my telling you we were unqualified to assume anything without knowing the bigger picture was profound,' she tutted. 'No wonder Gabriel used to get so frustrated with you!'

Norman felt his adrenalin kick in. 'I don't care how big a picture I need to look at. As far as I'm concerned... because of Gabriel's actions, the other side are out there with an Antichrist imbued with *our* sphere of knowledge.' He tried to raise his body. 'We've lost!'

Xanthia shook her head. 'No, we haven't.' she smiled, placing her hands on his shoulders and gently settling him back. 'Gabriel came up with the *perfect* decoy... because even the decoy didn't recognise that's what they were!'

Norman's brow creased.

'You see, Normy... the Americans weren't the decoy.' She looked at him affectionately. 'The decoy was *you*.'

His jaw fell.

'You were never supposed to receive the sphere of knowledge. You were simply a distraction for the final phase of the plan.'

He stared at her in disbelief.

'I know,' she sympathised. 'It's a shock, given everything else you've been through.'

He tried to take in what he'd just been told, but his head was spinning.

'Perhaps I should let you get some rest,' she suggested.

'Babe?' he said slowly and breathlessly. 'I just told you the Antichrist had been imbued with the sphere of knowledge and that we'd lost... and you replied that we hadn't.'

'You did... and I did,' she nodded.

'Aside from how you actually *know* all this... you didn't once ask who the Antichrist was... what the sphere of knowledge was... or what *imbued* meant. On top of that, you've used words like *compromised, completion,* and the phrase *final phase of the plan.* What's more... I haven't *once* had to pull you up on saying *fing.*' He hesitated before placing his next question. 'Xan... what *exactly* is going on?'

*   *   *

'So... what are you trying to tell me?' Bob struggled to reconcile the look of contentment on his partner's face with the troubled one he was used to. 'Are you sayin' that freakin' light display's somehow given you the answers to life, the Universe, and everything?'

Chad looked at him and grinned.

'Well... *has* it?'

'I only wish!' Chad snorted. 'D'ya think if I were *that* smart, I'd waste my time bothering to come back here and find you?' He shook his head. 'No. I'm afraid the truth is far more prosaic. I've spent the best part of today needing to be on my own... trying to come to terms with what it is I *am* feeling. It's been a day of mixed emotions. But any questions I have no longer matter in the greater scheme of things. *That's* the point! I don't have to fight it anymore. The battle's over. That light's freed me from the excruciating mental limbo I've been in these last five years. I finally accept... without question or doubt... there's something bigger out there... beyond our comprehension. That ball of light this morning was as close as I'll ever come to experiencing it. And knowing thousands of others experienced it too means I can at least be certain I ain't going crazy!'

'From where I'm standing, that's debatable,' said Bob.

Chad raised himself and took a long look at the stones and the deconstruction work taking place around them. 'There's one *other* thing I'm certain of... Penkridge ain't our problem anymore. He's done what he planned to do here and nobody got hurt.'

Bob raised an eyebrow.

'Excluding the stabbing you referred to, of course.'

Bob's eyebrow lowered.

'Instead... everyone's been treated to something incredibly beautiful. I can't explain it, but I know what we saw is a force for good. I don't know why or how he produced it, but he's *definitely* responsible for what we experienced here and outside his apartment. His presence on both occasions is as big a connection beyond coincidence as I'll ever need.'

'Are you saying we're *done* here?' exclaimed Bob.

'I see no point in hanging around.'

'And Penkridge?'

'I'm even *more* curious about him now,' Chad smiled. 'But I certainly don't wanna stop what he's up to... *whatever* that is.'

'But our *client* does,' pointed out Bob.

'Then he'll have to find someone else to do his dirty work for him,' said Chad.

Bob stared at his partner, mortified. 'But what about all that money he was prepared to pay us to investigate? It wasn't dirty before this morning! The reverse, in fact. It was our shiny, golden ticket. We were gonna retire on it... remember?'

Chad looked at him in amazement. 'I've just told you that I've finally found peace of mind, Bob. D'ya really think *any* amount of money could eclipse that?'

Bob frowned. 'But it might help me find *mine*.'

'Then... I'm afraid you'll have to do it alone. Whatever Penkridge is involved in has my blessing.'

Bob looked about himself hopelessly. 'So...what am I gonna tell our client?'

Chad gave the matter some thought. 'You can tell him that I say *"thank you"*... because without his intervention, I'd still be chasing demons.'

6

'This is ridiculous!' cried Bob, throwing his hands in the air. 'You make it sound like he was some kinda angel sent to rescue you!'

Chad placed an affectionate arm around his partner. 'Bob... *now* who's being ridiculous!'

* * *

'Somebody *did* receive the sphere of knowledge,' Xanthia announced. 'Somebody who was meant to do so right from the beginning... Somebody who would *never* be suspected and could slip undetected under the radar at the very last moment.'

Norman stared at her silently.

She gracefully displayed her hands.

'Xan?' he quivered, the cogs of his mind struggling to connect the way they were supposed to.

'*Ta dah!*' she sung quietly.

His jaw plummeted.

'I know,' she said. 'It was quite a shock for me too! I had no idea... just that Gabriel always looked at me as if he was hiding something... which he *was,* of course. That's why I always had the feeling I couldn't trust him. Call it women's intuition.'

Norman's mouth remained agape.

'I understand it's a lot to take in,' she sympathised. 'But imagine what it's been like for *me.*' She scrambled onto the side of his bed, excitedly. 'It's the weirdest feeling, Normy! I know *everything!* It's all a bit of a jumble at the moment, but I'm sure that'll sort itself out as I get the hang of it!' She giggled. 'Go on... ask me something!'

He looked at her, confused.

'A question. Go on... *anything!*'

'Am I dreaming?' he managed.

'No... a real one,' she laughed, playfully rocking his arm.

He stared at her warily. 'Alright... Who painted *David with the Head of Goliath?*'

'Michelangelo Merisi da Caravaggio.' she answered proudly, before he'd had time to draw his next breath.

Norman swallowed. 'When was he born?'

She leant back like a proud child demonstrating something learnt at school. 'The twenty-ninth of September, fifteen seventy-one.'

'What's the square of his birth year?' he blurted, as quickly as his stupefaction allowed.

'Two million, four hundred and sixty-eight thousand and forty-one,' she replied, even quicker. 'But you'll have to trust me on that, as I'm also aware *you* don't know the answer!'

Norman stared at her in disbelief. '*But... how?*' he struggled.

She gently placed his hand in her lap. 'Just as the sun started to appear, I had an urge to run to the centre of the monument. Of course, I didn't know at the time that's where *you* were supposed to be. It just felt like the right thing to do. When I got there, I found some people fighting. Two of them were the Americans Gabriel had hired... and another, that boy who attacked me at the Tower of London the other day. That's what I mean about seeing the bigger picture. If Gabriel *hadn't* hired those Americans, they wouldn't have been there to stop that boy claiming the sphere of knowledge for himself.' She paused for a moment, in reflection. 'And then it happened.'

'You received the sphere.'

She smiled.

'I can't believe it!' he gasped, shaking his head.

'Now I can see that I was an integral part of the plan all along,' she explained. 'Think about it, Normy... It was *me* who suggested you get Stone Deaf Pete to help you achieve the sound level required... and *me* who recognised that the two notes Gabriel needed you to play were exactly the same as those in Stump's song. You said *I* gave you the idea of using *Trouzerbulge* as a solution to getting them played at Stonehenge... and it was *me* who persuaded Stump to change his mind when he initially refused. It's also why Gabriel had you send me back to London. He realised I was beginning to sense things... and that if I latched on to the truth, those spirits who'd gathered around you in search of answers might discover it too!'

4

'And you haven't seen him since?'

'It's become increasingly dangerous for him to materialise. I doubt Heaven will want to upset the balance of things any more than they already have. Besides... there's no need. His work here is done. It's now up to *me* to see it to its ultimate conclusion.'

Norman stared at her in her lipstick and mascara, baby-pink nails, and bleached blonde hair and marvelled at such a prospect.

She pulled his hand as close to her chest as the drip attached to it allowed. 'But I'd like you to be there with me,' she said, her eyes twinkling. 'Having all this knowledge doesn't make my task any less scary. I'm now getting an insight into what Mankind is capable of and what's waiting out there for me. It's not gonna be pretty. I'll need someone holding my *own* hand.'

Her admission of vulnerability caught him by surprise. 'But are you sure you want that *someone* to be me?' he whispered. 'I mean... now you have knowledge of everything, you know the truth about me. You can see I'm a sorry patchwork of jealousy, insecurity, inferiority and deceitfulness. I've been living a lie and pretending I could be someone else ever since I met you.'

'Normy... I wasn't *that* blind before this happened!' she laughed. 'But I know the *real* you is a good man. And I also now know just how much you love me. I doubt many in your position would've done what you did for me.'

He looked at her, perplexed. 'What *did* I do?'

'You kept quiet about Lake Como... despite knowing it was the one thing that would've put a nail in the coffin of your love rival.' She smiled. 'You see... very little can escape me now! It would've benefited you to have shattered my trust in Stump. But you knew how much it would hurt *me* if I discovered the truth... so you elected to hold on to that pain for yourself. That makes you a *very* special person.'

He felt a wave of emotion catch in his throat.

'And given you're still wondering... It wasn't *me* with him when you called that night to discuss the incomplete ring of stones. Stump and I have only ever remained friends. I kept in

3

touch with him... yes... and thought it best not to tell you when I had... knowing you wouldn't understand.'

Norman's instinct was to object... until he realised there'd be very little point.

'I got that right,' she smiled. 'Though, whilst you accept I'm telling the truth now... you obviously still believe *Gabriel* has been dishonest with you.'

'He told me I'd be the new Saviour,' croaked Norman, his body finally objecting to the effort he'd been forcing it to make.

She pressed his hand tightly. 'He never did.'

He looked at her warily.

'He just let you assume it... along with those he knew would be watching your every move.'

Norman's mind raced back to the conversations he'd had with the Archangel... but his tiredness prevented him from focussing on them.

'Trust me,' she said softly, seeing him struggle.

He exhaled wearily. 'I do, Xan. But I still can't believe he thought it a good idea to risk having my finances stopped. It very nearly cost us the sphere of knowledge!'

'The bigger picture, Norman,' she counselled.

He shrugged his bafflement.

'Gabriel did what he did out of love... for you,' she expanded. 'Despite being the most difficult person he'd ever encountered, he had so much faith in you, he was certain you'd do the right thing. He took that risk in order to give you back *yourself*. He saw you'd become lost... and would never find your true self whilst distracted by what you thought your paintings and possessions made you. He realised it would take something extraordinary for you to give them up and be truly happy again. His action in facilitating such a situation was a remarkably unselfish gift... knowing what the unimaginable consequences would be if you didn't believe in him enough to let everything go. But he loved you so much he did it anyway. It was *his* Lake Como moment for *you*.'

Norman's lip quivered.

'He trusted you, Norman... and you didn't let him down.'

He sighed. 'You're right. At least what he did means I can now get back to living in the *real* world.'

'We'll need to secure it first,' she reminded him.

He flinched as reality struck. He watched her sitting sweetly on his bed and shook his head for the umpteenth time. 'Who'd have thought it... Julie Swanson... the new Saviour!'

'We just need to convince the rest of the world about that... *Pooey*.' She hoisted up her impressively stretched halter top. 'And let's face it... it was a given I was always gonna attract more media attention than you!'

'I take it you won't be wearing sandals, then?' he ventured.

She gave him a withering look. 'And what's wrong with stilettos?'

Norman considered the prospect. *This WILL be interesting*, he thought.

*   *   *

'You really *are* leaving, then,' said Worker Three, having stumbled upon Worker One taking a last look at the henge and the landscape around it.

Worker One picked up a small bag of possessions from the ground and slung it over his shoulder. 'I am,' he confirmed.

'Still trying to find all those answers, eh?' Worker Three smiled.

'That's what questions are there for,' Worker One replied.

Worker Three gazed at the incomplete structure rising eerily out of the morning mist. 'Do you think it'll ever get built... or do you think it's destined to remain in its half-finished state forever?'

Worker one took a final look at the monument and shrugged. 'Who knows?'

THE END... as if

1

Pssst...

If you've enjoyed reading this book and think others might too, please could you take a few seconds of your time to leave a review somewhere or say so on social media.
This would be *greatly* appreciated, as all authors need as much help as they can get.

Thank you!

Interested in finding out more about what goes on in the author's head?

For various "things"... including subscribing to his mailing list, so that you can be the first to know what he's up to, visit:

www.andydanenye.com

ARTAVIA AAA
PUBLISHING